THE GIRL FROM
KELLER'S

Harold Bindloss

The Girl From Keller's

Harold Bindloss

© 1st World Library, 2006
PO Box 2211
Fairfield, IA 52556
www.1stworldlibrary.com
First Edition

LCCN: 2006936201

Softcover ISBN: 978-1-4218-3063-6
Hardcover ISBN: 978-1-4218-2963-0
eBook ISBN: 978-1-4218-3163-3

Purchase *"The Girl From Keller's"*
as a traditional bound book at:
www.1stWorldLibrary.com/purchase.asp?ISBN=978-1-4218-3063-6

1st World Library is a literary, educational organization
dedicated to:

- Creating a free internet library of downloadable ebooks

- Hosting writing competitions and offering book
publishing scholarships.

Interested in more 1st World Library books?
contact: literacy@1stworldlibrary.com
Check us out at: www.1stworldlibrary.com

1st World Library Literary Society

Giving Back to the World

"If you want to work on the core problem, it's early school literacy."

- James Barksdale, former CEO of Netscape

"No skill is more crucial to the future of a child, or to a democratic and prosperous society, than literacy."

- Los Angeles Times

Literacy... means far more than learning how to read and write... The aim is to transmit... knowledge and promote social participation."

- UNESCO

"Literacy is not a luxury, it is a right and a responsibility. If our world is to meet the challenges of the twenty-first century we must harness the energy and creativity of all our citizens."

- President Bill Clinton

"Parents should be encouraged to read to their children, and teachers should be equipped with all available techniques for teaching literacy, so the varying needs and capacities of individual kids can be taken into account."

- Hugh Mackay

ORIGINAL PREPARER'S NOTE

This text was prepared from an edition, published by Frederick A. Stokes Company, New York, 1917. It was published in England under the title "Sadie's Conquest."

CHAPTER I

THE PORTRAIT

It was getting dark when Festing stopped at the edge of a ravine on the Saskatchewan prairie. The trail that led up through the leafless birches was steep, and he had walked fast since he left his work at the half-finished railroad bridge. Besides, he felt thoughtful, for something had happened during the visit of a Montreal superintendent engineer that had given him a hint. It was not exactly disturbing, because Festing had, to some extent, foreseen the line the superintendent would take; but a post to which he thought he had a claim had been offered to somebody else. The post was not remarkably well paid, but since he was passed over now, he would, no doubt, be disappointed when he applied for the next, and it was significant that as he stood at the top of the ravine he first looked back and then ahead.

In the distance, a dull red glow marked the bridge, where the glare of the throbbing blast-lamps flickered across a muddy river, swollen by melting snow. He heard the ring of the riveters' hammers and the clang of flung-down rails. The whistle of a gravel train came faintly across the grass, and he knew that for a long distance gangs of men were smoothing the roughly graded track.

In front, everything was quiet. The pale-green sky was streaked along the horizon by a band of smoky red, and the gray prairie rolled into the foreground, checkered by clumps of birches and patches of melting snow. In one place, the figures of a man and horses moved slowly across the fading light; but except for this, the wide landscape was without life and desolate. Festing, however, knew it would not long remain a silent waste. A change was coming with the railroad; in a few years, the wilderness would be covered with wheat; and noisy gasoline tractors would displace the plowman's teams. Moreover, a change was coming to him; he felt that he had reached the trail fork and now must choose his path.

He was thirty years of age and a railroad builder, though he hardly thought he had much talent for his profession. Hard work and stubborn perseverance had carried him on up to the present, but it looked as if he could not go much farther. It was eight years since he began by joining a shovel gang, and he felt the lack of scientific training. He might continue to fill subordinate posts, but the men who came to the front had been taught by famous engineers and held certificates.

Yet Festing was ambitious and had abilities that sprang rather from character than technical knowledge, and now wondered whether he should leave the railroad and join the breakers of virgin soil. He knew something about prairie farming and believed that success was largely a matter of temperament. One must be able to hold on if one meant to win. Then he dismissed the matter for a time, and set off again with a firm and vigorous tread.

Spring had come suddenly, as it does on the high Saskatchewan plains, and he was conscious of a strange, bracing but vaguely disturbing quality in the keen air. One felt moved to adventure and a longing for something new. Men with brain and muscle were needed in the wide, silent land that would soon waken to busy life; but one must not give way to romantic impulses. Stern experience had taught Festing caution, his views were utilitarian, and he distrusted sentiment. Still, looking back on years of strenuous effort that aimed at practical objects, he felt that there was something he had missed. One must work to live, but perhaps life had more to

Harold Bindloss

offer than the money one earned by toil.

The red glow on the horizon faded and an unbroken arch of dusky blue stretched above the plain. He passed a poplar bluff where the dead branches cut against the sky. The undergrowth had withered down and the wood was very quiet, with the snow-bleached grass growing about its edge, but he seemed to feel the pulse of returning life. The damp sod that the frost had lately left had a different smell. Then a faint measured throbbing came out of the distance, and he knew the beat of wings before a harsh, clanging call fell from the sky.

He stopped and watched a crescent of small dark bodies plane down on outstretched wings. The black geese were breaking their long journey to the marshes by the Arctic Sea; they would rest for a few days in the prairie sloos and then push on again. Their harsh clamor had a note of unrest and rang through the dark like a trumpet call, stirring the blood. The brant and bernicle beat their way North against the roaring winds, and man with a different instinct pressed on towards the West.

It was a rich land that rolled back before him towards the setting sun. Birch and poplar bluffs broke the wide expanse; there was good water in the winding creeks, a black soil that the wheat plant loved lay beneath the sod, and the hollows held shallow lakes that seldom quite dried up. Soon the land would be covered with grain; already there were scattered patches on which the small homesteaders labored to free themselves from debt. For the most part, their means and tools were inadequate, the haul to the elevators was long, and many would fall an easy prey to the mortgage robber. But things would soon be different; the railroad had come. For all that, Festing resolved that he would not be rash. His pay was good in the meantime, and he would wait.

By and by a cluster of buildings rose out of the grass. A light or two twinkled; a frame house, a sod stable, and straw-covered wheat bins that looked like huge beehives grew into shape. The homestead was good, as homesteads in the back townships went, but Festing knew the land was badly worked. Charnock had begun well, with money in the bank, but luck had been against him and he had got slack. Indeed this was Charnock's trouble; when a job got difficult, he did not stay with it.

Festing crossed the fall back-set, where the loam from the frost-split clods stuck to his boots, passed the sod stable, noting that one end was falling down, and was met on the veranda by Charnock's dogs. They sprang upon him with welcoming barks, and pushing through them, he entered the untidy living-room. Charnock sat at a table strewn with papers that looked like bills, and there was a smear of ink on his chin.

"Hallo!" he said. "Sit down and take a smoke while I get through with these."

Festing pulled a chair into his favorite corner by the stove and looked about when he had lighted his pipe. The room was comfortless and bare, with cracked, board walls, from which beads of resin exuded. A moose head hung above a rack of expensive English guns, a piano stood in a corner, and lumps of the *gumbo* soil that lay about the floor had gathered among its legs. Greasy supper plates occupied the end of the table, and the boards round the stove were blackened by the distillate that dripped from the joint where the pipe went through the ceiling. These things were significant, particularly the last, since one need not burn green wood, which had caused the tarry stain, and the joint could have been made tight.

Then Festing glanced at Charnock. The latter was a handsome man of about Festing's age. He had a high color and an easy smile, but he had, so to speak, degenerated since he came to Canada. Festing remembered his keenness and careless good-humor when he began to farm, but disappointment had blunted the first, though his carelessness remained. He had been fastidious, but one now got a hint of a coarse streak and there was something about his face that indicated dissipation. Yet Festing admitted that he had charm.

"You don't look happy," he remarked.

"I don't feel particularly happy," Charnock replied. "In fact, the reckoning I've just made looks very like a notice to quit." He threw Festing a paper and swept the others into a drawer. "You might examine the calculations and see if they're right. I'm not fond of figures."

"That was obvious long since. However, if you'll keep quiet for a few minutes—"

Festing studied the paper, which contained a rough statement of Charnock's affairs. The balance was against him, but Festing thought it might be wiped off, or at least pulled down, by economy and well-directed effort. The trouble was that Charnock disliked economy, and of late had declined to make a fight. Festing doubted if he could be roused, but meant to try.

"I see an error of a hundred dollars, but that doesn't make much difference. Things look pretty bad, but I imagine they could be straightened out."

"How long would it take you to put them straight?"

"Three years," said Festing, when he had made a rough calculation. "That is, if I got moderately good crops, but I'd cut out drinks, the pool game, and some other extravagances. You want to keep away from the settlement."

"You'd cut out all that makes life bearable," Charnock replied, and added while his face went hard: "Besides, three years is too long."

Festing thought he understood. The portrait of an English girl hung on the wall behind the stove, and Charnock had already been some time in Canada.

"Anyhow," the latter resumed, "you take much for granted if

you count upon a moderately good crop; I haven't got one yet. We're told this is a great country for the small farmer, and perhaps it is, so long as he escapes a dry June, summer hail, rust, and autumn frost. As a matter of fact, I've suffered from the lot!"

"So have others, but they're making good."

"At a price! They sweat, when it's light long enough, sixteen hours a day, deny themselves everything a man can go without, and when the grain is sold the storekeeper or implement dealer takes all they get. When the fellow's sure of their honesty he carried them on, for the sake of the interest, until, if they're unusually lucky, a bonanza crop helps them to wipe off the debt. But do you imagine any slave in the old days ever worked so hard?"

Festing knitted his brows. He felt that Charnock must be answered, and he was not a philosopher.

"Canada's a pretty hard country, and the man without much capital who undertakes to break new soil must have nerve. But he has a chance of making good, and a few years of self-denial do a man no harm. In fact, I expect he's better for it afterwards. A fool can take life easily and do himself well while his dollars last."

Charnock smiled sourly. "I've heard something of this kind before! You're a Spartan; but suppose we admit that a man might stand the strain, what about a woman?"

"That complicates the thing. I suppose you mean an Englishwoman?"

"I do. An Englishwoman of the kind you used to know at home, for example. Could she live on rancid pork, molasses, and damaged flour? You know the stuff the storekeepers supply their debtors. Would you expect a delicately brought-up girl to cook for you, and mend and wash your clothes, besides making hers? To struggle with chores that never end, and be content, for months, with your society?"

Festing pondered. Life on a small prairie farm was certainly hard for a woman; for a man it was bracing, although it needed pluck and resolution. Festing had both qualities, perhaps in an unusual degree, and his point of view was essentially practical. He had grappled with so many difficulties that he regarded them as problems to be solved and not troubles to complain about. He believed that what was necessary or desirable must be done, no matter how hard it was. One considered only the best way of removing an obstacle, not the effort of mind and body it cost. Still, he could not explain this to Charnock; he was not a moralizer or clever at argument.

Then half-consciously he fixed his eyes on the portrait which he had often studied when the talk flagged. The girl was young, but there was something in the poise of her head that have her an air of distinction. Festing did not know if distinction was quite what he meant, but could not think of a better term. She looked at one with steady eyes; her gaze was frank and fearless, as if she had confidence in herself. Yet it was not an aggressive confidence, but rather a calm that sprang from pride—the right kind of pride. In a way, he knew nothing about her, but he was sure she would disdain anything that was shabby and mean. He was not a judge of beauty, but thought the arch of her brows and the lines of nose and mouth were good. She was pretty, but in admitting this one did not go far enough. The pleasure he got from studying her picture was his only romantic weakness, and he could indulge it safely because if he ever saw her it would be when she had married his friend.

The curious thing was that she had promised to marry Charnock. Bob was a good sort, but he was not on this girl's level, and if she raised him to it, would probably feel uncomfortable there. He was slack and took the easiest way, while a hint of coarseness had recently got more marked. Festing was not fastidious, but he lived with clear-eyed, wiry men who could do all that one could expect from flesh and blood. They quarreled about their wages and sometimes struck a domineering boss, but they did their work, in spite of scorching heat and biting frost. Raging floods, snowslides, and rocks that rolled down the mountain side and smashed the track never daunted them. Their character had something of the clean hardness of finely tempered steel. But Charnock was different.

"So you think of quitting?" Festing said at length.

"I'm forced to quit; I'm in too deep to get straight. It's possible that the man I owe most money might give me time, but it would only mean that I'd slave for another year or two and come down after all. I don't see why I should sweat and deny myself for somebody else's benefit, particularly as I'm not fond of doing so for my own."

"Then you have made a plan?"

Charnock laughed. "I'd a notion of applying for a railroad job. The pay's pretty good, and I daresay you could put me on the track."

"I could. The trouble is that somebody else might afterwards put you off. However, if you'd like to try—"

"I'll wait a bit. I don't know that it's prudent to plunge into things."

"It is, if you plunge in and stop in until you struggle out with what you want. Come up to the track and ask for me when you decide to let the farm go."

"On the whole, I think not," said Charnock, whose look got somewhat strained. "You see, I expect an offer of another post though nothing's been fixed yet. We'll let the matter drop in the meantime. Are you going to the Long Lake picnic?"

Festing looked at him with surprise. "Certainly not! Did you ever know me leave my job to go to a picnic?"

"It might be better if you did! My opinion is you think too much about your job."

"You think too little about yours," Festing rejoined. "Anyhow, what amusement do you think I'd get from lounging round Long Lake all day?"

"The ducks ought to be plentiful and I'd lend you a gun. In fact, I'll lend you my second team, if you'll drive the Marvin girls over."

"No, thanks," said Festing firmly. "Somebody left Flora Marvin on my hands at the supper, and I imagine she got very tired. She certainly looked tired; the girls about the settlement don't hide their feelings. But who's going with you, since you want the other team?"

"I promised to take Sadie Keller."

"Sadie Keller?" Festing exclaimed and paused, rather awkwardly. "Well, of course, I don't see why you shouldn't take her, if she wants to go."

Charnock looked at him with amusement. "As she's the chief organizer of the picnic, Sadie does want to go. For that matter, it was her suggestion that I should bring you."

"I won't be there; for one thing, I'm too busy," Festing declared, and soon afterwards got up. "It's time I started back to camp."

Leaving the homestead, he walked thoughtfully across the plain. Charnock had his faults, but he was his friend and was now in trouble. However, as he had not the pluck to face his difficulties, Festing did not see how he could help. Then he did not like Bob's taking Miss Keller to the picnic, because he had met and thought her dangerous. It was not that she had tried to flirt with him, although she had done so; he felt that if he had played up, it might have been difficult afterwards to let the matter drop. Sadie was not a silly coquette. She had a calculating bent, ambition, and a resolute character. She would not flirt with anybody who was, so to speak, not worth powder and shot.

Festing did not know how Miss Keller rated his value, but he was satisfied to remain a bachelor, and had perhaps allowed her to understand this, because she had since treated him with cold politeness. Now it looked as if she had thrown Bob some favor, which was ominous, because Sadie had generally an object. Of course, if Bob were free and content to marry a girl from the settlement, Sadie would not be a bad choice. She certainly had some virtues. But Bob was not free, and it was unthinkable that a man who had won the love of the girl whose portrait Festing knew should be satisfied with another of Sadie's type.

Then Festing pulled himself up. He could not warn Bob to be cautious, or interfere with the girl's plans, supposing that she had made some. Besides, it was Charnock's affair, not his. By and by he dismissed the matter and thought about a troublesome job that must be undertaken in the morning.

Harold Bindloss

CHAPTER II

THE PICNIC

The picnic at Long Lake was an annual function, held as soon as the weather got warm enough, to celebrate the return of spring. Winter is long and tedious on the high Western plains, where the frost is often Arctic and little work can be done, and after sitting by the red-hot stove through the dark, cold months, the inhabitants of the scattered homesteads come out with joyful hearts to greet the sunshine. There is, however, no slow transition. Rushing winds from the North-west sweep the sky, the snow vanishes, and after a week or two, during which the prairie trails are impassable, the bleached grass dries and green blades and flowers spring from the steaming sod.

Moreover, the country round Long Lake has some beauty. To the east, it runs back, bare and level, with scarcely a tree to break the vast expanse; but to the west low undulations rise to the edge of the next tableland. Sandhills mark the summits, but the slopes are checkered with birches and poplars, and creeks of clear water flow through the hollows in the shadow of thick bluffs. There are many ponds, and here and there a shallow lake shines amidst the sweep of grass. The clear air and the distance the view commands give the landscape a distinctive charm. One has a sense of space and freedom; all the eye rests upon is clean-cut.

It was a bright morning when Charnock drove up to the door of Keller's hotel. The street was one-sided, and for the most part of its length, small, ship-lap-board houses boldly fronted the prairie. A few had shallow verandas that relieved their bareness, but the rest were frankly ugly, and in some the front was carried up level with the roof-ridge, giving them a harsh squareness of outline. A plank sidewalk, raised a foot or two above the ground, ran along the street, where the black soil was torn by wagon wheels.

There was nothing attractive about the settlement, and Charnock had once been repelled by its dreariness. He, however, liked society, and as the settlement was the only center of human intercourse, had acquired the habit of spending time there that ought to have been devoted to his farm. He enjoyed a game of pool, and to sit on the hotel veranda, bantering the loungers, was a pleasant change from driving the plow or plodding through the dust that rolled about the harrows. For all that, he knitted his brows as his light wagon lurched past the Chinese laundry and the poolroom in the next block. The place looked mean and shabby in the strong sunlight, and, with feelings he had thought dead re-awaking, he was conscious of a sharp distaste. There was a choice he must shortly make, and he knew what it would cost to take the line that might be forced on him.

It was with a certain shrinking he stopped his team in front of the hotel. The bare windows were open and the door was hooked back, so that one could see into the hall, where a row of tin wash-basins stood on a shelf. Dirty towels were scattered about, and the boarded floor was splashed. The veranda, on to which the hall opened, was strewn with cigar-ends and burnt matches, and occupied by a row of cheap wooden chairs. Above the door was painted *The Keller House*. The grocery in the next block, and the poolroom, bore the same owner's name.

When Charnock stopped, a man without a coat and with the sleeves of his fine white shirt rolled up came out. He as rather an old man and his movements were slack; his face was hard, but on the whole expressionless.

"Hallo!" he said. "Late again! The others have pulled out a quarter of an hour since."

"I saw them," Charnock answered with a languid hint of meaning. "Didn't want to join the procession and thought they might load up my rig if I got here on time."

Keller looked hard at him, as if he understood, and then asked: "Want a drink before you start?"

"No, thanks," said Charnock, with an effort; and Keller, going to the door, shouted: "Sadie!"

A girl came out on the veranda. She was a handsome girl, smartly dressed in white, with a fashionable hat that had a tall plume. Her hair and eyes were black, the latter marked by a rather hard sparkle; her nose was prominent and her mouth firm. Her face was colorless, but her skin had the clean smoothness of silk. She had a firmly lined, round figure, and her manner was easy and confident. Sadie Keller was then twenty-one years of age.

"I thought you had forgotten to come, Bob," she said with a smile.

"Then you were very foolish; you ought to have known me better," Charnock replied, and helped her into the wagon.

"Well, you do forget things," she resumed as he started the team.

"Not those I want to remember. Besides, if you really thought I had forgotten, you'd have been angry."

"How d'you know I'm not angry now?"

Charnock laughed. "When you're angry everybody in the neighborhood knows."

This was true. Sadie was young, but there was something imperious about her. She had a strong will, and when it was thwarted was subject to fits of rage. Reserve was not among her virtues, and Charnock's languid carelessness sometimes attracted and sometimes annoyed her. It marked him as different from the young men she knew and gave him what she called tone, but it had drawbacks.

"Let me have the reins; I want to drive," she said, and added as the horses trotted across the grass beside the torn-up trail: "You keep a smart team, but they're too light for much work about the farm."

"That's so. Still, you see, I like fast horses."

"They have to be paid for," Sadie rejoined.

"Very true, but I don't want to talk about such matters now. Then I've given up trying to make the farm pay. When you find a thing's impossible, it's better to let it go."

Sadie did not reply. She meant to talk about this later, but preferred to choose her time. Her education had been rudimentary, but she was naturally clever. She liked admiration, but was not to be led into foolishness by vanity. Sadie knew her value. It had for some time been obvious that a number of the young farmers who dealt at the store and frequented the hotel did so for her sake, and she was willing to extend her father's trade. In fact, she helped to manage both businesses as cleverly as she managed the customers. Her charm was largely physical, but she used it with caution. One might indulge in banter, and Sadie had a ringing laugh that young men liked, but there were limits that few who knew her overstepped. One or two had done so, but had been rebuked in a way they wished to forget. Sadie had the tricks of an accomplished coquette, but something of the heart of a prude.

The settlement got indistinct, and crossing a low rise, they drove past a birch bluff where the twigs were breaking into tiny points of green. Then they forded a creek and skirted a shallow lake, from which a flock of ducks rose and flew North in a straggling wedge. Sandhills gleamed on the ridges, tall cranes stalked about the hollows, and when the team, laboring through the loose soil, crossed an elevation one could see the plain roll back into the far distance. It was sharp-cut to the horizon; only the varying color that changed from soft blue to white and yellow in the foreground helped the eye to gage its vast extent. The snow had bleached the grass, which glittered like silver in the strong sunlight.

A boisterous wind from the North-west drove white-edged clouds across the sky, but the air was soft with a genial warmth that drew earthy smells from the drying sod. In places, an emerald flush had begun to spread across the withered grass and small flowers like crocuses were pushing through. The freshness and hint of returning life reacted on Charnock, and stirred his blood when he glanced at his companion. He felt her physical allurement as he had not felt it before, but now and then he resolutely looked away. Sadie had shown him marked favor, but there was much he might lose.

She would not have charmed him when he first came to the prairie with romantic hopes and vague ambitions. He had been fastidious then, and the image of a very different girl occupied his heart. Even now he knew the other stood for all that was best in life; for tender romances, and sweetness, and high purpose. Helen had gracious qualities he had once half-reverently admired. She loved pictures and books and music, and was marked by a calm serenity that was very different from Sadie's restless force. But it looked as if he had lost her, and Sadie, who could break a horse and manage a hotel, was nearer his level. Yet he hesitated; he must choose one of two paths, and when he had chosen could not turn back.

"You don't talk much," Sadie remarked at length. "Guess you must be thinking about your mortgage."

"I was, in a way. It was rather useless and very rude. However,

I won't think of it again until somebody makes me."

"That's a way of yours. You think too late."

"I'm afraid I sometimes do so," Charnock admitted. "Anyhow, to-day, I'm not going to think at all."

Sadie noted the reckless humor with which he began to talk, but she led him on, and they engaged in cheerful banter until Long Lake began to gleam among the woods ahead. Charnock skirted the trees and pulled up where a number of picketed teams and rigs stood near the water's edge. Farther along, a merry party was gathering wood to build a fire, and Charnock did not find Sadie alone again for some hours after he helped her down.

In summer, Long Lake has no great beauty and shrinks, leaving a white saline crust on its wide margin of sun-baked mud, but it is a picturesque stretch of water when the snow melts in spring and the reflections of the birches quiver on the smooth belt along its windward edge. Farther out, the shadows of flying clouds chase each other across the flashing surface. Two or three leaky canoes generally lie among the trees, and in the afternoon Charnock dragged one down, and helping Sadie on board, paddled up the lake.

As they crept round a point flocks of ducks left the water and the air throbbed with a beat of wings that gradually died away. The fire, round which the others sat, was out of sight, and the rustle of the tossing birches emphasized the quietness. Charnock let the canoe drift, and Sadie looked up at him from her low seat among the wagon robes he had brought.

"What are you going to do about your farm?" she asked.

"I don't know yet, and don't see why I should bore you with my troubles."

"Pshaw!" said Sadie. "You want to put the thing off; but you know you can't."

Charnock made a gesture of humorous resignation. "Very well! I expect I won't be able to carry on the farm."

"No," said Sadie, thoughtfully, "I don't think you could. There are men who would be able, but not you."

"I dare say you're right, but you're not flattering," Charnock rejoined with a smile.

Sadie gave him a steady look. "Your trouble is you laugh when you ought to set your lips and get busy. One has got to hustle in Canada."

"I have hustled. In fact, it's hustling that has brought me low. If I hadn't spent my money trying to break fresh land, I wouldn't have been so deep in debt."

"And you'd have had more time to loaf about the settlement?"

"On the whole, I don't think that's kind. If I hadn't come to the settlement, I wouldn't have seen you, and that's about the only comfort I have left."

A touch of color crept into Sadie's face, but her thoughtful look did not change.

"Well," she said, "I'd surely have liked you to make good, and don't know that we mightn't have got the mortgage held over; but it wouldn't have been much use. You'd have started again and then got tired and not have stayed with it." She spread out her hands impatiently. "That's the kind of man you are!"

"I'm afraid it's true," Charnock admitted. "But I hope you like me all the same."

Sadie was silent for a few moments, but her color was higher and Charnock mused. He supposed she meant she could have persuaded her father to come to his help, and it looked as if she well knew his failings. Still he felt rather amused than resentful.

"We'll let that go," she resumed. "I want you to quit joking and listen. We're going to have a boom at the settlement as soon as the railroad's opened, and I and the old man can hardly manage the store and hotel. We've got to have help; somebody the boys like and we can trust. Well, if you took hold the right way—"

She stopped, but Charnock understood. Keller was often ill and was getting old. He could not carry on his rapidly extending business much longer, and Charnock might presently take his place. But this was not all, and he hesitated.

"Do you think I'm fit for the job?" he asked.

"You could do it if you tried."

Charnock smiled. "It's comforting to feel somebody trusts me, and I see advantages in the plan. You keep the books, I think. It's very nice in the little back office when the lamps are lit and the store is shut. We could make up the bills together."

Sadie blushed, and he thought he had not seen her look so attractive. She was remarkably pretty, although there was now something about her that puzzled him. It was something elusive that acted like a barrier, keeping him away. Yet he knew the girl was fond of him; if he wanted her, he had but to ask, and it was not on this account he hesitated. He thought of a creeper-covered house in England; a house that had an air of quiet dignity. He remembered the old silver, the flowers in the shady rooms, and the pictures. The girl who moved about the rooms harmonized with her surroundings; her voice was low and clear, she had a touch of stateliness. Well, he was ruined, and she was far away, but Sadie was close by, waiting for him. For a moment he set his lips, and then, while his nerves tingled, banished the disturbing doubts.

Dropping the paddle, he leaned forward, put his hand on the girl's waist, and drew her towards him. He felt her yield, and heard her draw a fluttering breath. Her head drooped so that he could not see her face; she was slipping into his arms, and then, in the moment of surrender, he felt her body stiffen. She put her hands on his shoulder and pushed him back; the canoe lurched and he had some trouble to prevent a capsize. The water splashed against the rocking craft, and Sadie, drawing away, fixed her eyes on him. She was breathless, but rather from emotion than effort.

"Don't do that again!" she said.

Charnock saw she meant it, which was strange. Sadie knew and sometimes used her power of attraction, but it was obvious that she was angry. It looked as if he had chosen the wrong moment, and he felt worse baffled and disappointed than he had thought possible.

"I won't," he said as carelessly as he could. "You nearly threw us both into the water."

"I guess that's what I meant to do," she answered fiercely.

"Well, I expect I'd have been able to pull you out. Suppose I ought to say I'm sorry; but I'm not. In fact, Sadie, I don't quite understand—"

"No," she said, "you don't understand at all! That's the trouble."

Charnock took out his tobacco pouch and began to make a cigarette. Sadie's cold dignity was something new and he thought she could not keep it up. If she did not break out in passionate anger, she would soon come round. As he finished the cigarette she turned to him with flashing eyes.

"Put that tobacco away or I'll throw it in the lake! Do you think you can kiss me when you like?"

"I wish I could," said Charnock. "As a matter of fact, I haven't kissed you yet. But I'm sorry if you're vexed."

For a moment Sadie hesitated and then fixed him with a fierce, scornful gaze.

"Oh," she said, "you're cheap, and you'd make me as cheap as you! You want things for nothing; they must be given, where other men would work and fight. But you can't amuse yourself by making love to me."

Charnock felt humiliated. If he had really offended her, she could have rebuked him with a look or sign. Her unnecessary frankness jarred.

"Very well; I must ask you to forget it. Of course, I was wrong, but I'll try not to vex you again. What are we going to do now?"

"Paddle back to the others as quick as you can."

Throwing his cigarette into the water, Charnock turned the canoe. It was a relief to be energetic, because Sadie's demand for speed stung him. He glanced at her now and then, but she gave no sign of relenting; her face was whiter than usual and her look was strained. Getting angry, he drove the canoe down the lake with a curling wave at her bow, until the paddle snapped in a savage stroke and he flung the haft away. For a moment, he hoped Sadie would laugh, but she did not.

"Now you'll have to paddle with your hands until you pick up the broken blade," she said.

Charnock did so and afterwards awkwardly propelled the craft towards the camp fire. He thought Sadie might have suggested their landing and walking back, but she was silent and calmly watched his clumsy efforts. He was glad when they reached the beach where the others were and he helped her out. An hour or two later he drove her home, but she did not talk. Her anger had gone, but she seemed strangely distant. After helping her down at the hotel he waited a moment.

"Can't we make this up and be friends again?" he asked.

She gave him a curious steady glance. "Not now. It looks as if you didn't know me yet."

Then she left him, and Charnock drove home in a thoughtful mood. He had some idea about what she meant and had been rather surprised by the pride she had shown. Sadie had certainly led him on; but she was not altogether the girl he had thought.

CHAPTER III

KELLER INTERFERES

For two or three weeks after the picnic Charnock did not meet Sadie. The rebuff he had got did not rankle much, and was rather provocative than daunting, but he understood why she had told him he made her cheap. She meant to keep her caresses for her husband or declared lover, and if he wanted her, he must pay the regular price. This was very proper, from her point of view, but from his the price was high.

Sadie was pretty, capable, and amusing, but he was not sure he would like to see her every day, in his house and at his table. Besides, the house would really be hers, and Sadie would not forget this. She was determined and liked her own way. He had promised to marry another girl, of a very different stamp, but his conscience was clear on that point. It was better for Helen's sake that he should give her up, because he was on the edge of ruin and she was much too good for him. Irresolution, however, was perhaps his greatest failing, and now he must decide, he wavered and thought about what he had lost.

There were days when he would not admit that all was lost, and harnessing his team in the early morning, drove the gangplow through the soil until the red sunset faded off the plain. In his heart, he knew the fight was hopeless; Festing, for example, in his place, might perhaps make good, but he had not the stamina for the long struggle. All the same, he worked with savage energy until his mood changed and he went off to hunt sandhill cranes. He would sooner have gone to the poolroom, but there was a risk of his meeting Sadie at the settlement.

In the meantime the days got warmer and a flush of vivid green spread across the grass. The roaring wind that swept the tableland drove clouds that never broke across the dazzling sky, and where there were belts of plowed land the harrows clanked across the furrows amidst a haze of blowing dust. The ducks and geese had gone, and red lilies began to sway above the rolling waves of grass. Farmer and hired man worked with tense activity, but Charnock's efforts were spasmodic and often slack.

In the meantime, trade was brisk at the settlement, and Keller found his business made demands on him that he could hardly meet. It was rapidly growing, and his strength got less. Indeed, he would have sold out but for Sadie. The girl was clever and had tone; he wanted her to find life smooth and taste pleasure her mother had not enjoyed. The latter had helped him in a hard fight when dollars were very scarce, and died, worn out, just before the tide turned. Since then he had schemed and sweated to make her child's future safe.

Now he thought he had done so, but it had been a struggle, and he knew he had held on too long. Keeping store in a wheat-growing district was not a simple matter of selling groceries; one was in reality a banker. Bills were not often paid until the crop was harvested, farmers began without much money, and one must know whom to trust. Indeed, one often financed a hustler who had no capital, and kept an honest man who had lost a crop on his feet; but the risk was great, and one felt the strain when there was rust and autumn frost.

One bright afternoon Keller stood on the sidewalk in front of the store. He was not old, but his hair was gray and his face was pinched. It was rather a hard face, for Keller's glance was keen and his lips were generally firmly set. Yet he was liked by his customers. Now he was breathing hard because he had helped a farmer to put a heavy bag of flour in his wagon. The farmer drove away and a cloud of dust the team stirred up blew down the street. The fronts of the wooden houses were cracking in the hot sun; there was not a tree to relieve the bare ugliness of the place, and the glare was dazzling. Keller at first imagined this was why he could not see the wagon well, but after a few moments he knew better.

He went into the store with a staggering step, and the rank smell of cheese and salt-pork nauseated him. The room felt very hot and was full of flies that buzzed in a tormenting cloud round his head. He wanted quietness and made his way to the dark back office, where he dropped into a chair.

"Go to the hotel," he ordered the clerk who entered after him. "Tell Jake to give you a big glass of the special whisky. Be quick, but don't run and spill the stuff."

The clerk came back in a few minutes, and Keller pulled himself together when he had drained the glass, though his forehead was damp with sweat.

"Now where's the list of the truck Gascoyne got?" he said. "I'll look it up."

"Sure you feel all right?" the clerk inquired.

"Get the list," said Keller. "Take that glass away."

He picked up a pen, but put it down when he found his hand shook, and told the clerk to charge the goods. When the latter had gone, he sat still for some minutes and then opened a book of accounts. He had had another warning, sharper than the last, and had better put things straight while he could. With this object he worked later than usual, and when he returned to the hotel called Sadie into his private room. The girl sat down, and he studied her, leaning his elbow heavily on the table.

Sadie had a strained look and had been quiet for the last week or two except when she was angry. This indicated that her nerves were on edge, and Keller thought he knew why.

"I guess we've got to have a talk," he said. "I've put it off, but now's the time."

Sadie waited calmly. She had courage and knew she must be frank with her father. He did not, as a rule, say much, but he noted things and understood.

"Well," he resumed, "I've built up a pretty good business here, but I'll have to quit and leave you some day, and reckon you won't be satisfied to stop at the hotel all your life. You're smart and a looker, and I guess you want to go out and see the world. That's all right, and you'll be able, as far as dollars count; but I can't go with you and you can't go alone."

Sadie shivered. Keller's face was pinched, and she knew his health was not good, although she did not know how bad it really was.

"I couldn't leave you, anyway, and hope you'll be with me a long time yet."

"It's possible," said Keller. "All the same, I can't keep my grip on the business long and want a man to help. But I'm not going to trust a stranger or a hired man. You see where this leads?"

Sadie saw and made a vague gesture, though her glance was level.

"Very well. The man who carries on my business must be your husband. Now there are three or four of the boys in the settlement who could be taught to run the store and hotel, but I allow you don't want me to choose from them. Have I got that right?"

"Yes," said Sadie with quiet calm, although her heart beat. "None of them would suit."

Keller knitted his brows and his look was grave. "They're good boys, and if you had taken one of that bunch, I'd have been satisfied. I reckon the trouble is they're my kind and belong where I do, while you mean to go higher. Well, that's right; I've put up the dollars to give you a good time, but you can't get where you want on your own feet." He paused with a dry smile. "I allow you're smart enough to figure this out."

"I have," said Sadie. "There's much I don't know and couldn't learn here. If I'm to move up, my husband must help."

"Then I only know two men round the settlement who could help. Festing's my choice."

A wave of color flushed Sadie's white skin, but her voice was quiet. "He isn't mine. I allow, in some ways, he's the better man, but that doesn't count."

Keller looked hard at her. "I used to think your head would guide you, not your heart; but it seems you're like the rest— well, I was a very poor man when your mother married me! Now I like Charnock and he has tone; but if you take him, there's a risk—"

"I know the risk."

"It's plain! I'd stop the thing right now if you were a different girl, but you know what you want and how to keep it when it's got. It looks as if you had made up your mind?"

Sadie's hands moved nervously. She made a sign of agreement, but did not speak, and Keller went on:

"Anyhow, you'd better understand what you're up against. Sometimes you'll have to hustle Charnock and sometimes hold him tight. You must keep him off the liquor, and maybe stop him getting after other girls. Then when you sell out the business, you'll hold the dollars."

For a moment Sadie turned her head and then got up and stood by her father's chair. Her look was strained but resolute as she put her hand on his arm.

"I know all that! Bob has plenty of faults, but he's the man I love."

Keller took and pressed her hand. He had some misgivings, but he knew his daughter.

"We all like Charnock, and though I wouldn't trust him far, I can trust you. I think you've got that right and won't forget. Very well, since you want Charnock I'll get him for you."

Sadie stooped and kissed him and then went out. She was moved, but there was nothing to be said. Her father was not a sentimentalist, but he had never failed her and would not do so now. When she sat down in her room, however, her face was grave. Her courage was high, but she felt half afraid. Although she loved Bob Charnock, life with him might be difficult. He was older than she and knew much more, but she must lead him and be firm where he was weak. It was a hard task for an ignorant girl, but she resolved to carry it out.

Next morning Keller went down the street and entered a wooden building filled with gaudily painted mowers and plows. He was not the man to waste time when he had made a plan, and moreover felt that he had not much time to lose. Finding the implement dealer in his office, he sat down, breathing rather hard.

"You don't look very spry this morning," the dealer remarked.

"I don't feel so bright. The boys have been rushing me the last week or two. Say, trade is booming now!"

"It surely is. I could sell more machines than I've got, but I've got a lot of money standing out, and after the bad harvest last fall, don't know who to trust."

They compared notes about their customers, and presently the dealer remarked: "Charnock was in a few days ago, asking about a new wagon, a mower, and some small tools."

"Ah!" said Keller, rather sharply. "Then it looks as if he meant to hold on! He reckoned, not long since, that he'd have to quit. But what did you tell him?"

"To come again. I'd like to keep Bob Charnock up, but guess it's dangerous. Owes me a pile. How does he stand with you?"

Keller supplied the information, and the other looked thoughtful. "Didn't know it was quite so bad as that. I allow I'd better not let him have the goods."

"Well, I reckon he's trying the new man at Concord. Smith said he met him there yesterday."

The dealer frowned. He hated to think of a customer going to somebody else. In fact, this was, for a debtor, an unpardonable offense.

"Charnock's trouble is that he's not quite straight. Ought to have stayed with me, told me how he was fixed, and let me see what I could do. If he's going to deal with the new man, I'd better pull him up and try to get my money back."

"You can't get it," said Keller dryly. "He can't pay now, and if you let him go on until harvest, you'll have a crowd of others with long bills fighting for what's left."

"Looks like that," the dealer agreed. "Well, I'd have liked to keep him going if he'd stayed with me, but I can't stand for losing the dollars he owes. What are we going to do about the thing?"

Keller explained his plans, and after some argument the other agreed. The decision they came to would bring Charnock's farming to an end, but Keller left the office with some doubts. His scheme was going to succeed, but he wondered whether he had indulged Sadie too far. Much depended on her firmness, and she might find the job harder than she thought; but on the whole he imagined she would be equal to the strain.

A week later, Charnock sat, one afternoon, in the saddle of his gang-plow, tearing a row of furrows through the dusty sod. The sweating horses moved leisurely, and he did not urge them as he moodily watched the tangled grass part before the shares and vanish beneath the polished surface of the turned-up clods. He was breaking new soil, doing work that would be paid for in the future, and knew the reward of his labor might never be his. When he reached the end of the plowing he stopped and let the horses rest while he looked about.

One side of the long furrows gleamed in the strong light, and another team was moving towards him from the opposite end. The sun was hot, but the wind was fresh, and thin clouds of dust blew across the plain. Still the belt he was plowing was good soil; the firm black *gumbo* that holds the moisture the wheat plant needs. There was something exhilarating in the rushing breeze and glow of light, but Charnock frowned and wondered why he had worked so long. He had no real hope, and admitted that he had continued his spasmodic efforts because he could not face defeat.

For all that, he had not been fighting entirely for his farm. He wanted to keep his freedom; to break through trammels that were getting tighter, and try to regain something that he had lost. Sometimes he felt desperate, but now and then saw an elusive ray of hope. If he could hold out until harvest and reap a record crop—

Then his hired man, driving the other plow, waved his arm, and Charnock saw a rig lurch across a rise amidst a cloud of sand. It was the mail-carrier going his round, but he would not have come that way unless he had letters, and Charnock waited until the man arrived.

"Here's your lot," he said, taking out three or four envelopes.

Charnock's hand shook as he opened the first, it was large and had an official look, and he found a number of unpaid accounts inside. Besides these, there was a lawyer's letter, stating that certain dealers had instructed him to recover payment of the debts Charnock owed. He crushed the letter in his clenched hand and the veins stood out on his forehead, while his face got red. The blow he feared had fallen and he was ruined; but when the shock began to pass he felt a faint relief. It was something to be free from doubt and anxiety, and there were consolations. Now he was beaten, the line he must take was plain, and it had some advantages.

"You can quit plowing and put the teams in the stable," he said to the hired man.

"Quit now!" exclaimed the other. "What about the machines?"

"Let them stop," said Charnock. "It seems they belong to my creditors, who can look after them. I'm going to Concord and don't know when I'll be back."

He went off towards the homestead and half an hour later drove away across the plain.

CHAPTER IV

FESTING COMMITS THEFT

The air was sharp and wonderfully invigorating when Festing stopped for a few moments, one evening, outside Charnock's homestead. A row of sandhills glimmered faintly against the blue haze in the east, but the western edge of the plain ran in a hard black line beneath a blaze of smoky red. It was not dark, but the house was shadowy, and Festing noticed a smell of burning as he entered.

The top was off the stove in Charnock's room, and the flame that licked about the hole showed that the floor was strewn with torn paper. Charnock was busy picking up the pieces, and when he threw a handful into the stove a blaze streamed out and the light shone upon the wall. Festing noted that the portrait that had hung there had gone, and looking round in search of it, saw a piece of the broken frame lying on the stove. It was half burned and a thin streak of smoke rose from its glowing end. Festing remarked this with a sense of anger.

"What are you doing, Bob?" he asked.

"Cleaning up," Charnock answered, with a hoarse laugh, as he sat down among the litter. "Proper thing when you mean to make a fresh start! Suppose you take a drink and help."

A whisky bottle and a glass stood on the table, and Festing thought Charnock had taken some liquor, although he was not drunk. Stooping down, he began to pick up the papers, which, for the most part, looked like bills. There were, however, a few letters in a woman's hand, and by and by he found a bit of riband, a glove, and a locket that seemed to have been trampled on.

"Are these to be burned?" he asked.

"Yes," said Charnock. "Don't want them about to remind me—Burn the lot."

Festing, with some reluctance, threw them into the stove. He was not, as a rule, romantic, but it jarred him to see the things destroyed. They had, no doubt, once been valued for the giver's sake; dainty hands had touched them; the locket had rested on somebody's white skin. They were pledges of trust and affection, and he had found them, trampled by Charnock's heavy boots, among the dust and rubbish.

"You'd get on faster if you used a brush," he suggested.

"Can't find the brush. Confounded thing's hidden itself somewhere. Can't remember where I put anything to-night. Suppose you don't see a small lace handkerchief about?"

Festing said he did not, and Charnock made a gesture of resignation. "Looks as if I'd burned it with the other truck, but I got that from Sadie, and there'll be trouble if she wants to know where it's gone. She may want to know some time. Sadie doesn't forget."

"Did Sadie give you the locket?"

"She did not," said Charnock. "You're a tactless brute. But there's something else I want, and I don't know where it can have got."

He upset a chair as he turned over some rubbish near the table, under which he presently crawled, while Festing looking about, noted a small white square laying half hidden by the stove. Picking it up, he saw it was the portrait of the English girl, and resolved with a thrill of indignation that Charnock should not burn this. He felt that its destruction would be something of an outrage.

He glanced at Charnock, but the latter's legs alone stuck out from under the table, and as it was obvious that he could not see, Festing dusted the portrait and put it in his pocket. By and by Charnock crept out and got upon his feet. It was dark now, but the glow of the burning paper flickered about the room and touched his face. His hair was ruffled, his eyes were dull, and his mouth had a slack droop. Festing felt some pity for the man, though he was also sensible of scornful impatience. The smell of burned paper disturbed him with its hint of vanished romance. Putting the lid on the stove, he took the lamp from Charnock's unsteady hand, and, when he had lighted it, found a brush and set to work. Presently Charnock made a vague sign of relief as he looked at the swept floor.

"All gone!" he remarked. "There was something I couldn't find. Suppose I burned it, though I don't remember."

"There's nothing left," said Festing, who felt guilty. "Why did you destroy the things?"

Charnock sat down and awkwardly lighted his pipe. "Wanted to begin again with what they call a clean slate. Besides, the stove's the best place for bills that bother you."

"You can't get rid of the debts by burning the bills."

"That's true," said Charnock with a grin. "Unfortunately obvious, in fact! However, I cut up my account book."

"I don't see how that would help."

"My creditors can now amuse themselves by finding out how I stand."

Festing frowned impatiently. "A rather childish trick! It doesn't strike me as humorous."

"You're a disgustingly serious fellow," Charnock rejoined. "But you might be a bit sympathetic, because I've had a nasty knock. My creditors have come down on me, and I'm going to be married."

Festing smiled. He had some sense of humor, and Charnock's manner seemed to indicate that he felt he was confronted with two misfortunes.

"You must have known your creditors would pull you up unless you came to terms with them, but one would expect you to please yourself about getting married."

"I'm not sure your joke's in good taste," Charnock answered sullenly. "But in a way, one thing depended on the other. Perhaps I oughtn't to have said so, but I'm upset to-night. Though I did expect to be pulled up, it was a knock."

"No doubt. Are you going to marry Sadie?"

"I am. Have you any reason to disapprove?"

"Certainly not," said Festing. "Sadie's rather a friend of mine."

In a sense, this was true. When Festing first came to the prairie from a mountain construction camp, where he had not seen a woman for twelve months, he had felt Sadie's charm. Moreover, he imagined that the girl liked him and consciously used her power, although with a certain reserve and modesty. For all that, he fought against his inclination and conquered without much effort. Marriage had not much attraction for him, but if he did marry, he meant to choose a wife of a different type.

"Sadie's a very good sort," Charnock resumed. "She knows what we are, and doesn't expect too much; not the kind of girl to make ridiculous demands. In fact, Sadie can make allowances."

Festing thought this was doubtful praise, although it bore out his opinion of the girl. For all that, Sadie might not be so willing to make allowances for her husband as for a lover of whom she was not quite sure.

"Perhaps that kind of thing has advantages," he said. "But I don't know—"

"I do know," said Charnock; "I've tried the other way. The feeling that you're expected to keep on a high plane soon gets tiresome; besides, it isn't natural. It's better to be taken for what you are."

"I suppose so," Festing assented. "Anyway, if Sadie's satisfied—"

Charnock grinned, although there was a touch of color in his face.

"You're not given to flattery, but might use a little tact. I've had a knock and am not quite sober, so I can't argue the point. Then it isn't your business if Sadie's satisfied or not."

"That's so. But what are you going to do when your creditors turn you out?"

"Everything's arranged. I'm going to help Keller at the hotel and store."

Festing got up. "Well, I've stopped longer than I meant. I wish you good luck!"

"We'll have a drink," said Charnock, reaching for the bottle with an unsteady hand. Then he paused and gave Festing a suspicious look. "It's curious about that portrait! I used to see you gazing at it, and don't remember that I picked it up."

"No, thanks," said Festing, refusing the glass. "I think you've had enough. In fact, it might have been better when you were wiping the slate clean if you had put the bottle in the stove."

He went out and walked back to the camp in the moonlight, thinking hard. He was angry with Charnock, but vaguely sorry. Bob had some virtues and was throwing himself away, although, when one came to think of it, this was only true to some extent. What one meant was that he was throwing away his opportunities of rising to a higher plane; while Bob was satisfied with his present level Sadie was good enough for him, perhaps too good. Life together might be hard for both, and there was a touch of pathos in his burning all the tender tokens that bound him to the past, though it was ominous that he kept the whisky. He could, however, get as much liquor as he wanted at the hotel; that is, if Sadie allowed it, but there was some comfort in the thought that the girl was clever and firm.

Festing dismissed the matter, and when he reached his shack at the bridge put the portrait on the table and sat down opposite. He felt that he knew this girl, whom he had never met, very well. Something in her look had cheered him when he had difficulties to overcome; he felt that they were friends. She was calm and fearless and would face trouble with the level glance he knew, although now and then, when the lamp flickered in the draught, he had thought she smiled. They had been companions on evenings when Charnock wanted to read the newspaper or the talk had flagged. Sometimes the window and door were open and the smell of parched grass came in; sometimes the stove was red-hot and the house shook in the icy blast. Festing admitted that it was not altogether for Charnock's society he had visited the homestead.

Then he began to puzzle about a likeness to somebody he knew. He had remarked this before, but the likeness was faint and eluded him. Lighting his pipe, he tried to concentrate his thoughts, and by and by made an abrupt movement. He had it! When he was in British Columbia, engaged on the construction of a section of the railroad that was being built among the mountains, he met a young Englishman at a mining settlement. The lad had been ill and was not strong enough to undertake manual labor, which was the only occupation to be found in the neighborhood. Moreover, he had lost his money, in consequence, Festing gathered, of his trusting dangerous companions.

Festing, finding that he had been well educated and articled to a civil engineer, got him a post on the railroad, where he helped the surveyors. Dalton did well and showed himself grateful, but when Festing went to the prairie he lost touch with the lad. The latter wrote to him once or twice, but he was too busy to keep up the correspondence. Now he knew it was something in Dalton's face he found familiar in the portrait. The girl had a steady level glance, and the lad looked at one like that. Indeed, it was his air of frankness that had persuaded Festing to get him the post.

But this led him nowhere. He did not know the girl's name, and if it was the same as the lad's, it would not prove that they were related. He pushed back his chair and got up. It looked as if he was in some danger of becoming a romantic fool, but he put the portrait carefully away, Soon after he had done so a man came in, and sitting down, lighted a cigarette.

"I wanted to see you, Festing, but hadn't a chance all day," he said. "Probably you haven't heard that I've got orders where to send the staff when the bridge is finished, as it will be soon."

Festing looked up sharply. Kerr was his superior in the company's service, but they were on good terms.

"I haven't heard. I'm anxious to know."

Kerr told him, and Festing's face hardened.

"So Marvin and I go on to the next prairie section! Since they want the best men on the difficult work in the mountains, it means that we're passed over."

"It does, in a sense," Kerr agreed.

"Then I think I know why you came," said Festing, who pondered for a few moments. He had courage and decision, and it was his habit to face a crisis boldly. "Now," he resumed, "I'm going to ask your opinion of my prospects if I stay on the road?"

"Your record's good. You're sure of a post, so long as there's any construction work going on."

"A post of a kind! Not the best kind, where a man would have a chance of making his mark?"

"Well," said Kerr, "I think that's what I meant. The headquarters bosses don't know us personally, and judge by a man's training and the certificates he's got. Of course, in spite of this, talent will find its way, and sometimes one gets there by a stroke of luck."

Festing smiled, rather bitterly. "I have no marked talent, and haven't found it pay to trust to luck. In fact, my only recommendations are a kind of practical ability and a capacity for hard work. I got on the road by doing chores and fought my way up."

"You are practical," Kerr agreed. "It's your strong point, but I've thought it sometimes kept you back."

He paused when Festing looked at him with surprise, but resumed in a thoughtful voice: "When your job's in front of you, you see what must be done, and do it well; there's not a man on my section does that kind of thing better. Still, I'm not sure you always see quite far enough. You miss what lies ahead and sometimes, so to speak, what's lying all round. Concentration's good, but one can concentrate too much. However, I didn't come to find fault, but to let you know how matters are."

Harold Bindloss

"Thanks. I'm going to look ahead and all round now, and the situation strikes me as much like this: If I'm content with a second or third best post, I can stop; if I want to go as far as my power of concentration may take me and find a place where I can use my independent judgment, I'd better quit. Have I got that right?"

"It's what I tried to hint. You can count on my recommendation when it's likely to be of use, but you said something that was rather illuminating. You want to use your judgment?"

Festing laughed. "I don't know that I've thought much about these matters, but I am an individualist. You get up against useless rules, empty formalities, and much general stupidity in organized effort, and good work is often wasted. When you see things that demand to be done, you want to begin right there and get at the job. If you wait to see if it's yours or somebody else's, you're apt not to start at all."

"Your plan has drawbacks now and then," Kerr remarked. "But what are you going to do about the other matter?"

Festing was silent for a few moments. He had to make a momentous choice, but had known that he must do so and did not hesitate.

"I'm going to quit and try farming. After all, I don't know very much about railroad building; up to now I've got on rather by determination than knowledge. Then, if I stop with you, I'll come up against a locked door whenever I try to push ahead."

"There are locked doors in other professions."

"That's so; but in a big organization you must knock and ask somebody to let you through, and unless you have a properly stamped ticket, they turn you back. When the job's your own you beat down the door."

"I've seen farmers who tried that plan left outside with badly jarred hands. Frost and rust and driving sand are difficult obstacles."

"Oh, yes," said Festing. "But they're natural obstacles; you know what you're up against and can overcome them, if you're stubborn enough. What I really mean is, you don't trust to somebody else's good opinion; whether you fail or not depends upon yourself."

"Well," said Kerr, getting up, "I think you're making the right choice, but hope you won't forget me when you leave us. You'll have a friend in the company's service as long as I'm on the road."

He went out and Festing lighted his pipe. Now he had come to a decision, there was much that needed thought; but, to begin with, he knew of a suitable piece of land. Living in camp, he had saved the most part of his pay, and had inherited a small sum from an English relative. In consequence, he could buy the land, build a comfortable wooden house, and have something over to carry him on until he sold his first crop.

He resolved to buy the land and set the carpenters to work, but could not leave the railroad for a month, when it would be rather late to make a start. Then he had worked without a break for twelve years, for the most part at camps where no amusement was possible, and resolved to take a holiday. He would go back to England, where he had a few friends, although his relatives were dead. This was, of course, an extravagance; but after the self-denial he had practised there was some satisfaction in being rash. Lighting another pipe, he abandoned himself to pleasant dreams of his first holiday.

Harold Bindloss

CHAPTER V

A RASH PROMISE

A few days before he started for England, Festing went over to Charnock's homestead, which was shortly to be sold. The evenings were getting light, and although Festing had finished his day's work before he left the bridge, the glow of sunset flooded Charnock's living-room. The strong red light searched out the signs of neglect and dilapidation, the broken boots and harness that needed mending, the dust sticking to the resin-stains on the cracked walls, and the *gumbo* soil on the dirty floor. As Charnock glanced up a level ray touched his face and showed a certain sensual coarseness that one missed when the light was normal. Festing, however, knew the look, and although he had not remarked it when he first met Charnock, thought it had always been there.

The change he had noted in his friend was only on the surface. Charnock had not really deteriorated in Canada; the qualities that had brought him down had been overlaid by a spurious grace and charm, but it now looked as if moral slackness might develop into active vice. On the whole, he thought Sadie would have trouble with Bob, but this was not his business.

"I've come to say good-bye," he remarked. "I won't see you again until my return, and expect you'll be married then."

"Yes," said Charnock, shortly. "I suppose you have made some plans for your trip. Where are you going to stop in England?"

Festing told him and he looked surprised. "I didn't know you had friends in that neighborhood. Will you be with them some time?"

"A month, anyway. Then I may come and go."

Charnock pushed his chair back out of the light. "Well, this makes it easier; there's something I want to ask. We are friends and I've let you give me good advice, though I haven't always acted on it. I don't know if this gives me a claim."

"If there's anything I can do—"

"There is," said Charnock, who hesitated for a few moments. "I want you to go and see Helen Dalton. She's the girl I ought to have married, and doesn't live very far from your friends."

"Ah!" said Festing with a start. "It was her portrait you meant to burn?"

Charnock gave him a sharp glance. "Just so. I imagine I did burn it, because I couldn't find it afterwards."

There was silence for a few moments while Festing wondered whether the other suspected him. Bob had an air of frankness, but was sometimes cunning. This, however, was not important, and Festing was strongly moved by the thought that he might see the girl.

"Why do you want me to go?" he asked.

"In order that you can tell her how I was situated. I want her to know why I was forced to give her up."

"But you have written and stated your reasons."

"Of course. But I've no talent for explanation, and in a letter you say too little or too much; probably I didn't say enough. Then you can't tell how far the person written to will understand, and questions rise. But will you go?"

Festing wanted to go, although he saw his task might be embarrassing. He had been some time in Western Canada, where people are frank and do not shrink from dealing with delicate matters. Then Charnock was his friend.

"It will be an awkward job, but you can indicate the line you think I ought to take."

"The line is plain. You will tell Helen what it means to lose one's crop, and try to make her understand the struggle I've had—how the weather was against me, and the debts kept piling up until I was ruined. You can describe the havoc made by drought, and frost, and cutting sand. Then there's the other side of the matter; the hardships a woman must bear on the plains when money's scarce. The loneliness, the monotonous drudgery, the heat, the Arctic cold."

"Miss Dalton looks as if she had pluck. She wouldn't be easily daunted."

"Do you think I don't know? But when you meet her you'll see that the life we lead is impossible for a girl like that."

"It looks as if you wanted me to be your advocate," Festing remarked rather dryly. "I'm to make all the excuses for you I can, and prove that you were justified in breaking your engagement. I doubt if I'm clever enough—"

Charnock stopped him. "No! Perhaps I used excuses, but my object is not to clear myself." He paused and colored. "We'll admit that Helen lost nothing when I gave her up; but a girl, particularly a young, romantic girl, feels that kind of thing, and it might hurt worse if she thought she had loved a wastrel. I want her to feel that I broke my engagement for her sake, when nothing else was possible. That might soften the blow, and I really think it's true."

"How much of it is true?" Festing asked bluntly.

"Ah," said Charnock, "you're an uncompromising fellow. You meant that if you'd had my debts and difficulties, you could have made good?"

"I might; but we both know two or three other men whom I'd have backed to do so."

"For all that, you'll admit that the thing was impossible for me?"

Festing knitted his brows. "I believe you could have overcome your difficulties; that is, if you had really made an effort and faced the situation earlier. But since you hadn't nerve enough, I dare say it was impossible."

"You forget one thing; I hadn't time. At the best, it would have taken me three or four years to get straight, and as you haven't much imagination, I suppose you don't realize what Helen's trials would have been in the meanwhile. An engaged girl's situation isn't easy when her lover is away. She stands apart, forbidden much others may enjoy, and Helen would have had to bear her friends' contemptuous pity for being bound to a man who had turned out a failure or worse."

"I expect that's true," Festing agreed. "However, there's another difficulty. Suppose I persuade Miss Dalton that you made a plucky fight and only gave her up when you were beaten? She may refuse to let you go, and insist on coming out to help."

Charnock started, but with a rather obvious effort recovered his calm. "You must see your suggestion's stupid. Helen can't come out; I'm going to marry Sadie."

"I forgot," said Festing. "Well, since you urge me, I'll do what I can, although I don't like the job."

He left the homestead shortly afterwards, but felt puzzled as he walked across the plain. When he suggested that Miss Dalton might resolve to join and help her lover, Charnock had looked alarmed. This was strange, because although Festing had, for a moment, forgotten Sadie, it was ridiculous to imagine that Bob had done so. Then why had he started. There were, however, one or two other things that disturbed Festing, who felt that he had made a rash promise. But the promise had been made, and he must do his best to carry it out.

He had a fine voyage, and a week after his arrival in the Old Country walked up and down the terrace of a house among the hills in the North of England. His host was an old friend of the family who had shown Festing some kindness when he was young, and his daughter, Muriel, approved her father's guest. She liked the rather frank, brown-skinned, athletic man, whom she had joined on the terrace. He was a new and interesting type; but although she was two or three years the younger and attractive, their growing friendship was free from possible complications. Muriel, as Festing had learned, was going to marry the curate.

After the roar of activity at the bridge, where the hammers rang all day and often far into the night, he found his new surroundings strangely pleasant. In Canada, he had lived in the wilds; on the vast bare plains, and among snowy mountains where man grappled with Nature in her sternest mood. Thundering snowslides swept away one's work, icy rocks must be cut through, and savage green floods threatened the half-built track when the glaciers began to melt. Every day had brought a fresh anxiety, and now he welcomed the slackening of the strain. The struggle had left its mark on him; one saw it in his lean, muscular symmetry, his quiet alertness, and self-confidence. But he could relax, and found the English countryside had a soothing charm.

The sun was low and rugged hills cut against the pale-saffron sky. The valley between was filled with blue shadow, but in the foreground a river twinkled in the fading light. Feathery larches grew close up to the house, and a beck splashed in the gloom among their trunks. Farther off, a dog barked, and there was a confused bleating of sheep, but this seemed to emphasize the peaceful calm.

"It's wonderfully quiet," Festing remarked. "I can't get used to the stillness; I feel as if I was dreaming and would wake up to hear the din of the rivers and the ballast roaring off the gravel cars. However, I have some business to do to-morrow that I'm not keen about. Can one see Knott Scar from here?"

"It's the blue ridge, about six miles off. The dark patch on its slope is a big beech wood."

"Then do you know the Daltons?"

"Oh, yes," said Muriel. "Helen Dalton is a friend of mine. Although the Scar's some way off, I see her now and then. But are you going there?"

"I am; I wish it wasn't needful," Festing answered rather gloomily.

"Ah!" said Muriel, giving him a sharp glance. "Helen was to have married a man in Canada, but the engagement was broken off. Do you know him?"

"I do. That's why I'm going to the Scar. I've promised to explain matters as far as I can."

Muriel studied his disturbed face with a twinkle of amusement. "Well, I'm sorry for Helen; it must have been a shock. For all that, I thought the engagement a mistake."

"Then you have seen Charnock?"

"Once. He's a friend of some people Helen used to stay with in the South, but I met him at the Scar. Handsome, and charming, in a way, but I thought him weak."

"What are Miss Dalton's people like?"

"Don't you want to know what Helen is like?"

"No," said Festing. "I know her already; that is, I've seen her picture."

Muriel, glancing at him keenly, did not understand his look, but replied: "Helen lives with her mother and aunt, but it's hard to describe them. They are not old, but seem to date back to other times. In fact, they're rather unique nowadays. Like very dainty old china; you'd expect them to break if they were rudely jarred. You feel they ought to smell of orris and lavender."

"Ah," said Festing. "I was a fool to promise Charnock. I've never met people like that, and am afraid they'll get a jar to-morrow."

"I don't think you need be afraid," Muriel replied. "They're not really prudish or censorious, though they are fastidious."

"And is Miss Dalton like her mother and aunt?"

"In a way. Helen has their refinement, but she's made of harder stuff. She would wear better among strains and shocks."

Festing shook his head. "Girls like her ought to be sheltered and kept from shocks. After all, there's something to be said for Charnock's point of view. Your delicate English grace and bloom ought to be protected and not rubbed off by the rough cares of life."

"I don't know if you're nice or not," Muriel rejoined with a laugh. "Anyway, you don't know many English girls, and your ideas about us are old-fashioned. We are not kept in lavender now. Besides, it isn't the surface bloom that matters, and fine stuff does not wear out. It takes a keener edge and brighter polish from strenuous use. And Helen is fine stuff."

"So I thought," said Festing quietly, and stopped at the end of the terrace. The bleating of sheep had died away, and except for the splash of the beck a deep silence brooded over the dale. The sun had set and the landscape was steeped in soft blues and grays, into which woods and hills slowly melted.

"It's remarkably pleasant here," he said. "Not a sign of strain and hurry; things seem to run on well-oiled wheels! Perhaps the greatest change is to feel that one has nothing to do."

"But you had holidays now and then in Canada."

"No," said Festing. "Anyhow I've had none for a very long time. Of course there are lonely places, and in winter the homesteads on the plains are deadly quiet, but I was always where some big job was rushed along. Hauling logs across the snow, driving them down rivers, and after I joined the railroad, checking calculations, and track-grading in the rain. It was a fierce hustle from sunrise to dark, with all your senses highly strung and your efforts speeded up."

"Then one can understand why it's a relief to lounge. But would that satisfy you long?"

Festing laughed. "It would certainly satisfy me for a time, but after that I don't know. It's a busy world, and there's much to be done."

Muriel studied him as they walked back along the terrace. He wore no hat, and she liked the way he held his head and his light, springy step, though she smiled as she noted that he pulled himself up to keep pace with her. It was obvious that he was not used to moving leisurely. Then his figure, although spare, was well proportioned, and his rather thin face was frank. He had what she called a fined-down look, but concentrated effort of mind and body had given him a hint of distinction. He was a man who did things, and she wondered what Helen, who was something of a romantic dreamer, would think of him. Then she reflected with a touch of amusement that he would probably find the errand his friend had given him embarrassing.

"You don't look forward to seeing the Daltons to-morrow," she remarked.

"That's so," Festing admitted. "I didn't quite know what I'd undertaken when I gave my promise. The thing looks worse in England. In fact, it looks very nearly impossible just now."

"But you are going?"

Festing spread out his hands. "Certainly. What can I do? Charnock hustled me into it; he has a way of getting somebody else to do the things he shirks. But I gave him my word."

"And that's binding!" remarked Muriel, who was half amused by his indignation. She thought Charnock deserved it, but Festing could be trusted.

"I wish I could ask your advice," he resumed. "You could tell me what to say; but as I don't know if Charnock would approve, it mightn't be the proper thing."

Muriel was keenly curious to learn the truth about her friend's love affair, but she resisted the temptation. Because she liked Festing, she would not persuade him to do something for which he might afterwards reproach himself.

"No," she said, "perhaps you oughtn't to tell me. But I don't think you need be nervous. If you have the right feeling, you will take the proper line."

Then they went into the house where the curate was talking to Gardiner.

CHAPTER VI

FESTING KEEPS HIS WORD

Next afternoon Festing leaned his borrowed bicycle against the gate at Knott Scar and walked up the drive. He had grave misgivings, but it was too late to indulge them, and he braced himself and looked about with keen curiosity. The drive curved and a bank of shrubs on one side obstructed his view, but the Scar rose in front, with patches of heather glowing a rich crimson among the gray rocks. Beneath these, a dark beech wood rolled down the hill. On the other side there was a lawn that looked like green velvet. His trained eye could detect no unevenness; the smooth surface might have been laid with a spirit level. Festing had seen no grass like this in Canada and wondered how much labor it cost.

Then he came to the end of the shrubs and saw a small, creeper-covered house, with a low wall, pierced where shallow steps went up, along the terrace. The creeper was in full leaf and dark, but roses bloomed about the windows and bright-red geraniums in urns grew upon the wall. He heard bees humming and a faint wind in the beech tops, but the shadows scarcely moved upon the grass, and a strange, drowsy quietness brooded over the place. Indeed, the calm was daunting; he felt he belonged to another world and was intruding there, but went resolutely up the shallow steps.

Two white-haired ladies received him in a shady, old-fashioned room with a low ceiling. There was a smell of flowers, but it

Harold Bindloss

was faint, and he thought it harmonized with the subdued lighting of the room. A horizontal piano stood in a corner and the dark, polished rosewood had dull reflections; some music lay about, but not in disorder, and he noted the delicate modeling of the cabinet with diamond panes it had been taken from. He knew nothing about furniture, but he had an eye for line and remarked the taste that characterized the rest of the articles. There were a few landscapes in water-color, and one or two pieces of old china, of a deep blue that struck the right note of contrast with the pale-yellow wall.

Festing felt that the house had an influence; a gracious influence perhaps, but vaguely antagonistic to him. He had thought of a house as a place in which one ate and slept, but did not expect it to mold one's character. Surroundings like this were no doubt Helen Dalton's proper environment, but he came from the outside turmoil, where men sweated and struggled and took hard knocks.

In the meantime, he talked to and studied the two ladies. Although they had white hair, they were younger than he thought at first and much alike. It was as if they had faded prematurely from breathing too rarefied an atmosphere and shutting out rude but bracing blasts. Still they had a curious charm, and he had felt a hint of warmth in Mrs. Dalton's welcome that puzzled him.

"We have been expecting you. Bob told us you would come," she said in a low, sweet voice, and added with a smile: "I wanted to meet you."

Festing wondered what Bob had said about him, but for a time they tactfully avoided the object of his visit and asked him questions about his journey. Then Mrs. Dalton got up.

"Helen is in the garden. Shall we look for her?"

She took him across the lawn to a bench beneath a copper beech, and Festing braced himself when a girl got up. She wore white and the shadow of the leaves checkered the plain dress. He noted the unconscious grace of her pose as she turned towards him, and her warm color, which seemed to indicate a sanguine temperament. Helen Dalton was all that he had thought, and something more. He knew her level, penetrating glance, but she had a virility he had not expected. The girl was somehow stronger than he portrait.

"Perhaps I had better leave you to talk to Mr. Festing," Mrs. Dalton said presently and moved away.

Helen waited with a calm that Festing thought must cost her much, and moving a folding chair, he sat down opposite.

"I understand Bob told you I would come," he said. "You see, he is a friend of mine."

"Yes," she replied with a faint sparkle in her eyes. "He hinted that you would explain matters. I think he meant you would make some defense for him."

Festing noted that her voice was low like her mother's, but it had a firmer note. He could be frank with her, but there was a risk that he might say too much.

"Well," he said, "I may make mistakes. In fact, it was with much reluctance I promised to come, and if Bob hadn't insisted—" He paused and pulled himself together. "On the surface, of course, his conduct looks inexcusable, but he really has some defense, and I think you ought to hear it, for your own sake."

"Perhaps I ought," she agreed quietly. "Well, I am willing."

Festing began by relating Charnock's troubles. He meant her to understand the situation and supplied rather confusing particulars about prairie farming and mortgages. For all that, the line he took was strong; he showed how Charnock's embarrassments prevented his offering her comforts she would

Harold Bindloss

find needful and saving her from the monotonous toil an impoverished farmer's wife must undertake. In the meantime, but unconsciously, he threw some light on Charnock's vacillating character.

When he stopped Helen mused for a few minutes. Although she had got a shock when Charnock gave her up, she knew her lover better than when she had promised to marry him. He came home once in the winter and she had remarked a change. Bob was not altogether the man she had thought; there were things that jarred, and his letters gradually made this plainer. Still she had meant to keep her promise, and his withdrawal hurt. She had borne something for his sake, because her mother and her relations had not approved the engagement. Then she roused herself and turned to Festing.

"You have done your best for your friend and Bob ought to be grateful, but you both start from a wrong point. Why do you take it for granted that I would shrink from hardship?"

"I didn't imagine you would shrink," Festing declared. "For all that, Bob was right. The life is too hard for a girl brought up like you." He hesitated a moment. "I mean for a girl brought up in your surroundings."

Helen smiled and he knew it was a sign of courage, but had a vague feeling that he understood why she did so as he looked about. The sighing in the beech tops had died away and the shadows did not move upon the lawn. A heavy smell of flowers came from the borders and the house seemed to be sleeping in the hot sunshine. Everything was beautiful, well-ordered, and tranquil, but he knew if he stayed there long he would hear the cry of the black geese and the clang of flung-down rails ring through the soporific calm. Something in the girl's face indicated that she might find the calm oppressive and sympathize with him.

"What is Bob going to do now he has lost his farm?" she asked after a time.

"In one respect, he won't be much worse off. They expect a boom at the settlement, and he'll manage the hotel and store and poolroom for Keller. The old man will probably retire soon and Bob will get the business."

"But why should the proprietor give the business to Bob?"

"He's Sadie's father," Festing answered with some surprise.

"But who is Sadie?"

Festing looked up sharply and saw that Helen was puzzled and suspicious. Her eyes were harder and her mouth was set.

"Ah!" he said. "Don't you know?"

A wave of color flushed Helen's face, but her voice was level. "I don't know! It looks as if Bob had not told me the most important thing. Do you mean that he is going to marry Miss Keller?"

Festing felt pitiful. He saw that she had got a shock, but she bore it pluckily, and he tried to conquer his indignant rage. Charnock had let him believe he had told her; he ought to have realized that the fellow could not act straight.

"I thought you knew," he stammered.

"That's obvious," Helen replied with an effort for calm. "But tell me something about Miss Keller."

"Sadie runs the hotel and helps at the store. She's rather pretty and intelligent. In fact, she's generally capable and a good manager."

"You seem to know her well since you call her Sadie."

"Oh," said Festing, "everybody calls her Sadie!"

"You mean in the bar and poolroom? I understand the latter's a public billiard-saloon!"

Festing felt that he must do Sadie justice. She had her virtues, and although he was very angry with Charnock he did not want Helen to think the fellow had given her up for a worthless rival. Still he was not sure if his putting the girl in a favorable light would soften the blow or not.

"To begin with, they don't employ women in a Canadian bar. Then Sadie's quite a good sort and understands Bob—perhaps better than an English girl could. She was brought up on the plains and knows all about the life we lead."

"You imply that she is not fastidious, and will be lenient to her husband's faults? That she will bring him down to her level?"

"Well," said Festing, who thought Helen did not know Charnock's dissipated habits, "I imagine she'll keep him there, and that's something. I mean she won't let him sink below her level; Sadie's shrewd and determined. Then marriage is a problem to men like Bob farming the plains. Girls of the type they have been used to and would naturally choose couldn't stand the hardships."

"So they are satisfied with a lower type? With any girl who pleases their eye?"

"I don't think that's quite fair," Festing objected. "Besides, lower is rather vague."

"Then would you, for example, be satisfied with a girl like Miss Keller?"

"Certainly not," said Festing, with incautious firmness. "Anyway, not now I've seen a different kind in the Old Country."

Helen turned her head and said nothing for a few moments.

Then she got up.

"I think you have had a difficult task, Mr. Festing, and I must thank you for the way you have carried it out. We won't speak of it again; but perhaps if Muriel Gardiner—"

"She hasn't asked me any questions or hinted that she is curious."

There was a gleam of amusement in Helen's eyes. "So you imagined she wasn't interested! Well, you can tell her about Bob's losses and farming troubles. You understand these matters, and it will save me something."

Festing made a sign of agreement and Helen went with him to the terrace, where Mrs. Dalton told him when he would find them at home if he wished to come again. He was glad to leave because he thought the interview had been difficult for Helen, but her mother had made him feel that if he came back he would be welcome. This was not altogether conventional politeness; he imagined she wanted to see him, although she was obviously willing to let him go then.

He puzzled about it and other matters as he rode back. Helen Dalton was finer than her picture. He had, no doubt, been awkward and had hurt her by his clumsiness, while she had got a painful shock, but had borne it with unflinching pluck. Her calm had not deceived him, since he knew what it cost, and her smile had roused his pity because it was so brave. Then his anger against Charnock returned with extra force. The fellow, as usual, had shirked his duty, and left him to tell the girl he had really given her up because he meant to marry somebody else. Festing thought she was too just to blame him for Bob's fault, but he had been forced to witness her humiliation, and she would, no doubt, avoid him because of this. Well, he had done with Bob, although he would see him once on his return and tell him what he thought.

Then he heard a shout and saw a farmer trying to move a

loaded cart out of his way. He had not noticed that he was riding furiously down a hill, but he sped past the cart upon the grassy margin of the road and laughed as he went on. His mood had changed and he resolved that he would go back to the creeper-covered house when Helen had had time to recover and his society would be less disturbing. After all, Mrs. Dalton had told him he might come.

In the evening he walked up and down the terrace with Muriel, and told her why he had gone to Knott Scar, although he was satisfied with relating Charnock's financial troubles and said nothing about his engagement to Sadie. He could not say that Muriel actually led him on, but he felt that she would be disappointed if he did not take her into his confidence.

"Of course I saw you knew all about it," she said when he stopped. "Besides, I expected that Helen would give you leave to tell me. It would make things easier for her and be more authentic."

"I should expect Miss Dalton to think of that."

Muriel smiled. "Perhaps not. Well, I imagine it's lucky Charnock released her; Helen is much too good for him. I suppose you thought you took the proper line in laying all the stress you could upon the hardships?"

"I did. I thought she couldn't stand the strain she would have had to bear."

"How did she take that?"

"She seemed surprised, as if she didn't think it much of a reason for Charnock letting her go."

"Frankly, I don't think it was."

"You haven't been to Canada. The life is hard."

"It doesn't seem to have broken down your health or nerve."

"That's different. A man gets used to hardships and discomfort. They're sometimes bracing."

"A very masculine attitude! Then men alone have pluck and endurance?"

"There are two kinds of pluck," Festing rejoined. "I dare say you surpass us in the moral kind—I'm sure Miss Dalton has more than Charnock. But there's the other; physical courage, and if you like, physical strength."

Muriel looked amused. "And you imagine Helen is deficient there? Well, I suppose you don't know she's the best tennis player in the county and a daring rock-climber. Girls are taking to mountaineering now, you know. But are you going back to the Daltons?"

Festing thought she gave him a keen glance, but answered steadily: "I am going back, but not for some time. I want to go, but it might be kinder if I kept away."

"Well, it's a very proper feeling and you're rather nice. But you talked about going to see the mountains for a few days. When do you start?"

"I don't know yet. Everything here is so charming, and I'm getting the habit of lazy enjoyment. It will need an effort to go away."

"You're certainly nice," Muriel rejoined, smiling. "However, you might tell me when you do think of starting. I don't want you to be away when we have arranged something to amuse you; and then, as I know the mountains, I can indicate an interesting tour. You might miss much if you didn't know where to go and what you ought to see."

Festing promised, and she left him and went back to the house with a thoughtful smile that hinted that she had begun to make an amusing plan. Muriel was romantic and rather fond of managing her friends' affairs for their good.

CHAPTER VII

HELEN TAKES THE LEAD

Festing was glad to sit down when he reached the bottom of a chasm that divided the summits of two towering fells. He had crossed the higher of the two without much trouble except for a laborious scramble over large, rough stones, but the ascent of the other threatened to be difficult. It rose in front, a wall of splintered crag, seamed by deep gullies, for the strata was tilted up nearly perpendicular. All the gullies were climbed by expert mountaineers, but this needed a party and a rope, and the other way, round the shoulder of the great rock, was almost as hard. Festing knew the easiest plan was to descend a neighboring hollow, from which he would find a steep path to the top.

Lighting his pipe, he glanced at his watch. It was three o'clock in the afternoon, and having been on his feet since breakfast, he felt tired. The nails he had had driven into his light American boots hurt his feet, and the boots were much the worse for the last few days' wear. Muriel had carefully planned the trip, and then delayed his start by a week because she wanted to take him to a tennis party. Since he could not play tennis much, Festing did not see why she had done so, but agreed when she insisted.

So far, he had followed her instructions and admitted that she had directed him well, because it was hard to imagine there was anything in England finer than the country he had seen.

Harold Bindloss

The mountains had not the majestic grandeur of the British Columbian ranges, but they were wild enough, and pierced by dales steeped in sylvan beauty. The chasm in which he now rested had an impressive ruggedness.

Blinks of sunshine touched the lower face of the crag, and in their track the dark rock glittered with a steely luster, but trails of mist rolled among the crannies above. Below, a precipitous slope of small stones that the dalesmen call a scree ran down to a hollow strewn with broken rocks, and across this he could distinguish the blurred flat top of another height. The mountain dropped to a dale that looked profoundly deep, although he could not see its bottom.

The light was puzzling. For the most part, the sky was clear and the gleams of sun were hot, but heavy, black clouds drifted about, and a thick gray haze obscured the lower ground. Rain and mist would be dangerous obstacles, but Festing understood that he could reach the dale in about two hours' steady walking. Muriel had told him where to stop; indeed, she had been rather particular about this, and had recommended him to spend two days in the neighborhood. Luckily, there would be no crags to climb if he kept the path across the summit, for he had found it easier to reach the top of the hills than get down by a different line.

A rattle of stones made him look up, and he saw two girls silhouetted in a flash of sunshine against the face of the crag. They carried bulging rucksacks and were coming down towards him, picking their way among the tumbled rocks. He could not see the face of the first, but noticed her light poise and graceful movements as she sprang from stone to stone. The other followed cautiously and Festing thought she limped, but when the first stopped to wait for her and lifted her head he felt a curious thrill. It was Helen Dalton.

He sat still, knowing his gray clothes would be hard to distinguish among the stones, and wondering what to do. He did not want to force his society upon the girl just yet, but would be disappointed if she passed. She came on, and when her eyes rested on him he got up. A flush of embarrassment colored her face, but she stopped and greeted him with a smile.

"Mr. Festing! How did you get here?"

"I came over the Pike," said Festing. "I'm going to the dale."

"So are we," said Helen, who presented him to her companion.

Festing remarked that they wore jackets that had a tanned look, unusually short skirts, and thick nailed boots. Then he thought Helen's eyes twinkled.

"You would not have expected to find me engaged in anything so strenuous as this?"

"It is rather strenuous," Miss Jardine broke in. "You can stand if you like; I'm going to sit down."

They found a flat stone, and when Festing leaned against another Helen resumed: "We meant to try the Stairs, but have had a hard day and Alison is lame."

"I hurt my foot," Miss Jardine explained. "Besides, I'm from the level Midlands and we have been walking since breakfast. That doesn't matter to Helen; she is never tired."

Festing thought Helen looked remarkably fresh. Exertion and the mountain air had brought a fine color to her face, her eyes were bright, and there was a hint of vigor in her resting pose. Moreover, he had studied the Stairs, which led behind the shoulder of the crag to the summit. One could get up, if one was thin enough to squeeze through a gap between two rocks, but nerve and agility would be required.

"But you must climb pretty well, if you meant to get up the Stairs," he said.

"I know the Carnarvon range, but only go there now and then, and one needs some training to keep pace with people born among the fells who walk like mountain goats."

Had she said a mountain deer, Festing would have approved, for he had noted Helen's easy balance and fearless grace as she crossed the ragged blocks of stone. Then a rumble of distant thunder rolled among the crags and Miss Jardine resumed: "We ought to fix upon the best way down."

"The best is a rather elastic term," Helen rejoined. "The easiest would be to go back by the way we came."

"It's much too far."

"The shortest is up the crag by the Stairs or the gully on the other side. The regular track takes us down near the bottom of the next dale, and then back over the top."

"That's unthinkable," Miss Jardine declared.

"Well," said Helen thoughtfully, "there's a short line down the scree and across the shoulder of the fell below, but it's steep and rough. There are some small crags, too, but they're not much of an obstacle when they're dry."

They set off and Festing noticed Helen's confidence on the scree. The descent was safe, but looked daunting, because their figures made a sharp angle with the gravel slope, and now and then a mass of dislodged stones rushed down hill. Sometimes the girl allowed herself to slide, sometimes she ran a few yards and sprang, but she did not stumble or lose her balance. Miss Jardine was cautious, and Festing kept near her, carrying her sack.

At the bottom they came to a wide belt of massive stones, fallen from the heights above, and their progress was slow. One had to measure the gaps between the blocks and step carefully across, while the stones were ragged and had sharp corners.

Festing was unable to look up and followed Helen, but after a time Miss Jardine stopped, and he saw that the crags were smothered in leaden cloud and all the sky was dark.

"I must have a few minutes' rest," the tired girl declared.

As they sat down on the edge of a ponderous slab there was a crash of thunder that rolled from rock to rock, and a few big drops fell. Then as the echoes died away the hillside was hidden by a curtain of driving rain. One end of the slab was tilted and they crept into the hollow underneath.

"It will be awkward if this goes on," Miss Jardine remarked.

"These thunderstorms seldom last," said Helen. "I expect we have seen the worst, and we must start again as soon as we can see."

Festing thought she was anxious to get down, but Miss Jardine grumbled about the rain, and then turned to him.

"It was a relief to give you my sack, and I was glad to see it didn't bother you. I suppose you are used to these mountains."

"No," said Festing. "This is the first time I've climbed a hill for amusement."

"But you are a climber. You have balance, trust your feet and not your hands, and know how to step on a loose stone."

Festing laughed. "I used to do something of the kind as a matter of business. You see, I helped mark out the line for a new railroad in British Columbia, and rocks are plentiful in that country."

"It must be a wonderful place," said Helen. "I have a photograph of the gorge at the foot of the glacier, where the line went through. You had stern work when you laid the rails in winter."

Festing looked at her in surprise, for he had worked to the edge of exhaustion and run many risks at the spot, but while he wondered how she knew Helen got up.

"I think the rain is stopping and we can start," she said.

There was not much rain, but thick mist rolled across the top of the hill they were now level with, and everything below was blotted out. Leaving the stones, they crossed a belt of boggy grass where their feet sank, but Festing felt it a relief to have done with the rocks. The narrow tableland they were crossing was comfortingly flat, and he looked forward to descending a long grassy slope. When they reached the edge, however, he got a rude disappointment, for the mist rolled up in waves with intervals between, and when a white cloud passed a gray light shone down into the gulf at his feet.

In the foreground there was a steep slope where rock ledges broke through the wet turf, and in one place a chasm cleft the hill. He could not see the bottom, for it was filled with mist, but the height of the rock wall hinted at its depth. A transverse ravine ran into the chasm, and he could hear the roar of a waterfall. Then the mist rolled up in a white smother and blotted everything out.

"We cross the beck," said Helen. "Then we go nearly straight down, keeping this side of the big ghyll."

"As far away as possible, I hope. I don't like its look," Miss Jardine remarked.

Festing agreed with her. So far as he could see, the descent looked forbidding, but there was no sign of the sky's clearing, and it was obvious that they must get down. The thunder had gone, but the mist brought a curious, searching damp, and a cold wind had begun to blow. He was glad to think Helen knew the way.

She took them down a steep pitch where small rocky ledges

dropped nearly vertical among patches of rotten turf and it was needful to get a good grip with one's hands as well as with one's feet. Festing helped Miss Jardine when he could, but he had an unpleasant feeling that a rash step might take him over the edge of a precipice. Sometimes he could see Helen in front, and sometimes, for a few moments, her figure was lost in the mist. He was glad to note that she was apparently going down with confidence.

After a time the slope got easier and she stopped, lifting her hand. Festing found her looking into a ravine through which water flowed. It was not very deep, but its sides were perpendicular. Seeing that Miss Jardine was some distance behind, she looked at Festing with a quiet smile.

"There is a place where one can cross without much trouble, but I don't know whether to go up or down."

Festing felt his heart beat. It looked as if she had taken him into her confidence and asked his help.

"Not down, I think. That would take us to the big ghyll. Let's try up, and cross at the first practicable spot."

Helen made a sign of agreement, and when Miss Jardine joined them they turned back along the edge of the ravine. By and by Helen stopped where patches of wet soil checkered the steep rock and a mountain-ash offered a hold. Almost immediately below the spot, the stream plunged over a ledge and vanished into the mist.

Festing looked at Helen. The descent would be awkward, if not dangerous, but he could trust her judgment. It was the first time he had allowed a woman to give him a lead in a difficulty, and he admitted that he would not have done so had his guide been anybody else.

"I think we can get across, and I don't want to go too far up," she said. "If you don't mind helping Alison—"

Harold Bindloss

"I'll throw the sacks across first," Festing replied.

He swung them round by the straps and let them go, and when the last splashed into a boggy patch on the other side Miss Jardine laughed.

"I'm selfishly glad that one is yours. If Helen's had fallen a foot short, it would have gone over the fall, but I expect she had a reason for taking the risk. Where our clothes have gone we must follow."

Helen seized a tuft of heather, and sliding down, reached a narrow shelf four or five feet below. Then a small mountain-ash gave her a fresh hold and she dropped to the top of a projecting stone. Below this there was another shelf and some boggy grass, after which a bank of earth dropped nearly straight to the stream.

"How we shall get down the last pitch isn't very obvious," Miss Jardine remarked. "I suppose we will see when we arrive. It isn't my resolution that gives way, but my foot. You might go first."

Festing dropped on to the first shelf, and she came down into his arms. The shock nearly flung him off, but he steadied her with an effort and seized the stem of the small tree.

"Looks like a tight-wire trick," he said, glancing at the stone. "However, if we miss it, there's another ledge below."

He reached the stone, and balancing on it with one foot, kicked a hole in the spongy turf. Finding this would support him he held out his hand.

"Now. As lightly as you can!"

The girl came down, struck the stone with her foot, and slipped, but Festing had time to clutch her first. He could not hold her back, but he could steady her, and for a moment felt his muscles crack and the peat tear out from the hole in the bank. Then his hands slipped and he fell, gasping and red in face, upon the shelf beside the girl.

"Thank you; you did that rather well," she said. "It looks as if I were heavier than you thought."

While he had been occupied Festing imagined he had heard a splash, and now looking down saw Helen standing on a boulder in the stream. She gave him an approving nod before she sprang to the next stone, and he felt a thrill of pleasure. She knew his task was difficult and was satisfied with him.

When they came to the scar where the floods had torn away the bank he hesitated. It was some distance to the water, and there was no hold upon the wall of soil, which was studded with small round stones.

"Helen slid," his companion remarked. "I imagine she chose her time; the sitting glissade isn't elegant. But if you'll go first and wait—"

Festing leaned back with his shoulders against the bank and pushed off. He alighted in the water, and Miss Jardine, coming down, kicked his arm. He saved her from a plunge into the stream, but thought she looked something the worse for wear as they made their way from stone to stone. The other bank was easier, and for a time they had not much trouble in going down hill, but the mist was very thick, and presently the steep slope broke off close in front. Helen stopped and beckoned Festing.

Looking down, he saw the wet face of a crag drop into the rolling vapor. For eight or nine feet it was perpendicular, and afterwards ran down at a very steep slant, but immediately below there was a gully with a foot or two of level gravel at its top.

"This is not the regular track," Helen said. "However, I think I know the gully."

Festing pondered. The rock looked daunting, but one might get down to the patch of gravel. The trouble was that one could not see what lay below, and it might be difficult to climb back, if this was needful.

"I could get as far as the edge yonder," he suggested.

"No," said Helen. "You don't know the gully, and if I'm mistaken about it, you could help me up."

"That's true. Still I'd sooner go."

Helen shook her head, and although she did not speak, he felt there was something delightful in her consulting him. They had come to know each other on the misty hillside in a way that would not have been possible in conventional surroundings. He had seen a possibility of the girl, so to speak, shutting him out in self-defense because he had had some part in her humiliation, but he thought that risk had gone.

"Well," he resumed, "what do you propose?"

"I'm going to see if this is the place I think. You can steady me."

Festing lay down with his head over the edge and found a grip for his toes and knees. There were a few cracks in the rock and Helen had got half way down before she took his hands. He felt the strain and braced himself, determined that he would be pulled over before he let her fall.

"Loose me now," she said.

"Have you got a safe hold for your foot?" Festing gasped.

"I think I have. Let go."

"Make sure first," he answered with a sobbing breath.

She looked up into his set face, and although the strain was heavy he thrilled as he saw her smile. The smile indicated courage and trust.

"I'm quite safe," she said, and he let her go.

She leaned cautiously over the next edge, but after a moment or two turned and waved her hand.

"This is the way I thought. Send Alison down."

Miss Jardine descended with some help from both, and Festing dropped safely on the gravel. He leaned against the rock to get his breath, and Helen turned to him with a twinkle.

"You doubted my nerve once. I suppose that was why you didn't let go."

"I'm sometimes dull," said Festing. "Just now, however, I wanted to make certain I could help you back."

Helen laughed. "Well, I dare say you could have lifted me, but it would have been simpler to lower me your coat."

They went down the gully, where jambed stones made rude steps, and reaching the bottom found a belt of grass that led them to the head of a dale. The mist was thinner, and presently a few scattered houses appeared across the fields. The path they followed forked, and Helen stopped at the turning.

"The hotel is yonder to the right," she said. "We are going to the hall, where they sometimes take people in."

Festing remembered that Muriel had indicated the hall, which he understood was a well-built farm, as his stopping place. He wanted to go there, but thought there was some risk of its looking as if he meant to force his society on the girls. He took the path Helen indicated, and when he had gone some distance, stopped, hesitated, and then went on.

The girls noted this and Miss Jardine said: "I suppose he remembered that he has my sack, or else his heart failed him."

Helen looked at her in surprise. "Did you forget?"

"I did not," Miss Jardine admitted. "I thought I wouldn't spoil the plot. It looked as if he wanted an excuse for meeting us again, but I think I wronged him. That sudden stop was genuine."

"The sack is yours," said Helen dryly. "But you will need the things inside."

"I imagine I will get them before long, although it doesn't seem to have struck him that my clothes are damp. It's rather significant that he went on when he could have run across the field and caught us up. Have you known him long?"

"I met him once," said Helen with an impatient frown.

"Rather a good type," Miss Jardine remarked. "I think I should like Canadians, if they're all like that."

"He isn't a Canadian."

"Then he hasn't been in England for some time, and so far as my knowledge goes, men like variety. Of course, to some extent, he saw us under a disadvantage. Mountaineering clothes are comfortable, but one can't say much more."

"Don't be ridiculous," Helen rejoined and went on across the field.

CHAPTER VIII

A DEBT OF GRATITUDE

After dinner Festing walked across the fields to the farm. It was raining and a cold wind swept the dale, but a fire burned in the room into which he was shown and the curtains were drawn. Helen and Miss Jardine got up when he came in and put the rucksack on the table.

"I'm sorry I forgot this until I'd gone some distance," he said. "Then I couldn't find anybody to send with it."

"No doubt you wanted your dinner," Miss Jardine suggested.

Festing saw that she wore a different dress that looked rather large.

"No," he said, "it wasn't the dinner that stopped me. Besides, it didn't strike me that—"

"That I might need my clothes? Well, I don't suppose it would strike you; but since you have come across in the rain, won't you stop?"

Festing found an old leather chair, and sitting down, looked about with a sense of satisfaction, for the fire was cheerful after the raw cold outside. The room was large and old-fashioned, with heavy beams across the low ceiling. There was a tall clock, and a big, black oak chest; curled ram's horns and brass candlesticks twinkled on the mantel; an old copper kettle threw back red reflections near the fire. His companions occupied opposite sides of a large sheepskin rug, and he felt that both had charm, though they were different. The contrast added something to the charm.

Miss Jardine's skin was a pure white; her hair and eyes were nearly black, and she had a sparkling, and perhaps rather daring, humor. Helen's colors were rose and cream, her hair changed from warm brown to gold as it caught the light, and her eyes were calm and gray. She was younger than the other and he thought her smile delightful, but, as a rule, she was marked by a certain gravity. Her wide brows and the firm lines of her mouth and nose hinted at pride and resolution.

"I hope your foot is better," he said to Miss Jardine.

"Yes, thanks. It mainly needed rest, and I must confess that I didn't find it altogether a drawback when we stopped at the bottom of the big crag. I should have had to go up if I hadn't been lame."

"You were not disappointed because you couldn't reach the top?"

Miss Jardine laughed. "Helen was. She makes it a rule to accomplish what she undertakes. I wasn't disappointed then, though I am now. Perhaps one really enjoys mountaineering best afterwards. You like to think how adventurous you have been, but it's sometimes difficult while the adventure's going on."

"That's true," Festing agreed. "Still you feel sorry if, as we say, you are unable to put the thing over."

Helen gave him a sympathetic smile. "Yes; one feels that."

"It depends upon one's temperament," Miss Jardine objected. "I know my limits, though Helen does not know hers. When I can't get what I'm out for, I'm satisfied with less. One can't always have the best."

"It's worth trying for, anyway," Festing replied.

He was afraid this sounded priggish. Miss Jardine got up.

"Well, I'm not much of a philosopher and had better put out some of the clothes you brought to dry, although it was thoughtful of you to throw your bag into the bog instead of mine."

"That was an accident," Festing declared. "I meant to throw them both across."

Miss Jardine picked up the sack. "There's nobody else here and a wet evening's dreary. I hope you won't go before I come back."

"I won't," said Festing. "They have only a deaf tourist and two tired climbers, who seem sleepy and bad-tempered, at the hotel."

Miss Jardine's eyes twinkled. "Well," she said as she went out, "I suppose it's a fair retort."

Festing colored and looked at Helen apologetically. "You see, I have lived in the woods."

"I expect that has some advantages," said Helen, who liked his frank embarrassment. "However, it was lucky I met you to-day. You didn't come back to see us, and there is something—" She hesitated and then gave him a steady glance. "You are not so much a stranger to us as you imagine."

Festing wondered what she meant and whether she knew about the portrait, but she resumed: "As a matter of fact, my mother and I felt that we knew you rather well."

"I don't understand."

"Some time since, you found a young Englishmen in a Western mining town. He had been ill and things had gone against him."

"Ah," said Festing sharply. "Of course! I ought to have known—He looked like you. I mean I ought to have known the name. Was he a relative?"

"My brother," Helen replied.

She was silent for a moment or two, and then went on in a tone that made Festing's heart beat: "You gave him work and helped him to make a new start. He was too proud to tell us about his difficulties."

"It cost me nothing; there was a job waiting. Afterwards he got on by his own merits. I had nothing to do with that."

"But you gave him his chance. We can't forget this. George was younger than me. I have no other brother, and was very fond of him. Indeed, I think we owe you much, and my mother is anxious to give you her thanks."

"Is he all right now? I lost sight of him when they sent me to another part of the road. It was my fault—he wrote, but I'm not punctual at answering letters, and hadn't much time."

"He is in the chief construction office," Helen replied. "In his last letter he told us about the likelihood of his getting some new promotion." She paused and resumed with a smile: "I don't suppose you know you were a hero of his."

"I didn't know. As a rule, the young men we had on the road seemed to find their bosses amusing and rather patronized them. Of course, they were fresh from a scientific college or engineer's office, and, for the most part, we had learned what we knew upon the track."

"But you knew it well. George wrote long letters about the struggle you had at the canyon. Some fight, he called it."

"Well," said Festing quietly, "we were up against it then. The job was worth doing."

"I know. George told us how the snowslide came down and filled the head of the gorge with stones and broken trees, and wash-outs wrecked the line you built along its side. He said it was a job for giants; clinging to the face of the precipice while you blew out and built on—under-pinning, isn't it?—the first construction track. But he declared the leaders were fine. They were where the danger was, in the blinding rain and swirling snow—and the boys, as he called them, would always follow you."

Festing colored, but Helen went on: "We were glad, when the worst was over, that he had had this training. It was so clean a fight."

"We were dirty enough often," Festing objected with an effort at humor. "When things were humming we slept in our working clothes, which were generally stained with mud and engine grease. Then I don't suppose you know how dissipated a man looks and feels when he has breathed the fumes of giant-powder."

She stopped him with a half imperious glance. "I know it's the convention to talk of such things as a joke; but you didn't feel that in the canyon. Then it was a stubborn fight of the kind that man was meant to wage. If you win in trade and politics, somebody must lose, but a victory over Nature is a gain to all. And when your enemies are storms and floods, cheating and small cunning are not of much use."

"That is so," Festing agreed, smiling. "When you're sent to cut through an icy rock or re-lay the steel across the gap a snowslide has made, it's obvious if you have done the job or not. This has some drawbacks, because if you don't make good, you often get fired."

"But that was not what drove you on. You must have had a better motive for making good."

Festing felt embarrassed. The girl was obviously not indulging a sentimental vein. She felt what she frankly hinted at, and although he generally avoided imaginative talk, her remarks did not sound cheap or ridiculous.

"Well," he said, "the fear of getting fired is a pretty strong incentive to do one's best, but I suppose when one gets up against big things there is something else. After all, one hates to be beaten."

Helen's eyes sparkled and she gave him a sympathetic nod. "The hate of being beaten distinguishes man from the ape and puts him on the side of the angels."

Then Miss Jardine came in, somewhat to the relief of Festing, who felt he could not keep up long on Helen's plane. Besides, he was not altogether sure he understood her last remark.

"I heard," said Miss Jardine. "Helen's sometimes improving, but perhaps she was right just now. The ape is cunning but acquiescent and accepts things as they are. Man protests, and fights to make them better. At least, he ought to, though one can't say he always does."

Festing did not reply and she sat down and resumed: "But I suppose you haven't many shirkers in Canada?"

"I imagine we have as many wastrels as there are anywhere else, but as a rule one doesn't find them in the woods and on the plains. When they leave the cities they're apt to starve."

"You're a grim lot. Work or starve is a stern choice, particularly if one has never done either. It looks as if you hadn't much use for purely ornamental people. But what about the half-taught women who don't know how to work? What do you do with them?"

"They're not numerous. Then one can always learn, and I imagine every woman can cook and manage a house."

"You're taking much for granted, though yours seems to be the conventional view. But how did you learn railroad building, for example?"

"By unloading ties and shoveling ballast on the track. The trouble was that I began too late."

"What did you do before that?"

"Sometimes I worked in sawmills and sometimes packed—that means carrying things—for survey parties, and went prospecting."

"In the wilds? It sounds interesting. Won't you tell us about it?"

Festing complied; awkwardly at first, and then with growing confidence. He did not want to make much of his exploits, but there was a charm in talking about things he knew to two clever and attractive girls, and they helped him with tactful questions. Indeed, he was surprised to find they knew something about the rugged country in which he wandered. He told them about risky journeys up lonely rivers in the spring, adventurous thrusts into the wilderness where hardship was oftener to be found than valuable minerals, and retreats with provisions running out before the Arctic winter.

Something of the charm of the empty spaces colored his narratives as he drew from memory half-finished pictures of the mad riot of primitive forces when the ice broke up and the floods hurled the thundering floes among the rocks; and of tangled woods sinking into profound silence in the stinging frost. Moreover, he unconsciously delineated his own character, and when he stopped, the others understood something of the practical resource and stubbornness that had supported him.

It was encouraging to see they were not bored, but he did not know that Miss Jardine had found him an interesting study and had skilfully led him on. He was a new type to both girls, although Helen was nearer to him than the other and sympathized where her companion was amused. Festing's ideas were clean-cut, his honesty was obvious, and she noted that he did not know much about the lighter side of life. Yet she saw that, sternly practical as he was, he had a vague feeling for romance.

"Will you stay on the railroad when it's finished?" she asked presently.

"I've left it. I hadn't the proper training to carry me far, and as the road is opening up the country I've bought a prairie farm."

"But do you know much about farming?"

"I don't. As a matter of fact, not many of the boys do know much when they begin, but somehow they make progress. On the plains, it isn't what you know that counts, but the capacity for work and staying with your job. That's what one really needs, if you see what I mean."

"I think I do," Miss Jardine replied. "A Victorian philosopher, whose opinions you seem to hold, said something of the kind. He claims that genius takes many different forms, but is not different in itself. That is, if you have talent, you can do what you like. Build railroads, for example, and then succeed on a farm."

Festing laughed good-humoredly. "It's a pretty big thing to claim, but that man was near the mark; they live up to his theories on the plains, where shams don't count and efficiency's the test. I don't mean that the boys have genius, but gift and perseverance seem to be worth as much. Anyhow, one can generally trust them to make good when they undertake a job they don't know much about."

Helen mused. Charnock, who knew something about farming, had tried it and failed, but she thought Festing would succeed. The man looked determined and, in a way, ascetic; he could deny himself and concentrate. Knowledge was not worth as much as character. But she was content to let Miss Jardine lead the talk.

"One understands," said the latter, "that farming's laborious and not very profitable work."

"It's always laborious," Festing agreed. "It may be profitable; that depends. You see—"

He went on, using plain words but with some force of imagination, to picture the wheat-grower's hopes and struggles; but he did more, for as he talked Helen was conscious of the romance that underlay the patient effort. She saw the empty, silent land rolling back to the West; the ox-teams slowly breaking the first furrow, and then the big Percheron horses and gasoline tractors taking their place. Wooden shacks dotted the white grass, the belts of green wheat widened, wagons, and afterwards automobiles, lurched along the rutted trails. Then the railroad came, brick homestead and windmills rose, and cities sprang up, as it were, in a night. Everything was fluid, there was no permanence; rules and customs altered before they got familiar, a new nation, with new thoughts and aims, was rising from the welter of tense activity.

Then Festing got up with an apologetic air. "I'm afraid I've stopped too long and talked too much. Still the big movement out there is fascinating and people in this country don't grasp its significance. I felt I'd like to make you understand. Then you didn't seem—"

"If we had been bored, it would have been our fault, but we were not bored at all," Miss Jardine replied. "At least, I wasn't, and don't think Helen was."

Helen added her denial and gave Festing her hand. When he had gone Miss Jardine looked at her with a smile.

"He was interesting," she remarked. "Talks better than he knows, and I suppose we ought to feel flattered, because he took our comprehension for granted. After all, it was rash to talk about Canadian progress to two English girls."

"You made him talk," Helen rejoined. "It's the first time I've known you interested in geography."

Miss Jardine laughed. "I was interested in the man. He told us a good deal about himself, although it would have embarrassed him if he'd guessed. The curious thing is that he imagines he's practical, while he's really a reckless sentimentalist."

Helen did not answer and picked up a book, but she thought more about Festing than about what she read.

CHAPTER IX

FESTING LOSES HIS TEMPER

Next morning Festing got breakfast early and set off down the dale. This was not the way Muriel had indicated, but he thought it better to avoid temptation. The girls had received him graciously at the farm and had perhaps listened with unusual patience, but if he overtook them in the morning the thing might look too marked. Besides, he doubted if it was advisable that Helen should see him again so soon, since he might remind her of matters she wished to forget.

The self-denial cost him something, and he went down the dale irresolutely, stopping once or twice to look back. It was annoying to feel himself so weak, because he had seldom vacillated in Canada, but had chosen the proper line and then stuck to it. As a matter of fact, he had generally had a definite object and definite plans for its attainment. Although he had an object now, he was otherwise at a loss.

He meant to marry Helen. Life was strenuous on the plains, and at first there might be hardships, but if she loved him she would not flinch. Her portrait had not done her justice; he dwelt upon her fearless confidence as she came down the screes, her light, sure step, and agile pose. These things indicated strength of mind and body, and he knew, if the need came, she would make good use of both.

By and by he thought of Charnock with keener anger than he

Harold Bindloss

had yet felt. Bob was a weak fool and something worse. He had broken the promise and then tricked his friend. The fellow's character was warped; he could not go straight, but tried to escape the consequences of his folly in a maze of crooked ways. The worst was that consequences could not be shirked. If the real offender avoided them, they fell upon somebody else, and now Festing had to pay. Bob had prejudiced him with Helen. She would probably never quite forget that he knew what she had suffered.

Then he remembered that he had meant to spend a week or two in London, and made his way towards a valley through which a railway ran. Although he wanted to see Helen, he was half afraid, and imagined that the longer he waited the less risk he would run of his society jarring. Next day he left the hills, but did not greatly enjoy his visit to town. London was much like Montreal, where the buildings were as fine, only they did not dig up so many streets and fill the air with cement from the towering blocks of new offices. The English liked permanence, while the Canadians altered their cities from day to day. Besides he wanted to go back to the North as soon as it was prudent.

On the evening of his return it rained hard and he talked to Muriel in her drawing-room. He liked Muriel Gardiner and she frankly enjoyed his society. It did not matter that she sometimes seemed to find him amusing when he was serious. A fire burned in the grate, for the summer evening was cold, his low chair was comfortable, and Muriel, holding a fan to shield her face, sat opposite in the soft light of a shaded lamp that left much of the room in shadow. The circle of subdued illumination gave one a pleasant feeling of seclusion and made for mutual confidence, but Festing was silent for a time, thinking rather hard.

He was getting used to English comforts, which did not seem so enervating as he had imagined, but he could give them up, and would, indeed, be forced to do so when he occupied his prairie homestead. A man could go without much that people in England required, and be the better for the self-denial, but it might be different for a girl. Long habit might make comfort and artistic surroundings actual necessities. It was, however, encouraging to remember Helen's cheerfulness as she led him among the crags in the rain. She had pluck and could bear fatigue and hardship. Besides, there need not be much hardship after all.

Presently Muriel gave him a careless glance. "Helen told me she met you in the hills and you came over to the hall where she and Alison Jardine stopped. Now you have had an opportunity of correcting your first impression, what do you think of her?"

"What I have always thought," Festing replied.

Muriel looked at him with surprise, and then laughed. "Oh, yes; I remember you saw her portrait first. Well, you have more imagination than I thought. But I understand you didn't see Helen again, although she and Alison went over part of the route I marked out for you."

Festing thought her manner was too careless, and felt suspicious, but he said: "I changed my plans. I thought it might look significant if I overtook the girls. One doesn't expect an accident to happen twice."

"Perhaps you did the proper thing. But did you want to overtake them?"

"I did," said Festing quietly. "Still I felt I'd better not."

Muriel was silent for a few moments, and then remarked: "Self-denial such as you practised deserves a reward, and I met Mrs. Dalton while you were away. She asked me to bring you over when you came back. I suppose you know what she wants?"

"Yes," said Festing, who looked disturbed. "Do you?"

"Mrs. Dalton told me. You helped George when he needed help, although he had no particular claim."

"He was ill and unfit for hard work."

"Was that the only difficulty?"

"I don't see what you mean," said Festing, with some embarrassment.

"Then I'll be frank. In what kind of company did you find the lad? You see, I know something about him."

"If you insist, he'd got into bad hands."

"That was what I suspected, and I think Mrs. Dalton knows. George was not very steady when he was at home and got into some trouble before he left the office of a civil engineer. In fact, this was why he went to Canada."

"But I don't see what it has to do with me."

"I wonder whether you are as dull as you pretend. George is Mrs. Dalton's only son; although he had faults she and Helen are very fond of him. Now it would have been something if you had merely helped him out of a difficulty, but you did much more. You gave him his chance of making up for past follies. He has been steady ever since, and I understand is now getting on very well. It looks as if you had used some moral influence."

"I didn't try," said Festing dryly, "I gave him his job and told him I'd have him fired if he shirked."

"You didn't consciously try, but it's possible to influence people without knowing. However, as Mrs. Dalton has too much tact to overwhelm you by her gratitude, you needn't be afraid of going to the Scar with me, although you seem to hesitate about meeting Helen."

Festing, who pondered for a few moments, felt that the girl was studying him. She had shown a rather embarrassing curiosity, but he though she meant to be his friend.

"Did you know Miss Dalton was in the mountains when you planned my walking tour?" he asked.

"I did know," said Muriel with a direct glance. "Perhaps I was rash, but if so, I'm not afraid to own my fault. I suppose you understand why I sent you where I did?"

"In one way, your object's plain. For all that, I'm puzzled."

Muriel smiled. "As Helen is my friend, you ought to be flattered. Doesn't it look as if I was satisfied with you?"

"We'll let that go. You took something for granted. I suppose you see you might have been mistaken about my feelings?"

"Then no harm would have been done," Muriel rejoined, and putting down her fan, gave him a steady look. "Was I mistaken?"

"You were not," said Festing quietly. "I mean to marry Miss Dalton if she is willing. I'm anxious to know what chance I've got."

"I can't tell you that. Perhaps I have gone far enough; but George's reformation is a good certificate of your character, and Helen and her mother owe you a debt of gratitude."

Festing colored rather angrily. "My helping the lad was, so to speak, an accident; I don't want to be judged by this, and won't urge the debt. Miss Dalton must take me on my merits."

"You have pluck; it's a bold claim," said Muriel in a dry tone, and then got up as Gardiner and the curate came in.

Next day Festing went to the Scar, and when Mrs. Dalton

Harold Bindloss

received him she put her hand gently on his arm. She said enough, but not too much, and he was moved as he saw the moisture glisten in her eyes.

"I don't deserve this," he answered awkwardly. "I found the lad in some trouble, but hadn't to make much effort to help him out. In fact, it was the kind of thing one does without thinking and forgets."

"Ah," said Mrs. Dalton, "the consequences of one's deeds follow one, whether they're good or bad." Then she gave him a very friendly smile. "But perhaps we had better join the rest outside."

Festing found Helen in the garden with her aunt and some friends, but the others left them by and by, and they walked alone among the flowers. The day was calm, the light clear, and the shadow of the dark beeches on the hill crept slowly across the lawn. Beyond a low hedge, woods, smooth pastures, and fields of ripening corn rolled back and melted into the blue shadow beneath the rugged fells. It seemed to Festing that the peaceful sylvan landscape was touched by a glamour that centered in the fresh beauty of the girl. Sometimes they were silent, and sometimes they talked about the mountains, but when they went back to the house he thought they had got nearer.

He returned to the Scar without Muriel a week later, and went again, and one evening stood with Helen on the terrace. Gentle rain had fallen for most of the day, but it had stopped, and a band of pale-saffron glimmered under heavy clouds in the West. Moisture dripped from the motionless branches and the air was hot. The lamps had just been lighted in the house and a yellow glow streamed out.

"I've stayed longer than I meant and forgot my lamp," Festing remarked. "However, this has happened before, and I hope I haven't stayed longer than I ought."

"We will let you go now," said Helen. "For one thing, I must get up early."

"Eight o'clock?" Festing suggested.

"No," said Helen, smiling. "I am always up before, but it will be six o'clock to-morrow. I want to gather some mushrooms; they ought to be plentiful after a day like this."

"Is six o'clock a particularly suitable time?"

"Five o'clock might be better. If you don't go early, you often find that somebody has been round the fields first."

Festing asked where she expected to find the mushrooms, and when she told him said, "Very well; I'll meet you. It only means half an hour's journey on your fine English road; that is, if the bicycle holds up."

"But why do you want to gather mushrooms?"

"I don't want to gather mushrooms. I really want to see you where I think you belong."

"In the fields?" Helen suggested humorously.

"No," said Festing. "I don't mean in the fields. I've seen you in the afternoon when the sun's on the ripening corn and the leaves are dark and thick, but they stand for fulfilment, and that's not your proper setting. Once or twice I've stopped until evening, but you don't belong to the dusk."

"Then where do I belong?"

"To the sunrise, when the earth is fresh and the day is getting bright. Promise is your sign; fulfilment hasn't come."

Helen colored, and as she turned her head it struck her as portentous that she glanced towards the saffron streak that

Harold Bindloss

glimmered in the West. When she looked back, however, her face was calm.

"Ah!" she said, "I wonder how and where the fulfilment will come! Sometimes I think of it and feel afraid; my life has been so smooth."

"You won't flinch if you have to bear some strain."

Helen gave him her hand. "Well, you must go now. I will expect you to-morrow."

She stood looking towards the fading light for some time after his figure melted into the shadows on the drive. Her heart beat and she felt a thrill, for she admitted that the man had power to move her. As yet she would not ask herself how far his power went, but she knew the question must be answered soon. Other men had flattered her, and she had smiled, knowing what their compliments were worth, but she could not smile now. Then she roused herself and went in quietly.

Festing met her next morning while the sun rose above the rounded masses of the beech wood, and entering a dewy pasture they skirted a fence half-smothered in briars. Both felt invigorated by the freshness of the morning and brushed across the sparkling grass, engaged in careless talk. By and by as Helen stooped to pick a mushroom a shrill scream came from beyond the fence, and she rose with an angry color in her face.

"Oh!" she said; "that spoils everything!"

"What is it?" Festing asked as the pitiful scream rose again.

"A rabbit, choking, in a snare," she answered with a look of horror.

Festing leaped across a ditch and plunged into the briars. Helen heard the rotten fence-rails smash and he vanished behind the thorny branches that closed across the gap. She was glad he had gone so quickly; partly because it was her wish, and partly because she saw the cry of pain had moved him. She liked to think he was compassionate.

As a matter of fact, Festing's pity was soon mixed with rage as he came upon a scene of barbarous cruelty. Three or four rabbits lay quiet upon the grass, but there were others that struggled feebly at his approach; their eyes protruding and strangling wires cutting into their throats. He thought they were past his help, but one rolled round with half-choked screams and he ran to it first. It was difficult to hold the struggling animal while he opened the thin brass noose, but he set it free, and it lay paralyzed with fear for a few moments before it ran off.

Then he released the others as gently as he could. Their dew-draggled bodies felt cold and limp and the wire had bitten deep into the swollen flesh. Two, however, feebly crawled away and he carried another to the mouth of a burrow, after which he wiped the dew and blood from his hands, while his lips set in a firm line. He hoped he was not a sentimentalist, and admitted that man must kill to eat; moreover he had used the rifle in the Northern wilds. Once a hungry cinnamon bear had raided the camp, and he remembered a certain big bull moose. That was clean sport, for a man who faced such antagonists must shoot quick and straight, but this torturing of small defenseless creatures revolted him. Still he admitted that it might not have done so quite so much but for the pain it caused the girl.

Helen glanced at him with some surprise when he went back to the fence. She had not seen him look like that.

"I've let them go, but two or three are dead," he remarked. "I suppose they've been lying there all night."

"I'm afraid so. They come out to feed at dusk. It's horribly cruel."

"It's devilish! Why don't you stop it? Is the field yours?"

"It goes with the house, and when we let the grazing I stipulated that no snares should be laid, but there was some mistake and the tenant claimed the rabbits. We said he could shoot them, and I understand he's disputing with the agent. But where are you going?"

"I'm going back to finish the job; these particular snares won't be used again. If you like, I'll come over every evening and pull the blamed things up."

"I don't think that will be necessary," Helen answered with a strained laugh.

She felt disturbed and excited when Festing turned away. Her life had been smooth and she did not think she had seen a man seized by savage anger; certainly not a man she knew. Festing was angry, and no doubt justly, but at the Scar the primitive vein in human nature was decently hidden. Now she did not know if she were jarred or not. Then she heard voices, and going nearer the fence, tried to see through the briars.

Festing, with a pocket-knife and some brass wire in his hand, confronted a big slouching man who carried a heavy stick and a net bag. Bits of fur stuck to the fellow's clothes and there was blood on his dirty hands. A half-grown lad with another stick waited, rather uneasily, in the background.

"What might you be doing?" the man inquired.

"I'm cutting up your snares," Festing replied. "What have you got to say about it?"

The other gave him a slow, sullen look. "Only that you'd better leave the snares alone. How many rabbits?"

"Four," said Festing, pulling up another snare and cutting the noose.

"Then that will be five shillings. I'll say nothing about the snares; wire's cheap."

Festing laughed. "It's a dead bluff. Light out of this field before I put you off."

The man hesitated, his eyes fixed on Festing's hardset face. Perhaps a way out might have been found, but the lad precipitated matters. Running to the mouth of the burrow, he picked up a half-dead rabbit that was trying to crawl away, and leered at Festing as he raised his stick. The blow was not struck, for Festing leaped across the grass and next moment the boy fell beside the burrow. He was unhurt, but too surprised to move, because he had never seen anybody move as fast as the man who threw him down.

Then Festing heard steps behind, and turned in time to guard his head with his right arm. It felt numb and he was half dazed by a shock of pain, but he struck savagely with his left hand and his knuckles jarred on bone. The other's stick dropped, and when they grappled Festing was relieved to feel his arm was not broken. His muscles were hard and well trained, his blood was hot, and a struggle of the kind was not altogether a novelty. When liquor is smuggled into a construction camp, a section boss must sometimes use physical force or relinquish his command.

He staggered and nearly fell as his leg was seized. It looked as if the lad had come to his master's help; but one could not be fastidious, and a savage backward kick got rid of the new antagonist. The other was powerful and stubborn, and Festing spent a strenuous few minutes before he threw him into the sand beside the burrow.

"I'm pretty fresh and ready to start again if you are," he said. "Still I reckon you have had enough."

The fellow got up scowling and told the lad to bring his bag.

"You'll hear more about this," he rejoined and slouched off.

Festing went back, and Helen started when he jumped across the ditch. His jacket was torn, his lip was cut, and his face was bruised. He looked dishevelled, but not at all embarrassed. In fact, there was a gleam of half-humorous satisfaction in his eyes.

"The snares are all cut up," he said. "I broke the fellow's stick and threw away the pegs."

Helen felt a strange desire to laugh. There was something ridiculous in his naive triumph, but she was not really amused. In fact, her confused sensations were puzzling.

"Did you hurt him?" she asked.

"I hope so," said Festing. "I rather think I did and don't expect he'll come back while I'm about. However, as I can't come here as often as I'd like, it might be better to see your agent. In the meantime, we'll look for some mushrooms."

"But don't you want to bathe your face?"

"I forgot that I probably look the worse for wear," said Festing, who wiped his cut lip. "Still if I met your mother, she might get a shock, and now I come to think of it, I'm no doubt jarring you, so I'll go off and see your agent if you'll tell me where he lives."

"It's some distance, and we don't do things so quickly here. I must talk to my mother first. Besides, the agent may not have got up."

"Then I'll sit on the doorstep. But what is there to talk about? You don't want your rabbits tortured so that somebody may make thirty cents apiece. It has got to be stopped, and why not stop it now? Where does the fellow live?"

Helen told him, and added: "But you can't go like that."

"No; I suppose not," said Festing doubtfully. "It won't make a long round if I call at Gardiner's. I'll come back later and tell you how I've fixed things up."

He lifted his badly crushed hat, and when he turned away Helen laughed, a half-hysterical laugh. His fierce energy had, so to speak, left her breathless; she was shaken by confused emotions. It was for her sake he had plunged into the quarrel, but she felt disturbed by his savageness. For all that, something in her approved, and it was really this that troubled her. Picking up the basket, she crossed the field with a very thoughtful look.

CHAPTER X

HELEN DECIDES

Some weeks had passed since Festing went to gather mushrooms when he sat, one evening, on the terrace in front of Gardiner's house. His brows were knit and he had in his had a letter from Kerr at the construction camp. The back of the letter was covered with penciled calculations, but he presently put it down and looked moodily about.

The larches that sheltered the house had been in full leaf when he came, but now they were getting bare. One could see the hills through a fine network of twigs, dotted with minute tassels of gold. The beeches and oaks looked solid yet, but the former shone warm brown and red against the others' fading green. Withered leaves fluttered down, and the smell of a burning heap hung in the damp air.

The touches of brown and gold in the landscape hinted that time was passing. Winter was already advancing across the wastes of Northern Canada and the geese and ducks were flying south. Festing heard in fancy the brant's changing cry that always filled him with unrest, but the letter in his hand was a clearer call. Kerr had offered him a contract for hauling a quantity of telegraph posts and logs across the snow, and his calculations indicated that the work ought to be profitable. It would keep him occupied all winter; one could buy horses cheap when harvest was over and sell them advantageously when plowing began in the spring. Besides, the money he earned would help him to stock his farm and furnish his homestead well.

He had loitered in England long enough. He would never forget this holiday, for he had learned what happiness life might have in store; but it was a happiness that could not be attained by romantic dreams. He must earn it by tense effort, and was willing to pay the price; this was the reason he must get back to work. For all that, he had doubts, and was glad when Muriel came along the terrace and sat down on the bench.

"You look unusually thoughtful," she said.

"I have something to think about. I find I must go back to Canada very soon."

Muriel made an abrupt movement. "You are going away! But we thought—" She paused and resumed: "Does Helen know?"

"Not yet; I must tell her. It will cost me something to leave, but I've got to go. Perhaps you had better see what Kerr has to say."

He gave her the letter, and after waiting until she had read it, went on: "I can't let this chance pass; I want the money."

"I think I understand," said Muriel. "Still you haven't told me much."

He was silent for a few moments and looked very grave, but she had for some time imagined that he was bearing a strain.

"Well," he said, "I'm up against things and can't see my way. That is, I do see where I mean to go, but don't know if I ought."

"The problem's not exactly new. However, if you will state it clearly."

"I'll try," said Festing. "One can trust you; in fact, I wanted to tell you before."

He explained his difficulties, practical and moral, and when he finished Muriel said: "It comes to this—You are in love with Helen and mean to marry her, but hesitate because you fear she may find the life too hard."

"It's a big risk for an English girl. She must give up everything, while I have all to gain."

"But suppose she were willing?"

"The trouble is that she doesn't know what she may have to bear."

Muriel smiled. "It's a risk that many girls must run. But after all it depends upon what she values most."

"Comfort, leisure, refined friends, and other things you enjoy here are worth much to a girl."

"All this is true," Muriel agreed, and pausing, continued with a blush: "Still these things don't satisfy every need, and perhaps my example may be some encouragement. Fred isn't very clever and will probably never be rich, but I'd sooner face poverty with him than marry a prince."

Festing bowed. "Thank you for that! Fred's a very good sort. I knew you had pluck."

"I really think Helen is pluckier and stronger than me. But I imagine you have already made up your mind."

"I have; for all that, I'm afraid. If I have bad luck, Helen will have to pay. I know she was willing to marry Charnock, but she was very young then and he was rich compared with me."

"Then I suppose a little money would be a useful help?"

"It would, in one way," Festing agreed. "The trouble is that I haven't much; only enough to make a fair start if I'm economical."

For a moment Muriel looked amused, but her seriousness returned. "We'll let that go. You seem to forget that you don't stand alone. I should have found it hard to forgive Fred if he had decided whether he ought to marry or not, without consulting me. It's a girl's right, not her lover's, to say what she values most and how much she is willing to bear. If Helen loves you, she's entitled to be given the choice."

"Ah," said Festing, "I don't know if she loves me yet!"

Muriel's eyes twinkled. "That is something you must find out for yourself. But perhaps I have said enough."

She went back to the house and Festing sat still in the gathering dark. He had made up his mind and felt encouraged, but he saw difficulties that must be met.

Next day he went to the Scar and found that Helen was not at home, but Mrs. Dalton and her sister received him, and for a time he talked about things that did not matter. It was dull and damp outside, and a bright wood fire burned in the grate. The low-ceilinged room was very warm, its comfort seemed enervating, and he felt braced as he thought of the windswept prairie. Then he knew his remarks were vague and disconnected. It was a relief to plunge into the business he had come about.

"I had better tell you that I am going to ask Helen to marry me," he said.

Mrs. Dalton did not look surprised, and he thought Miss Graham smiled. Perhaps he had been abrupt, but he did not care.

"You have done what is proper in warning my sister first,"

Miss Graham remarked; but Mrs. Dalton was silent for a few moments.

"You imply that Helen doesn't know," she said.

"She does not; I've been careful not to give her a hint," Festing declared. "I was afraid to alarm her by, so to speak, rushing things. You're not used to it in England."

Miss Graham's amusement was plainer. "The caution you exercised must have cost you something."

"After all, you haven't known Helen long," Mrs. Dalton resumed.

"That's so, in a way, but five minutes was long enough. I knew I'd never marry anybody else when I saw her in the garden the first day I came."

He thought Miss Graham gave him an approving look, but he turned to Mrs. Dalton.

"I hope you will give your consent; but, of course, if you object, or there's anything you want to ask—"

Mrs. Dalton roused herself. She felt breathless, as if she had been carried along at an unusual pace.

"To begin with," she said quietly, "I cannot object to you. We know something about your character; you helped my son, helped him more than you perhaps thought. But there is something I must ask." She hesitated and then resumed: "You have seen the life Helen leads with us. She has never had to use much self-denial. What have you to offer her in Canada?"

"Not much. In fact, that's partly why I came first to you. I felt you should be warned; that's really what I meant."

"You are honest," Miss Graham interposed. "You want my

sister's approval, but don't think it essential."

Festing looked at Mrs. Dalton. "If you refused, I wouldn't be altogether daunted. I might wait, but that is all. This is a matter Helen must decide."

"Yes. All the same, it is my duty to guard her from a possible mistake."

"Very well; I'll make matters as plain as I can. To begin with, I haven't much money, and although I'm building a good homestead, a Western farm is very different from the Scar. There's none of the refinement you have round you; a man must work from sunrise until it's dark, and there are many demands upon a woman. For all that, I can guard against Helen suffering actual hardship. In fact, she shall suffer nothing I can save her from. It's the pressure of things one can't control and her own character that may cause the strain. If I know her, she won't stand by and watch when there's much that ought to be done."

"She would not. But how long do you expect the strain to last?"

"Not very long. Two years, three years; I can't tell. When you break new land you work hard and wait. The railroad throws out branches, elevators are built, small towns spring up, and while you improve your holding comfort and often prosperity comes to you."

"But in the meantime a little capital would help?"

"Of course," said Festing. "The trouble is I haven't much, but I think I have enough to provide all that's strictly necessary."

He thought Mrs. Dalton gave her sister a warning glance, but she said: "Well, you have my consent to ask Helen; but if she is willing to run the risk, there is a stipulation I must make."

"So long as you consent, I'll agree to anything," Festing declared. "I can't repay you for your trust, but I'll try to deserve it."

Mrs. Dalton told him where Helen had gone, and setting off to meet her, he presently saw her come round a bend in a lane. The sun had set and tall oaks, growing along the hedgerows, darkened the lane, but a faint crimson glow from the west shone between the trunks. To the east, the quiet countryside rolled back into deepening shadow. For a moment Festing hesitated as he watched the girl advance. It was rash to uproot this fair bloom of the sheltered English garden and transplant it in virgin soil, swept by the rushing winds. Then he went forward resolutely.

Helen gave him her hand and moved on with disturbed feelings, for there was something different in his look.

"If you don't mind, we'll stop a minute; I have something to say. To begin with, I'm going back to Canada."

She looked up sharply and then waited with forced calm until he resumed: "That precipitates matters, because I must learn if I've hoped for too much before I go. I was a stranger when I came here, and you were kind—"

"You were not a stranger," Helen said quietly. "George told us about you, and for his sake—"

"I don't want you to be kind for George's sake, but my own. I'd sooner you liked me for what I am, with all my faults."

"If it's any comfort, I think I really do like you," Helen admitted with a strained smile.

"Well enough to marry me?"

Helen colored, but gave him a level glance. "Ah," she said, "aren't you rash? You hardly know me yet."

"I'm not rash at all; I knew you long ago. Your portrait hung in Charnock's house and I used to study it on winter nights. It told me what you were, and when I saw you under the copper beech I knew you very well. Still now I have seen you, your picture had lost its charm."

"Then you have it?" Helen asked.

Festing gave her a Russia leather case and her face flushed red.

"Did Bob give you this?"

"No," said Festing quietly; "I stole it."

"And the case?"

"The case was made in Montreal. I went to Winnipeg, but could get nothing good enough."

Helen turned her head. It was a long way to Winnipeg from the prairie bridge, and she was moved that he had made the journey to find a proper covering for her picture.

"You must have valued the portrait," she remarked shyly.

"I did, but it won't satisfy me now. As soon as I met you I fell in love with you. Somehow I think you must have seen—"

"Yes," said Helen quietly, "I did see."

Festing summoned his self-control. "You must know what you decide. I must live in Canada; my homestead may seem rude and bare after your mother's beautiful house, and I tried to show you what a prairie farm is like."

"I think I know," Helen said, and gave him a quick tender look. "Still, such things don't really matter—"

Then Festing stepped forward and took her in his arms.

An hour later he sat talking to Mrs. Dalton and Miss Graham in the drawing-room.

"I am glad you have agreed to wait and come back for Helen in the spring, but I ought to tell you something now, because it may make a difference in your plans," Mrs. Dalton remarked "You admitted that some of the difficulties you and Helen would have to meet might be avoided if you had a little more capital."

"It would certainly make a difference, but I have got no more."

"Helen has some money," Mrs. Dalton replied.

Festing knitted his brows. "I didn't suspect this!"

"That is obvious," Miss Graham interposed.

Festing got up, moved a pace or two, and stopped. "How much has she got?"

Mrs. Dalton told him and he frowned. "Then she had better keep it. I'd sooner you tied it up."

"Isn't that unreasonable?" Miss Graham asked.

"It's a man's business to support his wife. I don't want to live on Helen's money. Besides, I've made my plans."

"I don't think you quite understand," Mrs. Dalton rejoined. "After all, it is not a large sum and can be used for Helen's benefit. It may save her from some discomfort and give her advantages you could not provide."

Festing pondered for a few moments, and then answered thoughtfully: "Yes, I see this, and can't refuse. Well, perhaps the safest way would be to transfer the land I bought to Helen and record it in her name. It's bound to go up in value and couldn't be taken from her unless she borrowed on a mortgage.

The arrangement would set free my capital and enable us to run the homestead on more comfortable lines." Then he paused and asked: "Did Charnock know about the money?"

"He did not," said Mrs. Dalton. "We thought it better not to tell him; but we can trust you."

"Thank you," said Festing, who was silent for a time.

He had wondered whether he had misjudged Charnock in one respect, but saw that he had not. The fellow was a cur and would not have married Sadie if he had known about Helen's money. But this did not matter.

"Well," he resumed, "if you agree to my proposition, we'll get a lawyer to fix it up. In a way, it's some relief to know Helen has enough, and now I'm going to talk to her."

He found her in the next room and she gave him a smile. "I expect mother has told you I'm not as poor as you thought. Are you pleased or not?"

"I'm pleased for your sake, because there's not much risk of your finding things too hard, but I'd have been proud to marry you if you had nothing at all."

"Not even a certain prettiness?" Helen asked.

"Your beauty's something to be thankful for; but after all it's, so to speak, an accident, like your money. It wasn't your beauty, but you, I fell in love with."

Helen blushed. "Ah!" she said, "now you're very nice indeed!"

CHAPTER XI

SADIE USES PRESSURE

It was getting cold in the small back office when Sadie put down her pen and went into the store. She was cramped with sitting, for she had been occupied with accounts for several hours and the stove had burned low.

"You can quit now, Steve," she said to the clerk. "Put out the lights, but don't lock up. I'm going to wait until the boss comes."

The clerk turned his head to hide a smile; because he knew where Charnock was, and thought Mrs. Charnock might have to wait some time; but he did as he was told, and when he went out Sadie stood shivering at the door. She had married Charnock late in the fall and now it was March, but there was no sign yet of returning spring. The sky was dark and a bitter wind from the prairie blew down the empty street. Blocks of square-fronted houses stood out harshly against the snow, which sparkled here and there in a ray of light. The settlement looked ugly and very desolate, and Sadie studied it with a feeling of weariness and disgust. It seemed strange that she had once thought it a lively place, but this was before she met Charnock, who had taught her much.

Shutting the door, she returned to the office and glanced critically at her reflection in a mirror on the wall. She had been ill, in consequence of the strain she had borne while her father was sick, and looked older. Her face was thin and she felt tired, but her skin had not lost its silky whiteness, and her black dress hung in becoming lines. It was a well-cut dress, for Sadie was extravagant in such matters and knew how to choose her clothes. She had lost the freshness that had marked her, but had gained something: a touch of dignity that she thought of as style.

Sitting down at the desk, she began to muse. Keller had fallen ill soon after her wedding. It was a painful illness, and as skilled help was scarce, she had nursed him until he died. He was a plain storekeeper, but she knew he was, in many ways, a bigger and better man than Bob. He demanded all that was his, but he kept his word, and when he undertook a thing put it over, which Bob seldom did. Shortly before he died he gave Sadie good advice.

"You got the man you wanted, and now it's your job to look after him. head him off the liquor, and keep your hands on the dollars. I've fixed things so's they belong to you."

Another time he asked for certain accounts, and after studying them remarked: "You want to watch the business and run it all it's worth. You have a husband to work for now, and I guess a man like Bob comes expensive. Still, if you can guild him right, he's not all a fool."

Sadie had not resented this. She knew it was true, and her father had not meant to sneer. He was a blunt man and generally talked like that, and Sadie sometimes did so. Well, she had not been cheated, because she knew what Bob was before they married; and although ambition had something to do with it, she loved him. For all that, she had got some rude jars, and now passion was dying, her love was colored by a certain half-maternal protection. Bob must be watched and guarded.

Her ambition, however, remained. She had beauty and intelligence and wanted to win a place in cultured society. Bob could help her, and she was tired of the dreary settlement. But she was practical. Money would be needed if they were to move to one of the cities, and although trade was good, gathering dollars was slow work when one had an extravagant husband. While she had been ill Bob was left in charge of the business, and on recovering her first task had been to find out how he had managed. Now she had found out and got something of a shock.

The room got colder, but Bob had made some entries in a cash-book she could not understand, and opening the book again, she spent some time in calculations that threw no fresh light on the matter. Then she heard steps and turned as Charnock came in.

He took off his fur-coat and Sadie frowned as he dropped it into a dusty corner. It was an expensive coat, but one could not teach Bob to take care of things. Then he kissed her and sat down on the edge of the table.

"You're getting prettier, Sadie; that thoughtful look of yours is particularly fetching. But I can see you're tired. Put those books away and let's get home."

Sadie knew what his compliments were worth, although they had not lost their charm. He wanted to put things off, but she must be firm.

"You make me tired, and I haven't finished with the books. We've got to have a talk."

"I like you best when you don't talk; you sometimes say too much," Charnock replied. "Besides a girl like you ought to be satisfied with being seen. You're worth looking at."

Sadie gave him a quick glance. He had recently become fastidious about his clothes and she did not grudge the dollars he spent on them. His taste was good, and he looked very graceful as he turned to her with a smile on his face. The hint of dissipation it had worn was not so marked, for she had some power over him and used it well, but she thought he had been indulging. There was, however, no use in getting angry with Bob.

"You were at Wilkinson's again," she said. "You promised you'd stop off going there. I suppose he set up the whisky!"

"I didn't take much. It wasn't good whisky; not like ours. That reminds me—I'm not much of a business man, but I've had a happy thought. My notion is we give the boys better liquor than they want. They wouldn't know the difference if we kept cheaper stuff."

Sadie frowned, because she had accepted her father's business code. His charges were high, but it had been his boast that Keller's delivered the goods one paid for. Then she realized that Bob had nearly succeeded in putting off the threatened talk.

"No," she said, "that's bad business in the end. When you'd had some whisky, Wilkinson got out the cards?"

"Oh, well, you know you stopped me playing a quiet game at home, and three or four of the boys were there. Then a Brandon real-estate man asked for the cards."

"How much were you out when you finished the game?"

"Not much," said Charnock with some hesitation.

"How much?"

"If you insist, about ten dollars."

Sadie made a gesture of impatience, but after all he might have had a heavier loss.

"Ten dollars and a headache next morning for an evening's

card game. You surely don't know much, Bob! But look at this statement and tell me where the money's gone."

Charnock took the paper she gave him and colored.

"I never thought it was as much as that. Upon my word, I didn't!"

"Where's it gone?" Sadie demanded.

"I've been unlucky," said Charnock, who began a confused explanation.

He had heard of a building lot on the outskirts of Winnipeg, to which he had been told a new street line would run. He had paid for a time option on the site, and now it appeared that the trolley scheme had been abandoned. Then somebody had given him a hint about a deal in grain that the speculators could not put over. It looked a safe snap and he had sold down, but the market had gone up and his margin was exhausted. When he stopped, Sadie's eyes flashed scornfully, but she controlled her anger.

"You're a fool, Bob; you never learn," she said wearily. "Anyhow, you have got to cut out this kind of thing; the business won't stand for it long. Well, as you can't be trusted with dollars, I'll have to put you on an allowance. I hate to be mean, but if you waste what I give you, you'll get no more."

Charnock's face got red. "This is rather a nasty knock. Not that I want your money, but the thing's humiliating."

"Do you think it isn't humiliating to me?"

"Perhaps it is," said Charnock, with a half-ashamed look. "I admit I have been something of an ass, but you are mean, in a sense. What are you going to do with your money, if you don't intend to spend it?"

"Use if for making more; anyhow, until I get enough."

"When will you have enough?"

"When I can sell out the business and live where I want; give you the friends you ought to have instead of low-down gamblers and whisky-tanks. If you'd take hold and work, Bob, we'd be rich in a few years. The boys like you, you could do all the trade, and the boom that's beginning will make this settlement a big place. But I guess there's no use in talking—and I'm ill and tired."

Sadie's pose got slack and she leaned her arms on the table with her face in her hands. Charnock, feeling penitent, tried to comfort her.

"You're a very good sort, Sadie, and mean well; I'll go steady and try not to bother you again. But we won't say any more about it now. Are those new letters? The mail hadn't come when I left."

She gave him two envelopes, and after reading part of the first letter he started and the paper rustled in his hand.

"What's the matter?" she asked. "Have you lost some money I don't know about?"

"I haven't," Charnock answered with a hoarse laugh. "The letter's from some English friends. You head that Festing had gone back to the Old Country. Well, he's going to be married soon and will bring his wife out."

"Do you know her? Who is she?"

"Yes; I know her very well. She's Helen Dalton."

"The girl you ought to have married!" Sadie exclaimed. "What's she like? I guess you have her picture, though you haven't shown it me."

"I had one, but haven't now. I meant to burn the thing, but suspect that Festing stole it. Confound him!"

Sadie was silent for a few moments and then gave Charnock a searching look. "Anyhow, I don't see why that should make you mad. You let her go and took me instead. Do you reckon she'd have been as patient with you as I am?"

"No," said Charnock, rather drearily. "Helen isn't patient, and I dare say I'd have broken her heart. You have done your best for me, and I expect you find it a hopeless job. For all that, I never thought Festing—"

"It's done with," Sadie rejoined quietly, although there was some color in her face. "If the girl likes Festing, what has it to do with you? Besides, as he has located some way back from the settlement, there's no reason you should meet him or his wife." Then she frowned and got up. "But the place is very cold; we'll go home."

Charnock put out the light and locked the door, but he was silent as they walked across the snow to the hotel, and Sadie wondered what he thought. There was no doubt he was disturbed, or he would have tried to coax her into abandoning her resolution to put him on an allowance. She meant to be firm about this.

For the next two or three weeks Charnock occupied himself with his duties and everything went smoothly at the store and hotel. He was popular in the neighborhood, since his weaknesses were rather attractive than repellent to people who did not suffer from them. Men who drove long distances from their lonely farms liked a cheerful talk and to hear the latest joke; others enjoyed a game of cards in the back office when Mrs. Charnock was not about. Besides, it was known that Keller's was straight; one got full weight and value when one dealt there.

Trade, moreover, was unusually good. Settlers looking for land filled the hotel, and now elevators were to be built, farmers hired extra labor and broke new soil. Household supplies were purchased on an unprecedented scale, and when snow melted the hotel stables were occupied by rough-coated teams, while wagons, foul with the mud of the prairie trails, waited for their loads in front of the store. Sadie felt cheered and encouraged, and although Bob sometimes spent in careless talk an hour or two that might have been better employed, she was willing to make up for his neglect by extra work in the office at night. He was doing well and she began to be hopeful.

One evening, however, when there were goods to be entered and bills written out, he went home for supper and did not come back. Sadie stopped in the office long after the clerk had gone, but when she put down her pen the stove was out and she was surprised to find how late it was. She felt tired and annoyed, for she had been busily occupied since morning, and suspected that Bob was telling amusing stories while she did his work. Then in shutting up the store she forgot her rubber over-shoes, and the sidewalk was plastered with sticky mud. She wore rather expensive slippers and thought they would be spoiled.

Charnock was not about when she entered the hotel, and the guests seemed to have gone to bed. The light was out in the office, and the big lounge room, where lumps of half-dry mud lay upon the board floor, was unoccupied. The bell-boy, who was using a brush amidst a cloud of dust, said he did not think the boss had gone upstairs, and with sudden suspicion Sadie entered a dark passage that led to a room where commercial travelers showed their goods. She opened the door and stopped just inside, her head tilted back and an angry sparkle in her eyes.

The room was very hot and smelt of liquor, tobacco, and kerosene; the lamp had been turned too high and its cracked chimney was black. Charnock and three others sat round a table on which stood a bottle and four glasses. One of the glasses had upset and there was a pool, bordered by soaked cigar-ash, on the boards. The men were playing cards, and a pile of paper money indicated that the stakes were high. Sadie knew them all and deeply distrusted one, whom she suspected of practising on her husband's weaknesses; she disliked another, and the third did not count. She looked up rather awkwardly, and she saw that Charnock had taken too much liquor.

"Good evening, boys," she said. "I want to lock the doors, and guess you don't know how late it is."

Wilkinson, the man she distrusted, took out his watch. He had a horse ranch some distance off, and the farmers called him a sport. As a matter of fact, he was a successful petty gambler, but generally lost his winnings by speculating in real-estate and wheat.

"It's surely late, Mrs. Charnock," he agreed. "Still, I dare say you can give us a quarter of an hour."

"Five minutes," Sadie answered. "You can cut the game you're playing when you like. I'm tired, but I'll wait."

Wilkinson looked at Charnock, but stopped arranging his cards. "Well, I'm ready to quit. Bob's made a scoop the last few deals, and I reckon I've not much chance of getting my money back."

"Go 'way, Sadie; go 'way right now!" Charnock interrupted. "You gotta put up a fair game, and I can't stop when I've all the boys' dollars in my pocket."

Sadie was sometimes tactful, but her anger was quick, and she disliked to hear her husband use Western idioms. Moreover she expected him to be polite.

"Well," she said, "I guess that's a change; your dollars are generally in their wallets. But this game has to stop."

Mossup, the man she did not like, turned in his chair. He was not sober and his manners were not polished at the best of times. He sold small tools and hardware for a Winnipeg wholesale firm.

"Say, you might call a bell-boy. That whisky's rank; I want a different drink."

Charnock got up with an awkward movement, but Sadie did not want his help.

"Drinks are served in the bar and the bar is shut," she said.

"I'm stopping here; I hired this room, and as long as I pay it's mine. We're not in Manitoba, and I guess the law—"

Sadie silenced him imperiously. She understood his reference to Manitoba, where regulations dealing with liquor are strictly enforced.

"I make the law at Keller's, and this hotel is not a gambling saloon. Mr. Wilkinson, cork that bottle and put it on the shelf."

As Wilkinson obeyed, Mossup put his hand on his arm to hold him back, but Charnock interfered:

"You sit down right now. Understand, everybody, what Mrs. Charnock says goes."

"Certainly," Wilkinson agreed. "Get off to bed Mossup; you'll have a swelled head all right to-morrow, as it is. I'll put out the light, Mrs. Charnock; guess I'll do it better than Bob."

"Think I can't put out a common old lamp?" Charnock inquired. "Destroy the blamed thing 'fore I let it beat me."

"You're not going to try," said Wilkinson, who hustled him and Mossup out of the room and then held the door open for Sadie.

She thanked him, but felt that if she had ground to fear resentment, it was not Mossup's but his. Wilkinson had manners, but she knew he did not like to be robbed of an easy victim, and it was possible that he had let Bob win until he was drunk enough to be fleeced. She waited a few moments to let the others go, and then went upstairs and stopped in a passage that led to her room. Her face was hot and she breathed fast, for her part in the scene had cost her something. It would have been different had Charnock not been there; she could have dealt with the others, but he had made her ashamed. Then she heard his step and turned with passionate anger as he came along the passage. He stopped and looked at her with drunken admiration.

"By George, you're a fine thing, Sadie! Handsomest and pluckiest woman in the township!"

Sadie said nothing, but her pose stiffened and her lips set tight.

"Look your best when you're angry," Charnock went on. "Not quite so 'tractive, too pale and want animation, when you're calm."

She did not answer, but felt a quiver of repulsion. His voice was thick, his eyes had a stupid amorous look, and he smelt of whisky. Sadie was not remarkably fastidious; she had, for several years, managed a hotel, and had used her physical charm to attract the man, but she was jarred. As yet, she made no appeal to the better side of Bob's nature, if it had a better side, and his sensual admiration revolted her.

Charnock felt puzzled and somewhat daunted, but tried to put his arm round her waist. Sadie seized his shoulders and pushed him violently back.

"Don't you touch me, you drunken hog!" she said.

He gazed at her in dull surprise and then braced himself. Sadie had moods, but generally came round if he made love to her. Besides, although she was in one of her rages, her attitude was irresistibly inciting.

"I'm your husband anyhow. Now don't be a silly little fool—"

She drew back as he advanced and picked up a mop. It was used for polishing board floors and had a long handle.

"You're my husband when you're sober; I didn't marry a whisky-tank. If you touch me, Bob, I'll knock you down!"

Charnock stopped. When Sadie spoke like that she meant what she said. She looked at him steadily for a moment or two, and then put down the mop and turned away. He durst not follow, and when she entered a room close by, he shrugged with half-bewildered resignation and stumbled off.

Sadie, leaning with labored breath against the rail of her bed, heard him fall down the three or four steps in the middle of the passage and afterwards get up and go on again. Then she laughed, a strained, hysterical laugh.

Harold Bindloss

CHAPTER XII

THE SACRIFICE

Charnock hesitated about meeting Sadie at breakfast, but found her calm and apparently good-humored. He felt embarrassed and his head ached, but she made him some strong coffee in a way he liked. Sadie did not often sulk, and he was grateful because she said nothing about what had happened on the previous night. Indeed, he was on the point of telling her so, but her careless manner discouraged him and he resolved instead that he would stop gambling and keep as steady as he could. After all, Sadie was really treating him well; she might, for example, have stopped his getting liquor. He meant to brace up and give her no more trouble.

He kept his resolve for a fortnight, and then, one morning, a man brought him a note from Wilkinson, asking him to drive over to the range. Charnock told the man he could not go, but presently put down his pen and looked out of the open window of the office of the store. The last of the snow had vanished some time since, and round white clouds drifted across the sky. Flying shadows streaked the wide plain, which gleamed like silver in the sunshine, and the bleached grass rolled in long waves before the breeze. There was something strangely exhilarating in the air and the dusty office smelt of salt-pork and cheese. It was a glorious day for a drive, he need not stay long at Wilkinson's, and the team needed exercise. Moreover, Sadie was not about and would not come home until afternoon; he might get back before her. He hesitated for a few minutes and then sent an order to the stable.

At midnight he had not returned, and Sadie sat in the office at the hotel, making futile efforts to fix her attention on a newspaper. The guests had gone to bed and the building was very quiet, but she had kept the ostler up. He might be needed and she could trust him not to talk.

At length she heard the sound she listened for. A beat of hoofs and rattle of wheels came down the street. It was their team, she knew their trot, but she wondered anxiously whether Bob was driving. When the rig stopped she went to the door, where the ostler stood with a lantern, and caught her breath as Wilkinson got down. There was nobody else on the seat of the light wagon, and Charnock had set off with a different rig.

"Where's Bob?" she asked in a strained voice.

"We put him inside," said Wilkinson. "He wasn't quite able to sit up. I'd have kept him all night only that I reckoned you might be scared."

Sadie, putting her foot on the wheel when the ostler held up the light, saw Charnock lying on a bundle of sacks. He was in a drunken stupor.

"Help Bill bring him, in," she said with stony calm.

Wilkinson and the other lifted the unconscious man, and staggering along a passage, awkwardly climbed the stairs. They put him on his bed and were going out when Sadie stopped them.

"Thank you, Bill; hold the team for a few minutes," she said and turned to Wilkinson. "I want you to wait in the office."

Then she shut the door, and after unfastening Charnock's collar and vest stood looking at him for a minute or two. He had not wakened, but she had seen him like this before and

Harold Bindloss

was not alarmed. His face was flushed and the veins on his forehead were prominent; his clothes were crumpled and sprinkled with bits of hay. Sadie studied him with a feeling of helplessness that changed to contemptuous pity. Her romantic dreams and ambitions had vanished and left her this—

As she turned away her mood changed again. After all, he was her husband and she had schemed to marry him. She was honest with herself about this and admitted that Bob had not really loved her much. But he needed her and she must not fail him. There was some comfort in remembering that he had sought no other woman; her rivals were cards and liquor, and she did not mean that they should win. Obeying a sudden impulse, she turned back and kissed his hot face, and then, noting the smell of whisky, flushed and went out with a firm step.

When she entered the office, however, her face was hard and white. She did not sit down, but leaned against a desk opposite Wilkinson.

"Why did you ask Bob out to the range?"

Wilkinson did not like her look. It hinted that she was in a dangerous mood, but he answered good-humoredly: "I thought he wanted a change. You hold him too tight, Mrs. Charnock. Bob won't stand for being kept busy indoors all day; he won't make a clerk."

"He won't," said Sadie. "I'm beginning to see it now. But you don't care a straw for Bob. You wanted a pick on me because I made you cut out your game that night."

"No," said Wilkinson, with a gesture of protest. "I certainly thought you were too smart, although it was not my business. Anyhow, if you let him have a quiet game with his friends at home—"

"Pshaw! I know you, Jake Wilkinson, better than Bob does.

You meant to make him drunk this evening and empty his wallet, and I guess you didn't find it hard."

Wilkinson's face got red, but he saw he would gain nothing by denial. Besides, there was a matter he was anxious about.

"It wasn't hard to empty his wallet, because he had only a few small bills."

"Yes; I fixed that. How much did you win from him when he was drunk?"

"He got drunk afterwards," Wilkinson objected. "Then I didn't win it all; there were three or four others."

Sadie smiled rather grimly. "How much?"

She got a jar when Wilkinson told her, but she fixed him with steady eyes.

"You knew what he had in his wallet, but let him go on? You thought Keller's would stand for the debt?"

"Yes," said Wilkinson, with some alarm; "we certainly thought so."

"Very well. Keller's makes good. Take the pen and right out a bill like this—R. Charnock, debtor in losses on a card game."

"You know it's never done."

"It's going to be done now, or you won't get your cheque. I know what I'm up against in you and your gang."

Wilkinson hesitated, but he needed the money and made out the bill. After examining it, Sadie wrote a cheque.

"I've paid you once, for Keller's sake, but you had better stop the card games after this. Bob's not my partner in the business, and no more of my dollars will go on gambling."

"Ah!" said Wilkinson sharply, "you're smarter than I thought!"

Sadie gave him a searching glance and he noted an ominous tenseness in her pose and her drawn-back lips. He said afterwards that she looked like a wild cat.

"Anyhow, I think I have you fixed. There's nothing doing in making Bob drunk again, but you had better understand what's going to happen if you try. The next time you drive over to the settlement after my husband I'll whip you in the street with a riding quirt."

Wilkinson put the cheque in his pocket and picked up his hat.

"On the whole, I guess I'd better not risk it," he said and went out.

Sadie let him go, and then went limply upstairs. She felt worn out and her brain was dull. She could not think, and a problem that demanded solving must wait until the morning. After looking into the room where Charnock lay and seeing that he was sleeping heavily, she went to bed.

Next morning she shut herself in the office at the store and gave the clerks strict orders that she was not to be disturbed. Opening a drawer, she took out a rough balance sheet, which showed that the business was profitable and expanding fast. Things were going very well, in spite of Bob's extravagance, and she thought she had prevented his wasting any more money. In three or four years she could sell the hotel and store for a large sum and, as she thought of it, give herself a chance.

She was young, clever, and attractive, and had recently tried to cultivate her mind. It was laborious work and she had not much time, but the clergyman of the little Episcopal church gave her some guidance and she made progress. For one thing, she was beginning to talk like Bob and thought he noticed this, although she had not told him about her studies. She meant to be ready to take her part in a wider and brighter life when she left the settlement. Knowing little about large towns, she exaggerated the pleasures they could offer. Montreal, for example, was a city of delight. She had been there twice and had seen the Ice Palace glitter against the frosty sky, the covered skating rinks, the jingling sleighs, and the toboggans rushing down the long, white slides. Then she remembered afternoon drives in summer on the wooded slopes of the Mountain, and evenings spent among the garish splendors of Dominion Park, where myriads of lights threw their colored reflections upon the river. Since then, however, her taste had got refined, and she now admitted that if she lived at Montreal it might be better to cut out Dominion Park.

But she pulled herself up. It looked as if these delights were not for her. She could enjoy them, if she wanted, in a few years' time, but the risk was great. Bob might go to pieces while she earned the money that would open the gate of fairyland. Although she had checked the pace a little, he was going the wrong way fast. Sadie knitted her dark brows as she nerved herself to make a momentous choice.

On the one hand there was everything she longed for; on the other much that she disliked—monotonous work, the loneliness of the frozen prairie in the bitter winter, the society, at very long intervals, of farmers who talked about nothing but their crops, and the unslackening strain of activity in the hot summer. Sadie thought of it with shrinking; she would soon get old and faded, and Bob, for whose sake she had done so, might turn from her. Yet there was danger for him if they stayed at the settlement. He had too many friends and whisky was always about. She must save him from the constant temptation and must do so now.

For all that, she struggled. There were specious arguments for taking the other course. Bob had failed as a farmer and would certainly fail again if left to himself; but farming was the only occupation on the lonely prairie. Loneliness was essential, because he must be kept away from the settlements. But she saw the weak point in this reasoning, because Bob need not be left to himself. She would, so to speak, stand over him and see he did his work. Well, it looked as if she must let her ambitions go, and she got up, straightening her body with a little resolute jerk.

"Tell the boss I want him," she said to the clerk.

Charnock came in, looking haggard and somewhat ashamed, and Sadie knew she had made the right choice when he sat down where the light touched his face. For a moment he blinked and frowned.

"I wish you'd pull down that blind," he said. "The sun's in my eyes, and I can't get round the desk."

Sadie did so, and then silently gave him Wilkinson's bill. He gazed at the paper with surprise, and colored.

"I'd no idea I lost so much. Why did you pay him?"

"Because you can't," said Sadie. "He thought you had a share in the business when he risked his dollars."

"I suppose that means you told him I wasn't your partner?"

"It does."

"I see," said Charnock, with some dryness. "You thought he'd leave me alone if he knew I wasn't worth powder and shot? Well, I believe it's very possible." Then he paused and smiled. "I can imagine his astonishment when you asked for a bill, and must admit that you're a sport. All the same, it's humiliating to have my friends told you don't trust me with money."

"The trouble is I can't trust you. Now you listen, Bob. This tanking and gambling has got to be stopped."

"I'm afraid I've given you some bother," Charnock answered penitently. "For all that, I'm not so bad as I was. In fact, I really think I'm steadying down by degrees, and since you have paid my debts I don't mind promising—"

"By degrees won't do; you have got to stop right off. Besides, you know how much your promises are worth."

Charnock colored. "That's rather cruel, Sadie, but I suppose it's deserved."

"I don't mean what you think; not your promise to Miss Dalton," Sadie answered with some embarrassment. "You told me you wouldn't drive over to Wilkinson's again, and the first time I wasn't about you went. Very well. Since I can't trust you round the settlement, we're going to quit. I've decided to sell out the business as soon as I can get the price I want."

"Sell the store and hotel!" Charnock exclaimed. "I suppose you know you'd get three or four times as much if you held on for a few years."

"That's so. But what's going to happen to you while I wait?"

Charnock turned his head for a moment, and then looked up with a contrite air.

"By George, Sadie, you are fine! But I can't allow this sacrifice."

"You won't be asked," Sadie rejoined with forced quietness. She was moved by Charnock's exclamation, but durst not trust him or herself. There was a risk of his persuading her to abandon the plan if he knew how deeply she was stirred.

"Well," he said, "what do you propose to do?"

"Take a farm far enough from town to make it hard for you to drive in and out. Donaldson's place would suit; he quits in the fall, you know, and we hold his mortgage."

Charnock got up and walked about the floor. Then he stopped opposite his wife.

"You mean well, Sadie, and you're very generous," he said with some emotion. "Still you ought to see the plan won't work. I had a good farm and made a horrible mess of things."

"You won't do that now. I'll be there," Sadie rejoined.

Charnock did not answer, but gave her a curious look, and she pondered for a moment or two. He was obviously moved, but one could not tell how far his emotions went, and she knew he did not want to listen. She understood her husband and knew he sometimes deceived himself.

"No!" He resumed; "it's too big a sacrifice! You like people about you and would see nobody but me and the hired man, while I admit I'm enough to jar a woman's nerves. Then think of the work; the manual work. You couldn't live as the bachelors live among dust and dirt, and it's a big undertaking to keep a homestead clean when you can't get proper help. Besides, there's the baking, cooking, and washing, while you have done nothing but superintend. I'd hate to see you worn and tired, and you know you're not so patient then. I get slack if things go wrong, and if I slouched about, brooding, when I ought to be at work, it would make you worse."

Sadie smiled. "That's very nice, Bob; but how much are you thinking about me and how much about yourself?"

"To tell the truth, I don't know," Charnock replied with naive honesty. "Anyhow, I am thinking about you."

"That is what I like, but there's no use in talking. Since I can make this business go I can run a farm, and see no other way. My plan's made and I'm going to put it over."

Charnock was silent for some moments and then turned to her with a look in his face she had not seen.

"I don't want to farm, but if you can stand it for my sake, I must try. You will need some patience, Sadie—I may break out at times if the strain gets too hard. One can't help running away when one is something of a cur. But I'll come back, ashamed and sorry, and pitch in again. Since you mean to stand by me, perhaps I'll win out in the end."

Bending down suddenly, he kissed her and then went to the door. She heard it shut, and sat still, but her eyes filled with tears. Bob had not promised much, but she thought he meant to keep his word now, and doubts that had troubled her melted away. She did not grudge the sacrifice she had made, for a ray of hope had begun to shine. It was, however, characteristic that after musing for a minute or two she took out some notepaper and began to write. Since the business must be sold, there was nothing to be gained by delay, and she gave a Winnipeg agent clear instructions. Then she went out and hid her annoyance when she saw Charnock sitting languidly on the hotel veranda.

"Has Wilkinson sent back our rig?" she asked.

"He has, but the team has done enough. Where are you going?"

"To look at Donaldson's farm. I want you to come along. Go across and ask Martin if he'll let you have his team."

Charnock got up with a resigned shrug. "You are a hustler, Sadie. It's not many minutes since you decided about the thing."

"I don't see what I'd get by waiting, and you may as well make up your mind that you're going to hustle, too. Now get busy and go for Martin's team."

CHAPTER XIII

AN UNEXPECTED MEETING

It was a bright afternoon and white-edged clouds rolled across the sky before a fresh north-west wind when Helen Festing rode up to a birch bluff on the prairie. The trees made a musical rustling as they tossed their branches, tufted with opening leaves. The sweep of white grass was checkered by patches of green that gleamed when the light touched them and faded as the shadows swept across the plain. There was something strangely invigorating in the air, but when she reached the bluff Helen pulled up her horse and looked about.

She missed the soft blue haze that mellowed the landscape among the English hills. Every feature was sharp and the colors were vivid; ocher, green, and silver gleaming with light. Distant bluffs stood out with sharp distinctness. She thought the new country was like its inhabitants; they were marked by a certain primitive vigor and their character was clearly defined. Neither the land nor the people had been tamed by cultivation yet. One missed the delicate half-tones on the prairie, but one heard and thrilled to the ringing note of endeavor.

When she looked west the land was empty to the horizon, and a flock of big sand-hill cranes planed down the wind. An animal she thought was an antelope moved swiftly through the waves of rippling grass. When she turned east she saw a plume of black smoke roll across the sky and the tops of three elevators above the edge of the plain. It was a portent, a warning of momentous change, in which she and her husband must play their part. What that part would be she could not tell, but the curtain was going up, and on the whole she approved the stage and scenery.

Helen had been some time in Canada and did not feel daunted. The sunshine and boisterous winds were bracing; one felt optimistic on the high plains, and the wide outlook gave a sense of freedom. She had many duties, but did not find them burdensome, or feel the strain of domestic labor she had been warned about. For one thing, her money had enabled Festing to arrange his household better than he had expected and hire useful help.

She took a rough trail through the bluff, picking her way among the holes and rotting stumps, and as she rode out the horse plunged. After calming the startled animal she saw a dirty handkerchief snapping in the wind at the top of a stick. Close by a team cropped the grass and the end of a big plow projected from the back of a wagon. There seemed to be nobody about, but after riding on a few yards she saw a man lying among some bushes with a pipe in his mouth. He looked half asleep, but got up as she advanced, and she stopped her horse with a jerk and tried to preserve her calm. Charnock stood looking at her with a half-embarrassed smile.

"Bob!" she exclaimed. "I didn't think I'd ever meet you."

"I hope it wasn't a shock, and we were bound to meet sooner or later. The distance between our homesteads isn't great."

Helen had heard where his homestead was. Indeed, Festing had told her that if he had known Charnock was coming to Donaldson's farm, he would have located farther off. She would sooner have avoided the meeting, but since it had happened, she must not cut it too short.

"But what is the handkerchief for?" she asked. "And why were

Harold Bindloss

you lying there?"

"It's a signal of distress. Another trail crosses the rise a mile off, and I was waiting in the hope that somebody might come along."

Helen now noted that a wheel of the wagon leaned to one side, and he remarked her glance.

"The patent bush has got loose in the hub," he resumed. "I took the pin out and then saw I might have trouble if the wheel came off. It has been threatening to play this trick for some time."

"Then why didn't you put the bush right before you started?"

"I don't know. I expect you think it's typical."

Helen laughed. Bob was taking the proper line, and she studied him with curiosity. He looked older than she thought, but remembering Festing's hints, she did not see the mark of dissipation she had expected. Indeed, Charnock, having spent a sober month or two under Sadie's strict supervision, looked very well. His face was brown, his eyes twinkled, and his figure was athletic. He did not seem to need her pity, but she felt compassionate. After all, she had loved him and he had married a girl from a bar.

"But where were you taking the plow?" she asked.

"To the smith's; one of the free preemptors has a forge some distance off, and if I'm lucky, I may find him at home."

"You won't find him at home if you stop here."

"That's obvious," said Charnock. "Still, you see, the plow's too heavy for me to lift out. Unless I do get it out, I can't try to put the wheel right."

"Then why not take it to pieces?"

"The trouble is you need a bent spanner to get at some of the bolts."

"They give you spanners with the plows, and there's a box on the frame to put them in. I've seen Stephen use the things."

"Just so," Charnock agreed. "Stephen's methodical, but when I want my spanner it isn't in the box."

"You never were very careful," Helen remarked.

"I don't know if there's much comfort in feeling that I've paid for my neglect."

Helen smiled; she was not going to be sentimental. "If you mean that you lost the spanner, you don't seem to have suffered much. I think you were asleep when I rode up. But I was surprised to hear you had begun to farm again. Do you like it? And how are you getting on?"

"I like a number of things better, but that's not allowed to make much difference. Sadie has decided that farming is good for me. However, I am making some progress, though as you know my temperament, I'll admit that I'm being firmly helped along."

There was silence for a few moments and Helen pondered. Bob had generally been tactful and she thought his humor was rather brave. He, no doubt, imagined she would soon learn all about his affairs and meant to make the best of things.

In the meantime, Charnock quietly studied her. She looked very fresh and prettier than he thought. Although she had not ridden much in England, he noted the grace and confidence with which she managed the spirited range horse. For all that, he was rather surprised by his sensations. He had expected to feel some embarrassment and sentimental tenderness when they met, but she left him cold; his pulse had not quickened a beat. Still it would be good for Sadie to know Helen, who could teach her much, and she unconsciously gave him a lead.

"Well," she said, "I must get home. I shall, no doubt, see you now and then."

"Not often, if you leave it to accident," he replied with a smile. "If you like to arrange the thing, there's a nice point of etiquette. You occupied your homestead before we came to ours, but you see we were on the prairie first. Anyhow, I'd be glad if you will let me bring Sadie over."

Helen thought he was going too far. She did not want to arrange for a meeting and would sooner not receive his wife. After all, the girl had supplanted her. Still she was curious and could not refuse.

"I'm often busy and daresay Mrs. Charnock is, while Stephen does not stop work until late. However, if you like to take your chance—"

"Thank you," said Charnock; "we'll take the risk of finding you not at home. Now perhaps it wouldn't be much trouble if you told Jasper I'm in difficulties. You'll see his place when you cross the ravine near the bluff."

Helen rode away, but when she saw Jasper's farm it was a mile off the trail and she had to cross a broken sandy belt. For all that, she smiled as she made the round. It was typical of Bob to send her. He might have tethered his horses and walked the distance, but he had a talent for leaving to somebody else the things he ought to do.

After supper she sat on the veranda, while Festing leaned against the rails. The house was built of ship-lap boards, with a roof of cedar shingles, and wooden pillars supporting the projecting eaves. It had been improved and made comfortable with Helen's money, and with the land about it, registered as belonging to her. Festing had insisted on this, rather against her will, because she had meant to make it a gift to him. The wind, as usual at sunset, had dropped, and clear green sky, touched with dull red on the horizon, overhung the plain. The air was cold and bracing; sound carried far, and the musical chime of cowbells came from a distant bluff. There were not many cattle in the neighborhood, but the Government was trying to encourage stock-raising and had begun to build creameries.

Helen meditatively studied her husband. Festing had been plowing since sunrise and looked tired. Something had gone wrong with his gasoline tractor, and she knew he had spent two or three hours finding out the fault. This had annoyed him, because time was valuable and he was impatient of delay. Helen approved his industry and the stubborn perseverance that led to his overcoming many obstacles, but sometimes thought he took things too hard and exaggerated their importance. Now as he leaned against the balustrade he had the physical grace of a well-trained athlete, but she thought his look was fretful and his mind too much occupied.

"I met Bob by the long bluff as I rode home," she said.

Festing looked up sharply. "Well, I suppose you were bound to meet him before long. What was he doing at the bluff?"

"Waiting for somebody to help him with his wagon," Helen answered with a laugh. "A wheel was coming off."

"That was like Bob. He has a rooted objection to helping himself when it means an effort."

"For all that, you were a friend of his."

"I'm not his friend now. I've done with the fellow."

"It's rather awkward," Helen remarked thoughtfully. "He asked if he might bring his wife over, and although I wasn't very gracious, I could not refuse."

"Oh, well, it doesn't matter. As I won't have a minute until the sowing is finished, I'll be out when he comes. If he stayed with his work just now, it would be better for him."

Helen was silent for a moment. Stephen was made of much finer stuff than Bob, but he had not the latter's graceful humor and his curtness jarred.

"There's no reason you should resume your friendship if you don't like," she said. "All the same, I think you ought to be polite to my guests."

"I can't pretend. The house is yours, but I don't want the fellow here."

"But why do you dislike him so much?"

"I don't think you need ask me that. It's dangerous ground, but you see—"

"I have forgiven him," Helen answered, smiling. "Indeed, if I hadn't done so long since, it would be easy to forgive him now. At first, I did feel dreadfully humiliated, but I soon saw what he had saved me from. And, of course, if he had kept his promise, I could not have married you."

Festing looked at her with surprise. In spite of her refinement, Helen would now and then talk calmly about matters he shrank from mentioning. But after the lead she had given him he could be frank.

"Well," he said, "I haven't forgiven him yet; I couldn't pretend friendship with anybody who had slighted you. Besides, when I found out how he had cheated me it was the worst moment of my life. I thought you would never speak to me again because, through the fellow's treachery, it was I who hurt you."

"You're very nice, Stephen," Helen replied, coloring. "But that's all finished. Don't you like Bob's wife? I really don't want to meet her, but one mustn't be a coward."

"You couldn't be a coward. Sadie has her virtues and is certainly much too good for Bob, but I don't want her here for all that. Frankly, she's not your sort, and she's meddlesome. I'm not afraid she'll make you discontented, but I can't have a girl like that telling you how your house ought to be run. Although you're a beginner, you manage very well, and I'd object to improvements on somebody else's plan."

Helen smiled. "When you talk like that, you're charming; but we'll say no more about it. You look tired. Are you sure you are not working too hard? The last time Jasper came he seemed surprised when he saw the ground you had broken. I imagined he thought you were trying to do too much."

As she spoke she glanced at the wide belt of plowing that broke the delicate green and silver of the grass. In the foreground, the rows of clods shone with an oily gleam in the fading light. Farther off, the rows converged and melted into a sweep of purple-brown that narrowed as it crossed a distant rise. There were two other belts; one where white grasses broke through the harrow-torn sod, and another flat and smooth where the land-packer had rolled in the seed. All told of strenuous effort in which sweating men and horses had been aided by tractor machines.

"Jasper's conservative and I feel I ought to do as much as I can," Festing replied. "When you bought the place you rather put me on my mettle."

Helen gave him a sharp glance. "I note that you spoke of it as my house when you ought to have said ours. I don't like that, Stephen."

"It is yours. I let you buy it because it's value must go up and the money's safe. I'm glad, of course, that you have comforts I couldn't have given you, but it's my business to support my wife, and I've got to increase my capital. I want to give you things you like, bought with money I have earned."

"You really want to feel independent of me," Helen suggested with a smile. "I suppose it's an honest ambition, but isn't the distinction you try to make ridiculous?"

"Perhaps, in a way," Festing agreed. "All the same, your help makes it my duty to do my best. I don't want to feel I might be forced to fall back on your dollars."

"You are ridiculous, Stephen," Helen rejoined. "However, let's talk about something else."

The talked good-humoredly until the dew and growing cold drove them in. Next morning Helen got up while the sun rose from behind a bluff on the edge of the plain, but when she went out on the veranda she saw the gasoline tractor and gang-plow lurch across the rise. This indicated that Festing had been at work for some time, and she looked thoughtful as she went back into the house.

Stephen was doing too much, and she wondered whether he could keep it up. Things, however, might be easier when the crop was sown, and if not she must insist upon his hiring extra help. She liked to see him keen about his work, but for the last few weeks he had scarcely had a minute to talk to her, and she could not allow him to wear himself out. After all, her money gave her some power, and there was no reason she should not use the power for her husband's benefit.

CHAPTER XIV

SADIE FINDS A FRIEND

The sun shone hot on the rippling grass, but it was cool on the shady veranda where Helen sat in a basket chair. A newspaper lay close by and the loose leaves fluttered now and then, but she did not notice that it was in some danger of blowing away. She had been occupied since early morning, but was not quite asleep, for she was vaguely conscious of a rhythmic drumming. By and by she raised her head with a jerk and glanced at the watch on her wrist. It was three o'clock and she had been dozing for an hour. Then the drumming fixed her attention and she saw a rig lurch along the uneven trail. The horses were trotting fast and there were two people in the light wagon.

Helen saw that one was Charnock. The other, who held the reins, was, no doubt, his wife, and Helen was sorry that Festing was at work beyond the rise. She would have liked him to be there when she received her visitors, but did not think it prudent to send for him. The rig was near the house now, and as she got up her dress moved the newspaper, which was caught by a draught and blew down the stairs and across the grass. It flapped in the fresh wind and fell near the horses' feet.

This was too much for the range-bred animals to stand, and they reared and plunged, and then began to back away from the fluttering white object. Charnock jumped out and ran towards their heads, but Sadie raised her whip with a gesture of command.

"Don't butt in, Bob; I'm going to take them past."

Charnock stood back obediently, though his alert pose hinted that he was ready to run forward if he were needed, and Helen studied his companion.

Sadie, dressed in black and white, with a black feather in her white hat, was braced back on the driving seat, with one hand on the reins while she used the whip. There was a patch of bright color in her face, her eyes flashed, and the rigidity of her figure gave her an air of savage resolution. She looked a handsome virago as she battled with the powerful horses, which plunged and kicked while the wagon rocked among the ruts. Helen watched the struggle with somewhat mixed feelings. This was the girl for whom Bob had given her up!

After an exciting minute or two Sadie forced the horses to pass the fluttering paper, and then pulled them up.

"Where's Stephen?" she asked.

Helen said he was harrowing on the other side of the rise, and Sadie, getting down, signed to Charnock.

"Put the team in the stable, and then go and look for Festing. Don't come back too soon."

Then she came towards the house and Helen felt half-annoyed and half-amused. Stephen did not like to be disturbed when he was busy, and she knew what he thought of Bob. Moreover, she wondered with some curiosity what Mrs. Charnock had to say to her. Sadie sat down and waited until she recovered breath.

"You know who I am," she remarked presently. "Bob can drive all right, but he's too easy with the team. I don't see why I should get down before I want because the horses are scared by a paper."

"Perhaps it was better to make them go on, but they nearly upset you," Helen agreed with a smile.

Sadie gave her a steady, criticizing glance, but her naive curiosity softened her rudeness.

"Well, I wanted to see you. Looks as if Bob was a fool, in one way, but I guess I can see him through what he's up against on the prairie better than you."

Helen had been prejudiced against Mrs. Charnock, but her blunt sincerity was disarming. Besides, she had expected something different; a hint of defiance, or suspicious antagonism.

"It's very possible," she said. "Everything is strange here. I feel rather lost sometimes and have much to learn."

Sadie studied her closely, and after pondering for a few moments resumed: "When I was driving over I didn't know how I was going to take you; in fact, I've been bothering about it for some time. I thought you might be dangerous."

"You thought I might be dangerous!" Helen exclaimed with rising color. "Surely you understand—"

"Now you wait a bit and let me finish! Well, I might have come now and then, found out what I could, and given you a hint or two, until we saw how things were going to be. But that's not my way, and I reckon it's not yours. Very well. We have got to have a talk and put the thing over. To begin with, I somehow feel I can trust you, and needn't be disturbed."

"Then I'm afraid you are rash," Helen rejoined with a resentment that was softened by a touch of humor. "You can't form a reliable opinion, because you don't know me."

"That's so, but I know Bob."

Helen laughed. She ought to be angry, for Mrs. Charnock was taking an extraordinary line. But perhaps it was the best line, because it would clear the ground. She said nothing and Sadie went on:

"How do you like it here?"

"Very much. I like the open country and the fresh air. Then I think I like the people, and one has so much to do that there is not time to feel moody. It's bracing to find every minute occupied by something useful."

"If you feel that way about it, you'll make good. And you've got a fine man for your husband. When Festing first came to the bridge I didn't know if I'd take him or Bob. In fact, I thought about it for quite a time."

Helen's eyes sparkled. Mrs. Charnock was going too far, but she controlled her resentment.

"After all, were you not taking something for granted?"

"Well," said Sadie thoughtfully, "if I'd tried hard, I might have got Steve then, but I don't know if I'd have been any happier with him. He'd have gone his own way and taken me along; a good way, perhaps, but it wouldn't have been mine. Bob's different; sometimes he has to be hustled and sometimes led, but you get fond of a man you must take care of. Then everybody likes Bob, and he kind of grows on you. I don't know how it is, but you can't get mad with him."

Helen thought there was something humiliating to Bob in his wife's patience, but she was moved. Mrs. Charnock loved her husband, though she knew his faults. Then Sadie resumed in a harder voice:

"Anyhow, he's mine and I know how to keep what belongs to me."

"I imagine you will keep him. I have no wish to take him away."

"Well, that's why I came. I wanted to see you, and now I'm satisfied. Bob needs a friend like your husband and he puts Steve pretty high. If you can see your way to let us drive over now and then evenings—"

Helen pondered this. Stephen might object, but he was not unreasonable, and his society would certainly be good for Bob. She was not altogether pleased by the thought of the Charnocks' visits, but Sadie's resolve to help her husband had touched her. Then there was something flattering in the hint that she and Stephen could take a part in his reformation.

"Very well," she said. "I hope you will come when you like. It will do Stephen no harm to get a rest instead of hurrying back to work after supper."

Sadie looked grateful. "We'll certainly come. I've talked to you as I'd have talked to nobody else, but you know Bob most as well as I do. But perhaps there's enough said. Won't you show me the house?"

Helen realized that she had made an alliance with Mrs. Charnock for Bob's protection, and was conscious of a virtuous thrill. The work she had undertaken was good, but she remembered with faint uneasiness that she had pledged her husband to it without his consent. She showed Sadie the house, and while there was much the latter admired, she made, from her larger knowledge of the plains, a number of suggestions that Helen thought useful. By and by Bob returned with Festing for supper, and stopped for another hour. When he and Sadie had gone Festing frowned as he glanced at his watch.

"It's too late to finish the job I wanted to do tonight," he said, and indicated the dark figures of a man and horses silhouetted against the sunset on the crest of the rise. "There's Jules coming home. He couldn't get on without me."

Helen pretended not to notice his annoyance. "After all, you're not often disturbed, and a little relaxation is good. I've no doubt you had an amusing talk with Bob."

"Bob bored me badly, though we didn't talk much. I was driving the disc-harrows and he lay in the grass. I had to stop for a few minutes every time I reached the turning and listen to his remarks."

"And you feel you deserve some sympathy?" Helen said with a laugh. "Well, I suppose it was an infliction to be forced to talk."

Festing's annoyance vanished. "I mustn't make too much of it. I really don't object to talking when I've finished my work."

"When do you finish your work, Stephen?"

"That's a fair shot! In summer, I stop when it's too dark to see. The annoying thing wasn't so much the stopping as Bob's attitude. He lay there with his pipe, looking as if nothing would persuade him to work, and his smile hinted that he thought delaying me an excellent joke. I believe I was polite, but certainly hope he won't come back."

Helen thought it was not the proper time to tell him about the invitation she had given Sadie, and she said, "Idleness seems to jar you."

"It does. I dislike the man who demands the best to eat and drink and won't use his brain or muscle if he can help. In this country, the thing's immoral; the fellow's obviously a cheat. We live by our labor, raising grain and cattle—"

"But what about the people in the towns?"

"A number of them handle our products and supply us with

tools. Of course, there are speculators and real-estate boomsters who gamble with our earnings, but their job is not as easy as it looks. They run big risks and bear some strain. Still, if it was left to me, I'd make them plow."

Helen laughed. "You're rather drastic, Stephen; but if one takes the long view, I dare say you are right."

"Then let's take the narrowest view we can. When a farmer who hasn't much money loafs about the poolroom and lies on his back, smoking, it's plain that he's taking advantage of somebody else. Perhaps the thing's shabbiest when he puts his responsibilities on his wife. That's what Bob does."

"I'm afraid he does," Helen admitted, and mused, while Festing lighted his pipe.

Stephen was not a prig and she recognized the justice of his arguments, but he was rather hard and his views were too clear-cut. He saw that a thing was good or bad, but could not see that faults and virtues sometimes merged and there was good in one and bad in the other.

"Well," she said, "I like Mrs. Charnock, and she is certainly energetic and practical. She went over the house and suggested some improvements. For example, you are building a windmill pump for the cattle, and it wouldn't cost very much to bring a pipe to the house. A tap is a great convenience and would save Jules' time filling up the tank."

"It will need a long pipe and cost more than Sadie thinks, but I'll have it done. However, I wish I had thought of it and she hadn't made the suggestion. I don't want Sadie interfering with our house."

"But you don't dislike Mrs. Charnock."

"Not in a way; but I don't know that I want to see her here. Sadie has a number of good points, but she's rather fond of managing other folks' affairs. Then she's not your kind."

On the whole, Helen was not displeased. Mrs. Charnock's bold statements that she could have got Stephen if she had wanted had jarred, but it looked as if she had made an empty boast.

"I thought you were a democrat," she remarked, smiling.

"So I am, in general; but when it's a matter of choosing my wife's friends, I'm an exclusive aristocrat. That's the worst of having theories; they don't apply all round."

Helen thought his utilitarian dislike of idleness was open to this objection, but it was not the time to urge Bob's cause. She would wait for another opportunity, when Stephen had not been delayed, and she made him a humorous curtsey.

"Sometimes you're rather bearish, and sometimes you're very nice," she said, and went into the house.

The Charnocks returned a week later and came again at regular intervals, while Helen rode over to their house now and then. Festing refused to accompany her and sometimes grumbled, but on the whole tolerated Charnock's visits so long as they did not delay his work. Nothing must be allowed to interfere with that, for he was uneasily conscious that he had set himself too big a task. His dislike to using his wife's money had spurred him on, and he had sown a very large crop at a heavy expense for labor, horses, and machines. Now he must spare no effort to get his money back, and much depended on the weather. Indeed, he was beginning to feel the strain of the unrelaxing exertion and care about details, and this sometimes reacted upon his temper. Still he must hold out until the crop was reaped, after which he could go easy during the winter months.

One hot afternoon, he lay under a mower in a sloo where the melted snow had run in spring and the wild grass now grew tall. It made good hay and the fierce sun had dried it well, so that he had only to cut and haul it home; but something had gone wrong with the machine, and after taking out the broken knife he dismantled the driving gear. When he crawled out, with a greasy cogwheel in his hand, he was soaked with perspiration and his overalls were stained by oil. The mosquitoes, that did not as a rule venture out in the strong wind and sun, had bitten him badly while he lay in the grass.

"You had better wait for ten minutes and take a smoke," said Charnock, who had come up quietly and sat in the shade of the partly-loaded wagon. "You'll get on faster when you have cooled down."

"You believe in waiting, don't you?" Festing rejoined.

Charnock laughed. "I feel justified in going slow just now. Sadie has given me a day off, and when she doesn't think I ought to work it certainly isn't necessary. It saves you some bother if you can leave that sort of thing to your wife."

"Pshaw!" said Festing. "You make me tired."

He picked up the broken knife and looked at Charnock. Bob was bantering him, exaggerating his slackness. As a matter of fact, the fellow was not so lazy as he pretended; Sadie was beginning to wake him up. Stephen did not know if he had forgiven him or not, but they had gradually dropped back into something like their old relations.

"You might take off the broken blades," he resumed. "You'll find new ones in the box. They ought to be riveted, but if you use the short bolts and file down the nuts, I dare say they'll run through the guides."

Then he crawled back under the machine and did not come out until he head a rattle of wheels. Wilkinson, whom he knew and disliked, stopped his team close by and began to talk to Charnock. This annoyed Festing, because he was nearly ready

Harold Bindloss

to replace the knife.

"I called at your place and found you were out," Wilkinson remarked. "They told me where you had gone, and when I saw Festing's wagon I reckoned you might have gone with him. You come here pretty often, don't you?"

"Steve's patient," Charnock replied with a twinkle. "I'm not sure he enjoys my visits, but he puts up with them."

"Well, I want you to drive over to-morrow evening. A man you know from Winnipeg is coming to see me about a deal in Brandon building lots. The thing looks good and ought to turn out a snap."

"The trouble is I haven't much money to invest," Charnock answered, and Festing thought he was hesitating. It looked as if Wilkinson had not seen him yet, for he was standing behind the machine.

"I understand you have a bigger interest in the farm than you had in the hotel and something might be arranged. Anyhow, come over and hear what our friend has to say."

"You'll be a fool if you go, Bob," Festing interposed.

"I don't know that this is your business," Wilkinson rejoined. "I haven't suggested that you should join us."

"You know I wouldn't join you. I had one deal with you, and that's enough. No doubt you remember selling me the brown horse."

"You tried the horse before you bought him."

"I did. He was quiet then, but I've since suspected that he was doped. Anyhow, he nearly killed my hired man."

Wilkinson laughed. "You had your trial and backed your

judgment. Know more about machines than horses, don't you?"

"I didn't know the man I dealt with then. You warranted the brute good-tempered and easy to drive. I'll give you five dollars if you'll take him out of the stable and harness him now."

"I haven't time," said Wilkinson. "Didn't charge you high and guess you've got to pay for learning your business. The trouble is you're too sure about yourself and reckoned you'd make a splash at farming without much trouble. Anyhow, I don't want to sell Charnock a horse; he's a better judge than you."

"He's not much judge of building lots. If your friend has got a safe snap, why do you want to let Charnock in?"

Wilkinson began to look impatient. "I came over to talk to Charnock, and if he likes the deal it's not your affair."

"It is my affair if you stop him when he's helping me," Festing rejoined. "If he's a fool, he'll talk to you some other time; if he's wise, he won't. Just now I'd sooner you drove off my farm."

Wilkinson gave him a curious look. "Very well. I reckon the place is yours; or your wife's." Then he turned to Charnock. "Are you coming over, Bob?"

"No," said Charnock, irresolutely, "I don't think I will."

He lighted his pipe when Wilkinson started his team, and presently remarked: "On the whole, I'm glad you headed him off, because I might have gone. You mean well, Stephen, but that man doesn't like you, and I've sometimes thought he doesn't like Sadie."

"It doesn't matter if he likes me or not," said Festing. "Let's get on with the mower."

CHAPTER XV

THE CHEQUE

The North-west breeze was fresher than usual when, one afternoon, Helen rode through a belt of sand-hills on her way to the Charnock farm. Clouds of dust blew about the horse's feet, and now and then fine grit whistled past her head. She had her back to the boisterous wind, but she urged the horse until they got behind a grove of scrub poplars. Then she rolled up her veil and wiped her face before she looked about.

Round, dark clouds rolled across the sky, as they had done since spring, but for nearly a month none had broken. A low ridge, streaked by flying shadows, ran across the foreground, and waves of dust rose and fell about its crest. Sandy belts are common on parts of the prairie, and when they fringe cultivated land are something of a danger in a dry season, because the loose sand travels far before the wind.

Beyond the sand-hills, the level grass was getting white and dry, and in the distance the figures of a man and horses stood out against a moving cloud of dust. Helen supposed he was summer-fallowing, but did not understand the dust, because when she last passed the spot the soil looked dark and firm. She remembered that Festing had been anxious about the weather.

Riding on, she saw the roof of the Charnock homestead above a straggling bluff, and her thoughts centered on its occupants.

Strange as the thing was, she had come to think of Sadie as her friend. Her loyalty and her patience with her husband commanded respect, and now it looked as if they would be rewarded. Bob was taking an interest in his farm and had worked with steady industry for the last month or two. Helen thought she deserved some credit for this; she had had a part in Bob's reformation and had made Stephen help.

Sadie trusted her, and no suspicion or jealousy marked their relations. Indeed, Helen wondered why she had at one time been drawn to Bob. Were she free to do so, she would certainly not marry him now. Still she had loved him, and this gave her thoughts about him a vague, sentimental gentleness. It was a comfort to feel that she had done something to turn his wandering feet into the right path.

When she reached the homestead she found Sadie looking disturbed. Her face was hard, but her eyes were red, and Helen suspected that she had been crying. It was obvious that something serious had happened, because Sadie's pluck seldom broke down.

"I'm glad you came," the latter said. "I'm surely in trouble."

Helen asked what the trouble was, and Sadie told her in jerky sentences. Charnock had started for the railroad early that morning, and after he left she discovered that he had written a cheque, payable to Wilkinson.

"It's not so much the money, but to feel he has cheated me and broken loose when I thought he was cured," she concluded. "He has been going steady, but now that brute has got hold of him he'll hang around the settlement, tanking and betting, for a week or two. Then he'll be slack and moody and leave the farm alone, and I'll have to begin the job again."

Sadie paused, with tears in her eyes, and then pulled herself together. "Pshaw!" she said, "I'm a silly fool. Before you came I thought I'd quit and let Bob go his own way; but I'm not beaten yet. If Wilkinson wants him, there's going to be some fight. Now, I want you to ride over with me to the fellow's place."

Helen felt sympathetic. Sadie's resentment was justified, and she looked rather refined when angry. Her stiff pose lent her a touch of dignity; her heightened color and the sparkle in her eyes gave her face the charm of animation. Moreover, her want of reserve no longer jarred. Reserve is not very common on the plains.

"But you must tell me something about it first," Helen replied. "How did you find out he had written the cheque?"

"I suspected something after he'd gone and looked for his cheque-book. He'd torn out a form, but hadn't filled up the tab. Bob's silly when he's cunning and didn't think about his blotter. The top sheet was nearly clean and I read what he'd written, in a looking-glass."

"Why did he give Wilkinson the money?"

"I guess it's to speculate in wheat or building-lots, and Bob will certainly lose it all; but that's not what makes me mad. After all, it's his money; he's been saving it since he steadied down. I can manage Bob if he's left alone, and thought I'd cut out the friends he shouldn't have. Wilkinson was the only danger left, but he's a blamed tough proposition."

Helen knew Festing disliked the man, but she felt puzzled. "The sum is not very large," she said. "I don't quite see why Wilkinson thought it worth while—"

"It shows he's pinched for money, and there's some hope in that. Then he doesn't like me, and I imagine he has a pick on your husband. Stephen froze him off one day when he was getting after Bob. Anyhow, I mean to get the money back."

"But can you? It is Bob's cheque."

"I'm going to try. The bank deals with *me*," Sadie answered. "But come along; I hear the hired man bringing the rig."

When they got into the vehicle, Helen remarked that Sadie had brought a flexible riding whip. Since the quirt was useless for driving, Helen wondered what she meant to do with it. The trail they took ran through the grass, a sinuous riband of hard-beaten soil that flashed where it caught the light. It was seamed by ruts and fringed by wild barley but in places the grass had spread across it, leaving gaps, into which the horses' legs and the wheel sank. The smell of wild peppermint rose from among the crackling stalks as the team brushed through. Now and then a prairie-hen got up, and small animals, like English squirrels, squatted by the trail until the wheels were nearly upon them, and then dived into holes.

"The gophers are surely plentiful," Sadie remarked. "Don't know that I've seen so many around before, and that's going to be bad for the grain. They're generally worst when the crop is poor."

"Do you think the crop will be poor?"

Sadie glanced at the sky, which was a dazzling blue, flooded with light, except where the scattered clouds drove by.

"We didn't get the June rains, and the frost-damp has gone down pretty deep. Then we have had very few thunder-storms, and the sand is blowing bad. It makes trouble in parts of Manitoba, but the scrub trees in our sand-hills generally hold it up. What does Steve think?"

"He hasn't told me. Sometimes he looks anxious, but he doesn't talk about it much."

"That's Steve's way. I don't know if it's a good way. He sees when he's up against a hard thing and makes his own plans. Now I want to know my husband's troubles. You feel better when you can talk."

Helen agreed with Sadie; she often wished Stephen would talk to her about his anxieties. He wanted to save her and had confidence in himself, but she felt that he left her out too much.

"How does the sand damage the wheat?" she asked.

"Cuts the stalk. Takes time, of course, but the sharp grit puts down the grain like a binder knife, if it blows through the field long enough. However, I'm not worrying much about that; there are worse things than the sand and drought. We're fools and make our real troubles; that's what's the matter with us."

Helen smiled. Sadie was amusing when philosophized, but Helen thought her views were sound. She had chosen a stern country, but its stinging cold and boisterous winds were invigorating, and with pluck one could overcome its material obstacles. It was human weaknesses that made for unhappiness.

"Well," she said, "we must hope the rain will come; but hadn't we better go by the long bluff? The new man has put a fence across the other trail."

Sadie left the trail, and as they crossed a hollow the tall grass rustled about the horses' legs. It had lost its verdure; the red lilies and banks of yellow flowers had withered on their parched stalks. When they reached the level the grass was only a few inches high and the wide plain rolled back in the strong light, shining pale-yellow and gray. It was only when the shadows passed that one could see streaks and patches of faded green. In the distance a cluster of roofs broke the bare expanse, and Helen knew they marked the Wilkinson ranch. A horse and buggy approached it, looking very small, and she glanced at Sadie, who said nothing, although her face was stern. By and by the latter stopped her team in front of the homestead and fastened the reins to a post.

"Now," she said, "you sit on the veranda and wait for me. It was Wilkinson's rig we saw, and I'll find him in."

Wilkinson looked up from the table at which he was writing when Sadie entered the room. He was, on the whole, a handsome man, but was rather fat, and his black eyes were unusually close together. This perhaps accounted for the obliquity of his glance, which, some believed, conveyed a useful hint about his character. He was neatly dressed in light, summer clothes, although the farmers generally wore brown overalls. As he got up his look indicated that he was trying to hide his annoyance.

"This is something of a surprise, Mrs. Charnock," he said politely. "However, if there's anything I can do—"

"You can sit down again in the meantime," Sadie replied, and occupied a chair opposite, with the quirt on her knee. "To begin with, if you're writing to your Winnipeg friend, you had better wait a bit."

"I'm not writing to Winnipeg; but don't see what this has to do with your visit."

"Then you haven't sent off Bob's cheque yet! I mean to get it back."

Wilkinson saw that he had made a rash admission. Mrs. Charnock was cleverer than he thought.

"If Bob wants it back, why didn't he come himself?"

"He doesn't know I have come," Sadie answered calmly.

Wilkinson studied her and did not like her look. Her face was hard, her color higher than usual, and her eyes sparkled ominously.

"Well," he said, "you told me you would pay no more of your husband's debts, but this is not a debt. Besides, the money must be Bob's, since he gave me the cheque."

"Why did he give it you?"

The question was awkward, because Wilkinson did not want to state that he had persuaded Bob to join him in a speculation. This was the best construction that could be put upon the matter, and he did not think it would satisfy Mrs. Charnock.

"Why does a man give another a cheque?" he rejoined, with a look of good-humor that he did not feel.

"The best reason I know of is—for value received. But this doesn't apply. You allowed it wasn't a debt, so Bob has got no value."

"One sometimes pays for value one expects to get."

Sadie laughed scornfully. "If that's what Bob has done, he'll get badly stung. There's nothing coming to him from a deal with you. I guess you don't claim he made you a present of the money?"

"I don't," said Wilkinson, with a frown, for he thought he saw where she was leading him.

"Very well. One pays for something one has got or is going to get, and as we can rule out both reasons, the cheque is bad. In fact, it's not worth keeping. Better give it me back."

"Your argument looks all right, Mrs. Charnock, but you don't start from sure ground. How do you know there's nothing coming to your husband?"

"I know you," Sadie rejoined. "Anyhow, the cheque is certainly bad. They'll turn it down if you take it to the bank."

Wilkinson made an abrupt movement. "You can't stop your

husband's cheque. You don't mean he hasn't the dollars to meet it?"

"I don't," said Sadie, with an angry flush. "Bob is honest. The money's there, but if you think the bank will pay when I tell them not, go and see. The manager knows me and he knows you."

Wilkinson saw that he was beaten, but tried to hide his anger. "Well, it looks as if Bob was lucky. He has a wife who will take care of him, and I reckon he needs something of the kind. However, here's the cheque; I want a receipt."

Sadie wrote the receipt and he noted that her hand shook. As she got up he glanced at the quirt.

"Did you ride over? I thought I heard a rig."

"I drove," said Sadie. "Looks as I needn't have brought the quirt. Well, I'm glad you agreed about the cheque being bad. I meant to get it anyhow."

Wilkinson gave her a curious look, but said nothing and she went out.

"I've saved Bob's money," she told Helen as she started the team. "Wilkinson saw my arguments and didn't kick as much as I expected, but he certainly doesn't like me any better. I think he'll make trouble if he can."

"That seems unlikely," Helen remarked. "I imagine that as you have beaten him he'll be glad to let the matter drop. No doubt he wanted the money and was vexed because he had to give it up, but I hardly think he'll try to revenge himself on you. Men don't do these things."

"My husband and yours don't, but Wilkinson is different," Sadie answered.

Charnock had not returned when she reached the farm, and after Helen left she sat on the veranda, feeling disturbed. Bob had told her he was going to the railroad to bring out some goods, but he could have got back two or three hours earlier. Then Wilkinson no doubt knew where he had gone. A small settlement, with two new hotels, had sprung up round the station, and as the place was easily reached by the construction gangs there was now and then some drunkenness and gambling. For all that, Sadie did not mean to anticipate trouble, and set about some household work that her drive had delayed. It got dark before she finished, but Bob did not come, and she went outside again.

The night was clear and refreshingly cold after the scorching day. The wind had dropped, everything was very quiet, and she could see for some distance across the plain. The hollows were picked out by belts of darker shadow, and the scattered bluffs made dim gray blurs, but nothing moved on the waste, and she did not hear the beat of hoofs she listened for.

For a time she sat still, lost in gloomy thought. Bob's relapse had been a bitter disappointment, because she had begun to hope that the danger of his resuming his former habits was past. He had stuck to his work, which seemed to absorb his interest, and had looked content. There was ground for believing that with a little judicious encouragement he might make a good farmer, and Sadie did not grudge the patient effort necessary to keep him in the proper path. Now he had left it again and might wander far before she could lead him back.

For all that, she did not mean to give up. She had fought hard for Bob and was resolved to win, while there was a ray of comfort. The woman she had at first thought a danger was her best friend, and she felt for Helen Festing a grateful admiration that sometimes moved her deeply. Helen had many advantages that she could not have combated had they been used against her: grace, polish, and a knowledge of the world in which Bob had lived. But Helen was on her side. Sadie's admiration was perhaps warranted, but she undervalued her own patience and courage.

At length she got drowsy and forgot her troubles. She did not think she really went to sleep, but after a time she got up with a start. A beat of hoofs and rattle of wheels had roused her, and she saw a rig coming towards the house. For a minute or two she stood shivering and trying to brace herself. If Bob was driving, things might be better than she thought; but when the horses stopped another man got down.

"Perhaps you'd better rouse out your hired man, Mrs. Charnock," he said awkwardly. "I've got your husband here, but it's going to take two of us to bring him in."

Sadie brought a lamp and, with her mouth firmly set, looked into the rig. Bob lay upon some sacks in an ungainly attitude, and the jolting had not broken his heavy sleep. It was some time since he had come home like this, and Sadie felt dejected and tired. Then with an effort she went to waken the hired man.

They carried Charnock in, and when she had given the driver some money she sat down and indulged her passionate indignation. Wilkinson had sent the rig, but had not been prompted by kindness when he told the man to drive Bob back; it was his revenge for his defeat. He had found Bob, made him drunk, when there was nothing to be gained by doing so, and sent him home like this. The fellow was poison-mean, but she thought him rash. He had struck her a cruel blow, but she did not mean to sit still and nurse the wound. She must strike back with all the force she could use and make him sorry he had provoked her to fight. Then, putting off her half-formed plans until next day, she went to bed.

CHAPTER XVI

A COUNTER-STROKE

When Sadie got up next morning she ordered the buggy to be brought round, and then went to look at Charnock. He was asleep, of which she was rather glad, because there was something to be said and she was highly strung. She could not trust her temper yet and might go too far. Bob was generally docile, particularly when repentant; but it was possible to drive him into an obstinate mood when nothing could be done with him. She was angry, but her anger was mainly directed against Wilkinson.

After breakfast she drove off across the plain. It was about eight o'clock, but the sun was hot. The breeze was not so fresh as usual, and a bank of dark clouds rolled up above the prairie's edge. They looked solid and their rounded masses shone an oily black, and she wondered whether they promised one of the thunder-storms that often broke upon the plains on summer afternoons. She would have welcomed the savage downpour, even if it had spoiled her clothes.

Sadie was getting anxious about the crop. Its failure would mean a serious loss, and she hated to see labor and money wasted; but this was not all. Knowing the risks the farmer ran on newly-broken land, she had not adventured too much of her capital on the first year's harvest; but success might encourage Bob, while failure would certainly daunt him. He would work for an object he was likely to gain, but if disappointed, regretted the exertions he had made, and refused, with humorous logic, to be stirred to fresh effort.

"I'm not convinced that farming's my particular duty," he once said. "When I plow it's in the expectation of cashing the elevator warrants for the grain. If I'm not to reap the crop, it seems to me that working fourteen hours a day is a waste of time that might be agreeably employed in shooting or riding about."

Sadie urged that one got nothing worth having without a struggle. Bob rejoined: "If you get the thing you aim at, the struggle's justified; if you don't you think of what you've missed while you were uselessly employed. Of course, if you like a struggle, you have the satisfaction of following your bent; but hustling is a habit that has no charm for me."

Sadie reflected that the last remark was true. Bob never hustled; his talk and movements were marked by a languid grace that sometimes pleased and sometimes irritated her. It was difficult to make him angry, and she was often silenced by his whimsical arguments when she knew she was right. But he was her husband, and she meant to baulk the man who hoped to profit by his carelessness.

Then she urged the horse. It was a long drive to the settlement where she had kept the hotel, and she had not been there for some time. The goods she and her neighbors bought came from the new settlement on the railroad, which was not far off; but she had an object in visiting the other. It was noon when she reached the hotel and sat down to dinner in the familiar room. She did not know if she was pleased or disappointed to find the meal served as well as before, but her thoughts were not cheerful while she ate. She remembered her ambitions and her resolve to leave the dreary plains and make her mark in Toronto or Montreal. Now her dreams had vanished and she must grapple with dull realities that jarred her worse than they had done.

The dining-room was clean, but unattractive, with its varnished board walls, bare floor, and wire-mesh filling the skeleton door, which a spring banged to before the mosquitoes could get in. There were no curtains or ventilator-fans, the room was very hot, and the glaring sunshine emphasized its ugliness. Then it was full of flies that fell upon boards and tables from the poisonous papers, and a big gramophone made a discordant noise. Sadie remembered Keller's pride in the machine and how he had bought it, to amuse the boys, after hearing an electric organ in a Montreal restaurant. Yet she knew her craving for society must be gratified at such places as this; a rare visit to the settlement was the only change from monotonous toil.

When she offered her meal-ticket at the desk the clerk shook his head.

"You don't need to open your wallet in this house. The boss left word he'd be glad to see you at the store."

Sadie, who had meant to see the proprietor, complied, and found him and his wife in the back office, where she and Bob had often sat. The woman gave Sadie a friendly smile.

"I hope they served you well. When you're in town we want you to use the house like it still belonged to you."

Sadie made a suitable reply. She had charged a good price for the business, but had stuck to the Keller traditions and made a straight deal. Stock and furniture had been justly valued, and when the buyers examined the accounts she had frankly told them which debts were doubtful and which were probably bad. It was about these things they wished to talk to her, and she meant to indulge them.

"How's trade?" she asked, to give them a lead.

"In one way, it's good," replied the man. "We're selling out as fast as we can get the truck; but there's a point I want your views about. The cheque I gave you wiped off most all the capital I had, wholesalers put up their prices if you make them wait, and a number of the boys have a bad habit of letting their bills run on. Now, if you can give me some advice—."

"Certainly," said Sadie, who thought the woman looked anxious. "Suppose you read out the names and what they owe?"

The man opened a ledger, and she told him what she knew about his customers; whom he could trust and whom he had better refuse further credit. Then she looked thoughtful when he said: "Wilkinson, of the range—"

"He didn't deal with us."

"But you know everybody round here and can tell me if he's likely to make good," the man urged.

"How much does he owe you?" Sadie asked.

The man named a rather large sum and she pretended to consider.

"Well," she replied, "the boys have probably told you that Wilkinson's not a friend of mine, and since that's so I'm not going to say much about his character."

"It's not his character we're curious about. Do you know how he's fixed?"

Sadie was silent for a few moments. The others were young and newly married and had admitted that the purchase of the business had strained their resources. It was plain that a large bad debt might involve them in difficulties. Wilkinson had forced her to fight, and she meant to show him no mercy, but she must say nothing that could afterwards be brought up against her.

"Character counts for as much as dollars," she remarked. "That was my father's motto, and he was never afraid to take steep chances by backing an honest man. Although he had debts on his books for three or four years, it was seldom a customer let him down. But he cut out a crook as soon as he suspected what the fellow was. However, you want to know how Wilkinson stands? Well, it's a sure thing he finds dollars tight."

"Anyhow, a man can't disown his debts in this country."

"That's so; but if he's a farmer, the homestead laws stop your seizing his house and land and part of his stock, unless he has mortgaged them to you. If somebody else holds a mortgage, you generally get stung."

"The trouble is that if you're too hard on a customer, he tells his friends, and the opposition gets his trade and theirs."

"Sure," said Sadie, "Keller's let the opposition have that kind of trade. A crook's friends are generally like himself, and there's not much profit in selling goods to folk who don't mean to pay."

"Has Wilkinson given a mortgage?" the man asked.

"If he had, it's got to be registered. You can find out at the record office, and I guess it would pay you to go and see."

"Well, I hear he's just sold a good bunch of horses. That means he'll have some money for a while."

"Then you had better take your bills over and get them paid before the money's gone," Sadie answered in a meaning tone.

"If you had the store, would you risk his being able to pay all right and afterwards dropping you?"

"I certainly would," said Sadie. "I'd harness my team and start for the range right now."

The woman looked at her husband. "That's my notion, Tom; you'd better go," she said, and turned to Sadie. "It would hit us hard if Wilkinson's bill got much longer and he let us down."

Sadie left them and went to a new store farther up the street, after which she called on an implement dealer who occasionally speculated in real estate and mortgages, and one or two others. She knew them all, and they knew that on business matters her judgment was sound. It was plain that they were suspicious about Wilkinson, but, so far, undecided what to do. They had doubts, but hesitated to admit that they had been rash, and shrank from using means that might cost them a customer. Sadie gave one information she had gathered from another, and added hints of what she herself knew. The tact she used prevented their guessing that she had an object, and she did little more than bring their own suspicions to a head; but she was satisfied when she returned to the hotel.

When the horse had rested she drove out of the settlement. For some distance a wire fence ran along the dusty, graded road, but it ended at a hollow, seamed by deep ruts that united on the other side, where a trail emerged. Then for a mile or two, she passed new scattered homesteads with their windmills and wooden barns, until these dropped behind and she drove across the empty wilderness. No rain had fallen, the sky was getting clear and green, and a vivid crimson sunset burned on the edge of the grass. The air was now cool, and although she was anxious about the weather, Sadie felt more cheerful than when she had come.

She had no scruples about what she had done. For one thing, she had kept to the truth when she might have made her hints more damaging by a little exaggeration. Her antagonist had struck her a treacherous blow; he was dangerous, and must be downed. Then she smiled with grim humor as she admitted that she had perhaps done enough for a time. Wilkinson's creditors were on his track; it would be amusing to watch them play her game.

Harold Bindloss

It was dark when she reached the farm and found Charnock waiting on the veranda. He looked dull but not embarrassed, and there was nothing to indicate that he had been disturbed by her absence. Sadie did not tell him where she had been and did not talk much. She had found out that it was better not to make things too easy for Bob.

"I suppose you have a headache; you deserve it," she said. "I'm tired and don't want to hear your excuses now."

"I really haven't begun to make excuses," Charnock answered.

"Then don't begin. It's late, and you have got to start for the bluff at sun-up and haul those fence-posts home. The job has been hanging on too long and must be finished to-morrow."

"It will be finished before dinner," Charnock replied. "As a matter of fact, I brought in most of the posts to-day."

Sadie's look softened, but she did not mean to be gracious yet.

"I reckoned you'd be loafing round the house and finding fault," she said and left him.

When she had gone Charnock smiled. Sadie would, no doubt, come round to-morrow, and it was lucky she knew nothing about the cheque he had given Wilkinson; but he wondered where she had been. Now he came to think of it, Wilkinson had said nothing abut the cheque when they met at the railroad settlement; but after all there was perhaps no reason he should do so.

About seven o'clock one evening a fortnight later, Festing threw down the cant-pole he had been using to move a big birch log, and lighting his pipe, stopped and looked about. A shallow creek flowed through a ravine at the edge of the tall wheat, and below the spot where he stood its channel was spanned by the stringers of an unfinished bridge. The creek had shrunk to a thread of water, but Festing, who had been wading about its bed, was wet and splashed with mire. Moreover he had torn his threadbare overalls and his hot face was smeared where he had rubbed off the mosquitoes with dirty hands.

The evening was hot, he felt tired and moody, and his depression was not relieved when he glanced at the wheat. There was no wind now, but the breeze had been fresh, and the ears of grain that were beginning to emerge from their sheaths dropped in a sickly manner. The stalks had a ragged look and fine sand lay among the roots. The crop was damaged, particularly along its exposed edge, although it might recover if there was rain. Festing, studying the sky, saw no hope of this. The soft blue to the east and the luminous green it melted into, with the harsh red glare of the sinking sun, threatened dry and boisterous weather. Unless a change came soon, the wheat would be spoiled.

It was obvious that he had sown too large a crop, and the work this implied had overtaxed his strength. He had felt the strain for some time, and now things were going against him it got worse. Hope might have braced him, but the thought of failure was depressing. For all that, there were economies he must practise at the cost of extra labor, and bridging the creek would lessen the cost of transport and enable him to sell one of his teams. He was late for supper, but wanted to finish part of the work before he went home.

By and by he saw Helen stop at the edge of the ravine. Her face was hot, as if she had been walking fast, and she looked vexed.

"You have kept us waiting half an hour and don't seem ready yet," she said.

"I'm not ready," Festing replied, and stopped abruptly. "Very sorry; I forgot all about it," he resumed.

Helen made a gesture of annoyance. She had invited some of

Harold Bindloss

their neighbors to supper and had spent the day preparing the feast. Things, however, had gone wrong; the stove had got too hot and spoiled her choicest dishes.

"You forgot!" she exclaimed. "It really isn't often I trouble you with guests."

"That's lucky, because I haven't much time for entertaining people. I'm overworked just now."

Helen hesitated because she was afraid she might say too much. She admired his persevering industry, but had begun to feel that he was slipping away from her and devoting himself to his farm. Sometimes she indulged an angry jealousy, and then tried to persuade herself it was illogical.

"Then why give yourself another task by building the bridge?" she asked.

"I tried to explain that. I can get the thing done with less trouble when the creek is nearly dry, and if we had to use the ford when hauling out the grain, it would mean starting with a light load or keeping a team of horses there. When I've built the bridge and graded back the road we can take the full number of bags across, and that makes for economy. It looks as if I'll have to be severely economical soon."

Helen colored. She thought he did not mean to vex her, but he had ventured on dangerous ground.

"You know that what is mine is yours," she said.

"In a way, it is, but I put all my capital into the stock and crop, and must try to get it back. I can't ask my wife for money if I loaf about and lose my own."

"You don't loaf," Helen rejoined. "But if you lose your crop from causes you can't prevent happening, there is no reason you shouldn't accept my help."

"I know you're generous and would give me all you had but—"

Helen shook her head. "You don't see the matter in the right way yet; but we'll let it go. Get your jacket and come back at once."

"Must I come?" Festing asked irresolutely.

"Isn't it obvious?"

"I don't think so. Can't you tell the folks I'd forgotten and started something I must finish?"

"I can't," said Helen sharply. "It hurts to know you had forgotten. The farm is lonely and I haven't many friends; but I can't tell outsiders how little that matters to you."

"I'm sorry," Festing answered with some embarrassment. "Still I think you're exaggerating; nobody would look at it like that. Our neighbors know one has to stay with one's work."

"Bob finds time to go about with his wife."

"He does," said Festing dryly. "Driving about is easier than farming, and Bob has no scruples about living on his wife's money. I expect that was his object when he married her. There's another thing I forgot; he's coming to-night."

"He and Sadie have been at the house some time."

Festing made a sign of resignation. "I could stand the others better. They know what we may have to face, but nothing bothers Bob, and it's hard to play up to his confounded cheerfulness when you're not in the mood. Then I suppose I've got to put on different clothes?"

Helen forced a smile. When they first came to the homestead, Stephen had changed his clothes for supper and afterwards devoted himself to her amusement, sometimes playing chess, and sometimes listening while she sang. Then, as the days got longer, he had gradually grown careless, contenting himself with changing his jacket and half an hour's talk, until at length he sat down to the meal in dusty overalls and hurried off afterwards. Helen had tried to make excuses for him, but felt hurt all the same. Stephen was getting slovenly and neglecting her.

"It's plain that you must take off those muddy overalls," she said.

They went back, and supper was delayed while Festing changed. He forced himself to be polite when he joined his guests, but it cost him something, and the dishes Helen had carefully prepared were spoiled. On the whole, he felt grateful to Sadie and Bob, who kept the others in good-humor and relieved him from the necessity of leading the talk; but he was glad when they left.

When the rigs melted into the shadowy plain he stood on the veranda and yawned.

"Well," he remarked, "that's over, and it will be some time before they need come back. I hope none of them will think they have to ask us out in return."

"You gave them a very plain hint," Helen said bitterly.

Festing did not answer and went into the house. He felt he had not been tactful, but he was very tired, and if he ventured an explanation might make things worse. Besides, he must get up at four o'clock next morning.

Helen sat still for some time, looking out on the prairie. She was beginning to feel daunted by its loneliness. Except for Sadie Charnock, visitors seldom came to the farm. Her neighbors lived at some distance, but she had hoped to plan a round of small reunions that would break the monotony.

Stephen, however, had shown her that she could expect no help from him, and had actually forgotten her first party. She felt wounded; it was hard to think that so long as he had work to do she must resign herself to being left alone.

CHAPTER XVII

FESTING USES FORCE

A week or so after the supper party Festing started for the settlement with some pieces of a binder in his wagon. He had bought the machine second-hand, and meant to replace certain worn parts before harvest began, although he doubted if this was worth while. The drought was ripening the grain prematurely and some of it was spoiled, but he must try to save as much as possible. Reaching the edge of the wheat, he stopped the team irresolutely, half tempted to turn back, because it seemed unlikely that the old binder need be used.

The wind had fallen; the mosquitoes were about and bit his face and neck. Everything was strangely quiet, it was very hot, and masses of leaden cloud darkened the horizon. Festing, however, had given up hoping for rain, which would not make much difference if it came now.

The front of the wide belt of grain was ragged and bitten into hollows by the driving sand. The torn stalks drooped and slanted away from the wind, while others that had fallen lay about their roots. Farther in, the damage was less, but the ears were half-filled and shriveled. The field was parti-colored, for the dull, dark green had changed to a dingy, sapless hue, and the riper patches had a sickly yellow tinge instead of a coppery gleam.

Festing's face hardened. If he thrashed out half the number of bushels he had expected, he would be lucky. He had staked all he had on the chances of the weather and had lost. It was his first failure and came as a rude shock to his self-confidence. He felt shaken and disgusted with himself, for it looked as if he had been a rash fool. Still, if rain came now, he might save enough to obviate the necessity of using Helen's money. She would give him all he asked for, but this was a matter about which he felt strongly, and she knew his point of view.

Driving on, he met the mail-carrier, who gave him a letter. It was from Kerr, his former chief on the railroad, who had been moved to a new section on the Pacific Slope. He told Festing about certain difficulties they had encountered, and the latter felt a curious interest. Indeed, he looked back with a touch of regret to the strenuous days he had spent at the construction camps. The work was hard, but one was provided with the material required and efficient tools. Then there was freedom from the responsibility he felt now; one did one's best and the company took the risk.

Festing's interest deepened when, at the end of the letter, Kerr told him about a contract for which nobody seemed anxious to tender. It was a difficult undertaking, but Kerr thought a bold, resourceful man could carry it out with profit. He did not know if it would appeal to Festing, although prairie farmers sometimes went to work with their teams on a new track when their harvest was poor. Kerr ended with the hope that this was not the case with Festing.

The latter sat still for a few minutes with his brows knit and then started his team. It was too late to think of railroad contracts; he had chosen his line and must stick to it, but his look was irresolute as he drove on.

Some time after Festing reached the settlement, Wilkinson and three or four others sat, smoking, in the poolroom. This supplied a useful hint about their character, because supper would not be ready for an hour or two, and industrious people were busily occupied. The room was hot, the floor and green tables were sprinkled with poisoned flies, and the wooden chairs were uncomfortably hard, but it was cooler than the sidewalk, and the men lounged with their feet on the empty stove.

"Does anybody feel like another game?" one asked.

"No," said the man he looked at. "I've lost three dollars, and that's all I can spare. Can't spare it, for that matter, but it's gone. I'm going broke if this weather lasts.

"That's nothing," remarked another. "Some of us have been broke since we came here; you get used to it. There'll be other folks in a tight place if the rain doesn't come; but it won't make much difference to you, Wilkinson. I guess the storekeepers have you fixed now."

Wilkinson frowned. He knew the remark was prompted by malice because he had won the money his companion had lost. The fellow, however, had not exaggerated. His creditors had recently stopped supplies and made demands with which he was unable to comply, and since they were obviously consulting each other, it looked as if he would be sold up and forced to leave the neighborhood. Somebody had put them on his track and he suspected Mrs. Charnock. He meant to punish her if he could.

"I've certainly got to sell off a bunch of young horses sooner than I meant; I expect you've seen the notices," he said, and added with a sneer: "They'd have made a much better price if I could have kept them until the spring, and now's your chance if you have any dollars to invest. It's a sure snap for anybody who'll help me hold them over."

One of the men laughed ironically and another asked: "Why don't you try Charnock? He used to be a partner of yours, and he's more money than the rest of us."

Wilkinson saw his opportunity. His companions were loafing

gossips, and those who were married would tell their wives. In a very short time the rumor he meant to start would travel about the neighborhood, and there was enough truth in it to make it dangerous and hard to deny.

"Charnock's deadbeat. He's as poor as you."

"His wife has plenty dollars, anyhow."

"That's so, but she's not going to give him any more," Wilkinson rejoined. "He married Sadie for her money, and now he hasn't sense enough to stick to her."

It was obvious that he had secured the others' attention, for they waited eagerly, with their eyes fixed on him. The room was quiet, but a rig came up the street and the rattle of wheels and harness drowned the sound of steps outside. Nobody noticed that the door, which was not quite shut, opened wider.

"What do you mean by that?" one asked.

"Bob's running after Mrs. Festing. Old sweetheart of his in England, though he turned her down to marry Sadie. Now she's got hold of him again—tired of Festing or has a pick on Mrs. Charnock, perhaps. Anyhow, Bob's round the Festing place all the time, and I don't know that I blame him much. Mrs. Festing's a looker and Sadie's a difficult woman to live with."

"But what has Festing got to say?"

Wilkinson laughed. "Festing's a bit of a sucker and doesn't know. He's scared about the big crop he has sown and thinks of nothing but the weather and his farm, while Bob goes over when he's off at work. But I guess there's trouble coming soon."

"It's coming now," said somebody, and Wilkinson's jaw fell slack, and he sat with his mouth open as Festing strode into

Harold Bindloss

the room.

The latter had come to look for a smith, and hearing Wilkinson's voice as he went up the steps, waited for a moment or two. He was too late, in one sense, because the harm had been done, but he could not steal away. Although the course he meant to take was not very logical, judgment would be given against him if he did nothing. His sunburned face was rather white and he stood very stiff, with muscles braced, looking down at Wilkinson.

"Get up, you slanderous brute, and tell them it's a lie," he said.

"I'll be shot if I will!" said Wilkinson, who got on his feet reluctantly. "You know it's true."

Then he flung up his arm, a second too late, for Festing struck him a smashing blow and he staggered, with the blood running down his face.

He recovered in a moment, and seizing a billiard cue brought the thick end down on Festing's head. Festing swayed, half-dazed, but grasped the cue, and they struggled for its possession, until it broke in the middle, and Wilkinson flung his end in the other's face. After this, for a minute or two, the fight was close and confused, and both made the most of any advantage that offered.

In Western Canada, personal combat is not hampered by rules. The main thing is to disable one's antagonist as quickly as possible, and Festing knew that Wilkinson would not be scrupulous. He must not be beaten, particularly since his defeat would, to some extent, confirm the slander.

He grappled with Wilkinson as a precaution, because another cue stood near, and with a tense effort threw him against the empty stove. The shock was heavy enough to bring the stove-pipe down, and a cloud of soot fell upon the struggling men, while the pipe rolled noisily across the floor. Wilkinson, however, stuck to him, and they reeled up and down between the wall and table, getting an arm loose now and then to strike a blow, and scattering the chairs. Nobody interfered or cleared the ground, and by and by Wilkinson caught his foot and fell down, bringing Festing with him. After this, they fought upon the floor, rolling over among the chairs, until their grip got slack. Both got up, breathing hard, and Festing gasped:

"Tell them you're a liar. It's the last chance you'll get!"

Wilkinson did not answer, but struck him before he could guard, and the fight went on again amidst a cloud of dust that rose from the dirty boards. Then it ended suddenly, for Festing got his left arm free as he forced his antagonist towards the open door. He struck with savage fury, and Wilkinson, reeling backwards across the narrow veranda, plunged down the stairs and fell into the street. He did not get up, and Festing leaned against the wall and wiped his bleeding face.

"Pick up the hog and take him to the hotel," he said, and tried to fill his pipe with shaking hands while the rest went out.

Other people joined them in the street, and Festing, stealing away as a crowd began to gather, went to the implement store, where he washed his face and brushed his damaged clothes. There was a cut on his forehead and his jacket was badly torn, while some of the soot that had fallen upon it would not come off. After a rest and a smoke, however, he did not feel much worse, and the dealer, going to the hotel, brought back news that Wilkinson had driven home.

"I guess you have done all you could and can let the fellow go," he said. "My notion is he won't be in the neighborhood long."

An hour later, Festing drove out of the settlement, with a strip of sticking plaster on his forehead and his jacket clumsily mended. The sky was now a curious leaden color, and the wild barley shone a livid white against the dark riband of the trail;

the air was very hot and there was not a breath of wind. Festing noted that the horses were nervous and trotted fast, although they had made a long journey. Now and then they threw up their heads and snorted, and swerved violently when a gopher ran across the trail or a prairie-hen got up. The flies seemed to have gone, but the mosquitoes were out in clouds, and the hand with which he slapped his face and neck was soon smeared with small red stains. He could not hold the whip; but it was not needed, because the team rather required to be checked than urged.

When the trail permitted he let them go, and swung, lost in gloomy thoughts, with the jolting of the rig. The damaging part of Wilkinson's statement was false, but since part was true the tale would spread and some would believe the worst. It was impossible to doubt Helen, but he was angry with her. She had let her ridiculous notion of reforming Bob carry her away. Festing did not think Bob could be reformed, but it was Sadie's business, not Helen's. Besides, he had objected to her encouraging the fellow to hang about the homestead, and she had disregarded his warnings. Now, the thing must be stopped, and it would be horribly disagreeable to tell her why. She had been obstinate and rash, but after all she meant well and would be badly hurt. He began to feel sorry for her, and his angry thought's centered on Charnock.

It was, of course, ridiculous to imagine that Bob was seriously trying to make love to Helen; he knew her character too well. All the same, the fellow might amuse himself by mild indulgence in romantic sentiment. He was a fool and a slacker, and had now humiliated Helen for the second time. The longer Festing thought about it, the angrier he got, and when he roused himself as the horses plunged down the side of a ravine he was surprised to note how far he had gone. He had just time to tighten the reins and guide the team across the open log bridge at the bottom, and as they plodded up the other side saw that he had better get home as soon as possible.

The drooping leaves of the birches in the hollow flittered

ominously, and when he reached the summit a bluff that stood out from the plain two or three miles off suddenly vanished. It looked as if a curtain had been drawn across the grass. The horses set off at a fast trot, and the rig jolted furiously among the ruts. It would not be dark for an hour, but the gray obscurity that had hidden the bluff was getting near. At its edge and about a mile off a pond shone with a strange sickly gleam.

Then a dazzling flash fell from the cloud bank overhead and touched the grass. A stunning crash of thunder rolled across the sky, and the team plunged into a frantic gallop. Festing braced himself in a vain attempt to hold them, for the trail was half covered with tall grass and broken by badger holes. He was soon breathless and dazzled, for the lightning fell in forked streaks that ran along the plain, and the trail blazed in front of the horses' feet. Thunder is common in Canada, but it is on the high central plains that the storms attain their greatest violence.

The team plunged on, and Festing, jolting to and fro, durst not lift his eyes from the trail. The storm would probably not last long and might do some good if it were followed by moderate rain. But he was not sure that moderate rain would fall. By and by a few large drops beat upon his hat, there was a roar in the distance, and a cool draught touched his face. It died away, but the next puff was icy cold, and the roar got louder. He looked up, for he knew what was coming, but there was not a bluff in sight that would shield him from the wind.

Turning down his hat-brim against the increasing rain, he let the horses go. He need not try to hold them; the storm would stop them soon. It broke upon him with a scream and a shower of sand and withered grass. He staggered as if he had got a blow, and then leaned forward to resist the pressure. The horses swerved, and he had trouble to keep them on the trail, but their speed slackened and they fell into a labored trot. For a few minutes they struggled against the gale, and then the roar Festing had heard behind the scream drowned the rumbling thunder. He threw up his arm to guard his face as the terrible hail of the plains drove down the blast.

It fell in oblique lines of ragged lumps of ice, hammering upon the wagon and bringing the horses to a stop. They began to plunge, turning half round, while one pressed against the other, in an effort to escape the savage buffeting. Festing let them have their way at the risk of upsetting the rig, and presently they stopped with their backs to the wind. He let the reins fall, and the hail beat upon his bowed head and shoulders like a shower of stones. The horses stood limp and trembling, as powerless as himself.

Their punishment did not last long. The hail got thinner and the lumps smaller; the roar diminished and Festing heard it recede across the plain. The wind was still savage, but it was falling, and the thunder sounded farther off. There was a savage downpour of drenching rain, and when this moderated he pulled himself together, and turning the horses, resumed his journey. He was wet to the skin, his shoulders were sore, and his face and hands were bruised and cut. Pieces of ice, some as large as hazelnuts, lay about the wagon, and the wild barley lay flat beside the trail. Not a blade of grass stood upright as far as he could see, and the ruts in which the wheels churned were full of melting hail and water.

It was getting dark when his homestead rose out of the plain; a shadowy group of buildings, marked by two or three twinkling lights. He was wet and cold, but he stopped by the wheat and nerved himself to see what had happened to the crop. He had not had much hope, but for all that got something of a shock. There was no standing grain; the great field looked as if it had been mown. Bruised stalks and torn blades lay flat in a tattered, tangled mass, splashed with sticky mud. The rain that might have saved him had come too late and was finishing the ruin the sand and hail had made.

Then the downpour thickened and the light died out, and he drove to the house. He could see in the morning if any remnant of the crop could be cut, but there would not be enough to make much difference. Hope had gone, and his face was stern when he called the hired man and got down stiffly from the dripping rig.

Harold Bindloss

CHAPTER XVIII

HELEN MAKES A MISTAKE

When Festing had changed his clothes he entered the small sitting-room with an effort at cheerfulness. The room was unusually comfortable for a prairie homestead. The floor was stained, rugs were spread on the polished boards, and Helen had drawn the curtains, which harmonized in color with the big easy chairs. There were books in well-made cases, and two or three good pictures on the painted walls, while a tall brass lamp with a deep shade threw down a soft light. Helen had put a meal on the table, and Festing sat down with a feeling that was half uneasiness and half content.

While he ate he glanced at his wife. She wore a pretty and rather fashionable dress that she kept for evenings. She looked fresh and vigorous, although the summer had been hot and she worked hard; the numerous petty difficulties she had to contend with had left no mark. Her courage had always been evident, but she had shown a resolution that Festing had not quite expected. He admired it, in a way, but it was sometimes awkward when they took a different point of view.

There was a charm in coming back to a home like this when he was tired and disappointed, but its taste and comfort were now disturbing. For one thing, he had perhaps not made the best use of his privileges, and, for another, Helen might have to be satisfied with a simpler mode of life. It hurt him to think of this, because he had hoped to beautify the house still further, so that she should miss nothing she had been used to in the Old Country. It was obvious that she understood something of his misfortune, for her look was sympathetic; but she let him finish his supper before she began to talk.

"Your jacket is badly torn, Stephen," she remarked when he lighted his pipe. "And how did you cut your face?"

"The hail was pretty fierce."

"It was terrible. We never had storms like that in England. I was frightened when I thought of your being out on the prairie. But I don't mean the small bruises. How did you cut your forehead?"

"Oh, that!" said Festing awkwardly. "I did it when I fell over a stove at the settlement. The pipe came down and I imagine the edge struck me."

"You would have known if it hit you nor not."

"Well, it might have been the top of the stove. The molding was sharp."

"But how did you fall against the stove?" Helen persisted.

Festing did not want to tell her about the fight with Wilkinson. He had resolved to say nothing about the matter until morning.

"I tripped. There was a chair in the way and it caught my foot."

Helen did not look altogether satisfied, but let the matter go.

"Has the hail done much damage to the wheat?"

"Yes," said Festing, with grim quietness. "I imagine it has done all the damage that was possible. So far as I could see, the crop's wiped out."

They were sitting near together, and Helen, leaning forward, put her hand on his arm with a gesture of sympathy.

"Poor Stephen! I'm dreadfully sorry. It must have been a blow."

Festing's hard look softened. "It was. When I stopped beside the wreck I felt knocked out, but getting home braced me up. I begin to feel I might have had a worse misfortune and mustn't exaggerate the importance of the loss."

Helen was silent for a few minutes, but she was sensible of a certain relief. She was sorry for her husband, but there was some compensation, since it looked as if a ray of light had dawned on him. Although she had struggled against the feeling, she was jealous of the farm that had kept him away from her.

"I think you sowed too large a crop, and you could not have gone on working as you have done," she said. "It would have worn you out."

Festing put down his pipe and looked at her with surprise. "You don't seem to understand that I'll have to work harder than before."

"I don't understand," said Helen, taking away her hand. "To begin with, it's impossible; then I'd hoped the loss of money, serious as it is, would have made you cautious and, in a sense, more content."

"You hoped the loss of the money—!" Festing exclaimed. "Did you ever know losing money make anybody content? The thing's absurd!"

Helen made a gesture of protest. "Stephen, dear, try to see what I mean. You have been doing too much, running too big risks, and fixing all your thought upon the farm. It has made you irritable and impatient, and the strain is telling on your health. This could not go on long, and although I'm truly sorry the wheat is spoiled, it's some relief to know you will be forced to be less ambitious. Besides, it's foolish to be disturbed. Neither of us is greedy, and we have enough. In fact, we have much that I hardly think you value as you ought."

"I haven't enough; that's the trouble."

"Oh," said Helen, "you know that all I have belongs to both."

"It doesn't," Festing answered in a stubborn tone. "You don't seem to realize yet that I can't change my views about this matter. I've lost most of my money, but that's no reason I should lose my wife's. Besides, since you bought the farm, you haven't a large sum left." He paused and indicated the handsome rugs and furniture. "Then it costs a good deal to live up to this kind of thing."

"We can change that; I can manage with less help and be more economical. There is much that we can go without. I wouldn't mind at all, Stephen, if it would help you to take things easily."

Festing colored. "No. I can't let you suffer for my rashness. It's my business to give you all the comforts you need."

"Ah," said Helen, "I like you to think of me. But something's due to pride. I wonder how much?"

"I don't know," said Festing, rather wearily. "I'm what I am and haven't much time to improve myself. For that matter, I'll have less time now."

"Then what do you mean to do?"

"Make the most of what I have left. I'd hoped to give you a change this winter—take you to Montreal and go skating and

Harold Bindloss

tobogganing, but that's done with. I believe I have money enough to begin again in a small way and work up. It may take me two or three years to get back to where I was, but somehow I will get back."

"Then you are going on as before; concentrating all your mind upon the farm, taking no rest, denying yourself every pleasure you might have had?"

"I'm afraid that's the only way. It's a pretty grim outlook, but I think I can stand the strain."

"Then I suppose I must try," said Helen, very quietly.

She was silent afterwards, and Festing lit his pipe. Something stood between them, and she felt that it was not less dangerous because their motives were good. Had they differed from selfishness, agreement might have been easier, but an estrangement that sprang from principle was hard to overcome. She wanted to help her husband and keep him to herself; he meant to save her hardship and carry out a task that was properly his. But perhaps their motives were not so fine as they looked. Suppose there was shabby jealousy on her side, and false pride on his? Well, Stephen was tired and could not see things in the proper light, and it was some relief when he got up and went out. Helen picked up a book, in the hope of banishing her uneasy thoughts.

Next morning Festing came in for breakfast, feeling gloomy and preoccupied. He had not slept much and got up early to examine the damaged grain. It looked worse than he had thought and, for the most part, must be burned off the ground. There were patches that might, with difficulty, be cut, but he hardly imagined the stooks would pay for thrashing. Moreover, he had bought and fed a number of expensive Percheron horses, which ought to have been used for harvesting and hauling the grain to the railroad, and had engaged men at lower wages than usual, on the understanding that he kept them through the winter. Now there was nothing for both to do, although their maintenance would cost as much as before.

He read Kerr's letter again. If he had not been married, it would have given him a chance of overcoming his difficulties. A man and a team of horses could do all that was required on the farm in winter, and he could have taken the others to British Columbia. Kerr would arrange for free transport, and, if he was lucky, he might earn enough on the railroad to cover part of his loss. But this was impossible. He could not leave Helen.

Then there was the other matter. He had not yet told her what Wilkinson had said, but she must be told, and Bob's visits must stop. The trouble was that he had already vexed her by refusing her help, and this would not make his delicate task easier. Besides, he was not in the mood to use much tact. His nerves were raw; the shock he had got had left him savage and physically tired. For all that, the thing could not be put off.

He said nothing until breakfast was over, and then, asking Helen to come with him, went on to the veranda. The sun was hot, the sky clear, and thin steam drifted across the drenched plain. Had the storm come without the hail a few weeks sooner, it would have saved his crop; but now the vivifying moisture seemed to mock him. It had come too late; the wheat had gone. Struggling with a feeling of depression, he turned to his wife.

"There's something we must talk about; and I hope you'll be patient with me if you get a jar."

He leaned against the balustrade, nervously fingering his pipe, and Helen sat down opposite. She felt curious and disturbed.

"Well?" she said.

"To begin with, I'll tell you what happened at the settlement yesterday. You must remember that the statements are Wilkinson's."

Helen's color rose, and when he stopped her face was flushed and her eyes were very bright.

"Ah," she said in a strained voice. "But what did you do?"

Festing smiled rather grimly. "I dragged the brute about the floor and threw him into the street. I don't know that it was a logical denial of the slander, but it was what the others expected and I had to indulge them."

"And that was how you cut your forehead?"

"Yes," said Festing, and for a few moments Helen tried to regulate her thoughts.

She felt shocked and disgusted, but did not mean to let her anger master her, because there were matters that must be carefully weighed. Indeed, it was something of a relief to dwell upon the first. To hear of Festing's thrashing her traducer had given her a pleasant thrill, but all the same she vaguely disapproved. He had not taken a dignified line and had really made things worse. It was humiliating to feel that she had been the subject of a vulgar poolroom brawl.

"Could you not have found a better way to silence him?" she asked.

"I could not. I was afraid you wouldn't like it, but you must try to understand that I was forced to play up to local sentiment. English notions of what is becoming don't hold good here; you can't stop a man like Wilkinson with a supercilious look. If I'd let the thing go, the boys would have thought his statements true, and the tale is bad enough to deal with."

Helen gave him a steady look, but her color was high and her face was hard.

"But you know it isn't true!"

"Of course," said Festing, with quiet scorn. "All that the brute insinuated is absolutely false. Bob's a fool, but he knows you, and I'm beginning to think he's a little in love with his wife."

"Ah," said Helen, "I knew you knew. But I felt I must hear you say so."

Festing hesitated. One difficulty had vanished, but there was another, and he hoped Helen would see his point of view.

"For all that, in a way, there was some truth in the story; enough, in fact, to make it dangerous, and I think you have been rash. Bob has been here too often, and you will remember I objected to his coming."

"You did," said Helen. "You were rather disagreeable about it; but you objected because he liked to talk and kept you from your work."

"He certainly talked. General conversation is all right in English country houses where nobody had much to do, but casual chatterers who insist on talking when you're busy are a disgusting nuisance in Canada. However, I don't think that's worth arguing about."

"It is not," said Helen, with a smile. "Besides, I know your opinions about that point. What do you wish me to do?"

"Warn Sadie to keep Bob at home. There's no reason she shouldn't visit you, but you can't go there."

The color returned to Helen's face and she got up. She looked stately with her air of injured pride.

"Do you mean that I should rule my conduct to suit the ideas of the drunken loafers at the settlement poolroom?"

"Oh!" said Festing impatiently, "try to be sensible! You have done a foolish thing, but you needn't make it worse. The trouble is that those loafers' opinions will be reflected all round the neighborhood. Wilkinson won't say anything more; at least, he won't when I'm about; but I can't keep on throwing out people who agree with him."

"That is plain. If you were not so angry, the remark would be humorous."

"I'm not angry," Festing rejoined.

"Well, I am," said Helen. "And I think I have some grounds. Must I let those tipsy gossips dictate when I may see my friends?"

"Does it matter if you see them or not? You don't really care for Bob."

"No," said Helen, trying to be calm. "In a way, I don't care for Bob; that is, I'm glad I didn't marry him. But I don't see why I should stop him coming here when Sadie wants to bring him. She's my friend, and she knows it does Bob good. I'm too angry to flatter you, Stephen, but you have some influence—"

Festing laughed. "All the influence I've got won't go far with Bob. I don't say the fellow's vicious, but he's an extravagant slacker and a fool, which is perhaps as bad. Anyhow, if he can be reformed at all, it's Sadie's business, and I've no doubt she finds it an arduous job. There's no use in an outsider meddling, and your anxiety for his improvement might be misunderstood. In fact, it has been seriously misunderstood."

"You seem to have made up your mind about the matter," Helen remarked with a curious look.

"I have. Perhaps the easiest way would be for you to give Sadie a hint."

"Suppose I refuse?"

"Then I shall have to talk to Bob. After all, that might be better."

Helen flushed, but her color faded and her face got white. "You are willing to let this scurrilous gossip influence you as far as that? Do you mean to forbid my friends coming to see me?"

"I won't have Bob hanging round my house. The wastrel has done you harm enough."

"You forget something," Helen rejoined in a strained, cold voice. "The house is mine."

She knew her mistake as she saw the change in Festing's look, and weakly turned her head. When she looked back it was too late. His hands were clenched and his gaze was fixed.

"I—I didn't quite mean that," she faltered.

"Anyhow, it's true," said Festing quietly. "The farm is yours as well, and I admit you have no grounds for being satisfied with the way I've managed your property. You won't have much trouble in getting a better steward."

Helen glanced at him, with a hint of fear. "But I don't want anybody else. Do you mean to give up the farm?"

"Yes. As soon as I can arrange things for you I'm going to British Columbia for a time. I've been offered a railroad contract, and as it's a job I know something about, I mayn't fail at that."

"And you will leave me alone to face this slander?"

"The remedy's in your hands. I'm powerless if you won't use it. I can't forbid Bob coming here; you can."

Helen hesitated. It was unfortunate that both were in an abnormal mood. They had borne some strain, and the shock of the disaster to the crop had left them with jangled nerves. This clouded Helen's judgment, but reenforced her pride. She had meant well when she tried to help Sadie with Bob, and could not give way to her husband's unreasonable prejudice. This was a matter of principle. She could help Bob and must not be daunted by vulgar gossip.

"No," she said; "I can't break my promise to Sadie for the reasons you give. You must do what you think best."

Festing made a sign of acquiescence and went down the steps, while Helen bit her lip. She wanted to call him back, but somehow could not. It might be easier if he would look round, but he went on across the grass and his step was resolute, although his head was bent. Then she got up, and going to her room, sat down trembling. She had let her best chance go; Stephen's resolve would stiffen, for when he had made a choice he was hard to move. Besides, he had wounded her deeply. He did not seem to understand that if he went away he would give people ground for thinking the slander true. He ought to have seen this if he had thought about her. Perhaps he had seen it and refused to let it influence him. Well, if he wanted a reconciliation, he must make the first offer.

In the meantime, Festing went to look for the foreman, whom he could trust. After some talk, the man agreed to manage the farm for the winter on the terms Festing indicated. Then the latter asked if the other men would go with him to the Pacific Slope, and finding them willing, went back to his office and carefully studied his accounts. He was glad to think that Helen had sufficient help and that the staid Scottish housekeeper would take care of her. By and by he wrote a note and then drove off to the settlement. He did not come back until next morning, but his plans were made and he only waited a telegram from Kerr. Three or four days later the telegram arrived.

"All fixed," it ran. "Pass for transport mailed. Come along soon as possible."

Harold Bindloss

CHAPTER XIX

SADIE SEES A WAY

Soon after Festing started for British Columbia Sadie drove over to the farm; because she had heard about the fight in the poolroom and suspected why he had gone. At first she found it difficult to break down Helen's reserve, but the latter could not resist her frank sympathy, and softening by degrees, allowed herself to be led into confidential talk. Sadie waited until she thought she understood the matter, and then remarked:

"So you stuck to your promise that you'd help me with Bob, although you saw what it would cost? Well, I wouldn't be surprised if you hated us."

"It wasn't altogether the promise," Helen replied. "We were both highly strung, and I thought Stephen hard and prejudiced; it seemed ridiculous that he should care what the loafers said. But I don't hate you. The fault was really mine, and I want a friend."

"Well," said Sadie, "I feel I've got to help put this trouble right, if I can." She paused and asked with some hesitation: "Will Steve be away long?"

"I don't know," Helen answered dejectedly. "He hinted that he might not come until spring; I think he means to stop until he has earned enough to make him independent. That's partly my fault—I said something rash. If I hadn't had more money than him, it wouldn't have happened."

Sadie smiled. "My having more money won't make trouble between me and Bob; he doesn't mind how much I've got. But I suppose you want Steve back?"

"Of course! It's all I want, but the matter is not as simple as it looks. I don't think he will come back as long as he's poor, and if he does, he won't use my capital, and things will be as before. If he earns some money, I should feel hurt because he was obstinate and wouldn't let me help. That's why I don't know what to do. I wish I'd never had the money!"

Sadie thought Helen had some ground she had not mentioned yet for her distress. Moreover, it looked as if she still felt she had a grievance against Festing, and their clashing ideas about the money did not altogether account for this.

"I guess you're keeping something back."

Helen's reserve had broken down. She was half ashamed because she had lost it, but she felt the need of sympathy, and Sadie could be trusted.

"He didn't see, or didn't mind, that his going away would bear out the wicked story!" she exclaimed with sparkling eyes. "I feel that was the worst."

"I don't know that it looks quite as bad as you think. It's a common thing for a farmer who has lost his crop to go off and work on a new railroad, particularly if he has teams the construction boss can use. Anyhow, I guess the thing will come right, and I'll help if I can. But I want to see my way before I move."

Helen did not answer, and soon afterwards Sadie left the homestead. She said nothing to Charnock about her visit, but started for the settlement next morning and informed herself about what had happened at the poolroom and what people thought. Then she drove home, and getting back at dusk, sat down opposite Charnock, who lounged in a basket chair with a pipe in his mouth. Her eyes twinkled with rather grim humor.

"You don't look as if anything bothered you," she said.

"It's possible," Charnock agreed. "I suppose I'm lucky because I have nothing much to bother about."

"You wouldn't bother about it, anyhow. You leave that kind of thing to me."

Charnock gave her a quick glance. She was not angry, which was something of a relief, because Sadie was difficult when she let herself go. Besides, he was not conscious of having done anything to vex her since he gave Wilkinson the cheque. But she looked resolute.

"I've a good excuse," he answered. "I've got a remarkably capable wife."

"We'll cut out the compliments. I don't think you have seen any of the boys from the settlement since Festing left."

Charnock said he had not done so, and she gave him a thoughtful look.

"I suppose you can't remember when you last did something useful; something that would help somebody else?"

"It's a painful confession, but I can't remember. Still I've some experience of being helped along a way I didn't want to go, which leads me to believe it's often kinder to leave folks alone."

"Anyhow, you have done some harm."

"I'm afraid that's true. I don't know that I meant to do much harm, but it's generally easier than doing good. For example, I've given you some trouble; but at the moment I can't think of a new offense."

"You can quit joking and put down that newspaper. It looks as if you didn't know why Festing left?"

Charnock said he could not guess, and got up abruptly when Sadie told him. He kicked the newspaper out of his way and crossed the floor with angry strides. His face was red when he stopped in front of his wife.

"You don't believe the lying tale!"

"No," said Sadie, calmly. "If I had believed it, I wouldn't have talked to you like this."

"Thank you! Now we have cleared the ground, I'm certainly going to do something. I'll begin by driving over to Wilkinson's to-morrow, and I'll take a whip."

"Festing 'tended to that matter before he left, and making another circus won't help. Besides, Wilkinson has got to quit. You'll see notices about his sale soon; I fixed that up."

Charnock laughed. "You're a marvel, Sadie, but the brute deserves it. Well, if I mustn't thrash him, what's your plan?"

"You'll go to British Columbia and bring Festing back."

"I will, by George!" said Charnock. "We owe him and Helen much, and the job is obviously mine—by joining Festing I give Wilkinson the lie. You're clever, and I expect you saw this. Anyhow, I'll start; but Festing's an obstinate fellow. Suppose he won't come back?"

"He mayn't at first. If so, you'll have to wait."

Charnock turned away and walked about the floor while Sadie

watched him, pleased but curious. Bob was rather hard to move, but he was moved now. He came back, and sitting down, looked at her thoughtfully.

"I imagine you are giving me a bigger job than you know. If Festing has taken the railroad contract, he'll probably stop until he had carried it out. Now I don't imagine I'd find it amusing to loaf about and watch him work; for one thing, it's pretty cold in the ranges after the snow comes."

"Well?" said Sadie.

Charnock leaned forward with an apologetic smile. "I'd like to take a share in the contract and help him through; that is, of course, if he won't come back at once. But there's a difficulty; I haven't the cash."

"You want me to give you some?"

"Yes. I shouldn't feel much surprised if you refused. I've squandered your money before, but this time I mean business. Can't you see that I have, so to speak, got my chance at last?"

"I don't quite see. You have had many chances."

"I have," Charnock agreed; but there was a new note in his voice and a look in his eyes that Sadie had not often seen. "I've been a fool, but perhaps it doesn't follow that I'm incapable of change. However, let's be practical. The crop is spoiled, we have no grain to haul in, and there'll be nothing doing here while the snow is on the ground. Well, if Festing can get some of his money back, why can't I? I've wasted yours long enough, and now, if I can't bring him home, I'll stop with him until we both make good."

"You mean that, Bob?"

"I do. Give me a chance to prove it."

Sadie got up, and putting her hands on his shoulders, kissed him. "Very well. You shall have all the money you want."

Then she went back to her chair and turned her head. She had borne with her husband's follies and fought hard for him, sometimes with hope and sometimes in desperation, but always with unflinching courage. Now it looked as if she had won. Victory was insecure yet, and there was a risk that it might turn to defeat, but Sadie never shrank from a daring venture. For a moment she could not speak; her heart was full.

"Hallo!" said Charnock, who got up and came towards her. "Crying, Sadie? Will you miss me as much as that?"

Sadie hastily wiped her eyes. "Yes, Bob; I'll miss you all the time. But if you'll come back the man you are now, I'll wait as long as you like."

"I'll try," said Charnock simply. "I'm not going to protest, but you deserve a much better husband than you've got. If I can't come back better fit to live with you, I won't come back at all."

"I wouldn't like that," Sadie answered, smiling uncertainly. "But I guess I know what you mean. I'll wait, dear, because I know you are going to make good."

Then, feeling that she had said enough, she began to make plans. Something might be saved from the ruined crop and she had better keep a heavy team, but Charnock could have the other horses if they were required. She could carry on whatever work was possible after the frost set in, and would pay off one of the hired men. Charnock approved, and after a time Sadie leaned back in her chair.

"It's all fixed, but perhaps we mayn't need these plans," she said. "Remember you're really going there to bring Festing home."

"That's understood. However, I don't think he'll come, and if so, it will be Helen's money that prevents him. If he's foolish enough to doubt her, I can put him right, which will be something."

"Yes," said Sadie, with a sigh. "Well, if he won't come, you must stop and do the best you can."

In the meantime, Festing reached the railroad camp. It was raining when the construction train rolled noisily through a mountain gorge, and he stood at the door of the caboose, looking out. Three or four hundred feet below, a green river, streaked with muddy foam, brawled among the rocks, for the track had been dug out of a steep hillside. Festing knew this was difficult work; one could deal with rock, although it cost much to cut, but it was another matter to bed the rails in treacherous gravel, and the fan-shaped mounds of shale and soil that ran down to the water's edge showed how loose the ground was and the abruptness of the slope. Above, the silver mist drifted about the black firs that clung to the side of the mountain, and in the distance there was a gleam of snow. Some of the trees had fallen, and it was significant that, for the most part, they did not lie where they fell. They had slipped down hill, and the channels in the ground indicated that the shock had been enough to start a miniature avalanche which had carried them away. The pitch was near the slant engineers call the angle of rest, but Festing thought there was rock not far beneath, which prevented the solidification of the superincumbent soil. It looked as if his contract would be difficult and he would earn his pay.

As the cars passed he saw the ballast creep about the ends of the ties, which reached to the edge of the descent, and in places small streams of gravel had run down, leaving hollows round the timber. The harsh jolting indicated the consequences, but he knew that in the West railroads are built as fast as possible and made safe afterwards. For that matter, he had often run risks that would have daunted engineers used to conservative English methods. In the meantime, the speed was slackening, and by and by the harsh tolling of the locomotive bell echoed among the pines. Tents, iron huts, and rude log shacks slipped past; men in muddy slickers drew back against the bank, and then the train stopped.

Festing got down into the water that flowed among the ties, and Kerr came forward in dripping slickers.

"If you want help to get the teams out, I'll send some of the boys," he said. "If not, you had better come along and I'll show you your shack. I told our cook to fix your supper, and I'll be glad to sit down for a time out of the wet."

Festing followed him along the descending track, which presently ended at a ledge of rock sixty or seventy feet above the river. Wire ropes spanned the gap between the banks, and near the middle a rock islet broke the surface of the savage flood. Here men were pouring cement into holes among the foundations of an iron frame, while suspended trollies clanged across the wires. On the other bank was a small flat where shacks of log and bark stood among dripping tents. The roar of the river filled the gorge, but its deep note was broken by the rattle of hammers, clash of shovels, and clang of thrown-down rails.

The sounds of keen activity stirred Festing's blood. He had a touch of constructive genius, but lack of specialized training had forced him into the ranks of the pioneers. Others must add the artistic finish and divide the prizes of ultimate victory; his part was to rough out the work and clear the way. But he was satisfied with this, and something in him thrilled as he heard in the crash of a blasting charge man's bold challenge to the wilderness. Kerr waited with a twinkle of understanding amusement while Festing looked about, and then took him up the hill.

"You have come back," he remarked. "Well, I guessed you would come. After all, this is your job; it's here you belong."

"That is so, in a sense," Festing dryly agreed. "It looks as if my job was to get tired and wet and dirty while others got the dollars; but it's a job with different sides. Farming's as much a part of it as this, and has very similar disadvantages."

"There's an altruistic theory that the dollars don't count; but it's easier to believe when you draw your wages regularly, and I've known it break down when an engineer was offered a more lucrative post. Anyhow, I reckon it's our business to make good, even if our pay isn't equal to our desserts, which happens pretty often when you work on the railroad."

"If you work on a farm, you often don't get paid at all."

Kerr laughed and indicated the pines that rolled up the hill in somber spires.

"Well, there's your raw material, and you won't have much trouble to bring the logs down, though you may find stopping them from plunging into the river a harder thing. However, you have some notion of what you're up against, and I'll show you the plans and specifications when we get out of the rain."

He stopped in front of a small log shack, and opening the door, beckoned Festing in. There was an earth floor, and a bunk, filled with swamp-hay, was fixed to the wall; two or three camp-chairs stood about, and a fire of scented cedar logs burned on the clay hearth. A Chinaman, dressed in very clean blue clothes, was putting a meal on the table. Festing hung up his wet slickers and sat down with a vague sense of satisfaction. It was plain that he must go without many comforts he had enjoyed at the farm, but he felt strangely at home.

Kerr took supper with him, and afterwards threw some papers on the table and lighted his pipe. Half an hour later Festing looked up.

"I imagine I've got the hang of things, and I'll make a start to-morrow. Your way of underpinning the track is pretty good, but I don't like that plan. You can't hold up the road long with lumber; the work won't stand."

"I don't know if your objection springs from artistic delight in a good job or British caution. Anyhow, you ought to know that in this country we don't want work to stand; our aim is to get it finished. If the track holds up until we can start the freight traffic running, it's as much as we expect. We'll improve it afterwards as the dollars come in."

"A freight train in a Canadian river isn't a very uncommon object," Festing rejoined. "However, it's my business to cut the logs and do the underpinning as well as I can. On the whole, and barring accidents, I see some profit on the job. I'm grateful to you for putting it in my way."

"Your thanks are really due to somebody else. The head contractor is not allowed to sub-let work without our approval, and although I recommended your being given a chance, the decision rested with another man."

"Who's that?"

"He'll probably look you up to-night," Kerr replied with a twinkle. "They sent him from headquarters to see how we're getting on. But I'll leave you the plans. We're working nights with the blast-lamps, and I've got to be about when the new shift makes a start."

He went away and Festing studied the drawings. He had undertaken to cut and dress to size the heavy logs required for the lower posts of trestles and foundation piles. So far, he did not apprehend much difficulty, but he would run some risk over the underpinning of part of the track. In order to make a secure and permanent road-bed, it would have been necessary to cut back the hillside for some distance and then distribute the spoil about the slope below, but the engineers had chosen a quicker and cheaper plan. Heavy timbers would be driven into the face of the hill to make a foundation for the track, which would be partly dug out of, and partly built on to, the declivity. Where the main piles reached the rock the plan would be safe, but where they were bedded in gravel there was danger of their giving way under a heavy load. Festing knew he must share the risk of this happening with the head contractor.

By and by somebody knocked at the door, and he got up abruptly as a man came in.

"Dalton!" he exclaimed.

The other smiled and threw off his wet slickers. It was getting dark, but the firelight touched his face and Festing studied him with surprise. The lad, whom he had not seen for some years, had grown into a man, and had moreover a look of quiet authority. He had made rapid progress if he had, as Kerr had stated, been sent to report upon the latter's work.

"You don't seem to have expected me, though, to some extent, I'm responsible for your being here," he said. "However, I'm remarkably glad we have met again."

Festing, awkwardly conscious that his welcome was somewhat cold, indicated a chair, and sitting down opposite began to fill his pipe. Dalton sometimes wrote to Helen, but had not mentioned his being sent to British Columbia.

"Well," he said, "I was glad to hear you had got a move up once or twice, but it looks as if you had gone farther than I thought."

"I had the advantage of a proper training, and the reputation of the engineer who gave it me counted for something, although I might never have got my chance in this country but for you. Now I'm happy if I've been able to show my gratitude. When Kerr brought your name forward I told him to see you got the contract."

"You did more than you knew," said Festing. "It looks as if you hadn't heard from Helen."

"Not for a time; I hope she's well. I'd thought about coming West to see you, but couldn't get away, and she talked about your going to Montreal this winter."

"That's off, of course. It's plain you don't know that Helen and I have quarreled."

Dalton looked up sharply, but was silent for a moment or two.

"This is a nasty knock," he said. "I don't know if my relation to you justifies my venturing on dangerous ground, but do you feel at liberty to tell me what you quarreled about?"

Festing decided that Charnock's part in the matter must be kept dark. It was unthinkable that Dalton should imagine he suspected his wife.

"To put it roughly, we differed about what you might call a principle, although Helen's money had something to do with the thing. You see, I lost my crop and she was hurt because I wouldn't use her capital."

"I don't see altogether," Dalton rejoined. "In fact, your objection seems unusual."

He pondered for a minute or two, and Festing marked the change in him. Dalton had a reserve and thoughtfulness he had not expected. He had grown very like Helen.

"A quarrel about a principle is apt to be dangerous," he resumed. "Although you are probably both wrong, you can persuade yourselves you are right. Then while I was glad to hear about your wedding, I'll admit that I saw some difficulties. Helen has a strong will and is sometimes rather exacting, while you're an obstinate fellow and a little too practical. I must wait until I know more than I do now, but might be of some use as a peacemaker. Isn't it possible to compromise? Can't you meet half way?"

"Not in the meantime. I can't go home until I'm able to run the farm without your sister's help. There's some risk of her despising me if I did go."

"You may be right; I can't judge," Dalton thoughtfully agreed. "Now I could, of course, find an excuse for getting you dismissed, but I know you both too well to imagine that plan would work. You would go somewhere else, while though Helen is generous there's a hard streak in her. I really think she'd like you better afterwards if you carried your intentions out."

He paused and smiled. "She got the money you object to in a very curious way—by refusing to indulge the wishes of our only rich relation. I was more compliant because his plans met my views, and he paid for my education, but when he died we found Helen had got her share and mine. I understand he told his lawyer that he still thought her wrong; but if she thought she was right, she was justified in refusing, and he admired her pluck."

"She has pluck," said Festing. "On the whole I don't think that makes things much better for me. Anyhow, I've taken this contract and I've got to stay with it."

"I'll help you as far as I can," said Dalton, who soon afterwards left the shack.

CHAPTER XX

FESTING GETS TO WORK

Mist rolled among the pines and it was raining hard when Festing led his team down the hill. He wore big rubber boots and slickers, and a heavy log trailed behind the horses through the mud. Some distance above the river the slope was gradual, and it was necessary to haul the logs to the skidway he had built. They would then run down without help; indeed, the difficulty was to stop them when they reached the track. Festing was wet and dirty, and the sweating horses were splashed. When he stopped to unhook the chain, three or four men came up with cant-poles, and struggling in the churned-up mire, rolled the log to the top of the incline.

A shallow, undulating trough scored the hillside, crossed at short intervals by small logs, split up the middle and laid with their round sides on top. It looked something like a switchback railway, only that while the incline varied, all the undulations ran down hill. A few logs rested insecurely on the top skids, and the men put the one Festing had brought below the rest. Then they threw down their poles and Festing looked about.

Water filled the hollows in the wavy line of skids, which vanished at the edge of a steeper dip and reappeared below, to plunge out of sight again. Its end was banked up with wet gravel near the track. Festing could not see the track, but the opposite side of the river was visible, with the island, near which two wire-ropes skimmed the surface of the flood. A man

Harold Bindloss

stood on the skids about half way down and presently waved his arm.

"Watch out below!" he shouted and signed to Festing. "All clear! You can start her off."

Festing seized a handspike and the skids groaned as the big log began to move. The men helped and sprang back as it gathered speed. Water flew up, the bark tore off in crumpled flakes, and the wet timber smoked. The other logs were smaller and easier launched, but they did not gain the momentum of the first, which plunged furiously down hill and flung up its thin end as it leaped over the edge of the dip.

"She's surely hitting up the pace," one of the men remarked.

"The mud is greasing the skids," said Festing, who began to run down the incline when the man below shouted.

Two of the others followed, but stopped at the top of the last pitch, which ended in the bank of gravel close above the track. The logs, spread out at intervals, rushed down, rising and falling on the uneven skids. Showers of mud and water marked their progress; there was a crash as a smashed skid was flung into the air, and a roar when the leading mass plowed through fallen gravel. Stones shot out and Festing saw smoke and sparks, but the logs rushed on, and he wondered anxiously whether the bank would stop them. So far, it had served its purpose, but he was doubtful about it now, and hoped there was nobody on the track beneath.

The big log reached the bank and ran half way up the short incline before its speed slackened much. Festing held his breath as he watched, for some gravel cars had come down the track, and he could not tell where they were. The log was going slower, but he doubted if it would stop.

It plowed on through the gravel, which shot up all round, and then the end of the bank seemed to fall away. There was a shower of stones; the butt of the log went down and its after end tilted up. Then it lurched out of sight and there was a heavy crash below. After this Festing heard a confused din, and imagined, though he could not see, the mass of timber plunging down the precipitous slope, smashing rocks and scattering gravel as it went. The noise stopped, he heard a splash, and as the following logs leaped the broken bank, the first shot half its length out of water, and falling again, drove down stream.

The rope at the island caught it while a trolley ran down, but the straining wire curved and parted, and the trolley fell into the river as the log swept on. The others followed and vanished in a turmoil of muddy foam, and Festing went down to the track. Things might have been worse, for nobody was hurt, although some yards of road-bed had been carried away and a derrick he had built to put the logs on the cars was smashed. As he studied the damage a wet and angry engineer ran up.

"You have got to stop your blamed logs jumping down like that! They've broken a steel rope and there's a new trolley-skip in the river!"

"I'm sorry," Festing answered. "I'll try to get the skip out as soon as possible, and you can trust me to stop more logs getting away, for my own sake."

"There'll be trouble if you let your lumber loose on me, and I want the skip soon," said the other. "A stranger asked for you a few minutes ago and I sent him up the hill."

He went away and Festing's men came up.

"Pretty rough luck, boss!" one remarked. "What are we going to do about it?"

"We'll grade up the gravel dump to begin with, and then make a new derrick," Festing answered gloomily. "It doesn't look as if I'd get much profit on the first week's work."

He moved off, and as he scrambled up the bank met a man coming down. Both stopped abruptly and Festing frowned.

"What in thunder has brought you, Bob?" he asked.

"They told me you were up the hill," Charnock said, smiling. "I came in on the last construction train."

"But why did you come?"

"I suppose you mean—Why did I come to bother you again? Well, the explanation will take some time, and it's confoundedly muddy and raining hard. When are you likely to be unoccupied?"

Festing tried to control his annoyance. The accident had disturbed him and he was not pleased to see Charnock, whom he did not wish to make free of his shack.

"What have you been doing since you arrived?" he asked.

"Sitting in the bunk-house and waiting for the rain to stop. Then I got dinner with the boys, and afterwards went to see a rather nice young fellow called Dalton. I told him I was a friend of yours, and he half promised to give me a job."

"You don't seem to know who he is?" Festing remarked.

"I don't; but I thought he looked hard at me when he heard my name. However, don't disturb yourself on my account; I'm pretty comfortable in the bunk-house."

"Very well. You had better come to my shack when work stops. I can't leave my men now."

Charnock strolled off with his usual languid air, and Festing resumed his work. He could not imagine what Charnock wanted, but wished he had stopped away. In the meantime, he had much to do and drove his men hard, until a steam-whistle hooted and they threw down their tools. His supper was ready when he reached the shack, but Charnock had not arrived, and although this was something of a relief, he felt annoyed. He had told him to come when work stopped, but the fellow was never punctual. An hour later Charnock walked in.

"I thought I'd better wait until after supper," he said. "My coming now leaves you more at liberty to turn me out."

"To begin with, I'd like to know why you came at all?"

"Sadie thought it was time I did something useful, and I agreed. It's obvious that if anything useful can be done, I'm the proper person to undertake the job. Now you understand me, shall I go on?"

Festing nodded. Charnock's careless good humor had vanished; he looked embarrassed but resolute, as if he meant to carry out a disagreeable task. This was something new for Bob.

"Very well," the latter resumed. "In order to clear the ground, do you imagine I'm in love with your wife?"

"I'm sure Helen is not in love with you," Festing rejoined.

"That's much, but we have got to talk about the other side of the matter," said Charnock quietly. "I went to your home with Sadie because I thought she and Helen could learn something from each other; while I suspect she thought your society was good for me. It's obvious that Helen agreed, and Sadie and I will always be grateful for her staunchness in sticking to us, although you disliked it. Whether I'm worth the quarrel or not is another thing. I hope you understand me as far as I've gone."

Festing made a sign and Charnock continued: "Very well. There was a time when I loved Helen, or honestly thought I did, but I imagine we had both found out our mistake when I gave her up. It's certain that she would not have been satisfied with me. Our romance came to nothing and was done with long since; there's now no woman who could rouse the feeling I have for my wife."

He got up and leaned upon his chair, with his eyes fixed on Festing. "When I told you I was going to be married, you showed your confounded supercilious pity! You thought I was making a fatal mistake. Well, you're not a clever fellow, Stephen, but that was the worst blunder you ever made. Marrying Sadie is perhaps the only wise thing I have done. She has borne with my follies, hustled me when I needed it, and helped me to fight my weaknesses; and if there's any hope of my being a useful man, I owe it to her. Now it's obvious that I can't draw comparisons, but I think you see where this leads."

"I do see," said Festing, who felt somewhat moved. He had not heard Charnock talk like this before, and the note in his voice was significant. He smiled, to ease the strain, as he replied: "Comparisons would be particularly awkward just now, Bob. Besides, they're unnecessary, I'm convinced!"

"Then there's no reason you shouldn't go home, and I've come to take you back."

Festing shook his head. "There are two reasons. In the first place, I've taken a contract."

"That fellow, Dalton, would probably let you off."

"It's uncertain, and I don't mean to ask. You don't seem to know that Dalton is Helen's brother."

Charnock laughed. "Then I've no doubt he knows who I am; his manner ought to have given me a hint. The situation has a touch of ironical humor, and perhaps the strangest thing is that we should now be better friends than we have been yet. But what still prevents your going back?"

"Helen's money. I can't beg from her, after refusing the only thing she has asked."

"You're a bit of a fool," Charnock remarked with a grin. "I've begged from Sadie often and imagine she liked me for it; anyhow she expected it. But if you have made up your mind, I expect I can't persuade you."

Festing's gesture indicated an unshaken resolve, and Charnock said: "Then I'm going to stop and see you through."

"That's ridiculous!" said Festing, who was strongly moved now. "You must think of Sadie. You can't stop; I won't allow it!"

Charnock's eyes twinkled. "I expect Sadie will bear the separation. For one thing, we lost our crop and she'll save money while I'm away. She's not parsimonious, but she hates to waste dollars, and must have found me expensive now and then. Then I mean to earn something, and can imagine her surprise when I show her my wages check."

On the surface, his mood was humorous, but Festing got a hint of something fine beneath. "But," he said, "you mustn't stay, and I'd sooner you didn't joke."

"Then I'll be serious; but after this there's no more to be said. Don't imagine it's altogether for your sake I'm going to stay. You know what I owe Sadie, and I want to show that her labor has not all been lost. in fact, I've got my opportunity and mean to seize it. Then if you feel some reparation is due to your wife, you can finish the work you made her drop. Help me to cut out liquor and stay with my job, and if you have trouble with your contract, I'll help all I can. Is it a bargain?"

"It's a bargain," said Festing quietly. "Now I think we'll talk about something else."

He sat still for some time after Charnock left. His bitterness against his wife had gone, and it was plain that he had been a fool. For all that, he could not go home yet; the money was still an obstacle. Pride forbade his letting Helen support him. Moreover, he felt that to act against his convictions now would cost him her respect. There was perhaps no ground for supposing she felt much respect for him, but he meant to keep all she had.

Then he got up and straightened the blankets in his bunk. The sooner he finished his contract, the sooner he could return, and there was much to be done next morning. The job had not begun well.

He got up at sunrise and spent several days repairing the damage the accident had caused, after which, for a time, things went smoothly. Then, one morning, he stood on a rocky ledge of the island, waiting while two of his men dragged an iron pulley backwards and forwards along a trolley wire.

The morning was clear and cold, and the snow had crept nearer the belt of dwindling pines that looked like matches tufted with moss. They grew in size as they rolled down the tremendous slopes, until they towered above the track in tall, dark spires. The mist had gone; rocks and trees and glistening summits were sharply cut, but the valley was rather marked by savage grandeur than beauty. There was something about its aspect that struck a warning note. It had a look of belonging to a half-finished world, into which man might only venture at his peril.

The river had fallen and its turbid green had faded, for the frost had touched the glaciers that fed it on the heights, but the stream ran fast, swirling round the island and breaking into eddies. In one place, a white streak marked a rebound of the current from an obstacle below, and it was across this spot the men dragged the pulley. A chain and hook hung from the latter, and they were fishing for the skip that was lost when the log broke the rope.

Festing had spent the most part of the previous day trying

different plans for grappling the skip, but the fast currents and smooth side of the big steel bucket had baffled him. His efforts had cost time and money, and he began to realize that he must give it up or try dangerous means. The chain stopped and tightened as the hook struck something below the surface, but next moment it moved on again, and when this had happened a number of times Festing raised his hand.

"You can quit, boys," he said, and turned to a man close by. "She must have fallen with the shackles where the hook can't get hold, but I think she's only about three feet under water."

The other studied the broken surface. The water was not transparent, but here and there a darker patch indicated a rock below. The eddies made a revolving slack along the bank, but near the skip joined the main current in its downstream rush.

"I've a notion there's a gully between her and us," he remarked. "Anyhow, we'll try to wade, if you like."

Festing threw off his jacket and plunged in. When he had gone a few feet he was up to his waist and it cost him an effort to keep his feet. After two or three more steps, the bottom fell away and, floundering savagely, he sank to his shoulders. Then his companion pulled him back.

"The gully's there all right," the man remarked when they clambered out. "Say, that water's surely cold."

"It will be colder soon when the ice comes down, and if the skip's to be got out, we must get her now. I think I could reach her by swimming."

The other looked doubtful, but Festing took off his heavy boots, and picking up the end of the rope they had used to move the pulley, walked to the edge of the island. He was now a short distance above the skip, and hoped the eddies would help him to reach the ledge it rested on before he was swept past; but he must avoid being drawn into the main stream, since there was not much chance of landing on the foam-swept rocks lower down. Making sure he had enough slack rope, he plunged in.

An eddy swung him out-shore, towards the dangerous rush; the cold cramped his muscles and cut his breath, but he was already below the spot he had left, and there was no time to lose. The white streak that marked the skip seemed to forge up-stream to meet him, and he swam savagely until he was in the broken water and something struck his foot. Then he arched his back and dived, groping with his hands. He grasped the slippery side of the skip and felt the shackle loop. With some trouble he got the rope through, and then tried to put his feet on the bottom. They were swept away and he came up gasping, knowing he had made a mistake that might cost him dear.

He held the end of the rope, but had been carried several yards down-stream, and the lost ground must be regained. The rope was rather a hindrance than a help, since the men on the bank could only haul him back to the skip and drag him under water, while he must pull the slack through the loop as he struggled to land. If he got out of the eddies he would be swept past the island, but he did not mean to let the rope go yet.

A revolving eddy swung him in-shore, but the reflux caught and drove him a few yards lower down. The men were shouting, but he could not tell what they said. The roar of water bewildered him, and he fixed his eyes upon the rocks that slid past until a wave washed across his face. For a moment or two he saw nothing, and then was vaguely conscious that a trolley was running down the wire above. An indistinct object hung from the trolley and next moment fell away from it. A dark body splashed into the water, vanished, and came up close by. Then he was seized by the shoulder and driven towards the bank.

The men had stopped shouting and ran into the water at the island's lower end. Festing drifted towards them, but it looked as if he would be carried past. The drag of the rope kept him back, and his strength was going, but he braced himself for an effort and felt a helping push. Then somebody seized his hand, he was pulled forward, and felt bottom as he dropped his feet. In another few moments he staggered up the bank and gave the nearest man the end of the rope.

"Stick to that," he gasped, and turned to see who had helped him.

"Bob!" he exclaimed.

Charnock dashed the water from his hair and face. "Thought you mightn't make it and jumped on a trolley they were loosing off. But we had better change our clothes."

"Come to my shack," said Festing. "Signal them to send a trolley, boys."

CHAPTER XXI

CHARNOCK TRIES HIS STRENGTH

The skip that crossed the river was loaded, and Charnock and Festing were forced to wait until it came back. They climbed to a platform on the bridge-pier and stood for some minutes, shivering in the wind. The skip would only carry one, and when it arrived Charnock made Festing get in.

"You were in the water longest," he said. "Get aboard as quick as you can!"

Festing was swung across the river, but waited until Charnock arrived, when they ran up the hill to the former's shack. The fire was out and Festing's face was blue, while Charnock's teeth chattered as he threw off his clothes. Festing gave him another suit.

"I'm afraid they're not very dry, but they're the best I've got," he said. "You did a plucky thing, Bob."

"Not at all, and you would, no doubt, have landed if I hadn't come. You see, the skip was starting and I didn't stop to think. But it's horribly cold. Where's your towel?"

He put on the half-dry clothes and went to the door. "I'm not often in such a hurry to get back to work, but if I don't move I'll freeze. See you later!"

"Stop a moment," Festing called. "Do you find the bunk-house comfortable?"

"It's not luxurious, but doesn't leak very much unless it rains unusually hard."

"Then why not come up here at night? I haven't another bunk or I'd have suggested it before, but a carload of ship-lap has arrived and I dare say Kerr will let me have a few boards."

"Thanks; I'd like that," said Charnock, who hurried away.

Soon afterwards Festing resumed his work. Kerr allowed him to take the boards, and when he had finished his supper Charnock came in. Sitting down by the fire, he filled his pipe.

"There's more room here and you can dry your clothes," he remarked, stretching out his legs to the blaze.

"We're going to talk about what happened this morning," Festing replied. "I was getting exhausted when you jumped off the skip."

"After all, I only gave you a push now and then. I was fresh, and imagine I swim better than you."

"It's possible. I don't swim very well."

"Then why did you go into the rapid? I call it a blamed silly thing!"

"I felt I had to recover the skip."

"Not at all," said Charnock, with a grin. "The skip could have stopped where it was. For a man who thinks much, you're ridiculously illogical; got no proper sense of relative values. Your business is to carry out your contract, and not risk your life for a rusty bucket."

"You risked yours!"

"I didn't. The only risk I ran was knocking your head off with my heavy boots. But if you hadn't begun the folly, I wouldn't have jumped, if the river had been full of the company's skips."

Then the door opened and the head contractor's engineer came in.

"You did a plucky thing to-day, Festing," he began; but Charnock interrupted.

"Don't spoil my argument, Mr. Norton. I've been proving he made a fool of himself."

"Then there were two of you," Norton rejoined. "The trolley was running fast, and if you had dropped a few yards farther out, you wouldn't have got back." He turned to Festing. "I was rather mad about it when you broke the wire, and of course wanted the skip. Still I didn't mean you to take a risk like that. We could have fixed the thing."

"A matter of bookkeeping?" Charnock suggested. "Much depends on how you charge up your costs, and one understands that doing it cleverly leads to promotion. The worst is when you come to the total—"

"I'll talk to you later. You're up against a big proposition, Festing; but if you find yourself in a tight place and I've a man or two to spare, or can help—"

"Thanks; I may take advantage of your promise," Festing replied, and Norton turned to Charnock.

"You are doing better than I expected when Dalton sent you along."

"I imagine my recent activity would surprise my friends, and you're a stranger. However, I suppose I've got to keep it up so long as I work on the road."

"That's sure," said the other dryly. "Well, I didn't think it prudent to give you much at first, and now I'll mark you up an extra fifty cents."

He stopped a few minutes, and when he went out Charnock laughed. "Not a bad sort, but I'm puzzled by my satisfaction at getting three dollars more a week. If I wanted a check not long since, I'd only to look penitent and go to Sadie."

After this, they sat smoking quietly for a time, and then Charnock drew up his legs and frowned.

"What's the matter?" Festing asked.

"Nothing much," said Charnock. "I've got a bit of a weakness I don't think you know about. Neuralgic, I imagine; it grips me here." He indicated the region between his belt and chest. "Comes and goes when I'm not quite up to my proper form."

"Then I expect jumping into the river and standing about in wet clothes brought it on."

"No; I have had it before. Besides, I've often been as wet; so have you. Anyhow, the pain's going, and there's a thing I forgot to mention. I met Wilkinson this afternoon."

Festing knitted his brows. "Wilkinson! What do you think has brought him?"

"Chance and Sadie's scheming. I've cause to suspect she forced him off his ranch, though she would probably wish she hadn't meddled if she knew she'd sent him here. As he looked surprised when he saw me, I imagine he'd no particular object in coming, except that he wanted a job."

"Did you speak to him?"

"I did not. It's very possible he'd have resented my remarks. Then I was on the company's business and the foreman was about."

"Well," said Festing thoughtfully, "it might be better to keep out of his way as far as you can. I don't know that he's likely to do us harm, but wish he had gone somewhere else."

They let the matter drop and talked about other things until they went to bed. Next morning broke bracingly cold, but thin mist rolled among the pines a few hundred feet above the track. For the most part the climate of the interior of British Columbia is dry, and there are belts where artificial irrigation is employed, but some of the valleys form channels for the moist winds from the Pacific. Except in the bitter cold-snaps, it was seldom that the white peaks above the track were visible, and now something in the atmosphere threatened heavy rain.

Charnock began his work as usual with the gravel gang. It was his business to spread the ballast thrown off the cars by the plow that traveled along the train, and although the labor was not exhausting it had tried his strength at first. His muscles, however, were hardening, and until the last few days, he had been able to scatter heavy shovelfuls of stones with a dexterous jerk that distributed them among the ties.

Streaks of dingy haze that looked like steam rose from the river. The fresh smell of pines hung about the track, and the clash of shovels and ringing of hammers mingled harmoniously with the deep-toned roar of the rapids. The cold braced the muscles and stirred the blood, and the sounds of activity had an invigorating influence while the day was young, but Charnock felt slack. His pain had gone, but he was conscious of a nervous tension and knew what it meant. A small blister on his hand annoyed him, he growled at comrades who got in his way, and swore when the gravel fell in the wrong place. Somehow he could not get the stuff to go where it ought.

For all that, he felt no serious inconvenience until about eleven o'clock, when a stinging pain spread across the front of his body. For a few moments he leaned on his shovel and gasped, but the pang moderated and he roused himself when the foreman looked his way. He must try to hold out for another hour, and he savagely attacked his pile of stones. When the echoes of the whistle filled the hollow he had some trouble in reaching the bunk-house, but felt better after dinner and a smoke, which he enjoyed sitting on a box by the stove; but the time for rest was short. The foreman drove him out, and feeling very sore and stiff, he resumed work.

About four o'clock another pang shot through him and he dropped his shovel and sat down on a heap of ties, hoping to get a few minutes' rest before the gravel train came up. The pain was troublesome, but not dangerous. It might only bother him for a day or two, but it might last a week. Rest was the best cure, but sick men were not wanted at the camp. One must work or go, and when a cascade of gravel poured off the cars as the plow moved along he pulled himself together.

It began to rain soon afterwards and he had left his slickers at the bunk-house, but he stuck to his work, while the sweat the effort caused him ran down his face, until the whistle blew. Then he went limply up the hill to Festing's shack.

"I thought I'd have supper with you, if you don't mind," he said. "Felt I couldn't stand for joining the boys. They've annoyed me all day and eat like hogs."

Festing gave him a sharp glance. Bob did not often lose his temper, but he looked morose.

"Of course I don't mind. Sit down."

Charnock did so, and when Festing had filled his plate resumed: "This food is decently cooked, and I like my supper served and not thrown at me. Still, in view of what we're charged for board, it's annoying to think the contractor will be richer for a meal I haven't got."

"It's a new thing to find you parsimonious. I hope you'll keep it up."

Charnock's gloomy face softened. "I mean to. I'm thinking of Sadie's feelings when I come home with a wad of five-dollar bills. She won't be surprised; she'll get a shock."

He talked with better humor during the meal, but was silent afterwards and sat with half-closed eyes, stretching out his feet towards the crackling logs. Although the pain had nearly gone, it would, no doubt, begin again in the morning, and he might have some trouble in hiding his weakness from the foreman. He could lay off for a day or two, but as his wages would stop and his board would be charged, it would cost him something. Besides, if he laid off once or twice, he would be told to leave.

This, however, did not account for his moodiness. He knew of no cure except rest, but it was easy to find relief; a small dose of spirit would banish the pain for a time. The remedy was dangerous, particularly to him, since it offered an excuse for repeated indulgence, and he struggled with the temptation. Liquor was difficult to get, because there was no settlement for some distance and the engineers had tried to cut off supplies, but it could be got. In fact, Charnock knew where he could buy as much whisky as he wanted, at something above its proper price. So far he had not done so, but continued self-denial would require a stern effort. A drink would banish the pain and enable him to work.

He had not known it fail since he drove over to Wilkinson's one afternoon, when he had been loading prairie hay since early morning and had forgotten his lunch. He reached the homestead scarcely able to sit upright on the driving seat, and a man asked him what was the matter. When Charnock told him he sent Wilkinson for whisky.

"I know all about it; the blamed thing grips me now and then if I work too hard and cut out a meal," he said. "I'll fix you up for the rest of the day, but won't answer for your feeling pert to-morrow."

As a matter of fact, Charnock had felt worse, but obtained relief by increasing the dose. Indeed, he had once or twice done so with unfortunate consequences; but after Sadie bought the farm and saw he led a regular life the pain had gone and had not returned until he went to work on the track. Now he was not going to give in, but did not want to talk, and was glad that Festing was occupied with some calculations and left him alone.

Next morning he felt better and had two days' ease, after which the pain wrung him for the rest of the week. Somehow he stuck to his work, and his comrades, who were rudely sympathetic, helped him to elude the foreman's watchfulness. It was obvious that he could not keep it up, but the trouble often ended suddenly. Then an evening came when he could scarcely drag himself to the bunk-house for supper. It had rained all day and the building was overheated by a glowing stove and filled with the smell of rank tobacco and steaming clothes. Charnock could not eat the roughly served food, and for a time sat slack and limp, with the sweat upon his face, and his arms on the table. Then he got on his feet awkwardly and set off for Festing's shack.

The rain and cold revived him, but walking was difficult, and when he reached the shack he fell into a chair. Festing was not in, and Charnock remembered he had said something about having extra work to do. It was dark, but the log fire threw out a red light, and by and by Charnock, glancing round as the shadows receded, thought there was something unusual on the table. It looked like a bottle, but they kept no liquor in the shack. Festing was abstemious but Charnock suspected that he had practised some self-denial for his sake.

He waited until a blaze sprung up, and then his relaxed pose stiffened. It was a bottle of whisky, better stuff than the railroaders generally drank, for he knew the label. Moreover, when the light touched the glass the yellow reflection showed that it was full. He got up and approached the table, wondering how the liquor came there, until he saw some writing on the label. Picking up the bottle, he read his own name.

He put it down abruptly and stood with his hand clenched. The veins swelled on his forehead and the pain nearly left him as he fought with temptation. It was some weeks since he had tasted liquor, but this was not all. A drink would give him relief from the gnawing ache and perhaps a night's sound sleep. If he could get that, he might be well for most of the next day. But he shrank from the remedy. There was liquor enough to last some days, but the next bottle would not last as long, and he knew there would be another. He must resist and conquer his craving now.

He opened the door and picked up the bottle by the neck. With a swing of his arm he could throw it among the pines; he wanted to hear it smash. Victory could be won by a quick movement; but afterwards? The touch of the glass and the way the yellow liquid gleamed in the light fired his blood. If he was to win an enduring victory, he must fight to a finish.

Leaving the bottle in the light, he moved his chair and sat down close by, after which he looked at his watch. He would give himself half an hour. If he could hold out now, he need not be afraid again, because the odds against him would never be so heavy. The craving was reenforced by pain and bodily fatigue; his jangled nerves demanded a stimulant. Yet to win would make the next conflict easier, and he had resources that he tried to marshal against the enemy.

The rough work on the track had given him confidence. He had always had physical courage and muscular strength, and it was something to feel he could hold his own with his comrades at a strenuous task. Moreover, his saving Festing from the river had restored his self-respect. But he had stronger allies, and his face got hot as he thought of the two women who had fought for him when he had scarcely tried to help himself.

Sadie had given up her ambitions and was content to live at the lonely farm because she thought it best for him. He remembered the bitter disappointments he had brought her and how he had found her sitting, depressed and tired, at his neglected work when he came home from some fresh extravagance. Sometimes she had met him with the anger he deserved, but as a rule she had shown a patience that troubled him now. Then there was Helen, who had borne slander and estrangement from her husband for his sake. Both had made costly sacrifices, of which he was unworthy; but it was unthinkable that the sacrifices should be made in vain.

Perhaps it was his imagination, or the proximity of relief, but the physical torment he suffered got worse. He could not sit straight, and leaned forward, with head bent and hands grasping the sides of his chair, until he looked at his watch. Ten minutes had gone, but he must hold out for twenty minutes more. Fumbling awkwardly in his pocket, he got his tobacco pouch. He did not want to smoke, but could occupy some time by filling his pipe, and did so with slow deliberation. Then he let the match go out as an idea dawned on him. The bottle had been put there with an object.

Wilkinson hated Sadie. He had struck at her and injured Helen, but had plotted a harder blow. The plot had, however, miscarried, for Charnock almost forgot his pain in his fury. The fellow was a dangerous reptile, and could not be allowed to hurt Sadie by his poisonous tricks. Charnock meant to punish him, but must first overcome the insidious ally the other had counted on. He looked at his watch again. A quarter of an hour had gone; he felt stronger, and more confident. For all that, the fight was stern, and at length Festing, entering quietly, was surprised to find Charnock sitting with his watch in his hand. His brows were knit; his face looked pinched and damp.

"What are you doing, Bob?" he asked.

"Trying my strength," said Charnock, who got up. "Three

Harold Bindloss

minutes yet to go, but I think we can take it that I've won."

"I don't understand. Is this a joke?"

"Do I look as if I'm joking?" Charnock rejoined, with a forced smile. "Anyhow, I'd like you to notice that I'm perfectly sober and this bottle has not been opened, although I've sat opposite it for nearly half an hour. I'd have finished the half-hour if you had not come in."

Festing picked up the bottle and read the writing. "Who brought the thing here?"

"I suspect Wilkinson. He knows a drink would stop the pain."

"Ah," said Festing quietly. "I think I understand! You have made a good fight, Bob, and I believe you've won. But we'll take precautions; it will be some satisfaction to throw out the stuff."

He went to the door, but Charnock stopped him.

"Hold on! I mean to keep the satisfaction to myself. Give me the cursed thing!"

Festing put the bottle in his hand, and opening the door Charnock swung it round his head and let it go. There was a crash as it struck a tree, and he went back to his chair.

"That's done with! It's remarkable, but I don't feel as sore as I did. Perhaps the effort of resisting was a counter-irritant. However, we have said enough about it. Tell me how you got on with the job that kept you late."

CHAPTER XXII

FESTING'S NEW PARTNER

Charnock felt better next morning and luck favored him. An accident to the gravel train disorganized the work, and he and some others were dismissed for the afternoon. He went to Festing's shack, and making himself comfortable by the fire, opened a tattered book and enjoyed several hours of luxurious idleness. After his exertions in the rain and mud, it was delightful to bask in warmth and comfort and rest his aching limbs. The next day was Sunday and he lounged about the shack, sometimes reading and sometimes bantering his comrade. The pain had gone and he felt cheerful.

When he returned to work on Monday he was sent with a bag of bolts to the bridge, and presently reached a spot where the heavy rain had washed away the track. For about a dozen yards the terrace cut in the hillside had slipped down, leaving a narrow shelf against the bank. The shelf broke off near the middle, where a gully had opened in the hill. Water flowed through the gap, and in order to get across one must pick a way carefully over the steep, wet slope. This, however, would save a toilsome climb, and Charnock, jerking the bag higher on his shoulders, went on.

A few minutes later he saw Wilkinson come round a corner. One of them would have to go back to let the other pass, and it would be difficult to turn if they met at the gully. Charnock did not mean to give way, and with his arms crooked to support his load, he required some room. There was no way up the torn bank, and on the other side a nearly perpendicular slope of wet soil and gravel ran down to the river. In places, the surface was broken by small, half-buried firs.

When both were near the gully Wilkinson stopped, and Charnock, whose head was bent, thought he had not known who he was. He certainly looked surprised, and Charnock was conscious of rather grim amusement as he guessed the reason. Wilkinson had, no doubt, not expected him to be capable of carrying a heavy bag along the dangerous ledge.

"Hallo!" he said. "The boys told me you were crippled by your pains."

"I was. The pain's gone."

"Rest's a good cure," said Wilkinson. "You got laid off on Saturday, didn't you?"

The curiosity that had made Charnock stop was satisfied. Since Wilkinson's work kept him at some distance from the gravel gang, it looked as if he had made inquiries about Charnock, and had probably been surprised to learn he had started with the others. There was, however, no use in taxing the fellow with trying to make him drunk, because he would deny that he knew anything about the whisky or declare that he had sent it with a friendly object.

"Yes," he said, "but I didn't need the cure as badly as you think. However, I'm not in a talkative mood and this bag is heavy. I'll trouble you to get out of the way."

Wilkinson looked hard at him. Charnock knew why he had sent the whisky and meant to quarrel, but was shrewd enough to choose his ground.

"You can dump your bag and wait until I get past."

"Not at all," said Charnock. "I don't see why I should pick up the load again to convenience you. Anyhow, I'm going on, and the thing takes up some room."

Wilkinson measured the distance across the gap. He imagined he could reach the other side first and squeeze against the bank, when Charnock must take the outside and would probably fall. He did not mean to be forced back, particularly as there were men at work not far off who had, no doubt, noted Charnock's aggressive attitude. The latter, however, was quicker than he thought, and reached the dangerous spot before Wilkinson got across. Splashing, and slipping in the mud, he advanced recklessly, and Wilkinson could not turn back. Moreover, he could not strike Charnock, because he was in the workmen's view, and the railroaders would not approve his attacking an apparently defenseless man. He thought Charnock knew this, but the fellow was not as defenseless as he looked. The heavy bag gave him a certain stability and momentum.

"If you come any farther before I find a hold, we'll both go down," he said.

"It looks like that," Charnock agreed. "I don't mean to stop."

Wilkinson clutched at the slippery bank but the wet gravel tore out. It was impossible to get up, and if he tried to scramble down, he might not stop until he fell into the river. He glanced at Charnock's set face and got something of a shock. He had thought the fellow meant to bluff and would give way if he were resolutely met; Charnock was impulsive, but never stayed with a thing. Now, however, he looked dangerous.

Driving his boots into the mud, Wilkinson braced himself, with one foot so placed that it might trip his antagonist. Then he set his lips as he met the shock. Charnock struck him with his shoulder and forced him backwards by the weight of the bag. The mud slipped under his feet; he staggered and clawed at the bank, but his fingers found no hold. They plowed through the miry gravel, and falling face downwards, he rolled down the hill.

Charnock lurched across the gully and stopped when he reached the shelf. Wilkinson had swung round on his descent and his head was lowest. He was sliding down rather slower, and there were some trees not far off. Charnock did not care if he brought up among them or not, and watched with a curious dispassionate interest. The fellow looked ridiculous as he went down, scattering the gravel with his hands. He was in some danger, but this was his affair.

Wilkinson rolled against the thin branches of a half-buried tree, which caught and turned him partly round. The branches broke and he went down sideways, until he and a wave of loosened gravel struck another tree. This stopped him, and Charnock plodded on until he was off the shelf.

"Better go down and fetch him, boys," he shouted to the other men. "I reckon he's not much the worse, except in temper, and you'll find a rope a piece back up the track."

He saw them start and then resumed his journey. Whether he was hurt or not, Wilkinson could talk, for he was pouring out scurrilous epithets. Charnock laughed as he stamped through the mud. His antagonist had got the worst of it, and there was a satisfactory explanation of their quarrel. They had met on a narrow path and neither would give way, but as Charnock was carrying the load he had put the other in the wrong. Wilkinson could not revenge himself by circulating the story he had told before because it would interest nobody at the camp, and Charnock's friendship with Festing would prove it untrue. In fact, he imagined Wilkinson would think it prudent to leave him alone.

He delivered the bag, and going back stopped at a spot where Festing and some others were fitting the end of a heavy beam into a pole. Charnock watched while the men dragged out the beam and then replaced it after deepening the hole. They were splashed and dirty, and presently Festing leaned upon his shovel while he got his breath.

"You seem determined to fix it properly," Charnock remarked.

Festing nodded. "There's no use in piling rock about half-bedded frames. It would mean trouble if they gave way under a freight train."

"You look ahead. The first difficulty is that if the frames don't hold up, you won't get paid. The engineers are responsible after the regular traffic starts, and I've no doubt they test a contractor's work. You would save something in wages if you built a pile-driver to sink those posts."

"I haven't the men or time. If I don't get this part of the work done before the frost comes, it's going to cost me more. It would mean using powder and making fires to thaw out the ground."

Charnock agreed and went on. He had been long enough over his errand and the foreman's tongue was sharp, but he mused about Festing as he picked his way across the pools between the ties. Festing's object was to make money, and he imagined, perhaps foolishly, that he had urgent ground for doing so, but he meant to make a good job. He felt his responsibility, and apart from this took a curious delight in doing things well. In fact, Festing's thoroughness was rather fine; he was an artist in his way. The artist's methods, however, were not as a rule profitable when applied to contract work. Then Charnock's meditations were rudely disturbed, for he heard a shout and saw the foreman had noted his cautious advance.

"Watch him coming, boys!" the latter remarked. "Like a blamed cat that's scared of wetting its pretty feet! Say, do you want a private car to move you along the track? Jump now and load up that trolley, you soft-bodied slob!"

Charnock obeyed, promptly and silently. He had, at first,

responded to encouragement of this kind by a witty retort, but had found the consequences unfortunate. There was no use in wasting delicate satire on a dolt. Besides, it was a relief to feel he was getting better and was able to work.

In the afternoon, he had occasion to pass the spot where Festing was occupied, and stopped to watch. The men were getting a big log on end; two steadying it and supporting part of the weight by a tackle fixed to its top, while Festing and another guided its foot into a hole. The ground was wet and slippery and their task looked almost beyond their strength, but Charnock knew he would get into trouble if he were seen going to their help. Since he was not in view of the foreman where he stood on top of the bank, it was prudent to remain there.

The log swayed as its point caught a stone, and Festing's hands slipped on the muddy bank. He shouted to the men at the tackle, who bent their backs and hauled, but the timber did not rise as it ought. Charnock, looking round, noted that the stake the tackle was fastened to was pulling out.

"Get from under! She's coming down on top of you!" he cried.

Festing looked up and saw the danger; but if the log fell it would not stop until it and the tackle plunged into the rapid below.

"Stay with it!" he gasped; and he and his companions braced themselves against the crushing weight.

The veins rose on his forehead. His back was arched and his wet slickers split, but it was plain to Charnock that the men could not hold up the timber, which would injure them if it fell. But with help they might perhaps move it enough for the point to sink into the hole before the tackle gave way, and Charnock leaped recklessly from the top of the bank. He knew what he was undertaking when he took hold. Festing would not let go; he meant to put the log into its socket, or let it start on its plunge to the river over his body.

For a few tense moments they struggled savagely, with slipping hands and labored breath, while Festing, using his head as a ram, pushed the point of the swaying mass nearer the hole. Then, when all could do no more, the strain suddenly slackened and there was a jar as the log, sliding through their arms, sank into the pit. After this, it was easier to hold it, while one threw in and beat down the gravel. Five minutes later, Charnock sat down on the bank. His face was crimson, his hands bled, and his chest heaved as he fought for breath, but he felt ridiculously satisfied.

"Thanks!" gasped Festing. "Lucky you came along. I thought she was going!"

"Blamed silly thing not to let her go," Charnock replied. "Some day your confounded obstinacy will ruin you. Anyhow, we've put her in. Not bad for a cripple!"

Then he sucked his torn fingers, and fearing that he might have to account for the delay, went about his business. It was curious that the tense exertion had not brought on the pain, but his back and shoulders were sore when he went to Festing's shack in the evening. The small, earth-floored room was dry and warm, and smelt pleasantly of resinous wood. They did not light the lamp, for although it was dark the red glow of the fire flickered about the walls. Charnock felt a comforting sensation of bodily ease as he lounged in his chair, and when he had smoked a pipe told Festing about his encounter with Wilkinson.

"I imagine the brute isn't hurt much, but don't know if I'm glad or not," he said. "He looked remarkably funny as he slid down the bank, with his arms and legs spread out like a frog. Suppose I should have thought about the risk of his tobogganing into the river, but I didn't."

"Well, I expect he deserves all he got, and remember the

satisfaction it gave me to throw him out of the poolroom. Looks as if we were primitive."

"We're all primitive in this country," Charnock rejoined. "They have no use for philosophical refinement in Canada. Their objects are plain and practical and they employ simple means. We're not bothered by the conventions that handicap you at home. If a man hurts you, and you're big enough, you knock him out."

"We have both knocked out Wilkinson, but I'm not sure that we have done with him. The simple plan's not always as easy as it looks."

"I don't think he can make much trouble. If he does, one of us will knock him out again. As it will hurt us less than it hurts him, he'll probably get tired first."

They let the matter drop, and Festing presently remarked: "The rain makes things difficult, but it's lucky the frost keeps off. I must try to get the frames up at the awkward places before it begins."

"You haven't enough men."

"I could use more. Still, one couldn't engage men to come here on short notices, and if we get a long cold-snap I might have trouble to keep them employed. I could, of course, use a number of men and teams hauling out logs across the snow, but the heavier stuff won't be needed for some time, and I can't lock up my money. The small man's trouble is generally to finance his undertaking."

Charnock looked thoughtful. "Yes; that's where the pinch comes. You can't work economically unless you have capital. Sadie's a good business woman, and she often said that if you want to save dollars, you must spend some."

"Much depends on how you spend."

"Just so," said Charnock, smiling. "Betting against marked cards doesn't pay, but I've stopped that kind of thing. However, I think I could get you the money you need."

Festing looked hard at him. "You have none."

"Sadie has a pile. She'd give me enough with pleasure if she thought it would help towards my reform. But if you take the dollars, you've got to take me."

"Ah!" said Festing. "But why do you want to join?"

"To begin with, I'm getting avaricious and want to go home with my wallet full. Then I'm tired of my job. I suppose it's a foreman's privilege to insult his gang, but the brute we've got is about the limit. He's truculent but not very big, and some day, if I stop on, I'll pitch the hog into the river. Then I'll certainly get fired, and there'll be an end to my dreams of wealth."

Festing was silent for a few moments. He understood Charnock better now, and knew that when he was serious he often used a careless tone. Bob wanted to help him as much as he wanted to help himself, and he saw no reason to reject his plan. He must, however, be warned.

"If you join me, you run some risk of losing your money."

"Of course. It's obvious that you don't think the risk very big, and I'm willing to take a fighting chance."

"I don't know how big it is. That depends on the weather and accidents."

"Exactly," said Charnock. "If I join you with some money and teams, will it lessen, or add to, the risk?"

"It will lessen the risk."

"Will it reduce, or increase, your working costs?"

"I think the answer's obvious."

"Then it looks as if you'd be foolish to turn my offer down."

Festing got up and walked about irresolutely for a moment or two. Then he stopped with some color in his face.

"I called you a shirker, Bob, and ordered Helen to leave you alone. Now I see you're the better man and I'm a confounded, fault-finding prig. But you're not vindictive, and we'll let that go. The trouble is, I'm obstinate and sure of what I can do—at least, I was, though my confidence has got shaken recently. Well, I think I can finish this contract, but don't know. I've lost a good deal of money, and would hate to feel I might lose yours."

"That's the line you took with Helen," Charnock rejoined. "I'm not surprised that she was vexed, and since we're being frank, you're a little too proud of yourself yet. Anyhow, I like a plunge; it's exhilarating, and there's not much excitement in betting on a certainty." He paused and resumed with a twinkle: "Besides, if there is a loss, Sadie will stand for it."

Festing gave him a puzzled look, and he laughed.

"You don't understand yet? You're dull, Stephen. Now I'm not a greedy fellow, and my chief use for dollars is to spend them. I want to take back some money to show Sadie I've made good, and if we put this contract over she'll be satisfied and you'll have her gratitude. That's why I mean to make a job if I join you, and I imagine you're with me there. Well, perhaps I've said enough. Is it a bargain?"

"Yes," said Festing quietly, and they shook hands.

CHAPTER XXIII

CHARNOCK MAKES PROGRESS

Deep snow covered the hillside and the pines, with lower branches bent, rose in somber spires against the dazzling background. The river had shrunk and the dark water rolled in angry turmoil between ice-glazed rocks. Streaks of gray haze rose a foot or two into the nipping air, and the clash of shovels had a new, harsh ring. It was nearly dinner time, and Festing noted that his men had not done much since breakfast as he walked down the beaten hollow in the middle of the track. One could not tell how long the cold-snap would last, but it had already embarrassed him.

He stopped above an excavation where Charnock and another were cutting a hole in the frozen gravel. The former held a steel bar in blue, frost-cracked hands and twisted it in the cavity while his companion struck the end. He knelt, in a cramped pose, in the snow, and Festing smiled. Bob was fond of comfort, and it was strange to see him occupied like this. Then, noting the length of the bar, he thought they would not sink the hole deep enough for the blasting charge before dinner, which was unfortunate, because the powder fumes are poisonous and would hang about the spot for some time.

A few moments later the whistle blew, but Charnock and his companion did not stop, and Festing heard the thud of the hammer as he went on. This rather puzzled him. The work was hard and he had not expected Charnock's assistant to

Harold Bindloss

continue his task longer than he need. Festing was fastidiously just, and thought it shabby to steal a workman's time; moreover, he imagined that if he had asked the fellow to go on after the whistle blew he would have refused.

Curiosity led him to wait farther along the track until the thud of the hammer stopped. It looked as if Charnock was putting in the dynamite, and Festing hoped he would be careful with the detonator. By and by he heard a warning shout, and a moment or two afterwards saw a blaze of light. Then there was a curious sharp report, and pieces of broken rock splashed into the river. The gorge rang with echoes and a mass of gravel roared down the slope. It was obviously a good shot and had moved more spoil than Festing expected. A glance at his watch showed that the others had given up a quarter of an hour of their short noon rest.

Festing set off again, and in the meantime, Charnock, holding his breath as he stood on the snowy bank, looked down into the hole the explosion had made.

"I think we've made a first-class job," he said, stepping back out of reach of the fumes. "I like the company's taste in powder."

"It's better than ours," his companion agreed with a chuckle.

"Much better. The company is richer than us. It would have saved us some hard work if you had hooked a few more sticks."

"They're a mean crowd," said the other. "Blamed suspicious how they tally out their stores, but I'll see what I can do. I'd sooner use good powder than cut frozen gravel with the pick."

"The pick's no tool for white men. We won't use it unless we're forced," Charnock answered, and both laughed.

He went to the shack, and while they were at dinner Festing asked: "How did you persuade Jim Brown to stop until you fired the shot?"

"I didn't persuade him. I took it for granted he would stop."

"He's a good man, but sometimes sulky if one wants him to do what he thinks is outside his job. I don't imagine I'd have found him so obliging if I'd asked him to keep on."

Charnock laughed. "Perhaps not; our methods are different. You would have explained logically why the thing ought to be finished; but that's a mistake. There are not so many logical people as you think. Instead of arguing, I made a silly joke."

"You certainly get on with the boys," said Festing thoughtfully.

"They're a careless, irresponsible crowd. I'm irresponsible, too, and they understand me. They trust you, but you sometimes puzzle them. Perhaps that accounts for the thing."

Festing talked about something else until they went back to work. Next morning he climbed the hill to a level bench where some of his men were busy hauling logs to the top of the skids. It was easier to move the big trunks across the snow, and he had seized the opportunity to get some out, but was surprised when he saw the number ready to be sent down. While he examined them, Charnock, sprinkled with dusty snow, came up, leading a heavy Percheron team. They dragged a log into place, and then Charnock unhooked the chain and beat his hands. His skin-coat was ragged and his fur-cap battered, but he looked alert and virile as he stood by the steaming horses' heads. The gray trunks of the pines made a good background for his tall figure, which had an almost statuesque grace.

"You look very well, Bob," Festing remarked. "It's obvious that the pain has gone."

"It won't come back while the dry weather lasts; I don't know about afterwards. These are pretty good logs."

"I was wondering how you were able to bring up so many."

"They're here; that's the main thing. You can look after other matters and leave this to me."

"If you don't mind, I'd like to see how you did it," Festing replied.

"Oh, well! You're a persistent fellow; I suppose you had better come along."

Festing went with him and stopped where a gang of men were at work among the fallen trees. Two, swaying backwards and forward with rhythmic precision, dragged a big crosscut-saw through a massive trunk. Others swung bright axes, and the wood rang with the noise of their activity. All were usefully employed, but there were more of them than Festing expected.

"The two boys with the cantpoles belong to the contractor's bridge-gang," he said. "What are they doing here?"

"I think I told you Norton said I could have them when we were moving the big poles," Charnock replied. "He saw I needed help."

"But that was some days since. He sent them to help at a particular job which you have finished."

"He hasn't asked me to send them back. Looks as if he'd forgotten them. Anyhow, they're useful."

"We have no right to keep the men. How did you get them to stop?"

"That was easy," said Charnock. "The cooking at the bunkhouse isn't very good, and I told our man to find out what they liked. In fact, I said we'd stand for it if he put up a better hash."

Festing laughed. The plan was characteristic of Bob's methods.

"You must send them back," he said, and went away, doubting if Bob would do so.

For all that, he admitted that Charnock was doing well. He stuck to his work, and had a talent for handling men. Nobody was at all afraid of him; but his sympathetic forbearance with his helpers' weaknesses and his whimsical humor seemed to pay much better than bullying. He made a joke where Festing frowned, but the latter felt thoughtful as he went down-hill. One must make allowance, but Bob was something of a responsibility.

A week later, he got a jar as he stood with Charnock beside a part of the track they had laboriously underpinned. The ballast train was coming down, filling the valley with its roar, and the beaten snow heaved among the ties as the big cars rolled by. The rails sank beneath the wheels and then sprang up until the load on the next axle pressed them down again; the snow flaked off the side of the road-bed, which was built up with broken rock. Festing thought the movement was too marked and waited for the locomotive, which was coupled to the back of the train.

The engine was of the ponderous, mountain type, but it ran smoothly, with steam cut off, and although the ground trembled and the rails groaned as it passed, there was no threatening disturbance.

"The bank's holding up, and this was about the worst spot," Charnock remarked. "We had some trouble in bedding the king posts in the slippery stuff."

Then Kerr gave them a nod as he went by. "Looks pretty good, and they have a full load on the cars."

"I think we'll wait until the train comes back," Festing said to Charnock. "The engineer will open the throttle wide to pull her up the grade."

They sat down in a hollow of the bank, for a bitter wind blew through the gorge, and after a time the roar of falling gravel echoed among the pines. Then there was a heavy snorting and the locomotive came round a curve, rocking and belching out black smoke. The cars banged and rattled, slowing with jarred couplings and rolling on when the driving wheels gripped. Festing waited anxiously, because the wheels of a locomotive when driven hard strikes what is called a hammer blow.

By and by the ground began to throb; the vibration got sharper, and Festing watched the track as the engine passed. Cinders rattled about him, there was a mist of snow, but he saw the cross-ties start and the rails spring up and down. Then the clanging cars sped past, and when they had gone he climbed down the side of the bank.

It was now bare of snow and one could see the stones. Two or three had fallen, and the edges of the others were a little out of line. The unevenness was marked, and although one or two of the heads of the timbers had moved, the movement might not have caught Festing's eye had he not known the treacherous nature of their support. He did not think anybody else would notice that they were not quite in their proper place.

"I'm afraid we're up against trouble, Bob," he said.

Charnock looked unusually thoughtful. "The engineer had to start from a dead stop and turn on full steam. That made the jarring worse, but it wouldn't happen with the ordinary traffic."

"Perhaps not," Festing agreed. "Still, you see, the frequent repetition of a smaller shock—"

Charnock stopped him. "It's those confounded posts! If we pull them out, we'll have to cut down to the rock to find a solid bed, and there's a mass of stone to move. What would the job cost?"

He said nothing for a minute after Festing told him, and then remarked: "It's Kerr's business to find fault, and he looked satisfied."

"He doesn't know as much about it as we do."

"Then I wish we knew less. How long do you think the track would stand if we left it alone?"

"Until we got paid," said Festing. "It might stand for some time afterwards."

He fixed his eyes on Charnock and waited. Bob had expressed some praiseworthy sentiments about making a good job, but this was a different thing from living up to them when it would cost him much. What they ought to do was plain, but Festing admitted that the sacrifice required an effort. Then, somewhat to his surprise, Charnock looked up with a smile.

"You're not sure of me yet, Stephen, and I don't know that you can be blamed. It's a nasty knock, but we have got to bear it. Stop there a few minutes."

"Where are you going?"

"To bring Kerr back and show him the damage. He'll have to lay off the gravel gang while we pull down the bank."

Festing waited. Bob would stand by him, but he felt anxious. It would be an expensive business to rebuild the track and the frost would make things worse. In fact, if they had any more trouble of the kind, they might be ruined. Then he got up as he saw Kerr coming along the line.

In an hour or two the rails were up and they began to pull down the rockwork that faced the bank. The ragged stones cut their numbed hands, their backs ached with lifting heavy weights, and they stumbled under the loads they carried up the snowy incline. They had, however, help enough, for Charnock went away for a time and came back with three or four men from the construction gang. Festing noted that although he made them useful, he did not give them the hardest work. He refrained from asking how Charnock got the men, but was not surprised when the foreman arrived and inquired in forcible language what they were doing there.

"Let me answer him," said Charnock. "I feel in the mood. It's my first chance of letting myself go; as long as you're working for wages the advantage is with the boss. Besides, I think I ought to do something for the boys, who can't talk back."

Festing admitted that he talked very well. Charnock had a keen eye for the ridiculous and a pretty wit, and was no longer handicapped by the fear of being dismissed. While the foreman replied with coarse but rather meaningless abuse, Charnock's retorts had a definite aim and hit their mark. He indicated with humorous skill the defects in his antagonist's looks and character, and Festing's gang laughed uproariously, while the borrowed workmen applauded as loudly as they durst. At length, the foreman, breathless and red in face, gave up the unequal contest and returned to his first question.

"If you came for an argument, you've got it, and I can go on for some time yet," Charnock replied. "However, if you really want to know why the boys are helping me, you can ask Mr. Norton at the bridge."

The foreman retired, muttering, but not towards the bridge, and Festing looked hard at Charnock.

"I was anxious for a moment," Charnock admitted. "But I didn't think he'd go. For one thing, I knew he knows Norton doesn't like him."

"Then I'll leave you to deal with Norton if he hears about the matter. Now you have had your amusement, we had better get on."

The short rest and laughter had refreshed the gang and they made good progress. As the holes between the frames deepened, the work got harder and the footing bad, because they were forced to stand on slippery ledges while they passed the heavy stones from man to man. Charnock was ready with jocular sympathy if one fell or a stone bruised somebody's hand, and his jokes spurred on the weary. It got dark soon in the hollow, but as the light faded the flame of a powerful blast-lamp sprang up and threw out a dazzling glare. The lamp belonged to the company, and Festing did not ask Charnock how he had got it. Bob had his own methods, and it was better to leave him alone. When the whistle blew, the latter turned to the borrowed men.

"Go to our shack, boys, and get supper there. I told the cook to fix up something extra, and dare say you'll find it better hash than yours. I'd like you to come back to-morrow, but am afraid it's risky."

Harold Bindloss

CHAPTER XXIV

THE CHINOOK WIND

The frost got more rigorous, drying the snow to a dusty powder in which Festing's lumber gang floundered awkwardly. Had there been a thaw, the surface would have hardened, but now they were forced to move the logs through loose, billowy drifts. The men sank to their knees, it was difficult to find a fulcrum for the handspikes, and the logs would not run well on the beaten roads. The latter broke into holes, and the dry snow retarded the smooth sliding of the lumber like dust. One could not touch a saw or ax-head with the naked hand.

Festing had seen that he might be embarrassed by hard frost, but had not expected it to continue. On the central tablelands of British Columbia winter is severe, but near the coast and in valleys open to the West the mitigating warmth of the Pacific is often felt. He had imagined that when his work upon the track was hindered the snow would help him to bring down lumber ready for use when a thaw set in. Now, however, wages were mounting up and little work was being done. He began to wonder what would happen if a change did not come.

One morning he knelt in a hole below the track, holding a drill. He wore mittens, but the back of one was split and showed a raw bruise on his skin. It needs practise to hit the end of a drill squarely, and Charnock, who swung the big hammer, had missed. The worst was that the bruise would not heal while the temperature kept low. They were sinking a hole through frozen gravel that was worse to cut than rock, because the drill jambed in the crevices and would not turn. But for the frost, they need not have used the tool; a hole for the post they meant to put in could have been made with a shovel, without using expensive powder.

When he thought they had gone deep enough Festing got up and looked about. White peaks glittered against a vivid blue sky. The pines sparkled with frost and the snow in their shadow was a soft gray. The river looked as black as ink, except where it foamed among the rocks, and the gorge echoed with the crash of drifting ice that shocked and splintered on the ledges. The light was strong, and rocks and trees far up the slopes stood out, harshly distinct. As he turned to the West, however, he noted a faint haziness and shading off in the outline of the hills.

"I don't know if that softness means anything, and hardly believe it does," he said. "When I made up the wages book last night and saw what the work we have been able to do has cost us, I got a shock. The boys are a pretty good crowd, and if we pay them off we won't get them back; but it's obvious we can't go on long like this."

Charnock nodded. "How much money have we left?"

When Festing told him he looked thoughtful. "I didn't know things were quite as bad! Well, I suppose I could get another cheque, but don't want to put too much strain on Sadie's generosity. She might imagine I'd got on a jag! There are drawbacks to having a character like mine; it's easier lived up to than got rid of. However, what do you suggest?"

"We'll hold on while the money lasts."

"The plan's simple, as far as it goes. It's remarkable how short a time money does last and how hard it is to earn. Sadie misled me about that; she used to hint that I had only to apply my talents and pick up the cash; but since she's a business woman, she ought to have known better. The virtuous path is about as rocky as luck can make it; but perhaps you take something for granted if you allow that making money is virtuous."

Festing frowned impatiently. "One ought to pay one's debts."

"One's generally forced," Charnock replied. "But I think I see what you mean. We undertook this contract and must carry it out if possible. Sadie would agree. She's like her father, and the old man often said: 'It's safe to deal with Keller's. When you put up the money, we put up the goods.' But let's get the powder."

Opening a box, he took out a stick of yellow material that looked rather like a thick candle. A big copper cap was squeezed into one end, and from the cap there trailed a length of black fuse. Festing put the stick into the hole and cautiously filled this up with frozen soil, leaving a short piece of fuse sticking out. While he was feeling for his matches Kerr arrived.

"You are making trouble for me," the latter began. "You did the square thing in pulling out the weak frames, but they're not replaced, and I can't run the gravel train across the spot. As the back track is nearly ballasted up, I don't know how I'm going to use the locomotive and cars."

"The frost is stopping us," said Festing. "It is not our fault."

"That's so, but my chiefs at headquarters don't want to know whose fault it is. Their method, as you ought to know, is statistical—we're given a number of men and tools, and the value of the work done must equal the expense. It's the only standard for judging an engineer. His business is to overcome the difficulties, and if he's unable he's obviously of no use."

Charnock grinned. "Employers' logic! Piffle of that kind only goes when there are more engineers than jobs. I imagine there'll be a change some day."

"I'm sorry Dalton's gone back," Kerr resumed. "He's a friend of yours, and would have seen what we're all up against. But there's another thing; the boys are beginning to kick. We have had to lay off the ballast gang for a day now and then, and they claim they're not getting a square deal. One fellow told me we oughtn't to have given the contract to a man without capital to carry him over a set-back. He said if you'd had money you could have hired extra labor and kept to schedule, and in the end it wouldn't have cost you more."

"The argument is sound," Festing agreed. "In fact, it shows more understanding than I'd expect the boys to use."

Kerr looked hard at him. "I suspect that somebody is stirring them up. You see, they haven't demanded more wages yet; they only claim that I ought to hustle you."

"The fellow's object isn't very plain, but I've no doubt the demand for bigger pay will come. Well, we can't hire more help, and if there's no change soon, the frost will break us without your bothering. We'll do our best until then."

"We'll leave it at that," said Kerr, with a sympathetic nod; and when he went away Charnock turned to Festing.

"Wilkinson's the man, and as the boys have a real grievance he'll find them easy to work on. That means I've got to write to Sadie."

"No," said Festing. "If you write, I stop. Your wife has sent you money enough, and I'm afraid some of it is lost. We must trust to luck, and in the meantime we'll fire the shot."

He blew a whistle and then striking a match lighted the fuse and hurried away. A minute or two later, lumps of frozen gravel flew about the track and showers of smaller fragments scattered the snow. As Festing came out of his shelter a man with an angry look advanced along the line.

"Why don't you warn folks before you shoot off your rocks?" he asked.

"My partner whistled," Charnock answered. "What's the matter, anyhow? Did the shot jar your nerves?"

"A rock a foot across mighty near jarred my head! A smaller piece got me plumb on the ribs."

Festing thought this unlikely, in view of the fellow's distance from the explosion, but could not be certain he was not struck.

"I'm sorry if you got hurt," he said. "You ought to have heard the whistle."

"Anyhow, I didn't. You want to stop shooting rocks when there are men around. Then you've mussed up the track and can't put her straight. Why don't you hire more boys and rush the job? Can't see why the bosses let two deadbeats like you and your partner have the contract!"

"We have got it. How we mean to carry it out is our business, not yours."

"Then it's certainly our business if we work or not," the other rejoined. "As the bosses will find out if they reckon we're going to lose our time to help you save your dollars!"

He went away grumbling, and Charnock looked at Festing.

"Was that bluff? Do you think he means it?"

"I don't know. They haven't lost much time through our fault, but the frost has interfered with other jobs, and I expect there'll be trouble if it lasts. I'm puzzled, because they're not a bad-tempered lot, and I understand that Wilkinson is not a favorite. Your throwing him down the bank wouldn't strengthen his influence."

"It's easy to work on men's feelings when they're discontented," Charnock replied. "The worst is that Kerr can't stand by us if the gang put down their tools. Labor's scarce in the mountains, and he'll be forced to do what they want."

Festing gloomily agreed. "I'm afraid so. However, we must do the best we can in the time we have left."

They worked by a blast-lamp until late at night and began again before daybreak in the morning. The weakened frame had been replaced, but others needed strengthening and the rockwork must be built up among the timbers. The stones required careful fitting, and it was impossible to dress them to rough shape. The frozen surface resisted the tool and they broke if much force was used. Fires were made, but the rock thawed irregularly and much time was lost.

Festing's bruised hand gave him trouble, his mittens wore to rags, and his numbed fingers cracked and bled, but he worked savagely until evening. Then he walked stiffly to the shack and sat, dejected and aching, looking at the food on the table. Although he had eaten little all day, it cost him something of an effort to begin his meal.

An hour afterward he heard steps and voices outside and opened the door. The light shone out from behind him and he saw a group of dark figures in the snow.

"Well, boys," he asked, "what do you want?"

"We want to know when you're going to fix the track," one replied.

"That's easily answered. We mean to put it right as soon as we can."

"Not good enough!" remarked another. "We've got to know when."

"Then I'm sorry I can't tell you. It depends on the weather."

Some of them growled, and Festing felt Charnock's hand close warningly on his arm.

"Won't you come into the light, boys?" the latter asked. "I'd like to know to whom I'm talking."

They did not move, and Charnock resumed: "Have you brought your foreman or Wilkinson?"

Somebody said neither had come, and Charnock nodded.

"Well, I reckon they know what's best for them! Wilkinson doesn't like me, but he's not looking for more trouble; I imagine he's had enough. Then the foreman's not a friend of mine, but he has a better job than yours and means to hold it down. If you get up against the bosses, he's not going to be fired."

There was silence, and he saw his remarks had not been wasted. He had hinted that the men were being used and given them ground to distrust their leaders.

"I half expected another fellow, a friend of Wilkinson's, who claimed he had been hit by a stone. Has he come along?"

"Said he was too sore and would have to lay off to-morrow," one replied. "That's another thing. When you shoot off your blasts you have got to watch out that nobody gets hurt."

"Sure," agreed Charnock. "We did watch out and blew the whistle; but we want to do the square thing. If Pearson got hurt and can't work, let him show you the bruise. We'll stand for his pay until you think he's fit to begin again."

"That's fair," admitted the other with a laugh. "He wasn't showing the bruise much. Say, you're pretty smart!"

"I hope so," said Charnock, modestly. "Looks as if I needed all the smartness I've got. We're up against the weather and a big awkward job, and then you come along and worry us! However, what are you going to do about it if we can't put the rails down as soon as you want?"

"We'll make the bosses break your contract."

Charnock pondered, keeping his hand on Festing's arm, because he thought he could handle the matter better than his comrade. Festing was too blunt and sometimes got angry. He saw that the men were determined, but while they had, no doubt, been worked upon, he thought they had no personal grudge against him or his partner.

"There's only one way you could put the screw to the bosses, and that way's dangerous. The *Colonist* states that they have a number of men unemployed in the coast towns. If Kerr wrote to a labor agent, he'd send him up a crowd."

"It would cost him high to bring the men here, and take some time."

"That is so," Charnock agreed. He saw the others had made their plans and calculated the pressure they could put upon the engineers. Time was important, and he thought the foreman had helped them to estimate the expense the company would incur by the delay before they could get new men.

"Putting down your tools would cost you something," he resumed. "How long do you imagine it would take to persuade Kerr?"

"I guess a week would fix him; he wouldn't stand for a fortnight."

"Very well! I don't suppose your object is to put us off the road; you want what you're entitled to. So do we all, and though it's often troublesome to get, there's no use in taking the hardest way. If you stop, you lose a fortnight's wages and somebody will get fired. Not now, of course, but afterwards; the bosses know their job. Well, give us ten days, and the time you miss won't run to many dollars. If we can't put the rails down then, we'll quit."

There was silence for a moment, and then somebody said, "We'll let it go at that. It's a deal!"

The others growled consent and Charnock waited until they moved away, after which he shut the door and sat down wearily.

"You took the right line," Festing said.

"I hesitated about fixing the time, but we can't go on much longer."

"No," said Festing. "Well, we have ten days!"

They said nothing more and soon afterwards went to bed. Next morning there was a marked haziness in the west, but the frost was keener. It looked as if they must be beaten, although they meant to fight until defeat was sure, and Festing was surprised when he glanced at his comrade. This was not the careless lounger he had known. Charnock's face was grim and somewhat pinched; his hands were torn and bruised. He picked the heaviest stones to lift and was the first to take hold of ponderous beams. Festing owned that he had misjudged Charnock, but not more than he had misjudged himself. His farming had been a rash experiment and the contract a reckless gamble; the one threatened to end as badly as the other. Then Bob had somehow kept his wife's love, and he, with senseless obstinacy, had estranged Helen.

His thoughts were depressing, but they drove him on. Hope was dead; he had made a horrible mess of things. All that was left was to take his punishment and hold on until he was knocked out, but he meant to do this. He did not stop for dinner with the rest, but occupied himself with something that needed doing, and forgot that he had gone without the meal. Afterwards a pain began in his left side, but he had other aches, and the extra discomfort did not trouble him much. In the afternoon he worked with a kind of sudden fury, and when at length the tired men dropped their tools found some difficulty in straightening his back. He had never used his muscles as he had done for the past few days, but the strain would soon be over.

It was unusually dark when he went up the hill to the shack. The pines rose in blurred masses from the shadowy snow and he could not see the hollow of the path. Supper was a melancholy meal, but he ate because he was hungry, and afterwards dragged his chair to the fire. There was a great pile of crackling logs and the blaze flickered about the room, but bitter draughts came in beneath the door.

"An open fire's of no use; I thought about getting a stove," he said, and paused with a dreary smile. "It's lucky I didn't send the order!"

"You may need it yet," Charnock replied. "Somehow we'll put the rails down in time."

Festing did not answer and picked up a newspaper. He did not want to read, but could not sleep, although he was very tired, and felt he must have some relief from his anxious thoughts. The newspaper was a *Colonist* that had left Victoria some days before, and he read it methodically from the first column, trying to fix his attention on things that had happened in remote mining settlements and market reports. His efforts were mechanical, but he long afterwards remembered what he read and how he dully followed the arguments in an article on political reform. Indeed, when he saw the *Colonist* his imagination carried him back to the log-walled hut, and he felt something of the dazed hopelessness that blunted his senses then.

In the meantime, Charnock, half asleep, lounged with his legs stretched out to the fire. The logs snapped and a fitful wind stirred the tops of the pines. Now and then some snow fell from a branch and a loose roofing shingle rattled, but by degrees the sounds died away. Everything was strangely quiet, except for the roar of the river, which had got more distinct. Charnock shivered and felt a puzzling tension. It was often calm at night, particularly in hard frost, but he felt as if something was going to happen. Looking up, he saw Festing nod with his eyes half shut, and felt for his tobacco.

While he cut the plug, the silence was broken. There was a humming in the pine tops and light branches began to toss. The draught from the door got stronger, but did not bite as keenly, and it sounded as if the snow was falling from the trees. Then some slipped down the roof, and getting up with tingling nerves, he opened the door. All the trees were rustling and waves of sound came up the valley. The sound swelled, the air felt damp, and a drop of moisture from the roof splashed upon his head. He drew a deep breath of relief, for a warm wind from the Pacific was roaring through the defile. Then Festing dropped the newspaper.

"Why have you opened the door?" he asked drowsily, and got up with a jerk as the draught swept the smoke about the room.

"A Chinook!" he exclaimed, and ran to the door. "We'll have rain and warmth while it blows."

"It's great!" said Charnock hoarsely. "We are through the worst!" Then he caught Festing's arm and laughed. "Say something wise, partner; I want to shout and dance."

"You had better go to bed. It will be thawing hard to-morrow, and there's much to be done. A Chinook doesn't last long in the mountains."

"This Chinook is going to last until we put the rails down," Charnock replied.

CHAPTER XXV

THE THAW

When Festing went out at daybreak the air was soft, and drops from the wet pines fell into the honeycombed snow. The surface was turning to slush, but he knew it would wear down into a slippery mass on which the logs would run. This was fortunate, because he doubted if labor could be usefully employed upon the stones just yet. For a few moments he pondered the matter and listened to the river's turmoil. The deep, booming note was sharper, water splashed noisily in the gullies, and there was a ringing crash as an ice-floe broke upon a rock. Then he turned as Charnock came up.

"Which is it—logs or stones?" the latter asked.

"Logs, I think; we can handle them easily," Festing replied. "The other job is urgent, but the thaw has only begun, and when the ground gets properly soft we'll do twice as much as we could now. Still, there's a risk. We could make some progress with the track, and the warm spell mayn't last."

"Take the risk," said Charnock with a laugh. "There's not much fun in playing for safety, and you don't get far that way, while when you try to foresee things you generally see them wrong. But let's be practical! As soon as the ground is soft enough we'll ask leave to hire half the gravel gang. That will make friends of the opposition and won't put up our wages bill. If you double your helpers, you halve the working hours."

"Obviously. But you have to pay the larger number all at once. Where's the money coming from?"

"From the head contractor. We'll try to make Norton sign for an interim payment. Let's go and see him."

Festing was doubtful, but they found Norton, the contractor's engineer, more compliant than he hoped.

"I suppose you are entitled to ask for a sum on account, but I'd take some responsibility in allowing the demand," he said. "Why did you come to me now?"

"We want to be just," Charnock answered modestly. "At present, there's no prospect of our finishing the work we ask the money for."

"It doesn't go much beyond a prospect yet," Norton rejoined. "However, I'll help you if I can, and will see what Kerr thinks. He's the man we have both to satisfy in the end."

They went to work up the hill in the melting snow, and soon their clothes were dripping and their long boots soaked. At first, the logs vanished in the drifts through which they tried to roll them, and the horses slipped and floundered in the slush, but this flowed away and left a harder layer that was presently beaten firm. The surface turned black and compressed into ice, and before long rows of heavy logs plunged down the skids. Every moment must be turned to good account, and Festing stopped and went down reluctantly when Kerr sent for him.

"I've seen Norton and he thinks we ought to help you out," Kerr remarked. "Though he argues from single instances, his judgment's often good, and he seems convinced you can be trusted because you saved a skip of his. Of course, I had my opinion; but as he represents the contractor you are working for, I couldn't urge him."

"Thanks!" said Festing. "I wish I'd brought Charnock; he'd

deal with this better."

Kerr laughed. "Your partner has some talents and seems to have made Norton and my storekeepers his friends. If he hadn't, there might have been trouble about certain irregularities. However, you can have the gravel gang if I'm forced to lay the boys off, and as soon as we can run the train over the repaired track you'll get your cheque."

Festing went away, feeling satisfied, but not without some anxiety. He could not urge Norton to go farther than his employer would approve, and the payment agreed upon was small. Besides, if the frost returned before he had made the track secure, he would have spent enough money in extra wages to prevent his going on, and should this happen it might be difficult to obtain payment for other work already completed. He would be at the mercy of Norton's employer, who might contend that by throwing up his contract he had forfeited his claim. It was obvious that he must make the utmost use of every hour of open weather, and for the rest of the day he worked with a stubborn energy that conquered fatigue.

For a time, the logs went screaming and grinding down the skids, but darkness made launching them dangerous, and they could not light the lumber road on the hill. They worked in the dark, rolling out the sawn trunks from among the brush and melting snow until there was room to hook on the team. Then the driver, walking by his horses' heads, felt with his feet for the hollowed track, and losing it now and then embedded his load in snow. Then he called for help, and men with cantpoles laboriously hove the ponderous mass back to the road.

The work was worse on the inclines, where the logs ran smoothly and there was a risk of their overtaking the horses. Rain had begun to fall and one could not see the obstacles, but there were pitches where one must go fast in order to keep in front of the dangerous loads. But risks must be run in lumbering, and Festing felt that rashness was justified. Speed was the thing that counted most.

When supper time drew near, men and horses were worn out, and Festing knew that if he urged the former to continue he could not do much without the teams. There were, however, a few logs he meant to haul to the skidway before he stopped, and he had some misgivings when he started with the last. It was an unusually large trunk, and the tired horses floundered as they tightened the chain. Thawing snow when beaten hard is as slippery as ice, but the animals kept their feet and the mass began to move. Festing got a firm grip on the near horse's bridle and plodded forward cautiously, with the rain in his face when he crossed the openings in the wood. The snow reflected a puzzling glimmer, but the darkness was thick among the trees, and drops from the shaking branches fell into his eyes. Turning his hat-brim down, he felt for the edge of the trail.

By and by he stopped at the top of a descent. The gray snow looked all the same, and the hollow track vanished a few yards in front; the rows of trunks had faded into a vague dark mass, and the branches met overhead in a thick canopy. The horses were big, valuable Percherons, but they were exhausted and stood slackly, with steam rising from their foam-flecked coats. Festing did not like the look of the dip, and knew the trees grew close upon the track at the bottom, but he must go down, and shouted to the hesitating animals.

They moved faster; the log grinding heavily across the snow behind. Then the strain on the chain slackened, and he dragged at the bridle as he began to run. The log could not be stopped now; it was moving faster than he had thought, and all that he could do was to keep the team in front. His feet slipped on the icy trail, and the horses floundered, but they knew the danger and broke into a clumsy trot. It was hard to keep up, but Festing must hold them to the track and steer them round a bend ahead.

The log lurched noisily across lumps and hollows, the chain

made a harsh clank, and the wood echoed the thud of heavy hoofs. Festing ran his best, and imagined that he was running for the horses' lives and perhaps for his. He durst not look round, and could only guess where the log was by the noise. The blurred trees rolled back to him in a thick dark mass, but he thought the gap he followed got narrower ahead. This was, no doubt, the awkward spot where the trunks closed on the track, and there was a corner. He must go on and trust to luck for getting round.

In a few moments he was almost at the corner, and although it was hard to see, thought he distinguished a break in the dark wall of trees. One must keep to the inside, on the right; but there was very little room, and if he miscalculated, he or the horses would collide with a trunk. He smashed through a bush that caught his foot, but his hold upon the bridle saved him from a fall. It looked as if he had left the track and was plunging into the wood. Then a black trunk became detached from the rest, apparently straight in front. He did not mean to let go, although he might be crushed between the horse's shoulder and the tree, and drew as close as possible to the animal. Something brushed his coat, he felt a button torn off, but the tree was passed. He knew where he was now, and thrusting hard against the horse urged the animal towards the other side of the road. The log ran into soft snow and slowed; there was more room here and the steepest pitch was behind. A few minutes later, he reached the top of the skids and sat down on the log, breathing fast and feeling badly shaken.

He frowned as he thought there was no physical reason he should feel shaken. He was used to strenuous effort, and danger could not be avoided when one engaged in construction work. It was mental strain that was wearing him out; the constant endeavor to finish a task in less than the necessary time. Want of money was, however, the main cause of his difficulties, and when he had got his cheque it would be possible to take things easier. Comforting himself with this reflection, he got up and led the horses down-hill.

The clang of hammers and rattle of shovels rose from the gorge, sharply distinct at times, but melting when the throb of the river swelled and a gust roared among the trees. A dark skeleton of steel that stood out against pulsating flame, with blurred reflections below, marked the central pier of the bridge; the line of track was picked out by twinkling fires. Then the scream of a whistle pierced the sound and the lights went out. The men were going back to the bunk-house and Festing envied them. Their work was finished for the day and they could rest, free from care, until the whistle roused them to begin again. Many were, no doubt, tired, but that was man's common lot, and muscular fatigue in moderation was no hardship. The strain came when one had to make the dollars go round and see that every effort paid its cost. Among the mountains, the cost was high.

Charnock joined him when he was grooming the horses in the rude stable, because the teams must be cared for before the men thought of food. Supper was ready when they went in, and when they had eaten they sat by the hearth, drying their damp clothes and enjoying the warmth. They had scarcely spoken to one another during the day; as a rule, it was only after supper one could indulge in talk.

Presently Charnock took his pipe from his mouth. "It's luxuriously warm, but one can't expect the Chinook to last. I imagine we'll have some use for a stove after all."

"We're not out of danger yet," Festing replied. "Norton's cheque has still to be earned, but I begin to feel hopeful. If we can hold out for a few more days, I think we'll turn the corner. Anyhow, the plan you made prevents any trouble from Wilkinson for a time. Do you think he has had enough and will leave us alone?"

"I can't tell, but it doesn't matter much. We mustn't exaggerate the fellow's importance; he's a very poor sample of the theatrical villain. Besides, I imagine you seldom meet the latter in real life; it's an unnecessary part."

"You mean we're up against enough without a plotting antagonist? Well, I must agree. Considering the weather—"

Charnock stopped him with a smile. "I don't mean the weather, though one can't leave that out. In a new country, man must make the best fight he can against Nature; but she's not his worst enemy. It's our passions, our virtues sometimes, that lead us into a coil. Looks as if they didn't want much help from outside."

"That kind of speculation's not much in my line."

"Just so. You're what you call practical, and your mind runs upon the number of yards of rockwork you can put up in a day or the logs you can cut. Very useful, but it doesn't take you far enough. In fact, if you had thought more about other matters, you wouldn't be here now. Nor would I."

"I'm not sure I see your drift," said Festing impatiently. "What's your explanation for our being here?"

Charnock's eyes twinkled. "If you want the truth, it's because you're something of an obstinate ass. Wilkinson had really nothing to do with it, and the weather hasn't much. Your pride brought you and keeps you. You took the wrong line with Helen, and then, knowing you were wrong, couldn't force yourself to accept her help. However, I'll admit that we are a pair of fools. I could have spent a lazy winter at the homestead if I'd liked."

"You came to look for me," Festing remarked with feeling.

"I did, but stayed to please myself. Thought I'd show Sadie what I could do; felt virtuous about it at the time, but begin to suspect that vanity pushed me on. Sadie would, no doubt, sooner have me safe at home. Anyhow, I think I've proved my argument—we're here, doing unthinkable things, freezing, sweating, getting thin, because of our own stupidity."

"In a way, that is so," Festing agreed. "Still, I can't go back until I have finished this job."

"Perhaps you had better not," said Charnock dryly. "I imagine you wouldn't be easy to live with it you felt you had come home because you had failed. You might make good resolutions, but the thing would spoil your temper all the same. The pinch comes when you try to carry good resolutions out."

Festing got up and threw fresh wood on the fire. "If you have finished philosophizing, we'll talk about something else."

"I'm not going to talk about logs and wages," Charnock replied.

"Very well. You haven't told me much about Wilkinson. He seems a clever rascal. Do you think we have ground for being afraid of him?"

"I don't imagine he'd run much risk or make a sacrifice for the sake of getting his revenge; that kind of thing isn't often done by normal people. All the same, he doesn't like us, and if he found he could do us an injury without much trouble, I dare say he'd seize the chance. On the whole, it might be prudent to watch him. Now we'll let the matter go."

Festing nodded, and they lounged in silence by the snapping fire.

Next morning they got to work upon the track, and on the following afternoon, when the thaw had gone far enough into the ground, Charnock went for the gravel gang. The men came willingly, although Wilkinson and the foreman did not appear, and with the connivance of one Charnock obtained several of the company's blast-lamps. They worked well, and when they went away Festing was satisfied with what they had done. He imagined that Kerr and Norton had put themselves to some inconvenience in order to let him have the gang, and for the next two or three days he redoubled his efforts. The strain was getting unbearable, but the thaw would not last, and he must finish all the work the frost would delay while he could get the men. When he dismissed his helpers, they parted on friendly terms; but his look was grave that evening when he made up his accounts.

The wages had been a heavy drain, and he could not meet his storekeeper's bills unless he got his cheque. The defective underpinning had, however, been replaced or strengthened, and he expected that Kerr would test it soon. If the work did not pass the test, he would be ruined, and would, moreover, have involved Charnock in a serious loss.

It was about the middle of the morning when he stood with Kerr and his partner beside the mended tract. Bright sunshine touched the hillside, leaving the gorge in shadow, and the air was clear and cold. The snow had gone for a few hundred feet above the rails; the pines stood out sharply from the dark background, and the hollows in the glittering slopes beyond were marked by lines of soft-blue shade. Festing thought a change was coming, and he had not finished the track too soon.

By and by a plume of smoke rose above the trees and something twinkled in an opening. A rhythmic snorting and a rumble pierced the throb of the river, and Kerr looked up the track.

"The engineer's bringing her along fast. Shall I flag him to snub her and shut the throttle before he runs across the new stuff?"

"No," said Festing quietly. "It won't be needful."

"The work hasn't had much time to settle, and a locomotive using steam hits the rails harder than when she's running loose."

Harold Bindloss

"We don't want our money until it's earned, and you'll have to haul heavy loads up the grade when the regular traffic begins."

"In the meantime, I'm not thinking about the rest, but about the gravel train."

"The track will stand," said Festing, in a steady voice.

The train came on; the long, low-sided cars rocking and banging down the incline. Small figures jolted up and down on the gravel, and at the far end the big plow flashed in the sun. The front of the engine got larger, and Festing fixed his eyes upon the rockwork he had built among the piles. All that could be done had been done; he had not spared money or labor, for Charnock had agreed that the job must stand. It was, no doubt, exaggerated sentiment, for he was highly strung, but he felt that he had staked his wife's respect and his future happiness on his work.

The ground shook, and flying fragments of ballast beat upon his turned-down hat; there was a deafening roar as the cars jolted past, and he saw the rails spring. Then the wind that buffeted him changed to eddying puffs, the noise receded, and he lifted his bent head. The rockwork stood firm, the ends of the timbers had not moved, and only a few small heaps of gravel had fallen from the road-bed. Festing felt that he was trembling, and Kerr put his hand on his arm.

"It's a good job; I'm quite satisfied. If you'll come along to Norton's office, I'll tell him he can give you an order on headquarters for your cheque."

"I'll come instead," said Charnock, who turned to Festing. "Go to the shack and take a smoke. If you come out before I return, I'll stop the gang."

Half an hour later he found Festing sitting slackly by the fire.

"The order is in the mail-bag and will go out on the first

train," he said. "It's lucky we got it, because we have cut things very fine. I had a note some days since from the fellow who sends us our stores, insisting on our settling his bill."

"Then why didn't you tell me?" Festing asked.

Charnock laughed. "I imagined you had enough to bother you, and his account is big. We couldn't have paid him without going broke, and wages have first claim. There was a way out, but you had given me strict orders not to write to Sadie."

"I couldn't have allowed that, but you're a good sort, Bob!"

"Well," said Charnock cheerfully, "it was, so to speak, touch and go; but we have turned the awkward corner, and I think are going to make good."

CHAPTER XXVI

A NEW UNDERTAKING

Soon after the rails were laid down the frost returned, and one cold morning Festing sat in his shack, studying a letter from Helen. Norton's cheque had helped him to overcome the worst of his difficulties, things were going better, and Charnock would superintend the workmen until he was ready to go out. Festing felt that he need not hurry, and wanted to think.

Helen had written to him before, without any hint of resentment, and he had told her what he was doing. She knew Bob was his partner, and no doubt understood what this implied. It was obvious that he had been wrong in disliking Bob and half suspecting him; besides Helen knew from the beginning that he had not suspected her, although he had insisted that she had been imprudent. This ground for difference had vanished, but he wondered what she thought, and could not gather much from her letter.

She wrote with apparent good-humor and stated that all was going satisfactorily at the farm, where, indeed, nothing of importance could be done until spring. For all that, there was some reserve. A personal explanation was needed before they could get back to their old relations of intimate confidence, and he was ready to own his mistakes. Unfortunately, the explanation must be put off, because there was one point on which he was still determined, although his resolve no longer altogether sprang from pride. He must, if possible, repair his damaged fortunes before he went home. Farming on a proper scale was expensive work, and Helen's capital was not large. In order to raise a big crop, one must speculate boldly, and he meant to do so with his own money.

He saw a danger in staying away too long, but his contract was only beginning to be profitable. Besides, one thing led to another, and a number of extras, for which the pay was good, had been added to the original plans. Then he had been asked to undertake another job and had arranged to go over the ground with Kerr and Norton that morning. In a way, he would sooner have left it alone, because it would keep him longer from home, but the terms offered a strong inducement to stop. Glancing at his watch, he saw it was nearly time to meet the engineers.

He found them and Charnock near the half-finished bridge, which crossed the river obliquely. The track approached its end in a curve and then stopped where a noisy steam-digger was at work. Between the machine and the bridge, the hillside fell in a very steep slope to the water, which rolled in angry turmoil past its foot, and the channel dividing the bank from the island that supported the central bridge-pier was deep. Here and there a slab of rock projected from the slope, but, for the most part, the latter consisted of small stones and soil. The surface was now frozen beneath a thin crust of snow and the pines were white.

"You know roughly what we want," said Kerr. "If you'll come along, you can look at the shot-holes we made to test the ground. Then I'll show you a car-load of the rock we want to use, but it's largely a lumber job and that's why we thought of offering it you. You have some good choppers besides the teams and plant required."

They climbed about the bank by dangerous paths, and then stopped at the end of the bridge.

"The thing can be done, but it will only make a temporary job," Festing remarked. "You will have to do it again, properly, in a year or two."

"That the Company's business," Kerr replied. "As soon as we start the traffic improvements can be paid for out of revenue instead of piling up construction costs."

"You can imagine the cost if we cut back the hill far enough to ease the curve and lay the track on solid ground," Norton interposed. "The half-measure of scooping out a shallow road-bed and dumping the stuff on the incline is ruled out, because the spoil wouldn't lie and the river would sweep the dirt away. If we filled up the channel with rock, we'd turn the current on the bridge-pier."

Then Charnock said something and Festing let them talk while he looked about. Since a temporary job was required, he thought the plan was perhaps the best that could be used. It called for a timber framework, beginning about half-way up the bank, although its height would vary with the ground. The gaps between the frames would be faced with rockwork and then filled with rubble in order to make a bed for the rails on top.

"If you will come to the office, I'll show you the detailed drawings," Norton said presently, and the others followed him.

When they reached the office Festing studied the drawings, and then giving them to Charnock, lighted his pipe. He wanted to undertake the contract, but hesitated. The work already on his hands would occupy him for some time, and a lengthy absence might prejudice him with Helen. Besides, he had taken risks enough and a new venture might prove a rash challenge to fortune; one could not foresee all the difficulties that might arise. But, if he succeeded, he would go home with the means to resume his farming on a profitable scale. Then he saw Charnock looking at him and knew he would agree to his decision. Festing put down his pipe and knitted his brows.

"Well?" said Charnock.

Festing got up with a quick, resolute movement, and turned to Norton.

"We'll undertake the job."

"That's all right," said Norton. "I'll get the papers drawn up and send them over for you to sign."

They went out, and as they climbed the hill Charnock remarked: "This may turn out a big thing, partner. Are you going home before we start?"

Festing looked up sharply, with a disturbed air. "No. To begin with, I've got to be about because the thing is big."

"Then, as matters are going smoothly now, I'll leave you for a week."

"I can manage for a week and one of us must stay. But why d'you want to leave?"

"On the whole, I think one of us had better go," Charnock answered with some dryness. "If you don't mind, I'll get off to-morrow."

He started next morning, in the caboose of a returning supply train, and Festing, who went to see him off, stood for a few minutes on the snowy track while the rattle of wheels and snorting of the locomotive died away. Bob had made a curious remark when he talked about going, and Festing wondered what he meant, but dismissed the matter and went back to his work.

It was a bitter afternoon when Charnock got down at the little prairie station that was marked by a water-tank, the agent's shack, and the lower frames of three unfinished grain elevators. He hired a rig at the livery stable, and borrowing a fur-robe started on his drive across the plain. The landscape was empty and featureless except for the gray smears of distant bluffs. Nothing moved on the white expanse, and there was no sound but the measured thud of the horses' feet; the air was still and keen with frost. When the cluster of wooden houses sank behind a gradual rise, the wavy, blue riband of the trail was the only sign of human activity in the frozen wilderness.

The snowfall, however, is generally light on the Western plains, and the trail was good. Its smooth surface was dusty rather than slippery and the team went fast. Everything was different from the varied grandeur of the mountains; the eye found no point to rest upon, and the level snow emphasized the loneliness. In spite of the thick driving-robe, the cold bit through Charnock's worn-out clothes, but he was conscious of a strange and almost poignant satisfaction. This was not because he was at heart still something of a sybarite and had borne many hardships on the railroad; he was going home and in an hour or two Sadie would welcome him. It was curious, but when he married Sadie he had not thought she could inspire him with the feeling he had now. But he had learned her value and understood something of what she had done for him.

When it got dark he urged the horses and tried to control his impatience. Later he felt his heart beat as he drove round the corner of a shadowy bluff and saw his home-lights twinkle across the snow. A hired man came out to take the team, he got down, nearly too numbed to move, and as he stumbled up the steps Sadie met him with a cry of delight. She drew him in and when he stood, half-dazed by the brightness and change of temperature, in the well-warmed room, she took her arm from round his neck and moved back a pace or two.

Charnock's skin-coat was ragged, his mittens were tattered, and his long boots badly worn. He looked tired and unkempt, but Sadie's eyes were soft as she studied him.

"Your face is very thin, but I don't like it less," she said. "You haven't come back the same, Bob; I think you have grown."

"Perhaps the pains account for the thinness," Charnock answered with a smile. "Anyway, you ought to be satisfied, because you tried to make me grow, and in a sense I was very small when I left you. But we won't be sentimental and I want to change my clothes."

He found fresh clothes ready, and when he came back his slippers, pipe, and a recent newspaper occupied their usual place. Sitting down with a smile of content, he lazily looked about.

"This is remarkably nice," he said. "The curious thing is that I feel as if I'd only left the house five minutes since. Everything I want is waiting, although you didn't know I was coming."

"I knew you would come some day, and come like this, without letting me know."

"And so you kept everything ready?" Charnock rejoined. "Well, I imagine that's significant! But you see, I didn't know I could leave camp until the day before I started, and then it looked as if I'd get here as soon as the mail."

Sadie gave him a quick glance. "Then something happened that made you leave?"

"Something did happen, but nothing bad. However, it's a long story and I've not had much to eat."

"Supper will be ready in five minutes, and I've got something that you like."

"Ah!" said Charnock, "I suppose that means you kept the thing I like ready, too?"

They talked about matters of no importance until the meal was over, and then Sadie made him sit down by the stove and light his pipe.

"Now," she said, "you can tell me all you did at the construction camp, and leave nothing out."

Charnock was frank. He knew Sadie understood him, perhaps better than he understood himself, and if his narrative gave her any pleasure, he thought she deserved it. Moreover, when he wanted he talked rather well, making his meaning clear without saying too much. When he finished she gave him a level glance.

"You're surely a bigger man, Bob! I see that, not only by what you have done but by what you think."

"Well," said Charnock, twinkling, "I'm glad you're satisfied, but you'll probably find out that there's room for improvement yet."

"I suppose you must joke," Sadie rejoined with mild reproof. "But what about Festing? Doesn't he meant to come back until the job's finished?"

"So far as I could gather, he does not. I tried tactfully to persuade him he was acting like a fool and imagine he sees a glimmer of the truth. All the same, he's obstinate."

Sadie was silent for a minute, knitting her brows, and then looked up.

"You have only three days; I suppose I mustn't keep you after that?"

"It mightn't be prudent. If I stay longer, I shall, no doubt, feel unequal to going back at all. My industrious fit's very recent and good resolutions fail."

"Pshaw!" said Sadie. "Try to be serious. I must see Helen to-morrow and can't take you. She may have a message for her husband."

"Couldn't she write the message, if you went after I had gone?"

"NO," said Sadie firmly. "She must send it now."

Charnock looked hard at her and nodded. "Well, perhaps it's a good plan. Meddling is sometimes dangerous, but one can trust you."

Sadie, wrapped in furs, drove across the prairie next afternoon, and found Helen at home. The latter looked rather forlorn and dispirited, and Sadie felt that she had undertaken a delicate task.

"Bob has come home for three days," she said by and by. "He can't stop longer, but I thought you'd like to know how they are getting on with their contract."

"Stephen writes to me," Helen replied with a hint of sharpness.

"I guess he does," Sadie agreed. "Still, from what Bob says, they haven't much time for letters, and he talked to me about the work all last evening. He could leave when Stephen couldn't because he's the junior partner and doesn't know much about railroading yet."

Helen smiled, rather curiously. "Do you feel you must explain why your husband came home and mine did not?"

For a moment or two Sadie hesitated. It looked as if she had not begun well, but she braced herself. If her tact were faulty, she would try frankness.

"Yes," she said; "in a way that was what I did come to explain, though it's difficult. In the first place, I know why Stephen couldn't come."

Helen waited, and then, as Sadie seemed to need some

encouragement, said, "Very well. I think I'd like to be convinced."

"The reason Bob came and Stephen stayed begins with the difference between them. We know them both, and I want to state that I'm quite satisfied with Bob. That had to be said, and now we'll let it go. But they are different. Bob will work for an object; for dollars, to feel he's making good, or to please me. Your husband must work, whether he had an object or not, because that's the kind of man he is."

"Bob's way is easier understood," Helen rejoined. "Besides, Stephen is working for money enough to farm again on the old large scale."

"He is; but you don't understand yet, and I want to show you why he feels he has got to farm. Stephen's the kind we have most use for in this country. In fact, he's my kind; perhaps I know him better than you. Give him a patch of pine-scrub or a bit of poor soil in a sand-belt and he'd feel it his duty to cultivate it, no matter how much work it cost. Show him good wheat land lying vacant or rocks that block a railroad, and he won't rest till he starts the gang-plow or gets to work with giant-powder. He can't help it; the thing's born in him. Like liquor or gambling, only cleaner!"

"But when such a man marries—"

"What about his wife? Well, she must help all she can or stand out and let him work alone. It's a sure thing she can't stop him."

Helen pondered, and then remarked: "Stephen is not your kind, as you said. You wanted to leave the prairie and live in a town."

"I certainly did, but I didn't know myself. Though I wanted to meet smart people and wear smart clothes, to push Bob on and see him make his mark in big business or perhaps in politics.

Now I know I really wanted power; to order folks about and get things done."

"You found you must give up your ambitions."

"I saw they had to be altered," Sadie replied. "But when you can't get things done by others, you can do them, in a smaller way, yourself, and I find I can be satisfied with running a prairie farm as it ought to be run." She paused and resumed with a soft laugh: "Looks as if neither of us was fixed quite as we like. I have a husband who must be hustled; you want to hold yours back. Well, I guess we can't change that; we must take the boys for what they are and make allowances. Besides, your man's fine energy is perhaps the best thing he has."

Helen was somewhat moved. Sadie's rude philosophy was founded on truth, and having made sacrifices, she had a right to preach. After all, to dull the fine edge of Stephen's energy would be an unworthy action and perhaps dangerous. Helen had been jealous of his farm, but admitted that she might have had worse rivals.

"Do you know 'The Sons of Martha'?" she asked and recited a verse.

"It's great," said Sadie simply. "That man has our folks placed. Well, I don't read much poetry, but there's a piece of Whitman's I like. When I watch an ox-team break the first furrow in virgin soil, or a construction train, loaded with new steel, go by, I hear him calling: 'Pioneers! Oh, Pioneers!'"

There was silence for a few moments, and then Sadie leaned forward. "I don't know if I've said enough, or said too much, but Bob goes back in three days and could take a message."

The color crept into Helen's face, and her look was strangely soft.

"Let him tell Stephen to finish his work as well as he can; say I understand."

CHAPTER XXVII

SNOW

Tossing snowflakes filled the air, and although it was three o'clock in the afternoon the light was fading, when Charnock opened the door of the caboose. A bitter wind rushed past him and eddied about the car, making the stove crackle. The iron was red-hot in places and a fierce twinkle shone out beneath the rattling door. Half-seen men lay in the bunks along the shadowy wall, tools jingled upon the throbbing boards, but the motion was gentler than usual and the wheels churned softly instead of hammering.

"Is she going to make it?" somebody asked.

Charnock leaned out of the door. Black smoke streamed about the cars and he heard a heavy snorting some distance off, but the caboose lurched slowly along the uneven track. The construction train was climbing a steep grade, the driving wheels slipped and he doubted if the locomotive could reach the summit, from which the line ran down to the camp. Dim pines, hardly distinguishable from the white hillside, drifted past; a shapeless rack loomed up and slowly drew abreast. It was some moments before Charnock lost it in the tossing white haze.

"I don't know if she'll make it or not, but rather think she won't," he said.

Harold Bindloss

"Then come in and shut the blamed door," another growled. "No need to worry about it, anyhow! Pay's as good for stopping in the caboose as for humping rails in the snow."

"You're luckier than me in that way," Charnock answered as he shut the door. "There are some drawbacks to being your own boss. When you can't get to work it's comforting to know that somebody else has to find the dollars and put up the hash."

He shivered as he sat down on a box. The snow was obviously deep and things would be unpleasant at the camp, but Festing would not let this interfere with work. Charnock thought he had been foolish to come back, but Festing expected him and Sadie agreed that he ought to go. It was something of an effort to live up to the standards of such a partner and such a wife. Sadie was a very good sort, better than he deserved, but he would not have minded it if she were not quite so anxious about his moral welfare. Besides, after the comfort of the homestead, the caboose jarred. It smelt of acrid soft-coal smoke, the air was full of dust, and rubbish jolted about the floor. Then Charnock grinned as he admitted that he had not expected to find the path of virtue smooth.

His reflections were rudely disturbed, for a violent jolt threw him off the box. The boards he fell upon no longer throbbed, and it was evident that the train had stopped. The others laughed as he got up.

"Loco's hit a big drift," said one. "I guess the engineer won't butt her through."

"He'll surely try; Jake hates to be beat," another remarked, and the caboose began to shake as the train ran backwards down the line.

A minute or two later there was a savage jerk and a furious snorting. The caboose rolled ahead again, faster than before, for the wheels had cut a channel through the snow, and somebody said, "Watch out! Hold tight when she jumps!"

The speed slackened, a jarring crash ran backwards along the train, and the caboose tilted as if the wheels had left the rails. Tools and sacks of provisions rolled across the inclined floor, which suddenly sank to a level, and a man who had fallen from his bunk got up and opened the door.

"She's bedded in good and fast. Guess Jake will be satisfied now," he said, and laughed when a whistle rang through the snow. "Nobody could hear that a mile ahead, and as she's not over the divide it's some way to camp. I reckon we'll stop here until they dig us out."

Soon afterwards some more men came in, covered with snow. Then the door was shut, the stove filled and a lamp lighted, and Charnock resigned himself to spending another night in the caboose. After all, it was as warm as the shack, and he reflected with some amusement that Festing probably did not expect him to be punctual. The latter knew his habits, and no doubt imagined that he would find the comfort of the homestead seductive. But Festing did not know Sadie, who had sent him back within the promised time. He enjoyed his supper and slept well afterwards. In fact, he did not waken until a stinging draught swept through the caboose and he saw that it was daylight. The door was open and he heard voices outside. He recognized one as the foreman's, and presently the fellow came in.

"D'you reckon you're here for good, you blamed hibernating deadbeats?" he asked the occupants of the bunks. "Turn out and get busy before I put a move on you!"

The men got up, grumbling, and Charnock buttoned his skin-coat and jumped down into the snow. He sank to his knees, but went deeper before he reached the engine, round which a gang of men were at work with shovels. It was not his business to help them and he floundered on up the track they had made until he crossed the summit and saw the bridge in the distance.

Half an hour afterwards he met Festing and thought he looked surprised.

"You didn't come with the boys to dig us out," Charnock remarked.

"No," said Festing. "We knew the train had passed the Butte, and guessed where she was held up. But I hardly thought—"

"You didn't think I'd be up to time?" Charnock suggested. "Well, it's remarkable what a good example does!"

"Did you see Helen?"

"Sadie saw her. I understand she was very well and sent you a message. You're to finish your job and make good—Helen understands."

Festing was silent a moment, and when he looked up his eyes were soft. "Thank you, Bob! Or perhaps it's Sadie I ought to thank?"

"I wouldn't bother about it. Sadie's fond of meddling," Charnock answered with some embarrassment. "But will the snow stop the work?"

"Not altogether. We can keep busy on the hill and I'm going up now. Will you come?"

"Presently," said Charnock, smiling. "Food's a thing you don't seem to need when you're occupied, but I want my breakfast before I start."

Festing went away, and after a time Charnock joined him on the hill, where fresh trees had been felled and roughly squared with the ax. Men and horses were working hard, but Charnock stopped for a minute or two before he began. The snow was different from the thin covering that scarcely hid the short grass on the plains. The pines were glittering white pyramids, with branches that bent beneath their load, and there were no inequalities on the drop to the river. Every projection was leveled up, the hollows were filled, and the snow ran unbroken among the trunks in a smooth white sheet. It was not drying and getting powdery, because the frost was not very keen, and he imagined that Festing meant to get as much lumber as possible down while the surface could be beaten into a smooth track.

"You might take Gordon's team and break a trail by hauling the lighter pieces to the top," Festing said. "They'll run down when they have worn a chute, but we'll have some trouble man-handling the first."

Charnock nodded as he glanced over the edge of the narrow tableland. The descent was not steep near the top, but farther on it dropped precipitously to the water, crossing the curve by the bridge.

"How will you stop the heavy stuff going into the river?" he asked.

Festing indicated two men moving about the waterside. They looked curiously stumpy with their legs buried in the snow.

"I sent them to make a chain fast to the rocks. We'll shackle up the first logs we run down and make a lumber pond. A few may shoot across the top, but we'll see what must be done as we get on."

Charnock hooked the chain round the smallest log he could find and started the horses. They slipped and floundered as they plodded through the soft snow. Sometimes the log ran for a few yards, crushing down the surface, but it often sank overhead and the team struggled hard to drag it out. For all that, Charnock reached the top of the slope, and turning back, widened the trail he had made. The next log ran easier, although it gave him trouble, but when he stopped at noon he had beaten down a road.

When they started again he left the team to somebody else and joined the men who were clearing out a trough down the hill. This was harder work, but the small contractor finds it pays to give his men a lead instead of orders, and for a time Charnock used the shovel and his feet. Then Festing said they had better move a few logs as far as they would go, and they worked the first trunk down hill with handspikes and tackles. The lumber scored the bottom of the trough and would not run, and they struggled through the banked-up snow, lifting the heavy mass when it sank. Now and then they fixed the tackle to a tree and dragged the log across short skids thrust under its end, and at length launched it from the brow of the steeper pitch.

It plunged down some distance, but stopped again, half buried in loose snow, and they scrambled after it, clinging to small trees. Then the work got dangerous. One could scarcely stand on the steep bank, and when the log started it rather leaped than slid. Spikes, torn from the men's hands, shot into the air, and those in front sprang back for their lives, but the mass seldom went far before loose snow brought it up and the struggle with the levers began again. At last, it slipped from a hummock and glided slowly down, crumpling the snow in front, while a man, clinging to the butt and shouting hoarse jokes, trailed down the track behind.

Moving the next was easier, and those that followed ran without much help for most of the way, while when dark came the bank at the top was empty and there was a pile of logs held up by the chain at the waterside. Their descent had worn the channel smooth, and it was now difficult to stop them going too far. In a day or two Festing brought the most part of his material to the spot where it would be used, and got ready to put up the frames.

Stinging frost set in, and on the morning they cleared the ground for the first post Charnock felt daunted as he beat his numbed hands. The sky was clear; a hard, dazzling blue, against which the white peaks were silhouetted with every ridge and pinnacle in sharp outline. They twinkled like steel in places, but there were patches of delicate gray, and here and there a dark rock broke through its covering. The bottom of the gorge was soft blue, and the river a streak of raw indigo, but there was no touch of warm color in the savage landscape. The glitter made Charnock's eyes ache and the reflected sunshine burned his skin.

Some of the construction gangs were laid off, but in places men were at work. They looked small and feeble on the vast white slope, and a few plumes of smoke seemed to curl futilely out of the hollow. Frost and snow defied man's engine power, and the rattle of the machines was lost in the din the river made. Its channel was full of snow that had frozen in the honey-combed masses, and the ragged floes broke with a harsh, ringing crash. Others screamed as they smashed among the rocks and ground across ledges, while the tall cliffs on the opposite bank flung the echoes far among the pines. The uproar rose and sank, but its throbbing note voiced a challenge to human effort, and Charnock admitted that had the choice been left to him, he would have gone back to the warm shack and waited for better conditions.

Festing, however, would wait for nothing, and Kerr and Norton were equally resolute. Just now Festing was clearing away the snow while three or four men cautiously descended the bank, dragging loads of branches. A big fire was soon lighted, and when the resinous wood broke into snapping flame Festing cleared a spot farther on for another. By and by he scattered the first, the thawed surface was pierced, and a hole dug. Then with half an hour's savage labor they got the first big post on end. The next broke the supporting tackle and a man narrowly escaped when it fell, but they raised it again and got to work upon the braces. The wood was unseasoned and hard with frozen sap. Saw and auger would scarcely bite, but somehow they cut the notches and bored the holes. When the first frame was roughly stayed Charnock sat down with a breathless laugh.

"I suppose it's the best job we can make and it's up to

specification. Still, when one comes to think of it, the optimism of these railroad men is remarkable. Green wood and uncovered bolts that will soon work loose in the rotting pine! If I was an engineer, the thing would frighten me."

"The track will stand while they want it," Festing answered with an impatient look. "Long before it gets shaky they'll pull it down."

"Pulling things down is a national habit. A man I met in Winnipeg bought a nearly new hotel because he thought he could put up a better building on the site. However, I suppose there's something to be said for his point of view. Progress implies continuous moving on!"

"It does," said Festing. "While you moralize, the men you ought to put to work are standing still."

Charnock got up and went off, beating his hands. He noted that there was a hole in the mittens he had brought from home. This was annoying because Sadie had given him the mittens. In spite of many difficulties, they braced the posts securely before they stopped work, and when supper was over Charnock reluctantly put on his coat. He wanted to ask Norton something, and when he left the latter's office came back along a narrow path above the track. After going a short distance he stopped to look down at the half-finished frames.

The moon had not risen, but a pale glow shone above a gray peak and the sky was clear. One could not see much in the hollow, but the snow reflected a faint light. The timbers they had erected rose like a black skeleton, and after glancing at them, Charnock's eyes were drawn towards the pile of logs in the pond at the water's edge. A log pond is generally made in a river, where the stream will carry the trunks into the containing chains. But Festing had made his on land, using the snow instead of the current. Charnock could not tell what had attracted his attention, but stood motionless for a moment or two.

He heard nothing but the roar of the current and the crash of splintering ice, and could hardly distinguish the logs. Their outline was blurred and the dark-colored mass melted into a dusky background of rock and water. Yet he thought something had moved beside the pond.

Then an indistinct object detached itself from the pile. It was shapeless and he lost it next moment, but it had been visible against a patch of snow. It was not a man's height, and, so far as he could see, moved like an animal, but no wild beast would haunt the outskirts of a noisy construction camp. Since he could not imagine why a man should crawl about the logs at night, he resolved to satisfy his curiosity.

This needed caution, and he lay down and rolled himself in the snow. It stuck to his shaggy skin-coat, and remembering that some drills had been left near the track he felt about until he found one. The short steel bar was easy to carry and might be useful. The next thing was to get down without being seen, and he crept to the log-slide and sitting down let himself go. His coat rolled up and acted like a brake, but he reached and shot over the top of the last pitch. Next moment he struck the logs at the bottom with a jar that left him breathless, and he lay still to recover. His coat was white; indeed, the snow had forced its way inside his clothes, but he must be careful about his background and avoid abrupt movements.

Getting on his hands and knees, he crawled along the bottom of the pile. The logs were not numerous, since some had been used, and when Charnock reached the end he crouched in the snow and looked about. Nobody was there and his ears were not of much use because the crash of ice drowned every other sound. This made silence needless, and he tried to get between the logs and the water, but found it dangerous. The chain had sagged with the strain, and the lowest tier was scarcely a foot from the bank, along which the ice-floes rasped.

He came back and crawled half-way up the pile, meaning to reach the top, but stopped and lay flat. An object moved along

Harold Bindloss

the highest row, and he knew it was a man. The fellow's figure showed against the sky, though Charnock imagined he would have been invisible from above. He waited and felt his heart beat as he clenched the bar. The other did not seem to know he was watched and Charnock resolved to find out what he meant to do. He thought of the chain that held the logs; if this were loosed, the pile would roll into the river and be washed away, but it would be impossible to slip the fastening toggle while the links were strained. Still one might be nicked with a hacksaw and left to break with the shock when the next log ran down the slide. The man, however, could not get at the chain from the top row.

He came nearer and then stopped abruptly, as if alarmed. Charnock lay close in the hollow between two logs, but his coat was snowy and it was possible that the other had noticed the white patch. He turned and began to move back, not fast but with caution. Charnock felt it was unthinkable that he should get away, and raising himself, swung the drill round his head and let it go. It flew over the other man and vanished without a sound because the turmoil of the water drowned the splash, but Charnock lost his balance and rolled off the logs. He fell into the snow, and when he got up the man had gone.

For a few moments he stood still, hesitating and abusing his folly. He did not know if the fellow had seen the drill fly past or not, but he had thrown away his weapon, and might have a dangerous antagonist. For all that, he meant to discover who his antagonist was. Floundering through the snow, he reached the end of the pile, but found nobody there. The lumber gang had made a path along the water's edge, but Charnock could see nobody among the scattered trees. He climbed to the top of the logs and looked down on the other side, but saw nothing between the water and the pile.

After this, he felt the fastening of the chain, which did not seem to have been tampered with, because the toggle was securely fixed across the strap-link. Then he crept about the pile again, with an uncomfortable feeling that the other might be lying in wait for him, but saw nothing suspicious, and there was no use in examining the trampled snow. By and by he gave up the search and returned to the path, feeling disturbed. It was impossible to guess what the man had meant to do, or who he was, but Charnock resolved to watch.

Harold Bindloss

CHAPTER XXVIII

THE LEWIS BOLT

Charnock went back next morning and examined the chain, but found none of the links or fastenings damaged. This was puzzling, and he wondered whether the man he had seen, knowing that somebody was about, had stolen away without beginning what he came to do. The explanation was plausible, but left Charnock uncertain who the fellow was. He suspected Wilkinson, but only because he could think of nobody else with any ground for wishing to do him or Festing an injury.

On the whole, he thought it better not to tell Festing. It was rather an improbable story, and Stephen might think him imaginative, but he would watch and try to catch the fellow if he came again. For a week, he made excuses for going out after supper, and Festing did not object although he looked surprised, but he saw nothing and it was very cold lurking about the track. Moreover he was generally tired after his day's hard work, and was glad to give up the search.

Some time later, he returned from Norton's office one night and had reached the track when he saw a man coming obliquely up the slope. There was moonlight, and the snow glittered between the shadows of the trees. Charnock saw the other plainly and drew back into the gloom along the bank. The fellow did not seem to mind whether he was seen or not, but Charnock thought he knew his walk and figure, and when he reached the track set off with the object of overtaking him.

The loose snow dulled his steps, and he was close upon the man when the latter stopped and turned. Then Charnock saw, without much surprise, that it was Wilkinson.

"What were you doing down there?" he asked.

"I don't see what that has to do with you," Wilkinson answered coolly.

"The logs in the pond are ours."

Wilkinson looked amused and Charnock tried to control his temper. He would gain nothing by using force, and thought the other meant to give him no excuse for doing so.

"You don't imagine I meant to steal your logs!" Wilkinson rejoined. "They're too large to carry away, and there's no sawmill to buy them if I sent them down the river."

"That's obvious," said Charnock, who thought it prudent not to hint that he had seen the fellow lurking about the pond before. For that matter, he was not certain he had seen Wilkinson.

"You're much more suspicious than you were when I first knew you," Wilkinson resumed in a mocking tone.

"I was a confiding fool then and trusted my friends. It cost me something."

"And now you're afraid to let anybody pass your logs in the dark? Well, caution's useful, but it can be overdone."

"Why did you want to pass the pond?"

"For one thing, because it's the easiest way of getting from the smithy to the track; then this piece of hillside doesn't belong to you. However, as I guess you don't claim it, you no doubt reckoned I meant to play you some shabby trick; turn your logs adrift, for example?"

"I don't think it's impossible."

Wilkinson laughed. "Well, I might do you an injury if the thing wasn't difficult, but don't let your suspicions make you ridiculous. If you feel uneasy, you can watch the pond. Anyhow, the cold's fierce and I'm going to the bunk-house."

Charnock let him go and returned thoughtfully to the shack. He did not doubt that Wilkinson had been to the smithy, because one could find out if he had not, but he felt disturbed. The fellow had somehow encouraged him to believe he might tamper with the logs; but would hardly have done so had he meant to set them adrift. He might, of course, have wanted to keep him uneasy without ground; but suppose it was a feint, intended to cover the real attack, made at another point? Charnock determined to be cautious and keep his eyes open.

He saw nothing to cause him fresh anxiety, although he once or twice visited the pond at night. In the daytime his work absorbed his attention, for they were now building a lofty frame on the steepest pitch of the dip. The foot of the longest timber, which was unusually massive, rested in a socket cut in the rock near the water's edge, and it cost them a very hard and dangerous day's work to get the log on end. Indeed, for a few anxious minutes Charnock imagined that the mass would break the tackles and come down. When fixed, it was nearly perpendicular, but its top inclined slightly toward the bank, and Festing sent for Norton and Kerr.

"It's a good post, but I'm not sure we have got spread enough," he said. "There's not much to resist the outward thrust a heavy train might cause. Still, I don't see how we could have carried the foot farther back."

"You'd have to go into the water," Norton agreed. "That would have meant a coffer dam, and the Company won't stand for expensive extras."

"The ice would have smashed the dam," said Kerr. "The job meets the plan, which calls for stays to stop the post canting out. Put in an extra king-tie half-way up and I'll pass your bill and find the ironwork."

Festing was satisfied with this, and the post was stayed with chains while they got the braces fixed. This took some days, for the men were forced to work on dangerous snowy ledges and boards, hung from the top. Where there was most risk and difficulty Festing went himself, but he looked anxious.

"It's the worst part of the job and perhaps the most awkward thing I've done," he said one night. "If the frame came down with the rockwork filling, it might start the rest and shake some length of road."

"But there's no reason it should come down," Charnock argued.

"Not in a way, but I'm glad Kerr authorized the extra brace. We'll use the heaviest stuff we can, and although the fastenings may give some trouble, we haven't come to them yet. Perhaps I'm getting nervous. We're up to schedule and doing pretty well, but it will be a relief to get the contract finished."

Charnock told him about Wilkinson, and he looked thoughtful.

"I can't see his object, particularly since he left the chain alone. Of course he may have meant some mischief, but gave it up when he found you on his track."

"Somehow I don't think that was it," said Charnock, who went to open the door.

Kerr came in and after a time began to talk about the fastenings for the main tie-beam.

"As the rock is sound and can be thawed, I think we could use

Harold Bindloss

a bolt on the Lewis plan. Give me some paper and I'll make a sketch you can take to the smith."

Charnock examined the drawing and noted that the holding part of the bolt was shaped like the letter Y, except that the stalk was split. A wedge was sketched to fit the split, and would obviously expand the upper arms to fit tightly into a fan-shaped hole with a narrow mouth.

"I've not seen this kind of fastening before," he said. "It ought to grip well, but something depends upon the wedge."

Kerr nodded. "The wedge must be properly forged and fit tight, but there's a cross bolt to stop it backing out. So long as it doesn't break under the hammer, it can't come loose. Something depends on the way the hole is cut and the rock, but the stuff you're working is hard enough."

Next morning Charnock took the drawing to the smith, and calling at the forge a day or two later, found Wilkinson sitting on a box. He had brought a pick to be mended and made a few ironical remarks, until the smith showed Charnock some irons he had forged.

"I guess that's what you want, but I haven't finished the Lewis yet. Reckoned I'd wait until I could get a bit of horseshoe iron for the wedge when the new stores come along."

"What's that bar in the corner?" Charnock asked.

"Steel," said the smith. "A bit off the end would make a wedge, but you want to be careful you don't overheat the steel in the forge if it's to stand hammering after. Horseshoe iron's better for your particular job. Come back in a day or two and I'll have the thing ready."

Charnock left him and one afternoon soon afterwards helped Festing to notch and bore the heavy cross-tie to fit the post and the ends of the timbers it was to hold in place. These were intended to strengthen the frame, of which the post and tie were the most important members, and Festing had waited until their other ends were securely fixed. When the light was fading he beckoned Charnock.

"You might get the Lewis bolt. The smith sent word it's ready and I want to fasten the tie before we stop."

When Charnock reached the forge the smith was absent, but he blew the fire until the light flickered about the shop and looked for the bolt. He found it in a corner and took the wedge to the hearth. It was properly shaped and slotted for a cross-bolt, but it looked rough and scaly, and giving the blower a few more strokes he tapped it once or twice. The scale fell off and the metal looked sound. Then while the flame spread about the fuel he glanced round the shop. There was no horseshoe iron, but the bar of steel had recently been cut, and he thought the wedge had been forged out of its end.

Charnock did not think this mattered much. Festing had urged the smith to finish the job, and the man knew his business. Since he had been forced to use steel, he had no doubt taken the necessary precautions. It was dark when Charnock got back to the frame, but a blast-lamp threw out a dazzling glare and he climbed to a beam on which Festing sat. At the timber's inner end a fire burned on a shelf of rock and a man was stirring something in an iron pot.

"We're melting lead to fill up the hole, though I don't know if it's necessary," Festing said. "Have you got the bolt?"

"It's here. He has made it out of steel; the iron he expected hasn't arrived."

"That's all right. They now use steel for many jobs instead of iron, and the softer kinds are quite as tough. Anyhow, we can trust the smith not to burn the metal. Help Black while I get the tie ready for fastening."

Half an hour later the big cross-beam was in position and Charnock watched Festing fit the bolt into its fan-shaped socket. He did so with fastidious care and then standing on the beam swung the hammer a workman gave him. The blast-lamp roared upon a timber overhead, throwing down waves of light that flooded the rock face, but the twinkling brightness rather puzzled the eye. For all that, Festing struck the wedge squarely and drove it home with a few heavy blows. Then he fastened the cross-bolt and Charnock filled a ladle with the melted lead. A blue flame flickered about the cavity as he poured in the stuff, there was an angry sputtering, and he afterwards found some holes in his coat. Festing dropped his hammer with a gesture of satisfaction.

"That's an awkward piece of work finished, and I feel happier now! You can put out the lamp and quit, boys; I'll mark you up full time."

Then they got down from the frame and went home to supper, earlier than usual. In the morning they began to build a wall of roughly-cut stones among the timber, filling in the space behind with rubble; and kept on until at noon, a day or two later, heavy snow began to fall. It was impossible to work, and they lounged about the shack, smoking and reading, all next day. Charnock was thankful for the rest, but Festing grumbled and now and then walked impatiently to the door. Late at night the former was wakened by a distant rumbling. It sounded like thunder, and he called to his comrade.

"What's that? Had we better get up?"

"Sounds like a big snow-slide," said Festing, raising himself in his bunk. "Won't harm us; shack's on top of the ridge and we're safer here than anywhere else." He stopped and listened to the swelling roar and then resumed: "I'm glad we got that frame braced. It's a big slide and will probably come down the gully near the bridge. They're going to snowshed that piece of track and we'll haul out the posts if we can't get on with the other job."

He lay down again, but Charnock waited. This was the first snow-slide he had heard and he felt awed by the din. Growing in a long crescendo, it rolled down the hill in a torrent of sound, but by and by he thought he could distinguish different notes; the crash of trees carried away by the avalanche and the scream of gravel grinding across rocky scraps. He could imagine the stones being planed away and the mass of broken trunks riding on top of the huge white billow.

It was impossible to sit still, and jumping down, he lighted the lamp, but found it hard to replace the glass. The shack throbbed, the table on which he put the matches shook, and there was a rattle of crockery, but this was drowned by an overwhelming roar. The avalanche was pouring down a gully near the shack, and he leaned against the table, deafened, until it passed. Then he heard the turmoil of a tremendous cataract and imagined the snow was plunging into the river and deflecting the current upon the other bank. The sound gradually died away and he could hear detached noises; great pines, broken rocks, and soil, rushing down behind the fallen mass. There were heavy splashes, and then a strange, unnatural silence.

"It's finished," Festing remarked. "Rather alarming for the first time, but one gets used to it. You can put out the light and go back to bed."

Charnock did so and soon went to sleep. In the morning they found that the most part of the avalanche had fallen into the river, but its tail remained, resting in a steep cone of snow and broken trees and soil, against the bank on which they had built the frames. The top of the cone extended far up the hill, but, owing to the sharpness of the pitch, its bottom, which covered the frames and rockwork, was thin. Festing sent half the men to cut this portion away, and the others up the hill to haul posts for the snowshed to the top of the slides. It was obvious that a very heavy weight rested on the buried work, but the pressure was uniform, unlike the jarring of a train, and he did not feel disturbed.

About four o'clock in the afternoon he came to see how much progress the shovel gang had made, and Charnock, who superintended their labor, showed him what they had done. They had cut a gap in the cone, and part of the rockwork was exposed nearly to the bottom. On each side, the snow ran down to the water in a uniform smooth slant, except where broken trees projected from the surface. Above, the mass of snow rested on the shelf that would carry the track and on the top of the half-finished work. It glittered with a yellow flush where it caught the fading light, but in the hollow its color was a dull, cold blue.

By and by they examined the wall. So far as they could see, the stonework bore the unusual load well, but in one spot there was a crack between two courses.

"I'll get up there in the morning and see if it's worth while to drive in a few wedges," Festing remarked. "You had better watch that bank of snow. Some of it will probably break away."

"We have had two or three small falls," said Charnock, and Festing beckoned one of the men.

"Come up the hill in the morning, Tom. I'm going to clear the log-slide or break a new one. Which d'you think would be best?"

While they talked about it, a shower of snow fell on Charnock, who stepped back.

"Watch out!" he cried. "There's more coming!"

Festing moved a pace or two and went on talking, but Charnock fixed his eyes on the snow. The part above the track overhung the gap in a bulging cornice, as if it was moving down hill, and in a few moments a heavier shower began. The bulge got more prominent, but the cornice did not break off, and while he watched it, wondering whether he should call out the men, a stone fell from the wall and dropped at his feet. This was ominous, but next moment a mass of snow struck his head, nearly knocking him down, and when he recovered his balance and wiped his face he noted with alarm that the stones were opening and the big post leaned outwards.

"Jump for your lives, boys!" he shouted, and throwing himself on Festing, drove him back.

Then there was a roar of falling stones and a crash. The massive post lurched towards him and the air was filled with snow. He heard struts and braces crack as the post tore them out, and thought Festing turned round in order to see what was happening. He pushed him away, and then sank into loose snow and fell. Before he could get up there was a deafening noise, something struck him a heavy blow, and he was buried.

After a short struggle he got his head out, and finding that he was thinly covered, made an effort to extricate himself. When he had done so, he saw the men some distance up the bank. They were all there except Festing, but he noticed a heap of big stones and broken beams close by.

"Back here, boys! The boss is underneath!" he shouted, and threw himself upon the stones as the others ran up.

For a minute or two they worked desperately, flinging the lumps of rock about and dragging away the beams; and then stopped as they uncovered Festing. His face looked very white, although a red stain ran down his forehead. Charnock shivered and glanced at the break in the white mass above the track.

"It's risky, but we've got to pull him out before some more snow comes down," he said in a hoarse voice. "Scrape the snow off carefully, Tom. Get hold here with me, Pete."

After two or three minutes' cautious work they lifted Festing out of the hole. He was unconscious and his arm looked short and distorted. Charnock felt horror-struck and dizzy, but pulled himself together.

"Go for Kerr, one of you," he said. "Then I want the stretcher and a hand-sledge. Bring a blast-lamp; ours is smashed."

The men scattered, except for one who stayed with him, and kneeling in the snow he opened Festing's fur-coat and took off his cap. His head was cut and his arm broken, but Charnock did not think this altogether accounted for his unconsciousness. He suspected broken ribs, but could detect nothing unusual when he felt his comrade's side.

Kerr arrived first and looked at Festing.

"Unconscious all the time?" he asked, and when Charnock nodded resumed: "Most important thing's to get a doctor, and I'll see to that. Then I'll get some brandy."

As he hurried away three or four men came down the hill with the sledge and stretcher, and one rigged and lighted a powerful lamp. Accidents are common at construction camps, and one of Norton's gang examined Festing.

"He's sure got it badly; arm's not the worst," he said. "We'll tend to that and then slide him gently on the stretcher. Carrying him might be dangerous; we'll fix the whole outfit on the sled."

While they were occupied a plume of smoke shot up above the pines, and Charnock knew Kerr had sent off a locomotive to bring help. When they had put Festing on the stretcher a man arrived with brandy, but Festing could not swallow, and seizing the sledge traces, they started up the hill. Norton was in the shack when they reached it, and felt Festing's clothes.

"Not damp; it would be safer to let him lie until the doctor comes," he said, and sent the men away. Then he turned to Charnock sharply. "Sit right down!"

Charnock swayed, clutched the chair, and sank limply into the seat. The floor heaved and the quiet figure on the stretcher got indistinct. Then Norton held out a glass.

"Drink it quick!"

Charnock's teeth rattled against the glass, but he swallowed the liquor, and sat motionless for a moment or two.

"Seemed to lose my balance. Bit of a shock you know, and I expect that stone hit me pretty hard."

"So I imagine; there's an ugly bruise on your face," said Norton, giving him back the glass. "The first dose braced you. Take some more."

"I think not," said Charnock, with a forced smile. "Dangerous remedy if you have suffered from my complaint. Didn't know my face was hurt until you told me. When d'you think the doctor will come?"

"There's a man at Jackson's Bench. Loco ought to make the double trip in about two hours."

"Two hours!" said Charnock faintly, and braced himself to wait.

CHAPTER XXIX

FOUL PLAY

Some time after the accident a doctor arrived and set Festing's arm. He found two ribs were broken and suspected other injuries, but could not question his half conscious patient. When he had done all that was possible in the meantime and had seen Festing lifted carefully into his bunk, he put a dressing on Charnock's bruised face and pulled a chair to the fire.

"I'll keep watch; your partner has got an ugly knock," he said. "Don't think I'll want anything, and you had better go to bed."

Charnock could not sleep and spent the night uncomfortably on a chair. He was sore and dazed, but his anxiety would not let him rest, and once or twice he softly crossed the floor to his comrade's bunk. The last time he did so the doctor, whose head had fallen forward, looked up with a jerk and frowned as he signed him to go back. After this, Charnock kept as still as his jarred nerves would permit. Sometimes Festing groaned, and sometimes made a feeble movement, but so far as Charnock could see, his eyes were shut.

About three o'clock in the morning, the doctor stood for some minutes beside the bunk, and Charnock shivered as he watched his face. The shack seemed very quiet except for the throb of the river and the grinding of the ice. Then the doctor gave him a nod that hinted at satisfaction, and told him to refill the iron drum at Festing's feet with hot water. By and by he put fresh wood in the stove, moving cautiously and taking as long as possible, because it was a relief to do something after sitting still in suspense.

At daybreak there was a knock at the door, and Charnock, finding Kerr and Norton outside, looked at the doctor, who put on his fur-coat and went out to them.

"Have you any news for us?" Norton asked.

"No change yet. That's encouraging, as far as it goes."

"What about breakfast? Ours is ready. Will you join us?"

"I think not. If my patient doesn't come out of his stupor, I must try to rouse him soon. Send a man here and take Mr. Charnock. I expect he needs food."

"Very well," said Kerr. "We'll see the cook looks after you; but can you give us no idea about Festing? You see, there are matters, business matters—"

"He has had a bad shock and it will be a long job; a month anyway. I can't stop long and he ought to have a nurse, although it would be difficult to get one to come here. But I can't form an opinion yet."

He dismissed them and Kerr took Charnock away. It was very cold. The white pines were growing into shape; their tops caught the light in the east and glimmered with a faint warm flush against the dim blue shadow. Smoke and puffs of steam floated up from the gorge, and the ringing clang of steel pierced the turmoil of the river. Charnock felt braced but dizzy. Now he came to think of it, he had eaten no supper, and after a day of laborious effort the night's watch had fatigued him. Besides, his face smarted under the bandage, and his back was sore.

When he sat down in Norton's shack, where a plate was put for Kerr, he felt ravenously hungry and did not talk much until the meal was over. Then Norton made him sit near the stove.

"It's an awkward business," he said. "To begin with, what are we going to do about a nurse? This is hardly the place for a woman, and I doubt if we could get anybody to undertake the job."

"I'll write to Mrs. Festing."

"Would she come out?"

"I imagine so," said Charnock thoughtfully. "Still she doesn't know much about nursing."

"His wife is the proper person to look after him," Kerr interposed. "Then I have a young fellow in the rail gang who could help; found him useful once or twice when the boys got hurt. In fact, I suspect he's had some medical training, though I didn't ask why he quit."

Norton smiled. It is not unusual to find men whose professional career has been cut short working on a Western track.

"That simplifies matters. If you had wanted a lawyer or an accountant, I could have sent a man. However, there's another thing—"

"There is; it's important," Kerr agreed. "Who's going to carry on the contract?"

Charnock leaned forward eagerly. "I'll try. Give me a chance. I think I know my job."

There was silence for a few moments and Norton looked at Kerr, who slowly filled his pipe.

"I'd like to consent," he said, "but I'm the Company's servant and there's a risk." He paused and turned to Norton. "However, it's really your business. If things go wrong, the trouble's coming to you first."

"Sure. I'm willing to take the risk. I don't expect Charnock will fool the job, but if he does you can get after me. I'll stand for it."

"Very well! We'll let it go at that."

Charnock got up, with some color in his bandaged face, because he knew what Norton's confidence meant. He was, so to speak, an unknown man and the contract had been given to Festing, who was an engineer. If he failed, the men who trusted him would be held accountable.

"Thank you both," he said with feeling. "If labor and money can put the thing over, I won't let you down."

He went out, for he had, in his anxiety about other matters, forgotten his men, and it was now important that no time, which must be paid for, should be wasted. Finding some of the gang at work clearing away the fallen material and some hauling lumber on the hill, he gave them a few orders and returned to the shack. When he got there Festing was conscious and the doctor said he might speak to him.

"How do you feel?" Charnock asked.

"Better than the doctor thinks I ought to feel," Festing answered with a feeble smile. "You seem to have got knocked about!"

Charnock said he was not much the worse, and Festing resumed: "Have you seen Norton? What does he say about the contract?"

"I have seen him; you needn't bother. He has left the job to me; I'll finish it somehow."

A look of relief came into Festing's face. "That's comforting news; I was afraid—You're a good partner, Bob!"

"I don't know if I've been of much help so far, and the money I put into the undertaking wasn't mine. There's a third partner, Stephen, and I think she'd like me to see you through."

Festing gave him a grateful glance and closed his eyes. After a time, he opened them feebly and asked: "Do you know why the frame gave way?"

"Not yet," said Charnock with some dryness. "I mean to find out!"

Then the doctor interrupted and sent him away. Going back to the scene of the accident, he found the damage less serious than he thought. Part of the wall had fallen and the post, which had broken, had pulled down the timbers attached, but these could be replaced, and Charnock, calling two men, began to clear the snow from the king-tie, which he imagined had given way first. He found the Lewis bolt fixed to its end, but the wedge had gone, and he climbed to the spot where the end of the beam had been fixed. The stone socket had not broken, but pieces of crushed lead lay near the hole. The soft metal had not much holding power and had been used to fill up the crevices.

Sitting down, he began with methodical patience to turn over the snow and loose rubble that remained on the shelf after the large stones had fallen. The odds were against his finding what he sought, but he persevered for an hour and then picked up a piece of broken metal a few inches long. It was half of the wedge, which had broken at the slot, but although he searched carefully he could not find the other part. Putting the piece in his pocket, he went to the forge and, seeing the smith was occupied, sat down and filled his pipe. The door was open and the light reflected from the snow was strong. Charnock was glad of this, because he wanted to see the smith, who presently dropped his hammer and leaned against the hearth.

"How's your partner getting on?" he asked. "Mr. Festing's the kind of man I like; I was sorry to hear he had got hurt."

Charnock studied the man. His face was pale and wrinkled under the grime, but he looked honest, and if his statement was sincere, as Charnock thought, it seemed to clear the ground. After giving him a few particulars about Festing's injuries, he lighted his pipe.

"Wilkinson's not here to-day," he remarked.

"He's not always here," said the smith. "He comes when there are picks and drills that want sharpening."

"I saw him once or twice when I was in, and thought he was a friend of yours."

"He can swap a good yarn; kind of handy man and sometimes helps me with the hammer, but I guess that's all there is to it."

"Just so," said Charnock carelessly. "This is a warm place for a quiet smoke, and the foreman can't tell how long one ought to stop, particularly as you're sometimes out at the machine-shop. Do you find the boys meddle with your tools if they come in while you're away?"

"No, sir; there'd be trouble if I did! Besides, nobody comes but Wilkinson, and if I'm out he waits."

Charnock nodded, as if it did not matter. He had found out what he wanted to know and thought he had not excited the smith's suspicions. Taking the broken wedge from his pocket, he put it on the hearth.

"I expect you know what that is! The Lewis smashed when the

Harold Bindloss

frame came down."

"It's the wedge. Don't see why it broke; plenty metal left, though the slot weakened it."

"What's it made of?"

"Steel. The iron I wanted didn't come; but this is mild, low-carbon stuff."

"Then what's the matter with it. It did break."

The smith put the piece into a socket in the anvil and struck it with a hammer. The end broke short, and picking up the fragment he went to the door.

"Nature's gone out of it; I sure can't understand the thing," he said with a puzzled look. "If I hadn't forged the stuff myself, I'd allow it was burned."

"You don't often overheat the steel you work."

"No, sir," said the smith, who took up a piece of metal, pierced with holes. "Made this out of the same bar, and it took more forging. Now you watch!"

He put the object in a vise and hammered down the end, which did not break. "That's all right, anyhow; tough and most as soft as iron. But steel's sometimes treacherous; you want to be careful—"

"Could you tell by looking at it if a piece was burned?"

"Well," said the smith thoughtfully, "it's not always easy, but if the thing was badly scaled, I'd be suspicious. Of course, there might be some scale—"

"But the wedge looked all right when you finished it?"

"It certainly did," said the smith, who hesitated. "Say do you reckon it was the bolt going that let down your frame?"

"So far, I imagine it was the weight of snow. The pile ran back up the hill and must have made a crushing load. For all that, I'm curious about the wedge."

"Well," said the other, "If it was the wedge, I'm surely sorry! The blamed thing is burned, though I don't know how. But if she was loaded up too much, she might have broken anyhow, burned or not."

"I expect so," said Charnock, getting up. "You needn't bother about the matter; I'm not blaming you."

His face got very grim when he went out, for what he had learned fitted in with his suspicions. Wilkinson had heard the smith say that steel could be easily spoiled, and sometimes came to the forge when the man was away. Then there was the rough, scaly look of the wedge, which had been put out of the smith's sight, inside the split shank of the bolt. Everything was plain; Charnock knew why the tie gave way and allowed the frame to fall.

The thought of the treacherous injury made his blood boil. The thing had been so easily done; five minutes' work at the blower, a few strokes with a big hammer when the steel was dangerously hot, and then, perhaps, a sudden quenching in the snow, when the steel ought to have slowly cooled. He had been wrong in thinking men would not risk much for the sake of revenge. Wilkinson had foully struck his comrade and perhaps crippled him for life. But the cunning brute must be punished, and driven from the camp, and when he left should carry marks that would make it difficult to forget his offense.

Charnock, however, could not at once seek out his antagonist. He had promised Festing to carry on the contract; they had had a number of setbacks, and the accident would cost them much. Wages were high and it was essential that the men should be usefully employed, while there was now nobody but himself to superintend the work. Besides, the doctor might want him and he must call at the shack every now and then to see how Festing was getting on. It looked as if he must leave Wilkinson alone until he had more leisure in the evening.

It was a trying day. The doctor sent him errands and sometimes allowed him to come in for a few minutes, but his reports were not favorable, and Festing was either asleep or too feeble to talk. When work stopped and Charnock went to the shack after some hours' absence the doctor looked very grave.

"I'm sorry I must keep you out," he said. "You mean well, but you're clumsy, while the young fellow Mr. Kerr sent has had some training and knows his job."

"Then my partner's worse?"

"Well, I'll own that I'm anxious about to-night; but if he gets over the early morning, I'll have hope. Go to the engineer's shack and I'll send you a report, if possible."

Charnock tried to brace himself as he went away. So far, he had not imagined that Festing might die. He had got a shock, but must not let it overwhelm him. Thinking hard, he walked to Norton's shack to get some food. He was worn out and felt some pain.

Norton gave him supper and offered him room for the night, and Charnock forced himself to eat. When the meal was over he lounged in a comfortable chair with his eyes shut for a time, and then got up and put on his coat.

"Where are you going?" Norton asked.

"I've some business at the camp," Charnock replied in a very grim voice.

He went out and as he walked down the track met the

locomotive engineer, who stopped.

"Is that you, Mr. Charnock? Cold's pretty fierce to-night. How's Mr. Festing?"

Charnock had not felt the cold until then, but he shivered and beat his hands as he replied that Festing was badly hurt. Then he asked: "Are you going out with the loco?"

"Thought I'd finished, but they've wired that the cars are wanted on the next section and I've got to run them along."

"Ah," said Charnock. "Have you seen Wilkinson?"

"Met him going to the bunk-house just before you came up."

Charnock went on, and presently entered the big wooden shed, which was full of tobacco smoke and the smell of hot iron and food. The warmth made him dizzy after the cold outside. A group of men had gathered about the stove, others sat at the dirty table with pipes and newspapers, and a few were quarreling about a game of cards, but Charnock could not see them distinctly.

One or two looked round as he stopped near the door, dazzled by the light. He had pulled off the bandage, and there was a large, dark bruise on his face, which was set. His mouth made a firm line and his eyes glittered. Then the foreman got up.

"Well," he asked harshly, "what do you want?"

Charnock gave him a careless glance. The fellow was truculent and had bullied Charnock when he worked in his gang, while the latter had sometimes replied to his abuse with witty retorts that left a sting. Afterwards, he had beaten his persecutor badly in the dispute about the borrowed workmen.

"I'm looking for Wilkinson."

"What d'you want him for?" the foreman asked suspiciously.

"That's my business."

"Then this is my bunk-house; anyhow, I'm in charge. Guess you'd better get back to the bosses' shacks, where you belong."

Charnock noted the sneer, but said quietly, "I'll go as soon as I've had a word with Wilkinson."

He tried to see if Wilkinson was there, and did not think he was, but could not be certain. The foreman's manner hinted that he meant to protect the fellow.

"You'll go now! D'you want me to put you out?"

For a moment Charnock stood still, and then suddenly lost his self-control in a fit of savage rage. He had suffered at the hands of the brute, who was trying to prevent his finding Wilkinson. But he did not mean to be baulked, and stepped forward with his fists clenched.

He could not remember who struck first, but got a blow on his body that made him gasp. Then he felt his knuckles jar on his antagonist's face, and the next moment staggered and fell against a bench that upset with a crash. He recovered, bent from the waist to dodge a blow that would have felled him, and struck over the other's arm.

The foreman reeled, but did not fall, and closed with Charnock, who could not get away because of the table. The latter felt his antagonist's strength, and there was no room for skill. When he tried to break loose his feet struck the upset bench, and the wall was close by. Breathing hard, they rocked to and fro in a furious grapple, striking when a hand could be loosed, and then fell apart, exhausted. Both were bleeding but determined, for deep-rooted dislike had suddenly changed to overpowering hate. Moreover Charnock knew the foreman was Wilkinson's friend, and half suspected him of a share in the plot.

In the meantime the men gathered round, scarcely giving the fighters room, and some, crowded off the floor, mounted the table. Nobody, however, interfered. They had no part in the quarrel and did not know what it was about, but while a number sympathized with Charnock, it was dangerous to offend their boss.

Charnock resumed the attack, advancing with a savage rush. The foreman gave ground, but stretched out his foot and Charnock, tripping over it, plunged forward and fell among the legs of the nearest men. They crowded back, and as he got up awkwardly the foreman seized a heavy billet of cordwood and flung it at his head. The billet struck his shoulder, but he was on his feet, his face set and white, and his eyes vindictively hard. It was a foul blow, but there are few rules to hamper men who fight in a Western construction camp, and Charnock thought his antagonist meant to use a stove-iron that lay close by. Feinting at the other, he dodged and seized a pick-handle he had noticed on the floor. He was just in time, for the foreman struck at him with the iron. It clashed upon the pick-handle, but Charnock got the next blow home and the foreman fell upon the table, on which Charnock pinned him down. Then getting his right arm loose, he struck with blind fury.

He was seized from behind, and while he struggled to get loose somebody gasped: "That's enough! Do you want to kill the man?"

"Yes," said Charnock hoarsely. "Let me go!"

"Help me choke him off! He's surely mad!" cried the man behind.

Somebody else got hold of Charnock. He was dragged back, hustled away from the table and towards the door. Then the bar was torn from his hands and a man pushed him out in the snow.

"You have fixed him good," said somebody in a breathless voice. "Go home and cool off!"

"If Wilkinson's inside, I'm coming back," Charnock declared.

The man laughed. "Wilkinson lit out through the store-shed 'bout a minute after you came in."

Charnock felt faint and dizzy, but tried to think when the fellow banged the door. It looked as if Wilkinson knew why he had come, and had stolen away after seeing the struggle begin. Moreover he had friends who might go after him and tell him what had happened to the foreman. Then he remembered that the locomotive engineer had been ordered to move some cars, and set off for the track.

The snow was rough, he fell into holes, and stubbed his feet against the ties, but stumbled on until he heard the locomotive snort. Then there was a jar of iron, wheels rattled, and a dark mass in front began to roll away. He was too late, and when he stopped and tried to get his breath two men came down the track.

"Did any of the boys go out on the train?" he asked.

"Only Wilkinson," one replied.

"Where's he going?"

"I don't know," said the other. "As he took his clothes-bag, it doesn't look as if he was coming back."

Charnock set off for Norton's office. He did not know how he got there, because a reaction had begun, and he sat down feeling powerless and badly shaken.

CHAPTER XXX

UNDERSTANDING

At midnight, Charnock, sitting drowsily in a chair in Norton's office, roused himself with a jerk. He was too anxious about Festing to go to bed, but bodily fatigue reacted on his brain and dulled his senses. For all that, he thought he heard steps in the snow, and getting up quickly went to the door. The bitter cold pierced him like a knife and he shivered. A man stood outside, and his dark figure, silhouetted against the snow, was somehow ominous. Charnock tried to brace himself, for he feared bad news.

"Well?" he said hoarsely.

"It's Musgrave; the doctor sent me along. Your partner's taken a turn. He's going the right way now."

Charnock looked at the messenger. His relief was overwhelming and he could not speak.

"That's all, but I guess it's good enough, and you can go to sleep," the other resumed, and went away.

When he vanished among the trees Charnock returned to his chair. He thought he ought to have brought the man in and made him some coffee, but he was horribly tired and did not want to move about and talk. Besides, he was conscious of a poignant satisfaction that prevented his thinking about

Harold Bindloss

anything else. While he indulged it a wave of fatigue swept over him and his head drooped. He tried to open his eyes but could not, and a few minutes later he was sound asleep.

When he awoke the sun shone into the office and he felt stiff and cramped, but not cold. This was strange, and he glanced at the stove, which he had expected to find nearly out. The iron, however, glowed a dull red and he could hear the cordwood snapping. Somebody must have put in fresh fuel, and looking at his watch he got up with a start. The men had been at work for two hours, with nobody to superintend them. Then he heard a movement and turning round saw one in the room.

"Feeling better, boss?" the fellow asked. "Mr. Kerr told me to come and see if you were awake. Said you'd find breakfast ready if you went to his place."

"I expect you thought waiting for me to wake was easier than rolling logs," Charnock suggested.

"Oh, well!" said the other; "you won't find we've fooled away much time."

Charnock went to Festing's shack and the doctor nodded and indicated his comrade's bunk. As Charnock stopped beside it Festing turned his head.

"Things going all right, Bob?"

"They were last night," said Charnock, with some embarrassment. "I don't know about this morning because I've just got up. But how are you?"

Festing smiled. "Much better; imagine I'm not knocked out yet. You needn't bother about being late. The boys are a pretty good crowd, and they like you. I'm rather glad you didn't hustle them as much as I wanted."

"That's enough," said the doctor, who followed Charnock to

the door and gave him a hopeful report.

Charnock ate a very good breakfast in Kerr's shack, but his face was grave when he began his work. Luck had put upon him a heavy responsibility, but he must shoulder the load. Sadie and Helen and Festing had given him much, and now the time had come to pay them back. Moreover, with the responsibility had come a chance of proving and, so to speak reinstating, himself. He was entangled in a coil from which there was but one way out; he must stand by his comrade and finish the contract, or own himself a wastrel. The difficulties were obvious, but there was some encouragement. Perhaps the hardest battle had been fought, for he had grappled with his craving for liquor and thought he had won. Then the pain had not troubled him for some time.

The men gave him no trouble, and he imagined they worked with more energy than usual. Now and then one or another stopped to ask, with obvious sincerity, how the boss was getting on; men from the railroad gangs, some of whom he scarcely knew, made inquiries, and Charnock felt moved. His partner's justice had won him respect, but he saw that some of the sympathy was meant for himself.

Two days later he heard the rumble of an approaching supply train and walked up the track to meet it. The locomotive stopped farther off than he expected, and a woman got down. Running forward, he saw that it was Helen.

"Stephen's doing well; that's the first thing you'll want to know," he said when they met.

"I know it already. A man told me as soon as the train stopped; he seemed to guess who I am."

"Ah!" said Charnock; "the boys are very good! It makes me proud to feel they all like Stephen. But why didn't you telegraph us? The Company would have sent on the message."

Helen smiled. "I didn't see much use in doing so. You knew when your letter would arrive and how long it would take me to come. It's significant that you came to meet the train."

"Perhaps it's characteristic that I came too late to help you down! But the engineer stopped short of the usual place, and I really have much to do just now."

Helen gave him a quick glance. Bob had not lost his humor, but had gained something else. He was thin and haggard, but looked determined. Although his smile was frank, his mouth was firm and his eyes were steady.

"I know!" she answered quickly; "I know what you have done for Stephen and what you mean to do. There is nobody else who can help him and if there was, the help would not be like yours."

"Thank you," said Charnock. "I'm afraid you're mistaken about one point, but I have an extra reason for doing the best I can." Then he paused and smiled. "We tried to make the place comfortable, but you'll find things rough. One lives in a rather primitive way at a construction camp."

"Perhaps, so far, I have found things too smooth."

Then Helen asked him about the accident and he told her as much as he thought advisable, until they reached the shack, where the doctor met them at the door.

"I expect you're Mrs. Festing," he said. "You'll find your husband able to talk, but remember that he must be kept calm. I'm going out, but will be back soon, and we'll see about getting you some food."

He took Charnock away, and Festing looked up with a strained expression as Helen crossed the floor. Her eyes were wonderfully gentle, and stooping beside the bunk she kissed him and put her arm round his neck.

"My dear!" she said softly. "My poor hurt dear! I have come to take care of you until you get well."

"I imagine I'll need to be taken care of afterwards," Festing answered, with a forced smile. "It looks as if I hadn't much ground for self-confidence."

Helen pressed his arm. "We have both made mistakes; but we won't talk about that now. Do you really feel you're getting better?"

"Of course," said Festing, smiling. "Very much better! I'll get well remarkably fast now you have come."

Helen brought a chair and for a time they engaged in happy but careless talk. Both knew there was much to be said, but Helen skilfully avoided striking a serious note. The time for that had not arrived yet.

When it got dark the doctor came in and joined them at a meal.

"The engineers have promised to put me up to-night, and I must leave to-morrow when the train goes out," he said. "I'll try to get back, but Musgrave knows what to do and will send for me if necessary. The most important thing is to keep Mr. Festing quiet."

"I'm afraid it will be difficult," Helen answered.

The doctor's eyes twinkled. "So I imagine, but it's your job. If you find it too hard, Musgrave will put your husband in plaster."

He went East next morning with the supply train, and Helen was sorry to see him go. He had done what was needed with quiet efficiency, but she knew he had other patients scattered about a wide district.

Charnock came in for a few minutes now and then during the day, and Musgrave was often about, but Helen was content to be left alone with her husband. His helplessness moved her; he had been marked by such vigor and energy, and it was strange to see him unable to move. Yet, while very pitiful, she felt a vague satisfaction because she could help him and he needed her.

When it was getting dark she went to the door and looked out. The evening was calm and belts of pale-yellow broke the soft gray clouds. The eastern peaks were touched with an orange glow, but the snow lower down faded through shades of blue and purple into gloom. To the west, the pines were black and sharp, with white smears on their lower branches, and a thin haze rose from the river. The coloring of the landscape was harmoniously subdued, but its rugged grandeur of outline caught Helen's eye, and she stood for a few minutes, looking about with half-awed admiration.

"Do you feel the cold, Stephen?" she asked.

"No," said Festing. "Wonderful view, isn't it? But what's it like outside?"

"Very still. Everything has a soft look; the harsh glitter's gone and the air has not the sting it had. Somehow the calm's majestic. The pictures one sees of the mountains hardly give a hint; one feels this is the grandest country in the world, but it looks strangely unfinished."

Festing laughed. "A few ranches, roads, and cornfields would make a difference? Well, they follow the Steel in Canada and it's my job to clear the way. But the soft look promises warmer weather, and Bob will get ahead if a Chinook wind begins to blow. I imagine he hasn't done very much the last few days."

"You mustn't bother about what Bob is doing," Helen said firmly.

"Very well. Light the lamp and sit where I can see you. There's something I want to say."

Helen did so and waited until Festing resumed: "To begin with, I've been a short-sighted, censorious fool about Bob. I'm ashamed to remember that I said he was a shiftless wastrel. The worst is I can't apologize; it wouldn't make things better to tell him what I thought."

"That's obvious," said Helen, with a smile. "Still, in a way perhaps, you were not so very wrong. Bob was something of a wastrel; his wife has made him a useful man."

"Another thing I was mistaken about! I rather despised Sadie. Now I want to take off my hat when I think of her. But it's puzzling. A girl without polish, taste, or accomplishments marries a man who has them all. She has no particular talents; nothing, in fact, except some beauty, rude integrity, and native shrewdness. Yet she, so to speak, works wonders. Puts Bob on his feet and leads him on, when nobody else could have pulled him out of the mire!"

"She loved him," said Helen softly. "Love gave her patience and cleverness. However, I think Sadie did not always lead Bob. She knew when to drive."

Festing was silent for a few moments and then went on: "Well, I have confessed two blunders and think it has done me good; but I'm getting nearer what I want to say. Bob's something of a philosopher and once remarked that events and people seldom force us into coils; our passions and characters entangle us. He was scoffing at the power of the theatrical villain and used Wilkinson for an example."

"But Wilkinson had something to do with our troubles."

"Not very much, after all. Perhaps he's accountable for my broken bones, but it was my obstinacy and ridiculous self-confidence that sent me here. That's what I really mean to talk about."

"Is it necessary?" Helen asked. "I was foolish to be jealous of the farm. Women have sometimes worse grounds for jealousy."

"That would have been impossible for us! Nobody who knew you could be attracted by another woman."

"Bob was attracted," said Helen with a blush. "One must own that he was prudent. I haven't Sadie's courage and patience."

"In those days, Bob was a besotted whisky-tank; but we are not going to talk about him. I'm afraid I was forgetful and went my own way like an obstinate fool. It was wrong, ridiculously wrong; I'm not going to excuse myself, but I want you to understand."

He paused, for effort and emotion had tired him, but presently resumed: "I wouldn't use your money, but this wasn't altogether because I was too proud to let you help. I wanted to keep you safe; farming's a risky business, and I couldn't play a niggardly, cautious game. There was the land, waiting to be worked; I couldn't spare labor or money. But since both might be lost, I was afraid to use your fortune as a stake."

"I understand," said Helen. "All the same, I would have been glad to take the risk. I don't think I'm very much afraid of hardship—"

Festing smiled. "You have pluck, but don't know the strain that the wives of the struggling farmers have to bear. My object is to see that you don't know. But there's another thing, harder to explain; you felt that I neglected you, and I fear I did!"

"You didn't mean to neglect me. Perhaps I was foolish, Stephen, but I felt you left me out. There were ways I could have helped."

"I took the wrong line; that's plain now, but we must think of the future and not make the same mistake. You are first with me, Helen, but I must work; it's all I'm fit for. I can't play games and am not an amusing talker—though I'm talking at large to-night. Well, we have made our home on the prairie, and all round us the best wheat-soil in the world is lying waste. They're getting short of food in Europe, America will soon use all she grows, and folks in the older countries fix their eyes on us. Then we have room for an industrious population on our wide plains, cities are waiting to spring up, a new nation is being born. I and the others who were given the land must clear the way. It's our business, our only justification for being there. Sounds romantic and exaggerated, but I think it's true!"

"It is true," said Helen. "Your views are larger than mine."

"Well," said Festing, smiling. "I don't often let myself go and look far ahead. It's my share to tackle the job before my eyes; to drive the tractor plow, and the grading scoop along the road reserve. For all that, it's not a vague sense of duty that really drives me on; I must work, I'm unhappy when I stop! I'm afraid I'll always feel like that. what are we going to do about it?"

"You must let me help more."

"I need help; that's something I have learned, and nobody can help like you. But the strain will slacken soon. The things that will make life easier for you are coming fast; branch railroads, telephones, busy little towns, neighbors, and social amusements. Much that you enjoyed in England will surround you on the plains. But it will not come as a gift, as it did at home; we will have worked for and made it possible."

Helen got up. Her color was higher than usual and her eyes sparkled. She was romantic and Festing had struck the right note, with rude sincerity and unconscious power. She saw visions of the future and the dignity of the immediate task. In this wide, new country, man needed woman's help, and her part was as large as his. Like Sadie, and many another, she heard the call for Pioneers. Crossing the door she stood by Festing's bunk.

"I understand it all, Stephen. We must be patient and allow for small differences in our points of view, for I think, in the main, we see together. You must never leave me out again; I want to do my part."

Festing said nothing, but he pressed her hand and she kissed him.

CHAPTER XXXI

CHARNOCK'S TRIUMPH

Six weeks after the accident Musgrave and Charnock came into the shack one evening. The former had examined Festing in the afternoon, and Helen gave him a meaning look. It hinted that she had expected his visit and meant to encourage him.

"Come near the stove and smoke if you like. It is very cold."

"No sign of the frost's breaking, I suppose?" said Festing, who lay propped up with pillows. "Did you get the particulars I asked for, Bob?"

Charnock gave him a paper with some calculations, and after a time he nodded.

"On the whole, this is satisfactory; things are going better than I thought. But what about the new job across the river?"

"Things are going better than he thought! Isn't that like Stephen?" Charnock remarked to the others, and then turned to Festing. "However, I expect you didn't mean to be rude and you never were very tactful. We haven't begun the job you mentioned, but I don't know that it matters since we're busy at something else, and that's not what I want to talk about. Musgrave has examined you and gives us an encouraging report."

"My opinion is that he can be moved and the journey home won't hurt him if proper care is used."

"But I don't want to be moved just yet," Festing objected.

"No doubt," said Musgrave dryly. "You are an obstinate fellow, but you're in our hands now, and we have to think what is best for you. To begin with, you won't be able to get about in time to be of much use, and you don't get better as fast as you ought. Then I understood you were resigned to going home before the contract is finished."

"If I must; but I don't want to go now. I'm able to arrange things with Charnock in the evenings."

"The fact is he doesn't trust me yet," Charnock remarked with a grin.

"You know that isn't true, Bob!"

"Then prove you trust me by going home with Helen. She has been plucky to stay so long, and now you're fit to be moved, you oughtn't to keep her. There's another thing; to be frank, you don't help much. We need a boss to superintend, which you can't do, and when I want advice I can go to Norton. As a matter of fact, when I come here in the evenings you find fault with what I've done. When I undertake a job I like to feel I'm carrying it out."

Festing stopped him and looked at Helen, for he was not deceived by Charnock's injured tone.

"I imagine this is something like a plot to get me away."

"I think you would get better much faster at home, Stephen. You cannot do anything useful here, and you cannot rest. Mr. Musgrave agrees."

"Certainly. If he stays, Festing will do himself harm and bother his partner."

Festing knitted his brows and was silent for a moment or two. Then he said, "Since it looks as if you had made your plans, I had better go. You're a very good fellow, Bob; but if you can't keep things straight, I'll come back and superintend from a stretcher."

They talked about other matters, but when Charnock left, Helen put on her furs and told Festing she wanted fresh air. Moonlight shone upon the dark pines and sparkled on the snow, and when they came out of the shadow of the trees she thought Charnock's face was grave.

"I'm grateful, Bob," she said. "It's a big thing you have undertaken!"

"I frankly wish it was smaller," Charnock answered. "I fact, I feel I have been horribly rash. I haven't Stephen's constructive talent or, for that matter, his energy, but somehow I mustn't be beaten."

Helen gave him a gentle look. "You won't be beaten. It's unthinkable! We trust you."

Then she went back and read a newspaper to Festing, who was carried down to the supply train next day and made comfortable in the caboose. Charnock talked to him carelessly until the couplings tightened and the locomotive began to snort, but his mouth was firm and his face set as he went back to his work. He knew what he was up against, and there were difficulties he had not told Festing about.

The days got longer, and the frost was relaxing its grip on the white prairie, when Festing left his homestead and walked to the trail-fork to meet the mail-carrier. He returned with some letters and sat down limply. His face was thin and pale.

"I get tired soon, and there's nothing from Bob yet," he

grumbled as he turned over the envelopes. "It's curious, because he told us the job was nearly finished and some of the big engineers were coming out to examine the track. They ought to have arrived some days ago, and I've no doubt they'd test the work thoroughly when they were there."

"You get too anxious," Helen replied. "If you had a calmer temperament, you would be stronger now. The engineers can hardly have had time to make a proper test."

"I have some grounds for being anxious. If the fellows aren't satisfied, we won't get paid."

Helen smiled. "You're really afraid that Bob may have been careless and neglected something!"

"Bob's a very good partner; I've confessed that I misjudged him," Festing answered with a touch of embarrassment. "Still, you see, I know his drawbacks, and I know mine. There were two or three pieces of work, done before I left, that I now see might have been better planned."

Helen went to the door, for she heard a soft drumming of hoofs on beaten snow.

"Sadie's coming," she said. "Perhaps she has some news."

Festing followed her and Sadie stopped the horses, but did not get down.

"I've a telegram from Bob; he'll be home to-morrow," she said. "He wants you both to meet him at the station."

"Did he say anything about the job being finished?" Festing asked as he went down the steps.

"No," said Sadie. "He seemed particularly anxious to see you at the depot; my hands are too numb or I'd show you the telegram. I haven't time to come in and don't want the team to stand in the cold."

Then she waved her hand to Helen and drove away.

About six o'clock next evening Helen and Festing walked up and down beside the track at the railroad settlement. There was no platform, but the agent's office stood near the rails, with a baggage shed, and a big tank for filtering saline water near the locomotive pipe. Behind these, three tall grain-elevators, which had not been finished when Festing saw them last, rose against the sky, dwarfing the skeleton frame of a new hotel. The ugly wooden houses had extended some distance across the snow, and Festing knew the significance of this. It was not dark yet, but the headlamp of a locomotive in the side-track flung a glittering beam a quarter of a mile down the line. In the west, a belt of saffron light, cut by the black smear of a bluff, glimmered on the horizon. Festing indicated the settlement.

"It has grown fast, but if things go as some of us expect, the change will soon be magical. In a year or two you'll see a post-office like a palace, and probably an opera-house, besides street cars running north and south from the track."

"I think I should like that," Helen remarked. "When it comes, you will have an office and a telephone, and be satisfied to superintend."

Festing laughed. "It's possible, but there's much to be done first, and I'm not getting on very fast just now. Still I don't feel knocked out and I've walked half a mile."

Glancing at the elevator towers and blocks of square-fronted houses that rose abruptly from the snow, Helen mused. The settlement jarred her fastidious taste, but she had seen Western towns that had, in a few years, grown out of their raw ugliness and blossomed in an efflorescence of ambitious architecture. Such beauty as they then possessed was not refined or subdued, but it was somehow characteristic of the country and harmonized with the builders' optimism. There was no permanence on the prairie; everything was in a fluid state of change and marked by a bold, but sometime misguided, striving for something better. Then she turned to her husband. His face was thin and she noted lines that came from mental strain and physical suffering, but his eyes were calm. She liked his look of quiet resolution.

"You are getting stronger fast," she said. "The days are lengthening, spring is near, and you will soon be able to work again. Well, I will not try to stop you. When the prairie is plowed and covered with wheat I want you to feel that you have done your part. The change that is coming will bring the things women like; comfort, amusements, society. But what about you and the others, the pioneers, when there is no more ground to be broken and the way is cleared?"

Festing smiled. "As a rule, the pioneer sells his homestead and goes on into the wilds to blaze another trail, but I imagine I shall be glad to rest. If not, we're an adaptable people and there are different ways of helping things along. One can learn to use other tools than the ax and plow."

"Ah," said Helen, "You are getting broader. You see clearly, Stephen, and your views are often long, but I sometimes thought you focused them too narrowly on the object in front. Perhaps I shall have done something if I have taught you to look all round. But here's Sadie and the train."

A light sprang out from the distant bluff and grew into a dazzling fan-shaped beam. Then the roar of wheels slackened, and Sadie joined the others as a bell began to toll, and with smoke streaming back along the cars the train rolled into the station. Somebody leaned out from the rails of a vestibule, and Sadie began to run beside the track.

"Come along!" she cried. "It's Bob!"

Festing and Helen followed, and when they reached the

vestibule Charnock pushed a door open and took them inside. The car was brightly lighted, but not furnished on the usual plan. A table stood in the middle, the curtained berths were at one end, and there were cases holding books and surveying instruments. It was obviously meant for the use of railroad managers and engineers, and three or four gentlemen stood near the table, as if they had just got up. Festing saw that one was Dalton, who advanced eagerly as Helen came in. He presented his companions to her and Sadie, and a gentleman who was well known on Canadian railroads gave Festing his hand. Another was Norton's employer, a famous contractor.

"Sit down," said the first. "The engineer wants to fill his tank, and they won't pull out until we are ready." Then he turned to Festing. "We have examined a piece of tract you helped build and I must compliment you on a first-class job. As a rule, we are glad to get our contract work up to specification, but you have done better."

"My partner is really responsible for that," Festing replied. "I got knocked out soon after we made a good start and had to leave him to carry on."

The contractor smiled as he interposed: "A good beginning counts for much, and I'm glad to state that Mr. Charnock has kept to your lines. When you were forced to leave it seemed prudent to make some inquiries, but we found that your partner was doing high-grade work, and now we have inspected it, I must admit that Norton's favorable reports were deserved." He paused and turned to Sadie. "If your husband's as good a farmer as an engineer, he'll make progress."

Sadie flushed with pride. "Looks as if he'd made some already, but you didn't run much risk when you trusted him."

"My wife's the farmer and my partner the engineer," Charnock remarked. "I know my limits, but try to keep going when somebody starts me well."

"You have gone farther than our bargain demanded, which doesn't often happen," said the contractor, who turned to Festing. "Mr. Charnock has my cheque for the main job, but there are some accounts to make up and you won't find my cashier disputes the extras. Perhaps that's all I need say, except that you have satisfied me, and, I gather, satisfied your men. In fact, you and Mr. Charnock leave us with general good feeling."

Then they talked about something else until a man came in to say that the locomotive tank was filled, and the engineer and contractor went to the vestibule with their guests. For a minute or two the group stood on the platform, exchanging farewell compliments, while the station agent waited in the snow. Then the engineer said:

"I wanted to meet your husband, Mrs. Festing, and if we have any more difficult work, hope you will let me have him again."

"He came back the worse last time," Helen answered smiling. "I'm not sure I would have the courage to let him go. Besides, he has other work at home. A farm makes many demands on one."

"I have no doubt it does," agreed the engineer. "One imagines that on the Festing farm all demands will be met."

He signed to the agent, the others went down the steps, and the bell began to toll as the lighted cars rolled by. The rattle of wheels got louder, and a plume of smoke trailed back and spread in a dingy cloud, but Helen and Festing stood, a little way from the others, watching the receding train. They felt that something was finished; satisfactorily finished amidst well-earned praise, but done with for good. Festing looked at Helen with a comprehending smile.

"You answered right; I'm not going back! Our work is waiting, here on the plains."

"Ah," said Helen softly, "how much easier you make it when you call it ours!"

They went to the hotel where they had left the team, and as the others followed Sadie turned to her husband with a glow of happy pride. He had come back, so to speak, triumphant, the guest of famous men who had said flattering things about him, and for his sake the train had been held up while the great contractor talked to her.

"Bob," she said, "you have made good! I can't tell you all I feel about it. Some day you'll be a famous man."

Choose from Thousands of 1stWorldLibrary Classics By

A. M. Barnard
Ada Leverson
Adolphus William Ward
Aesop
Agatha Christie
Alexander Aaronsohn
Alexander Kielland
Alexandre Dumas
Alfred Gatty
Alfred Ollivant
Alice Duer Miller
Alice Turner Curtis
Alice Dunbar
Allen Chapman
Alleyne Ireland
Ambrose Bierce
Amelia E. Barr
Amory H. Bradford
Andrew Lang
Andrew McFarland Davis
Andy Adams
Angela Brazil
Anna Alice Chapin
Anna Sewell
Annie Besant
Annie Hamilton Donnell
Annie Payson Call
Annie Roe Carr
Annonaymous
Anton Chekhov
Archibald Lee Fletcher
Arnold Bennett
Arthur C. Benson
Arthur Conan Doyle
Arthur M. Winfield
Arthur Ransome
Arthur Schnitzler
Arthur Train
Atticus
B.H. Baden-Powell
B. M. Bower
B. C. Chatterjee
Baroness Emmuska Orczy
Baroness Orczy
Basil King
Bayard Taylor
Ben Macomber
Bertha Muzzy Bower
Bjornstjerne Bjornson

Booth Tarkington
Boyd Cable
Bram Stoker
C. Collodi
C. E. Orr
C. M. Ingleby
Carolyn Wells
Catherine Parr Traill
Charles A. Eastman
Charles Amory Beach
Charles Dickens
Charles Dudley Warner
Charles Farrar Browne
Charles Ives
Charles Kingsley
Charles Klein
Charles Hanson Towne
Charles Lathrop Pack
Charles Romyn Dake
Charles Whibley
Charles Willing Beale
Charlotte M. Braeme
Charlotte M. Yonge
Charlotte Perkins Stetson
Clair W. Hayes
Clarence Day Jr.
Clarence E. Mulford
Clemence Housman
Confucius
Coningsby Dawson
Cornelis DeWitt Wilcox
Cyril Burleigh
D. H. Lawrence
Daniel Defoe
David Garnett
Dinah Craik
Don Carlos Janes
Donald Keyhoe
Dorothy Kilner
Dougan Clark
Douglas Fairbanks
E. Nesbit
E. P. Roe
E. Phillips Oppenheim
E. S. Brooks
Earl Barnes
Edgar Rice Burroughs
Edith Van Dyne
Edith Wharton

Edward Everett Hale
Edward J. O'Biren
Edward S. Ellis
Edwin L. Arnold
Eleanor Atkins
Eleanor Hallowell Abbott
Eliot Gregory
Elizabeth Gaskell
Elizabeth McCracken
Elizabeth Von Arnim
Ellem Key
Emerson Hough
Emilie F. Carlen
Emily Bronte
Emily Dickinson
Enid Bagnold
Enilor Macartney Lane
Erasmus W. Jones
Ernie Howard Pie
Ethel May Dell
Ethel Turner
Ethel Watts Mumford
Eugene Sue
Eugenie Foa
Eugene Wood
Eustace Hale Ball
Evelyn Everett-green
Everard Cotes
F. H. Cheley
F. J. Cross
F. Marion Crawford
Fannie E. Newberry
Federick Austin Ogg
Ferdinand Ossendowski
Fergus Hume
Florence A. Kilpatrick
Fremont B. Deering
Francis Bacon
Francis Darwin
Frances Hodgson Burnett
Frances Parkinson Keyes
Frank Gee Patchin
Frank Harris
Frank Jewett Mather
Frank L. Packard
Frank V. Webster
Frederic Stewart Isham
Frederick Trevor Hill
Frederick Winslow Taylor

Friedrich Kerst
Friedrich Nietzsche
Fyodor Dostoyevsky
G.A. Henty
G.K. Chesterton
Gabrielle E. Jackson
Garrett P. Serviss
Gaston Leroux
George A. Warren
George Ade
Geroge Bernard Shaw
George Cary Eggleston
George Durston
George Ebers
George Eliot
George Gissing
George MacDonald
George Meredith
George Orwell
George Sylvester Viereck
George Tucker
George W. Cable
George Wharton James
Gertrude Atherton
Gordon Casserly
Grace E. King
Grace Gallatin
Grace Greenwood
Grant Allen
Guillermo A. Sherwell
Gulielma Zollinger
Gustav Flaubert
H. A. Cody
H. B. Irving
H.C. Bailey
H. G. Wells
H. H. Munro
H. Irving Hancock
H. R. Naylor
H. Rider Haggard
H. W. C. Davis
Haldeman Julius
Hall Caine
Hamilton Wright Mabie
Hans Christian Andersen
Harold Avery
Harold McGrath
Harriet Beecher Stowe
Harry Castlemon
Harry Coghill
Harry Houidini

Hayden Carruth
Helent Hunt Jackson
Helen Nicolay
Hendrik Conscience
Hendy David Thoreau
Henri Barbusse
Henrik Ibsen
Henry Adams
Henry Ford
Henry Frost
Henry James
Henry Jones Ford
Henry Seton Merriman
Henry W Longfellow
Herbert A. Giles
Herbert Carter
Herbert N. Casson
Herman Hesse
Hildegard G. Frey
Homer
Honore De Balzac
Horace B. Day
Horace Walpole
Horatio Alger Jr.
Howard Pyle
Howard R. Garis
Hugh Lofting
Hugh Walpole
Humphry Ward
Ian Maclaren
Inez Haynes Gillmore
Irving Bacheller
Isabel Cecilia Williams
Isabel Hornibrook
Israel Abrahams
Ivan Turgenev
J.G.Austin
J. Henri Fabre
J. M. Barrie
J. M. Walsh
J. Macdonald Oxley
J. R. Miller
J. S. Fletcher
J. S. Knowles
J. Storer Clouston
J. W. Duffield
Jack London
Jacob Abbott
James Allen
James Andrews
James Baldwin

James Branch Cabell
James DeMille
James Joyce
James Lane Allen
James Lane Allen
James Oliver Curwood
James Oppenheim
James Otis
James R. Driscoll
Jane Abbott
Jane Austen
Jane L. Stewart
Janet Aldridge
Jens Peter Jacobsen
Jerome K. Jerome
Jessie Graham Flower
John Buchan
John Burroughs
John Cournos
John F. Kennedy
John Gay
John Glasworthy
John Habberton
John Joy Bell
John Kendrick Bangs
John Milton
John Philip Sousa
John Taintor Foote
Jonas Lauritz Idemil Lie
Jonathan Swift
Joseph A. Altsheler
Joseph Carey
Joseph Conrad
Joseph E. Badger Jr
Joseph Hergesheimer
Joseph Jacobs
Jules Vernes
Julian Hawthrone
Julie A Lippmann
Justin Huntly McCarthy
Kakuzo Okakura
Karle Wilson Baker
Kate Chopin
Kenneth Grahame
Kenneth McGaffey
Kate Langley Bosher
Kate Langley Bosher
Katherine Cecil Thurston
Katherine Stokes
L. A. Abbot
L. T. Meade

L. Frank Baum
Latta Griswold
Laura Dent Crane
Laura Lee Hope
Laurence Housman
Lawrence Beasley
Leo Tolstoy
Leonid Andreyev
Lewis Carroll
Lewis Sperry Chafer
Lilian Bell
Lloyd Osbourne
Louis Hughes
Louis Joseph Vance
Louis Tracy
Louisa May Alcott
Lucy Fitch Perkins
Lucy Maud Montgomery
Luther Benson
Lydia Miller Middleton
Lyndon Orr
M. Corvus
M. H. Adams
Margaret E. Sangster
Margret Howth
Margaret Vandercook
Margaret W. Hungerford
Margret Penrose
Maria Edgeworth
Maria Thompson Daviess
Mariano Azuela
Marion Polk Angellotti
Mark Overton
Mark Twain
Mary Austin
Mary Catherine Crowley
Mary Cole
Mary Hastings Bradley
Mary Roberts Rinehart
Mary Rowlandson
M. Wollstonecraft Shelley
Maud Lindsay
Max Beerbohm
Myra Kelly
Nathaniel Hawthrone
Nicolo Machiavelli
O. F. Walton
Oscar Wilde
Owen Johnson
P.G. Wodehouse
Paul and Mabel Thorne

Paul G. Tomlinson
Paul Severing
Percy Brebner
Percy Keese Fitzhugh
Peter B. Kyne
Plato
Quincy Allen
R. Derby Holmes
R. L. Stevenson
R. S. Ball
Rabindranath Tagore
Rahul Alvares
Ralph Bonehill
Ralph Henry Barbour
Ralph Victor
Ralph Waldo Emmerson
Rene Descartes
Ray Cummings
Rex Beach
Rex E. Beach
Richard Harding Davis
Richard Jefferies
Richard Le Gallienne
Robert Barr
Robert Frost
Robert Gordon Anderson
Robert L. Drake
Robert Lansing
Robert Lynd
Robert Michael Ballantyne
Robert W. Chambers
Rosa Nouchette Carey
Rudyard Kipling
Saint Augustine
Samuel B. Allison
Samuel Hopkins Adams
Sarah Bernhardt
Sarah C. Hallowell
Selma Lagerlof
Sherwood Anderson
Sigmund Freud
Standish O'Grady
Stanley Weyman
Stella Benson
Stella M. Francis
Stephen Crane
Stewart Edward White
Stijn Streuvels
Swami Abhedananda
Swami Parmananda
T. S. Ackland

T. S. Arthur
The Princess Der Ling
Thomas A. Janvier
Thomas A Kempis
Thomas Anderton
Thomas Bailey Aldrich
Thomas Bulfinch
Thomas De Quincey
Thomas Dixon
Thomas H. Huxley
Thomas Hardy
Thomas More
Thornton W. Burgess
U. S. Grant
Upton Sinclair
Valentine Williams
Various Authors
Vaughan Kester
Victor Appleton
Victor G. Durham
Victoria Cross
Virginia Woolf
Wadsworth Camp
Walter Camp
Walter Scott
Washington Irving
Wilbur Lawton
Wilkie Collins
Willa Cather
Willard F. Baker
William Dean Howells
William le Queux
W. Makepeace Thackeray
William W. Walter
William Shakespeare
Winston Churchill
Yei Theodora Ozaki
Yogi Ramacharaka
Young E. Allison
Zane Grey

www.ingramcontent.com/pod-product-compliance
Lightning Source LLC
Chambersburg PA
CBHW031059260626
47172CB00001B/131